HER DARKEST DEVILS

THE SEVEN SINNERS OF HELL'S KINGDOM, BOOK THREE

by

GINNA MORAN

ISBN 978-1-951314-50-7 (soft cover)
ISBN 978-1-951314-51-4 (hard cover)

Cover design by Silver Starlight Designs
Cover images copyright Depositphotos

For Inquiries Contact:
Sunny Palms Press
9663 Santa Monica Blvd Suite 1158
Beverly Hills, CA 90210, USA
www.sunnypalmspress.com
www.GinnaMoran.com

DEDICATION

This book is for those who have embraced their freaky sides! Those who no longer hesitate to answer if asked tails or horns. This is for those of you who are like, "If it fits, it sticks. I don't care if it's some weird-ass appendage. Bring it on!" This is for those who are brave and adventurous, and for those who just love the hell out of reading twisted adventures. Get your kinks on, pretty souls! Life is more fun that way.

1

RAVEN

GO TO HELL

"THERE WERE WARDS set against the divine not unlike the ones that disallow me from entering this estate. I'm sorry, Raven. I could only get within the block without Lucifer's notice. He set them up and would know if I crossed." Zade ruffles his hand through his blond hair, balancing on the outer ledge of the balcony.

I blink a few times, trying to keep my wave of emotions

in check. This is so fucked up. How could the bastard get away with this? "I don't care if he notices or not. It's not like he could do much about it. You could've—"

"Raven," he says, cutting me off. Lines cut across his forehead with his frown. Damn pouty angel. "I don't think you understand. I've interfered enough with Hell's affairs. I shouldn't have even come here tonight. I've risked a lot, so please, accept that I've done all that I'm comfortable with. I have the nearest streets memorized, which you can pass on to your soul keepers. They can handle things from here."

His glassy eyes plead with me to understand, but my wild frustration burns through me. How can I understand? My soulmate and my eternity are both in jeopardy because of this. He made me a deal and hasn't kept good on his word.

"You've done nothing! I knew I should've confronted Lucian when I had the chance. Fought him. Done something besides trust that you could've helped me. This is your fault. He's off doing some shit, and you wasted my chance." I swivel on the balls of my feet, unable to face him. "You angels find such mercies impossible to give."

Anger boils under my skin the longer I stare at the heavenly glow radiating from Zade in his reflection on the glass door. I can't look into his sad eyes. He looks so pathetic, and because of his inability to do something more than spy, I might be doomed. I might never see Elias again. My heart hurts thinking about it. Even though it's only been an hour, knowing he isn't asleep in his room but possibly being tortured by his previous demonic master sends panic squeezing my heart. I know what Vincent is capable of. He'll do things that'll make Elias want to die.

"Raven, please look at me," Zade murmurs, the light reflecting from his wings brighter as he inches closer. He risks stepping onto the balcony. "Maybe if you allow me to use your Hell-touched soul to go to Andre—"

Spinning around, I shove my palms into Zade's chest. "Get the fuck out of here. I have too much at stake to let you use me. Andre doesn't even want to see you. He told me so."

Zade's eyes glass over, and I steel myself to his sorrow. I know I'm acting like a bitch, but I don't have time to deal with angels who are no help to me. Elias is my priority and I can't lose him.

He tightens his jaw, refusing to budge another foot despite my efforts to push him off the balcony. "Please, Raven. I'm lost without knowing he's okay. Cassius—"

I narrow my eyes and jab him in the chest with my finger. How dare he try to make me pity him. Is he so naïve that he doesn't understand what a little give and take means? Only finding a half-assed location for Elias does not even compare to what he asks of me. "Fuck you. Fuck Cassius."

Surprising me, Zade grabs my hand, tightening his fingers to stop me from running inside to slam the door in his face. "Give me something else I can do. I know this is unfair of me to request, but there has to be something else I can help with."

I study his blue eyes, half-expecting firelight to burst across his irises. He sounds a bit more devilish than angel. Desperate. Is that enough to make him jump from grace? I don't know. It might if I just keep giving him a push and withhold what he wants. I'm willing to try anything.

But his eyes remain glossy and blue. Disappointment washes through me that it doesn't happen like I want. I should know better than to think things could be that easy. If anything, they're only going to get harder than Kase and Dante's morning woods.

Zade's light illuminates the world around us, bathing me in a heavenly glow. It stings my skin the longer I stand in front of him, using my furious silence to make him uncomfortable. Usually, the angelic light doesn't faze me, but I think with Lucian's presence here in the Mortal World things have shifted a bit. I'm more sensitive.

I shiver and hug my arms around me. Now I'm only torturing myself. "If you want me to even consider allowing you to see Andre, there is one thing you can do."

"I can't jump from grace," he says, pursing his lips. His wings twitch, and he reaches up and touches them like he must assure himself they're still there and the same.

"Things would be a helluva lot easier on us if you just did, but that's not what I need from you. I need you to find Kase, Dante, or Micah. I've tried calling for them, but they're not here. Lucian steals my phone during our time, so I can't text them either. If you can find them—"

A low growl sounds through the air from behind me. Micah's familiar protectiveness kicks my heartbeat into chaotic thrums, and I spin on the balls of my feet to catch sight of him filling the doorframe to Lucian's suite without entering. No one is allowed within Lucian's quarters except for me unless they want to get in a fight. And with hours left on my time, I don't think Micah will. Lucian could take shit out on me.

Another growl escapes Micah's mouth. "Leave, savior! Don't make me fight you."

Zade launches into the air without a word, disappearing before Micah can threaten to tear his wings off next. I suck my bottom lip into my mouth and slowly look from the sky to Micah's fiery gaze. The orange in his eyes disappears, bringing back the beautiful brown color, and I offer him a smile.

He doesn't return it, glowering.

I can't hide my pout. "Hey, I—"

"Raven, you must be careful opening yourself to another angel while you're in Lucian's care. I fear he will hurt you if he catches you." Micah's muscles bulge as he grips the doorframe. "None of us are allowed a moment of your time. I shouldn't even be talking to you."

It takes everything in me not to flip my shit and destroy everything in Lucian's room. Fisting my hands, I bite my palms with my nails. I don't have time for this. Lucian has Elias.

I stride closer. "Fuck him. He's not your boss. He's your equal. You're just as powerful as that bastard."

A smirk tugs the side of his mouth. "I'm aware of that, heathen, but I'm also aware of your safety. I can't risk it. I've agreed not to test boundaries. It's not Lucian who concerns me as much as Kase and Dante."

He's full of shit and we both know it. A part of him still thinks of Lucian as the all-powerful devil tethered to Hell.

I stride closer to him, wanting to force him to come in. "None of that's important right now. Lucian took—"

The room shakes and the putrid scent of Hell permeates through the air. I don't have to look to know that someone opens a portal. I know it's not Andre because it's not his time, and he can visit my dreams. Kase and Dante don't travel often enough by Hell portal for it to be them either. Which means the dickhole, annoying, stupid shit fucking bastard has finally returned.

"Fuck, he's back. I'm sorry, Raven. We can talk about everything later. Maybe there is something I can do to make this less torturous for you." Micah grabs the knob and swings the door closed, his last comment sounding as if it was intended for himself.

Rushing forward, I bang my hands on the wood as I hear him lock it from the outside. "Micah, wait. Please! It's about Elias."

He doesn't respond, his heavy footsteps fleeting and fading. I rush to the balcony door and peek outside, watching the flaming circle vanish. I duck, hiding before Lucian catches sight of me. I don't want him to know that I'm up. If he knows that I know about Elias already, he could do something rash like have Vincent kill him. Fuck, what if he's already dead? I can't handle this.

"Lucian, I thought you were upstairs. You know you shouldn't leave Raven and Elias alone. Something could've happened to them while you were gone." Micah's voice murmurs through the air, coming from the backdoor below.

I squeeze my eyes shut, trying to suppress my raging emotions. Micah must've come straight to Lucian's room after returning home. Of course he had. He'd have sensed Lucian's absence, which is why he came to check on me. Micah's telepathic ability might not break into the other devils' heads, but it gives him an awareness of everyone.

"I can leave them alone if I want, and it's none of your damn business about what I do and where I go. Now fuck off." The backdoor slams, cutting off their voices from me.

Rushing toward my pile of blankets on the floor, I get to my knees and quickly arrange my make-shift bed, hearing something thud loud enough to be heard through the door. Something shatters next. I swear it better not be my favorite glass dick statue Dante had custom made of his cock for me.

Lucian's voice rumbles and reverberates across my soul as

he stomps his way down the hall in the direction of his room. "I don't care what you think. You can't see her or talk to her. I have another four hours and will do as I please. She will stay in my room and away from you. She is mine."

"I was only offering to help. You will continue to push her away acting like this," Micah says, remaining even in tone. "I don't understand why you must insist on trying to keep her isolated. And sending us all out to ensure it? That's not helping. We should be together to work through things."

"You sound like a blasted savior. Do I need to remind you that you're not?" Growling, Lucian turns the doorknob and hesitates.

"No, that won't be necessary. Call me if you need anything," Micah says. I was hoping he'd stand up to him, but he's letting me the fuck down. "I'll let you know when Kase and Dante return."

"Actually, I do need something. I have a few souls that need to be marked. I want the bastards brought here to do so in front of Raven. It's time she sees the true extent of my power." Lucian widens the door a bit more.

I glimpse him staring at Micah standing a dozen feet away, since this room is at the end of the hall. Micah flicks his eyes toward me for a quick second, a blip of anger on his face. I know it's not directed at me, but it doesn't sting any less. He's pissed about getting sent out again. I have a feeling it's because Lucian wants to give Vincent more time to ensure we can't find Elias. Fuck. I hope Zade comes through for me.

I flip on my side with my back toward the door. I clutch the pillow I've hidden a couple of useful things in to my stomach. At least it's something. I obviously can only rely on myself in this moment, and I'll do what I have to.

Micah groans, his voice louder with the opening door. "Yes, Lucian. I'll do that, but beware. Raven—"

"Just shut the fuck up and go. You've stolen enough of my time with Raven." Lucian's words snap across my eardrums at the same time he purposely slams the door shut.

I startle and cringe, wishing with everything in me that my body wouldn't have reacted at all. The bastard. He's being loud on purpose. Holding my breath, I wait to see if he notices my movement. Heat burns across my back under the weight of his attention. I sense him studying me from a few feet away, but he's so quiet now that it feels as if I'm actually alone. I hate being under his scrutiny.

And fuck. My nose itches, and it feels as if bugs crawl across my body. I want so badly to move.

This is torture.

"Raven, are you awake?" he asks, not bothering to keep his voice low.

I refuse to respond and remain frozen in my spot, clutching my pillow.

The ground trembles beneath my body. He purposefully stomps across the floor, testing me. Again, I don't move. I concentrate on keeping my breathing even, hoping he leaves me alone.

No such luck. I hear him settling on the floor behind me.

A hot arm slings across my side, sending my heart thudding harder against my ribs. Lucian pulls me against his chest and blows a warm breath in my ear. I clench as he pushes his hard-on against my ass, acting as if spooning with me will lead to fucking me from behind or some shit. Right now, all it's going to lead to is a punch in his junk—after I let him think he can mess with me, of course.

Easing my hips away from him, I slowly lift my leg until his cock stops poking me and slips between my thighs. He hums his contentment and tightens his arms, being the total perv that he is, testing my boundaries. He doesn't have to call me out about fake sleeping, because I know he knows I'm awake. I can't control my body's reaction, the sensation of his infuriating closeness buzzing across my skin.

"Tell me you want it," Lucian mutters, digging his fingers into my hip. "If you tell me, I'll let you join me on the bed. I'll make you realize that I'm who you want and need the most."

I squeeze my legs together, trapping him to me. There is no way I'm going to let him use my attraction toward his darkness against me. He's not my type of psycho. If anything, I'm only letting him get close enough for me to turn against him. He set us up. He doesn't want Hell to rise. He wants Earth and Heaven and everyone in this universe to fall at his feet. He had a demon kidnap Elias for that reason. The only thing I'm going to do in this moment is force him to return my soulmate to me or face getting sent back to Hell. It'll give me time to run.

"Sorry, that's a no. I only like sweet psychos. You're a controlling, sadistic asshole." I whisper my words to ensure my voice remains even. Lucian could impale me with his horns—fuck, probably even his cock—if he wanted too, and I just want to make it through the next few hours, so I don't have to be in this prison of a room.

"You enjoy being controlled." His fingers leave my hip and slide along my pelvis. "You just want to believe you have a choice. Freewill. The gift from the Higher Power that disobedient mortals think is owed to them." He presses harder to me, and I now realize he must've dropped his pants, because I feel the heat of his exposed skin between my legs with his tip right near my hand that I hug close to my body.

Fisting my fingers, I punch him on the top of his hand and cock in the same swing, stopping him from trying to touch me. He pushes the boundaries to extremes and will continue to do so unless I fight back. No response is a yes to him, which infuriates me.

"Don't touch me," I snap, thrashing away from him.

Howling a laugh, Lucian flips onto his back and watches me scramble from the floor. I wish he'd react with a little grunt to the pain I try to inflict, but hitting his groin doesn't bother him. It's like he loves it.

"You know you like it, Raven. Don't be a cunt for the sake of being a cunt. Things would be a lot more pleasant if you'd give in." Lucian stretches his arms, showing off his massive boner, now pointing at the ceiling. "I feel your soul and desires. You only resist because you know I'm right and you hate that."

Goddamn it.

"Stop looking at my fucking soul. You're so far out of line right now. Put your cock away and get off my blankets." I place my hands on my hips and glower at him.

It would be nice if I had some power to prove to him that he can't bully me into giving in to him. Who fucking cares if he's hot? He's intolerable on every other level. No wonder he got the reputation he did while Kase and Dante were left in his shadow.

"No, I don't think so. Maybe I'll just have a good time with myself." Lucian strokes his fingers over his hard-on, offering me a wicked grin. "When I'm through, maybe then you'll join me in bed."

I intake a sharp breath, disgust and fury rushing through me. He just threatened to cum all over my blankets.

The edges of my vision shadow, and before my mind has a chance to process what my rebel body is doing, I find myself snatching my pillow from the ground. The contents I've hidden inside it rattle against each other, drawing Lucian's attention to my hand. He tries to fly to his knees, but it's too late. The asshole will pay for everything he's done. For the position he put me in.

Flipping the top of the water bottle open, I squeeze it hard, sending a stream of holy water right into Lucian's face. Real, legit holy water, courtesy of Elias. At first I was upset that he managed to sneak in a jug among his things, but now I'm thankful.

And terrified.

Shit.

What the fuck did I just do?

Lucian hollers, his face burning and blistering from the gush of blessed liquid in his eyes. It's enough to slow him down, and he misses grabbing me. Dodging out of the way, I dig my hand into my pillowcase and pull out the container of salt.

I never expected I'd attempt to create my own summoning circle, but here I am, trying to remember the steps Elias taught me. I've only seen him do it once, and I laughed when he tried to teach me a second time, but shit. I pray I get this right.

Lucian needs to get his ass back to Hell.

"Raven, I'm going to fucking—"

I squirt him in the face again, shutting him up. I wonder how much holy water it would take to melt him, but I clearly don't have enough to find out. And I'm running out of time.

The room quakes as Lucian's true body explodes from his human façade, and I run around him in a circle, spilling the salt as quickly as I can. Fire erupts in his palms, and he chucks it in my direction, setting the pile of blankets on fire.

Thank God for small miracles. I needed a light.

Scrambling to grab Elias's banishing candle, marked with divine runes, I hold it to the smoldering fabric, igniting the candle aglow.

"You're dead, Raven!" Lucian shouts. "I will fucking destroy you!"

The floor shudders, and Lucian stomps his hooves, trying to knock me off my feet. I drop down and crawl toward him, clutching the candle for dear life.

All I have to do is say the words and touch him with the blessed flame. If I can manage, a portal will open and swallow him whole.

"Lucian, Raven! Both of you stop!" Micah's voice booms through the air, trying to distract me.

I ignore him and get within a foot of Lucian. "God, please help me. I can't live with him like this. Please."

"Micah, grab her! Stop her!" Lucian shouts, gathering hellfire in between his hands. "You have five seconds to get her under control, or this is it. I will no longer try to make this work."

My heart hammers, the beats pounding in my ears. Micah says something, but I can't hear him any longer. The world fades around me as I concentrate on my task.

Using my knuckles, I push the candle, rolling it on its side toward Lucian. "Ad quos eieci te ad infernum," I whisper, hoping with everything in me that it works. That I said it right.

"Raven!" Micah hollers, transforming into his devil self, his gigantic body filling the room so much so that he must bend his neck not to hit his head on the ceiling. "Raven, run!"

The world quivers, the floor rumbling until flames burst through the air in front of me. I jerk my attention toward Lucian. My heart sinks into my stomach. It isn't the blessed candle that sets the world aglow. It's Lucian.

The candle wax seeps out from under his hoof, melted completely by his hellfire.

"Lucian, please," Micah says. "She's not ready."

Ready?

I slowly turn my head to meet Micah's wide eyes.

"Let's find out how strong she truly is." Lucian's clawed hands rip through my night clothes as he drags me off the floor. "If she makes it out, maybe she'll learn her place."

"Makes it out?" I question, my voice a mere whisper over the sound of the flames.

The scent of sulfur assaults my nose, and I realize what Lucian means.

"Please, Lucian," Micah says again. "Raven, beg for forgiveness. Ask for mercy. Make a deal. Do something. Fight."

But it's too late.

Lucian hangs me over a portal to Hell.

He releases me.

Fire consumes everything.

2

RAVEN

WRATH'S KINGDOM

AM I DEAD? How the fuck am I here? Where exactly in Hell is here? I have no idea. I've only really been to Micah's kingdom, but that was through visions and his bond to my soul. I feel weird, and I'm nearly certain I'm here in mind *and* body. Confusion washes over me as I stare at the blood-red ground. I would know if I were dead, right? I've died before. I felt it.

Something about this is different.

Screams and shouts fill the air, startling me, and I force my body to get its shit together and work with my mind. The disconnect I had before—my body and mind warring with each other—is why I am here in the first place. I was stupid as fuck to think I could create a banishing circle to send Lucian back here. He'd have just returned anyway. I was just so fucking mad. I still am.

Now, Elias could be lost to me. I could be lost.

Micah wouldn't have freaked out like he had if he thought I'd be okay.

Shit.

Pushing my palms into the hot, squishy ground, I get to my knees and peer around. Tall, gnarled trees litter the landscape, creating the creepiest forest I have ever seen. The yells of pain and anguish continue to fill the air, but I can't see anything amid the trees. It's like people are here but aren't. Like they're figments of my imagination.

I'd believe as much if the blur of a massive figure didn't materialize several dozen feet in front of me. Oh shit.

Rushing to my feet, I race toward the nearest tree and duck behind the thick trunk. The mangled branches climb toward the orange sky with thick brown clouds. Everything looks off like I've lost the ability to see certain colors, but it might be because they just don't exist here in Hell.

The beastly demon snarls, the ear-shattering sound whipping through my head. I hold my breath like it could make a difference and slowly peek in its direction. I wish I hadn't. Jabbing its clawed fingers into its gut, the demon yanks out something from inside and drops it to the ground.

It's not just something. It's a figure. A man.

Fuck. Fuck. Fuck.

I recognize him.

Joel pushes up on one arm, his other one a bloody, partial limb, missing from where Kase bit it off. Hollering, he tries to drag himself from the demon, but it's no use. He can't escape. This is part of his eternal punishment from the twisted, murderous life he led.

And he's here because Kase wanted to ensure his damnation. I think that's where I am. Wrath's Kingdom. Now how to call upon the king of its throne? Shit. I'm guessing there aren't phones here. Or maps.

If I survive this bullshit, I'm going to need my devils to show me around. I really fucking didn't want the grand tour until I cemented my place in Purgatory, but if Lucian is capable of sending me here while I'm alive...

That's it. I need to find Andre. My time with him was supposed to be in his kingdom. That's where I need to go.

"Leave me alone! Please!" Joel's howl of agony whips my attention back in his direction.

Could I dare intervene? Maybe he knows his way around these creepy forest lands. He might be remorseful enough to help me in exchange for...who the fuck am I kidding? The asshole will try to get me back. He probably blames me for all of this.

Summoning my courage, I peer at the gnarled tree branches and find one that looks sturdy yet easy enough to break. If I'm going to travel through Hell, I need something to defend myself with. I'm sure screaming and telling any bastard demons or damned souls that I'm the one the devils want beside them will only leave me in danger. They'll try to use me to their benefit.

I stretch up and grab on to a branch nearly out of my reach. Swinging and throwing my weight forward, I snap it from the tree, using all my strength. Thank unholy Hell for my devilish strength, enhanced by my contract. Without it, I don't think I could even break a twig here.

A loud crack reverberates through the air, and a wave of liquid shoots from the jagged stump of the branch. My eyes widen, and I stumble away in shock. The tree gushes a waterfall of blood. I gasp and drop the mangled branch, realizing it might not be a tree at all—at least, not completely. A hunk of what could possibly be bone peeks from the end of the branch, dripping the same red liquid still pouring from the tree. I study the bark. I'm nearly fucking certain I see a face within the strange, rough texture like it could possibly have been a human or soul or something at one point.

Squeezing my eyes shut, I inhale a soft breath. "Just fucking pick it up. What's done is done, and you need a damn weapon. Who cares if it's some weird-ass limb and bleeding."

Damn, I'm twisted. My devils would be so proud. It's the thought that pushes me forward. I can't back down now. There is no fucking way I'm going to cower. If I want to help rule Hell, I need to act like the queen my devils want and need me to be.

Wiggling my fingers, I take a small breath and snatch the bloody branch from the ground. It's heavier than I expect it to be, so I flip it vertically and hold it like I would a walking stick. At least one side doesn't drip the blood. I wonder what the soul or whatever had done in life to deserve this sort of eternal torture.

"A living mortal. How curious." The gurgling voice booms from behind me as a demon creeps away from the other side of an enormous tree with several silently screaming faces protruding from the dry, cracked bark. "I've never seen such a sight."

Jagged, yellow teeth fill its lipless mouth as it regards me. I recognize the demon. It's the same one who pulled Joel from its stomach. Shit. Straightening its back, the demon towers over me, blocking out the view of the world. I shift on my feet, flicking my attention to my surroundings. I can try to run and hide, but I doubt I'll get far. The fucker's legs are as tall as my stomach.

"Get the fuck away from me," I snap, swinging the severed branch toward the demon.

It startles and jumps back, clutching its hands to its bulbous belly. "Feisty, aren't you."

The demon's mouth widens. I settle on thinking it's a male, considering the strange cluster of appendages whipping around just above the apex of his legs. Shivering, I swing the branch again, not giving him a chance to try to step closer.

"I said get away. I will bludgeon you until the ruler of Wrath's Kingdom comes and tears you apart for even speaking to me." I swing the branch again, clocking him in his swollen stomach.

It shudders and screams, suddenly exploding open. Joel tumbles onto the ground in front of me, and I jump back, shrieking uncontrollably. Roaring, the demon skulks toward me, gnashing his teeth. I do the only thing I can think of. I dodge around him and whack him with the branch in the back of the head. Then I do it again and again, my hellish strength giving the branch enough force to knock the demon's head off.

"Raven, hurry! Run! I know where we can go!" Joel's voice snatches ahold of my good senses.

Facing the now hollering, flailing demon or my ex? This really is fucking Hell. What kind of choices are those? Sucky ones. Impossible ones.

Screw this.

"Raven, seriously. We have to go. Now!" Joel shouts.

He extends his hand to me, and I automatically recoil and swing the branch, smacking him in the shoulder.

"The only place you're going is back in that demon's gut." I shove my hands into Joel's chest and knock him toward the demon.

His eyes widen, his arm pin-wheeling, but he manages to catch his damn self a foot away from the monstrous demon. Throwing himself forward, he charges toward me, using the side of a tree trunk to keep balanced. I don't have a chance to react as he slings his arm around me and drags me with him.

"You're fucking coming with me whether you want to or not. I'm not letting that demon get either of us. Now let me take care of you." Joel's voice digs under my skin, reminding me of our relationship, or our break up, of my desperation and return to him. It reminds me of the moment I realized he was drugging me to keep me with him. How he beat me so badly that I almost died alone in a dumpster.

"Joel, stop. I don't need you to take care of me. Just put me down. You'll only make things worse for you." I ram my fist into his chest, trying to force him into dropping me.

Joel doesn't relent, only adjusting me over his shoulder. "Please, Raven. I forgive you, you know. Those assholes pushed you into—"

I thrash and kick, doing everything in my power to break from his hold. Fury whips through me at his comment. He forgives me? Is he fucking serious? Of course he is. I'm more aware of his manipulative attitude and how he would gaslight me, making me feel crazy and unreasonable and like everything was my fault.

The world jerks, and I smack into the ground, landing on my ass. It barely fazes me. Dante's spanked me far harder, and I want to kiss him so badly for desensitizing me toward a little ass-ault.

"You fucking bitch! You've always been so selfish. I gave you everything, and this is how you repay me? None of this would've happened if you had just been—"

Sweeping my leg out, I knock him off his feet. Joel doesn't have a chance to get up. He doesn't even have the chance to block my attack. Wrath ignites inside me, turning my vision red. It's like I can feel the heat and power of Kase's wrath exploding through me on a soul-deep level.

I punch him in the nose hard enough to feel the cartilage crack under the force of my hand. I don't know exactly how this works, but he feels as real as I do. He obviously feels pain too. There is no resting in peace for the damned. They can't even rest in pieces. And as for Joel? I want to ensure it more so than anything in the world.

"This is for ruining my life!" I throttle him in the face again. "For all the years of making me feel like I wasn't worth better. For isolating me from my friends and family. For nearly killing me." I punch him over and over again, the overwhelming desire to get vengeance for the bullshit he put me through consuming me.

I only feel the quiver of the ground shaking when it's too late. A massive shadow swallows the red light around me as the hulking demon prepares to attack me.

Once again, Joel will be the reason life as I know it will end.

Fuck me.

Cracking his jaw, the demon widens his mouth like a damn snake. Wider than I've ever seen Dante do, and it freaks me the hell out. He stomps his feet and pounds his fists against his chest. Slamming my hands into Joel's chest, I shove myself away and somersault. And damn it. I barely get a foot away. If I make it out of Hell, I need to work out. I need to train. That's how I should spend the rest of my mortal life. Because this shit is hard, and I'm unprepared.

"My soul!" the demon shouts, his voice echoing like he calls through a megaphone.

Joel groans and raises his hands. "Not me! Take her! She's who you want. The king of this kingdom thinks he has a claim on her. Prove him wrong."

This fucking bastard.

"Several kings," Joel adds. "With her, you can get power. I swear. You have to believe me."

What the hell? How does he know this? He hasn't been around to see that I've built a relationship with my devils.

"They've told me as much, thinking they could use it to

torture me." Joel digs his feet into the ground, trying to put space between him and the monstrous fucker, hell-bent on taking someone.

The demon's attention turns away from Joel.

Shit. That someone is me.

"You sound like you have a connection to their majesties, soul. I think I'll be keeping both of you now. Come on. Get in." Snatching Joel by his feet, the demon lifts Joel up.

"No! No!" Joel thrashes, trying to break free.

I stare in shock, watching as the demon silences Joel by shoving his head into his mouth. Like a snake eating its prey, the demon swallows Joel inch by inch. I don't stick around to enjoy the show and instead haul my ass to my feet and make a mad dash away. The demon said he planned to keep the both of us, and there is no fucking way I'm about to join Joel in some demon's gut.

The ground quakes, rumbling under my feet. I stumble, nearly crashing into one of the gnarled trees. Whipping my hair, I crane my neck and catch sight of the demon fucking chasing me as he still swallows Joel, his waist and legs still kicking. How such a thing is possible? Well, this is Hell after all.

I pick up my pace and run, wishing with everything in me that I knew how to call one of my devils. I swear to God, the saviors, and every damn holy thing in the world that if I make it out of here, I will chop Lucian's balls off. I'll then take his cock and slap him in the damn face with it. And then when that's over, I'll figure out how to summon Joel from here and figure out how to shove his head up Lucian's ass. Am I psychotic? Most likely. But I have to be. I have to embrace the darkness shoved into my soul by a shitty deal. By the devil who plans to break my bonds with the others and force me away from the man who had given me his angelic light.

My breath heaves, and I clutch my side, trying to push through my body cramping. Anger lashes over my skin in waves of heat. This was not how I wanted to start my day. I shouldn't be running from demons in Hell. I should be controlling them by my devils' sides in the Mortal World.

A loud crack echoes through the air, and one of the high mangled branches of a tree falls from above. It misses me by inches, but I trip over some sort of root sticking out of the ground. I crash to the ground, scraping my palms. Another snap of a branch sounds out, and I propel back to my feet in time to spin around to find the demon within a dozen feet. The demon's neck swells with Joel's feet inside it and his stomach bulges. I nearly puke at how his skin thins, revealing Joel's silently screaming face stretching the demon's flesh.

"There's plenty of room for you, mortal. It'll be easier if you die. I'd prefer just your soul." The demon stretches his arms forward, widening his mouth.

I screech and scramble away, but I fall on another root—no, not a root. It's a fucking bone of some sort. And I realize they're everywhere. The trees seem to be dropping their branches, littering the world with pieces of what most definitely look like dry, disgusting limbs. I'm going to have to have a fucking talk with Kase about this bullshit.

"That's good. Don't run," the demon says, cracking his jaw and widening his mouth. Ugh. I can see the bottom of Joel's soles peeking from the back of the demon's throat as he stomps closer, moving faster than I thought possible.

"Stay away!" I grab the nearest branch and swing it as hard as I can, whipping it across the demon's face.

But he doesn't stop.

He growls and launches at me like a damn rabid animal. My dumbass loses my goddamn senses, and all I can think about is how I don't want this monster touching me, but the thoughts do nothing to increase my ability to defend myself. I can't even swing the branch again, because the demon snatches it right from my hands.

He snatches me from the ground.

"Help! God, please! Fuck!" I scream, trying to jab my fingers into the demon's eyes. But it's pointless. His eyes are protected by some weird clear shell.

"God doesn't exist here," the demon says, his voice humming.

And fuck. I can see down his throat. I can see Joel's shoes. Along the inside of the demon's mouth and from what I can see of his esophagus, a strange collection of what looks like suction cups expand, ready to clamp to my skin to suck me into this monster.

I clench my jaw and brace myself. I have no idea whether I can die in Hell, but I'm sure I'll want to. But then again...

"Release her!" a familiar voice bellows, tightening my chest.

Bright light engulfs me, blinding me.

I fall from the demon's grip and land on my back. Brilliant white wings with golden tips expand above me, shielding me protectively. I watch in awe as heavenly light glows from Zade's skin.

Raising his arm, he ignites his sword with angel fire.

I've never seen something so satisfying.

The fucking demon will have Heaven to pay.

3

RAVEN

ANGELIC ADVENTURE

GOD, MY DEVILS are going to want to fuck my mouth until I quit whispering holy words that they want to spank from my vocabulary. Shit. I can't help myself. An avenging angel is seriously glorious when their damn sword isn't directed at me or anyone I've bonded with. And Zade is more than glorious. He's fucking as hot as the burning world around us.

Swinging his sword, Zade cuts off the demon's head,

sending strange black goo squirting over him. His smiting turns his soft features hard and sexy, so broody and intimidating, that it takes me a good pep-talk not to crawl forward and climb his muscular legs to force myself into his protective arms.

He just destroyed a demon on my behalf. He saved me when he could've let the demon swallow me whole. It would've solved the saviors' biggest problem of Hell trying to rise. Instead, he granted me mercy. As for his reason for it? I don't even fucking care. I'm just so damn thankful.

Zade's muscles ripple, his skin smoldering from getting splashed with the demon's blood. Tugging his shirt off, he uses it to swipe away the residue. I can't take my eyes off of him. His muscular chest rises and falls with his deep breaths as he gets himself under control. My breathing slows to match his, and I lick my lips, getting trapped by his startling blue gaze. He doesn't move from his spot, drinking me in for what feels like a torturously long amount of time. The world seems to still around us. It takes everything in me to get myself together.

I should kick myself for having to be rescued by an angel.

I should be pissed off that I wasn't capable of fighting off a demon.

But damn. Sometimes, I just want to be saved and protected. Taken care of after having to take care of myself.

If only it wasn't Zade and instead Andre, Kase, Dante, or

Micah.

"Raven, I'm so sorry," Zade says, concealing his flaming sword and brilliant wings in a blink of my eyes.

Like breaking my eye contact gets him to act, he strides toward me. What if it wasn't me trapped in his gaze and it was him frozen in mine? My heartbeat picks up speed as the thoughts swirl through my mind. I shouldn't be feeling...excited? I can't put my finger on it. It just feels so much better than the emotions beating me up only moments ago.

"Here, let me help you." Zade kneels on one knee and uses a clean section of his shirt to wipe my face, carefully cleaning the demon guts I had no idea splashed me too.

My tongue sticks to the roof of my mouth, my whole body humming at his closeness. All I can do is remain utterly still and allow him to clean me off the best he can. Our eyes meet again, and I search his gaze, trying to find some answers. Why is he here? What is he doing?

Reaching his hand up, he brushes my frazzled hair out of my face with his fingers. "That's better. Are you okay? I could feel how terrified you were."

The closer he leans into me, the more I can smell the sweet toasted marshmallow fragrance of his skin.

Again, I can't find my voice. All I can do is force myself to look from his eyes. My gaze travels to the pentagram brand burned into his cheek, and something inside me hypnotizes me. I find my hand an inch from his face and trace my finger along the circle and draw over the lines until he snatches my wrist.

"Raven? Say something." Concern lines his voice. "I can't decipher your feelings, but they're making me anxious."

He can feel my emotions?

A strange gurgle of a groan sounds through the air, snapping my attention away from Zade. I watch in shock as Joel claws his way out of the demon's...nope. I can't even think about it. It's enough to make me gag.

And help me find my voice.

"Fuck, get me out of here," I say, my voice rising in pitch, practically shrieking. "Take me home."

Without thinking, I throw myself at him. Zade catches me in his arms and unfurls his wings, flapping them to stop us from crashing to the ground. Our chests meet. The sensation sends a zing of energy through me. It's the strangest thing, feeling the soft thuds of his heartbeat on my breasts like I've kicked his body into overdrive. His eyes widen in surprise, and I half-expect him to shove me away, but all he does is straighten his back and stand tall.

"Ra-Raven." The grumbly voice sounds from behind Zade as Joel gets to his knees.

I clutch Zade tighter. "Please. Please. I need to go home. I can't be here. Fucking Lucian threw me into a portal."

Zade bounces on his feet, adjusting me in his arms. "You're afraid. I'm not sure I understand why. You've aligned with the devils. This is your eternity. How can you carry such fear when it was you who made the decision?"

I dig my fingers in Zade's bare shoulders, keeping my eyes locked on Joel. "You are so oblivious. It kills me. Now let's go. You're wasting time. I just—fuck. Can't you see the asshole behind you? That's why I'm fucking afraid."

Spinning, Zade whips around, leaving my back open and facing Joel. I turn my torso, fisting my hand. Joel stumbles closer like his sole purpose in Hell is to torment me. He doesn't even care that I'm in the arms of an angel. Why would he? He doesn't have anything to lose.

Joel clenches his jaw and stretches out his hand. "Ra—"

Zade finally reacts to Joel's presence. His muscles bulge, and he reaches behind him and unsheathes his sword, setting the world aglow in heavenly light. Joel's scream pierces my ears, and I squeeze Zade's torso between my thighs, holding him with my legs to free my hands to cover my ears.

"I might not be a ruler of Hell but I am a vessel for the Higher Power and will seek justice where the devils have failed. If you step another inch closer or say Raven's name again, you will face my holy vengeance." Zade's voice booms through the air, filling me up with something I can't fathom. What is going on? Again, why is he doing this? Protecting me. Is it because of Andre? I have so many questions.

"No! Please!" Joel screams, smartening up. He stumbles away from us and trips over the demon's remains.

No, not remains.

Oh shit. Zade might've decapitated the bastard, but the demon starts healing and putting himself together.

"Zade, please. We have to go," I whisper. "Please." My pleas come out so softly, but I pray the words, hoping that he'll take me back to the Mortal Realm.

My heart jumps as Zade expands his wings. Whoa. He is going to answer my prayers again.

"My soul." The guttural sound of the demon's voice stakes into my very being.

"Angel, help! You can save—" Joel's words snap off.

I don't have a chance to look behind me. Bending his knees, Zade launches us into the air, sending my midnight hair flying around us. I cling to him tightly, burying my face in the crook of his neck to ease the sting of the hot wind whipping across my body. If it's hot to me, I imagine it being even hotter for him. But he doesn't complain or sweat, soaring with me higher and higher until...oh, fuck. We're going back down. There is no portal or anything. All he does is relocate us, landing near a blood-filled river.

"Zade, what are you doing?" I ask, squeezing my eyes shut, praying that when I open them our surroundings will change.

"Getting you away from the soul who tried to consume your light. I felt his desire to destroy you. It was unpleasant." Zade's voice remains even, and he strokes one of his big hands along the length of my back.

It shouldn't feel so good, but it's like my body and soul just know that unless my devils find me that I might only have safety in Zade's arms, no matter how annoyed I am by it. He got here, and he should be able to leave.

"No, I meant why aren't we leaving? Let's get out of here. Lucian—" My stomach flies to my throat, the sudden freefall stealing my words. I can only tense and hold on. I can't even get myself to open my eyes to see what's happening.

The rush of falling from the sky subsides, and I gasp, trying to catch my breath. I open my eyes and stare at the smoldering world around us. A red stone road, like it's made of garnet, winds through an expansive burning landscape. Zade lands in the middle of it, touching his boots to the ground with a thump.

And then I see them.

There are souls everywhere.

Men and women fight monstrous demons in a horrendous battle. The hellish warzone goes on for miles, the yells and shouts of fury resonating through the air. Here, there aren't guns or knives or any human-made weapons. These people are using their bodies, using each other, and even using the parts of bottom feeder demons trying to up their power in Hell.

Cool fingers touch my chin, and Zade guides my face to look at him instead of the war surrounding us. "Raven, you're safe. Despite Andre abandoning his purpose on your behalf, I do not blame you and don't want to see you hurt. He wouldn't want that. I know it."

I suck my bottom lip into my mouth and nod my head. I know it hurts him, knowing his eternal companion jumped from grace because of me but he's too pure to place the blame on me. He empathizes on a soul-deep level unlike the rest of his brethren. He always stood by Andre's side and would try to warn him, but he never truly did much to stop him. It's like he only prayed or held his faith in Andre. He didn't fight for Andre, which is why I'm surprised he's now going through the effort.

"I don't understand why you're going through this trouble, but I think he would want you to do as I ask and take me out of here," I finally say, covering his hands with my own. "He would want you to help me find Elias."

I press gently, feeling the weight of his fingers against my cheeks. The exhilarating spark of being so close to him helps staunch the fear inside me. I don't know if it's his presence alone or something more, but whatever it is excites me. It feels as if it breathes life into me amid the fiery darkness around us.

Blinking a few times, Zade shakes his head. "I can't. I'm sorry. I won't risk my grace. I won't betray the Higher Power or Cassius."

My chest tightens. I should be used to angels giving me a blip of hope only to steal it away. "Zade, please. I'm scared.

Elias could die and be lost forever. He was once part of your brethren. Can't you summon an ounce of mercy to help him? He can't end up in Hell and unable to claim a throne. This place will destroy him."

Tears burn my eyes at the thought. He might not be bound by contract to a demon any longer, but he's still destined for Hell—but it must be by my hands. No one told me exactly why, but I assume it has something to do with our shared soul and my contract with Lucian. Regardless, I already die inside thinking about it. But to not be there to do what must be done? I'll let everyone down. I can't stand the thought.

Zade releases a long breath and strokes his thumbs across my cheeks, smearing my tears. "You care about him." He says it like the idea is impossible to comprehend. "You've asked for me to show him mercy instead of you."

"He's my soulmate," I say, the words ringing more true than ever before.

"You're too pure and light for all of this." Tipping his head back, Zade closes his eyes. He remains silent as if he's praying or thinking or just trying to process everything that happened involving me. "I wish you would accept Cassius's terms and let us help you. I don't understand why you fight so fiercely for a place that will consume you."

Annoyance sizzles through me. He is as dense as Cassius to even think that I would humor such a bargain. Maybe if it were destroying only Lucian. But he wants Kase and Dante too. I'll do anything to protect my psycho sweet devils, even if it means I'm lost here.

"Because it won't. My devils won't let it. It's not about Hell, Zade. It's about Kase and Dante. I'm sorry if you can't get it through your thick, righteous head, but I...I love them. I want to spend eternity by their sides. By Micah and Andre's. By Elias's. We have a plan, and I don't give a fuck about what Cassius thinks—or what you think—for that matter." I tug myself away from him.

Zade tries to grab my hand but I cross my arms. "Raven—"

"I'm not done, Zade. You claim that you can't help me out of here because you don't want to risk losing your wings, but I think it's something more. You wanted to use me to come here to see Andre. You're not helping me leave because of it. You love him, don't you? More than just as your companion."

"It's different than what your mortal brain tries to comprehend," he snaps, his voice growing deeper. Heavenly light radiates from his skin, the holiness of it stinging my eyes.

I squint, remaining strong and stubborn, not letting his grace scare me. "Then explain it. I'm trying to understand why you're putting yourself through all this. Why torture yourself? You could help us. I want nothing more than to reunite you with Andre, but right now? He doesn't want to see you. He knows you don't understand why he chose me. If you coul—"

Blinding light engulfs me, zinging me through the core. Zade pulls me to him before I have a chance to process that his lips brush mine as he kisses me so softly it feels like a whisper of angelic grace.

His lips taste exactly how he smells, and they're softer than I could've imagined. My body reacts to his closeness. Tingles burst between my legs to send goosebumps over my skin. I slide my fingers into his blond hair, guiding him to kiss me harder, more fiercely. I want my lips to sting and ache with passion, touched by his grace.

Fuck. I can almost imagine Dante and Kase joking about angel corruption now and how of course the fucker couldn't resist me, even in Hell.

Zade moans deep in his throat, gliding his hands down my sides until his fingers dig into my hips, pulling me so close that I can feel the hard length of his massive boner flexing between us. Gasping, I jerk myself away, my good senses returning to me in a moment all is usually lost. Zade's hand flies down to his cock, and he rubs it, trying to adjust it in his pants. He doesn't have to say anything for me to know this might be his very first boner. And damn. For an angel who seems to rely on the universe to do shit for him, he really surprised me. In a good way. I hadn't realized how attracted I was to him because of how infuriating he's been.

I touch my buzzing lips. "What the hell was that for? I'd

think an angel would ask me for permission before jabbing me with his cock."

Heat flushes up Zade's sun-kissed skin and into his cheeks, turning his turquoise eyes even brighter. "I'm sorry. You're right. Forgive me. I only wanted to understand."

"Understand what? Andre didn't abandon Heaven to freely kiss me. He kissed me with all of his angelic glory beforehand. Hell, I even sucked his cock." Damn my mouth. What is it about Zade that makes me not only want to overshare but also convince him that it's more than about a devil's lust.

Zade's face reddens even more, and I'm nearly certain he will launch into the air and disappear, leaving me to fend for myself. "Oh," he finally says, rubbing his hand over his smooth jaw. "I still think it helped him make the decision. He was so enthralled with your soul."

"So why kiss me? Why risk your wings?" I can't stop from asking him the questions. "It seems neither of us understands any of this."

Zade unfurls his wings, expanding them out. "I think I do, but not only because of our intimacy." Oh-fucking-God. Intimacy? He didn't even use tongue. The sweet, innocent bastard. "It is more than that. The longer I'm with you, the more I—"

Zade's face twists in agony, and he hollers as he unsheathes his sword and sets it ablaze. We were so focused on each other that the rest of the world disappeared, leaving us open for an attack.

A hot hand slaps over my mouth. "What a delicious soul."

I can't move or scream.

Zade hollers again.

Staring with wide eyes, I scream against the sweaty palm of...another soul, I think. Zade drops to his knees and bows forward. Blood pours from a wound on his upper back, just above his wings.

"Kill him!" a woman shouts.

Zade whips his head up and locks his gaze to mine. I watch several men charge him.

They aim their strange weapons at his wings.

"No!" I scream against the sweaty hand of the asshole pinning me to his chest. "Zade!"

The demon jerks me around, grabbing my shoulders. His sallow eyes rove over my face as he studies me. I struggle to yank away from him, but it's like he has just as much Hell strength as I do.

Opening his mouth, the demon unrolls his strange white tongue and drags the disgusting thing from my chin to my forehead. Firelight flickers in his eyes, his pupils expanding within his yellow irises until his eyes turn black.

"Can't let that angelic bastard take you. No one leaves Hell except the kings," he says, slurping his tongue across my cheek next.

My skin stings, and I ram my knee as hard as I can into the fucker's groin, but he doesn't move. I'm not even sure he has a sensitive spot on his grotesque humanoid body. "He's not taking me from Hell, you fucker. He's taking me to Andre."

"Andre? I better get you broken and ready then. The ruler of the lustful has his own desires to quench. Maybe I'll find myself as part of his legion." The demon wags his thick, black brows. Ugh. Nasty. "I wouldn't doubt if he gives me you as a reward for taking care of the angel too."

"Take me to him and find out," I snap, grinding my teeth.

His pupils retract and he flicks his long tongue back out, gliding it along my neck. "Like I said, after I've had my fill."

Oh-fucking-no.

Sweeping his leg, he knocks my feet out from under me, pushing me to the ground. I scrape my palms on the hot ground, trying to get away, to do anything, but his heavy body lands on top of me. Every goddamned horrible situation I can think of tumbles through my mind in my fit of panic. He's going to rape me. He's going to fucking rape me.

I scream, kicking and bucking my body, doing everything I can to get this evil, disgusting demon off me.

His hot hand slams into my back, winding me. My shouts cut off, and the edges of my vision shadow. I pray to succumb to the darkness. I don't know if I can survive this. If I can live past it.

"No!" The world around me erupts in blinding light with Zade's holler.

The weight suffocating me vanishes. I gasp and rest my head on the ground, giving in to the shuddering relief coursing through me. Silence fills the air, the sounds of the battle, or the lost, wrathful souls no longer piercing my ears. A wave of tranquility covers me like a cozy blanket, calming my racing heart.

"Raven, can I pick you up?" Zade murmurs, his familiar sweet scent wafting around me from his closeness. "I need to make sure you're unhurt."

I'm so stunned by everything that happened that all I can do is nod. Zade lifts me from the ground and hugs me in his arms.

"That demon will never hurt you again. I promise." Expanding his wings, he flaps them a few times but doesn't launch us from the ground.

"Please, if you can't get me out of here, help me find Andre. I'm afraid if I don't, there won't be anything else you can do. The demons won't stop. They won't acknowledge me as anything but a contracted soul until I fulfill my end of the bargain." I lick my dry lips, my throat burning from my screams.

Zade sighs and nods his head. "Raven, I—"

"Now," I say, my words sharper. "I don't want you trying to give me hope. Because right now, seeing how much you resist and also not knowing what's happening with Elias...I'm hopeless. I'm lost."

All feels lost.

4

ZADE

HEAVEN'S LOSS

SOMETIMES I THINK I know something, but then it turns out that I have no idea. The Higher Power tests me and the other brethren over and over, but it's not because It doesn't believe in us. These tests help us work through difficulties, and right now, Raven is my number one problem.

At least, that's what I've been telling myself.

What Cassius has been telling me.

How our brethren could go from five to four at the heart of the particular soul so long ago baffled me. Apart from Lucifer, Kase, and Dante abandoning their purposes to start their own paths with such a vile place as Hell, a place the Higher Power cursed them with instead of the paradise they sought, Elias was the only other angel I've ever known to leave home. How he found himself entangled with a mortal soul was hard to fathom. It was not our place to get involved as we watched humanity. But he got too close. And then he disappeared. All for the soul.

I thought that was the end of it, and his departure an anomaly. We all thought it.

Then the soul returned. I could expect Micah to fall. He had a bond with Elias, and they were close. It wouldn't be unthinkable.

But Andre? My closest, most trusted companion?

I never imagined it until the moment I saw him touch her soul.

I feared it wouldn't be long. I had hoped to keep him on his path, but I wasn't enough. My light isn't as bright as hers.

Now that I stare deeply into Raven's eyes, searching the light of her soul for the answers of questions I don't even know how to ask, I realize why. She reminds me of home, of Heaven, of the things in the world we fight to protect. If only I could figure out why she does and how it's possible with the chains of darkness imprisoning her to a place I can hardly tolerate.

"If you keep staring at me like this, I'm going to kiss you to make you stop." Raven's eyes shift as she studies my face.

I continue to stroll down the hellacious path in the expanse of souls lost to their own personal Hell just below the surface of the road. I've never seen such a sight. There are hundreds of souls trapped under my boots in currents of Hell water only accessible by the demons who control this place for Kase.

"As much as I'd like to continue learning the reasons why Andre gave up his divine purpose for you, I must decline. Your emotions are far too fragile, and I'm nearly certain if I allow another demon to get within a foot of you, your cheeks will be forever branded with your tears. The sorrow and fear over being defiled by such a monstrous entity still blazes in my heart. I'm not sure either of us can survive any more trauma." I inhale a small breath, forcing my gaze away from Raven's. "You might be strong and resilient, but not every unfortunate thing adds to your strength. Mortals only say that to feel better. Sometimes, a soul just gets hurt and healing could last a lifetime. I do not want to be the reason for that."

I shudder, pushing the thought away. I hope she doesn't hold my need to guard her precious body and soul against me. Raven is the only way I can safely gain access to this realm. I can tether to her light and follow her here, since she crossed over in death and was dragged out by Andre. Without her, I would risk losing my wings. I can't. It pains me so much knowing that I'll never see light within Andre again.

"I don't even know how to respond to that, Zade. I thought you were a dickhead, you know. A righteous bastard. Is that only around Cassius? And what do you mean about you can feel my trauma?" Her bluish-green stare burns into the side of my face, but not in a painful way. The weight of her attention helps distract me from my own wandering thoughts and I stroll with her in my arms through a valley of the damned.

"Your emotions run rampant through me as if they are my own. I'm not used to it. I hadn't realized how...messy it is to connect with a soul not at peace. It's perplexing. Like now, you smile at me, but your soul weeps. You hurt on a deep level." I adjust her in my arms. "But you are also so guarded that I can't help you."

Her smile widens, her eyes crinkling in the corners. Among her pain, a bit of humor breaks through. "Silly angel. You've been around literally forever. Don't you understand the concept of putting on a brave face? And why do you think you can help me? You haven't been much help to my soul. Thanks for protecting my body, though. I'll give you that."

I open and close my mouth, trying to think of a way to convince her that I am more than the brute strength that comes with my angelic warrior power. I'm not sure why I feel the need to. I shouldn't care how she feels about me. She's not among Heaven's beloved. But a deep part of me craves to show her that I'm not a being who lives purely for vengeance and keeping Hell at bay. I am here for humankind. Her thoughts are tangled by the darkness, so she thinks our light is the problem. I can sense it. Heaven is her enemy. Hell is her captor. All she wants is to find a balance and peace.

Purgatory.

I'm beginning to understand her reasons...I think. But comprehending them is another story. God help me. If only I had Andre by my side. It was these types of situations we would ponder together. He shut me out before we could. Heaven is not the only one feeling his loss. It buries deep in my very essence, and I have no clue how to fix it. Everything I could try will jeopardize me. I will not abandon grace. I won't.

"Zade? I'm sorry. I was a bit harsh. I'm just so upset and scared. I'm pissed the fuck off at Lucian. I didn't mean to upset you." Raven's soft voice coaxes me from my thoughts. Her warm fingers touch my cheek, and she wipes my tears away. I hadn't realized I was crying.

I use the back of my hand to dry the rest of my face and blink a few times. "There is no need to apologize. It is not your fault. I appreciate your honesty. I'm sure with a bit more time, I will learn how to...put on a brave face, like you. No more tears."

Her brows knit together, her pouty mouth drawing my attention away from her eyes. "You don't have to do that. Being sensitive isn't a bad thing. You don't need to fake things. I just—it caught me off guard. I like being able to tell what you're feeling."

How curious. I feel the same. I'd prefer she not confuse me with smiles that do not match what's going on inside her, no matter how beautiful she looks doing so. And right now, frowning in concern, she remains just as stunning. If not more so. Not because I like seeing her sad. I like knowing that she isn't cold to me. She's opening up her fiery protective walls.

A zap of heat strikes me in my chest, and I gasp.

She unexpectedly lets me in completely, and my angelic sight kicks on, setting her aglow. A small gasp escapes her. Trailing her hands from my cheeks, she glides them down my neck and back up into my hair. Her hot lips shock me, sending sparks across my skin. One second she's pouting and now her mouth is on mine, her fingers curling in my hair, her body shifting until her legs wrap around me.

It feels like Heaven comes to Hell, here to put this wretched world in its place.

I unfurl my wings, wrapping them around the two of us protectively, ensuring that if some monstrous demon wants to ruin this strange and exciting moment of getting completely lost in Raven's emotions, then all trauma will fall on me. She has been through enough. She has faced too much in her life, and suddenly, I have the urge to...

I yank my head back and groan, my whole body rippling

with an emotion I've never felt before. The sensitivity pulsing from my groin tests my ability to continue to carry Raven when I have the urge to touch myself. It's mystifying. We were both fine only a moment ago.

"Fuck. What the fuck," Raven says, wiggling in my arms. "Oh, God. Are we...?"

I shake off the all-consuming need of what I realize is desire coursing through my body and look around. "We are in Lust's Kingdom," I murmur, my eyes widening at the sight before me.

A gust of hot wind nearly knocks me over, and I stand firm on the road, bracing myself. Raven tightens her arms around me like if I blow away, she wants to go with me. Together, we stare at the crowded landscape before us. Souls twist and tangle in an endless expanse of bodies. Desire and need rage inside me the longer I clutch onto Raven and peer around. The punishment lies in the passion of every soul, so close yet frozen, only moving with the gusts of hot wind.

And then there are the demons risen from the crowd in grotesque forms not quite like mortal bodies but enough to distinguish them apart as they march along the naked souls, bare and exposed, begging and pleading for...relief. Their passion pains them, and they beg for intimacy. They're hungry for it. Starved.

"Um, Zade?" Raven asks, wiggling in my arms. "We need to keep moving before they notice our arrival...not to mention, I'm weirded out by how fucking horny I feel."

"It's the winds. They're laced with some sort of aphrodisiac." I flare my nostrils and inhale a deep breath. "Andre was quite clever in the construction of his kingdom and its punishment. It probably reflects his own desperate needs. The devils get their strength from their sins."

Raven grimaces. Her sudden worry over Andre consumes me and blends with my own. My words trigger fear inside her, but I don't exactly know what about. She surely knows that the devils design their kingdoms, so I don't think it's that.

"You don't think he'd fuck others here, do you?" Raven asks, her voice a whisper on the wind. "Like, if that's how he gets power..."

"I don't know my companion as a devil." Forcing my legs to work, I stroll along the path again. This kingdom seems endless, but I know once I get a sense of Andre, things will shift for us. Like Heaven, Hell doesn't apply to the same laws as the Mortal Realm. Things just are and they adjust for individual souls. What I see might not be the same as what the souls do.

Raven tightens her jaw. "He's not much different, Zade. He still feels the same to me in my dreams. Maybe a little naughtier, but it isn't bad. I just—I don't know."

"You don't want him with anyone else," I say, meeting her gaze. "Intimately."

"If this is how he survives...it's unfair of me to assume,

right? Fuck. I never thought much about this and now that I am—"

A gust of hot, smoky wind cuts off Raven's comment, and I stumble, trying to move with it instead of fighting against it. Just when I find my balance, a cross wind knocks into my back. Raven's midnight hair whips in my face, and the world trembles around us. I can't do anything as the winds pick up so fiercely that I can no longer stay on the ground. I automatically stretch my arms wide, bracing myself against the fiery tornado that whips dozens of bodies into the air.

Raven gets caught in the whirlwind, and she screams, flying into the air and away from me. I yell her name, the horror of seeing her amid the masses of naked bodies shocks me to the core. I had promised to keep her safe and failed her.

Bending my knees, I launch into the air, praying that the Higher Power gives me the strength and endurance to conquer these hellish winds to save her. Her shrieks pierce the air, echoing through the world and striking me in the chest.

A bloated naked man flies from another tornado and crashes into my chest, sending the both of us to the road. Hot, dry lips caress my cheek at the same time a hand slides down my chest and over my stomach on a mission to touch me in a regrettable, unwanted way. I swing my hand and punch the soul, knocking him off me. I cannot believe his bold, demented attempt to satisfy his starving lust.

I catapult to my feet, jumping out of the way of his

plump fingers, his tongue licking his lips as if I'm some sort of delicious dinner for the taking. Another soul falls from the sky and thuds on the ground next to him, and I back away, averting my eyes at the sight unfolding in front of me. I had never thought an anus could be used like that, the knowledge of mortal sexual endeavors never my priority.

"Help!" Raven's call whips my attention to her high above the world as the wind settles, releasing every soul to freefall back to the ground.

Her voice snaps off, her breath stolen from her. I can feel her terror of splattering among the naked souls as if it were my own. Dozens of bodies smash into the ground around me, the sky too crowded for me to launch into the air fast enough.

My heart slams against my ribcage, and I cover my mouth with my hand. Tears blur my eyes. I've never felt so helpless.

And then Andre appears.

His expansive black wings, free of feathers and now made of something that reminds me of leather, spread out wider than before. He soars so gracefully through the falling bodies like they just automatically part for him as he dives toward Raven. She flails her body, getting closer and closer to the ground. I suck in a breath and hold it, praying to the Higher Power that Andre catches her. I can't bear to see what happens if he doesn't.

This is my fault.

Andre nosedives, zooming so quickly that he surpasses the

falling bodies and locks his fingers around Raven's wrist. He throws her into the air in front of him, engulfing her in his muscular arms.

I release my breath and watch as their lips meet as he blindly navigates the sky and skids to a stop a few dozen feet away from me. My body awakens, and I grab myself, feeling the hardening pulse of my erection through my pants. Desire seeps into my essence, ignited by the sight of the most beautiful light radiating from Raven and the new shadows slithering from Andre's essence, wrapping around her. Even as a devil, he's still handsome.

My feet get a mind of their own, and I shuffle closer, hypnotized by watching Andre's tongue slip into Raven's mouth—a mouth I had just kissed and experienced. One I want to experience again. And then there is Andre in all his hellish glory.

What am I thinking? Why am I thinking this?

Lust's Kingdom is getting to me.

It's in this moment I realize I'm afraid. I thought I wanted to see Andre, to confront him and try to understand his choices. But now? It's clear. He's in love with Raven and believes in her purpose over the Higher Power's.

I have to leave.

I unfurl my wings and prepare to take flight, keeping my eyes on Andre and Raven. Like he senses the weight of my stare, Andre jerks away from Raven. The dark depths of his brown eyes light with the flames of Hell, igniting inside him. Lava-like veins glow under his skin, traveling to his heart and what keeps Hell together with him as its anchor.

"Zade." The sound of my name on his lips washes a wave of foreign emotions over me.

I cringe at the toxic anger and hatred whipping from Andre to me. "Andre, I..." What do I say to him?

"You kissed the soul that belongs to Hell. And in my kingdom." Andre's comment stops me from trying to say anything else.

His black wings, glowing with red veins, expand out, and he sets Raven on her feet. She tries to block his way, pressing her palms to his naked chest. It doesn't work. It angers him even more, and surprisingly, I grow afraid for her.

"Raven, stop. Be careful," I say, holding my palms up. "You don't have to—"

Andre explodes into his devil form, proving to me that he truly has lost his grace. The giant beast before me isn't my brethren. He's gone. Our eternity sharing Heaven's grace has been destroyed.

Tears blur my vision as he charges at me, all rock and armor and full of hatred.

And it's all aimed at me.

"You fucking bastard! I should take your wings." Andre's deep voice booms through the air as he scurries toward me, his extra legs moving him impossibly fast. He snaps giant pinchers in his fury, sending a high-pitched whistle with every thunderous clap.

I straighten my back and face him head on.

This isn't who he truly is, and I won't back down.

I will remind him.

His massive tail curls over his head, aiming at me.

Raven screams.

5

ANDRE

DARK DESIRES

"ANDRE, STOP! PLEASE!" Cool arms hug around my tail as Raven tries to stop me from impaling Zade. "Calm down. He's been helping me. Lucian dropped me into a portal, and he answered my prayer. He only wanted to see you. He misses you."

I roar, my deadly need to get my former brethren out of my kingdom and away from Raven's soul all-consuming.

Slamming the sharp point of my stinger into the ground, I rip up the road beneath Zade's boots and send him sprawling backward. Raven dangles before me, swinging a few feet in the air.

I heave a few deep breaths, focusing on the sensation of her hands around my most powerful weapon. If she continues to mess with me, I might accidentally shoot venom from my retractable stinger. If that happens...I shiver in anticipation. All it would take is one prick to have a soul writhing on the ground in desperate lust, aching but never fully satisfied. Like me. At least, until now. I've been waiting what feels like forever for Raven to enter my kingdom in her physical form, because the lust I've been arousing in her during her sleep isn't enough.

But she's all I want. I will not accept anything less than her in all her delicious beauty. She is mine, and I'd rather starve and feel as if I live in torturous anticipation than find another relief. I just hope I'm not too much for her, because I know I'll never get enough. I already want her so badly that I'm willing to release Zade, so he leaves and she stops worrying about the blasted bastard.

I can barely look at him. At his judgmental face. Surely he thinks of me as an abomination and a traitor, but I don't regret my choice to save Raven.

"Andre," Raven whispers. She releases my tail and drops down, stumbling back and falling on her butt. She doesn't stay down long. Getting up, she raises her palms to me. "Andre, please. Just let him go. He was only helping me get to you, so you could open a portal to send me home."

My body shudders as I gather my power and suppress my devilish nature. Striding forward, I gather Raven in my arms, pulling her up until she hooks her legs around me. The thought of her leaving so soon makes me ache everywhere but especially in my cock. My balls throb like I've been punched in them, and it takes her touching my cheeks to get me to focus on her instead of what she does to my body.

"You want to leave me already?" I murmur, groaning under my breath. "You just got here."

"Of course I don't want to leave you. I just—I need to get back to the Mortal Realm because Lucian gave Elias to Vincent. He is supposed to hide him until he dies. Kase and Dante—"

"If you let me go, I will find them and inform them for you," Zade says, interrupting Raven's pleas. "I want you to know that I'm not a threat, Andre."

Raven's heartbeat picks up speed, her mouth turning incredibly sexy with her pout. I imagine her lips parting for me to taste my body like she had done before. My muscles tense and flex, my desire eating away at my good senses. A sudden sweet fragrance permeates the air, wafting from Raven to me, and I lower her a few inches, letting her feel what she does to me. I realize the fragrance intoxicating me belongs to her, her body reacting to mine, and it gets more potent. I want to gulp in breath after breath. Just her lust helps settle the burning in my soul.

"Okay," Raven says, her voice breathy. "You promise you'll get them right away?"

Zade nods his head. "I do."

Raven shudders a breath, her eyelids closing partially. She can sense my lust too. She craves me. Needs me. I can feel it in my carnal instincts. "Andre, please. If you let him go. I'll stay until someone comes for me."

"If you stay, I can't promise not do with you as I please, Raven. You don't understand what's happening to me," I mutter, locking my fingers through her hair and tilting her head to the side.

"But I do. You need me," she whispers. "Your power comes from the sin you embody. Zade said so."

I swallow and lick my lips, forcing myself to glance at Zade, but he's already gone. Raven is now mine and mine alone in my kingdom. I've thought about this moment over and over since the second I claimed my throne and the energy that comes with it, zinging through every molecule on my body.

"I've been starving without you, little hellion," I say, spinning on my feet. I've never been so excited to return to my empty palace, kept clear of anything that could test my restraint in ways I refuse to think about.

"You haven't found...sustenance elsewhere?" Her voice

remains soft like she's afraid to ask or know the answer. "I understand if you did what you had to."

I cock my head and look at her. Her beautiful eyes look toward the browning sky, the winds of lust separating the damned souls again, ensuring they'll never get their fill for their wrong-doings—those who've done vile things in life fueled by their passion and desire. All here for eternal punishment. And I make it hurt.

"Are you suggesting that I could possibly find a cure for my unrelenting ache for you through one of these miserable souls? Or a bottom feeder demon? You're it for me, little hellion. I would never betray you." I search her eyes, wishing I could listen to her thoughts. "I'd rather go weak and suffer."

Her frown softens as she thinks about what I say, and then she graces me with the most stunning smile that lights up her soul so brightly that it helps keep my urge to take her as my mate in the most intimate way in control.

"Thank-fucking-fuck," she says, giggling in my arms.

She plants her palms to my cheeks and pulls me to her face, crashing her lips to mine in a kiss that quickens my pace. I will not give any of the damned the satisfaction of me getting my fill.

I chuckle against her soft lips. "I should punish you for even thinking for one second that me being with another could possibly be okay. Your soul is mine. My brethren didn't even have to warn me about the rules of our eternity together if I chose a place by your side, which I have, Raven."

She crinkles her nose, narrowing her eyes. "Fuck no, I didn't think it was okay. I hated the thought. I wanted to cut a dick or bitch or whatever damn thing that could get you off. You think I'm yours, but you're mine. That intimidating, rock-hard, enormous cock is mine. I licked it, so you know I'm serious." She laughs with her words, her playfulness so endearing that I could let her take control of me however she wants. "I earned it. Corrupting you as an angel, and now I'm getting my reward by corrupting a devil too. Your virginity is mine."

"You naughty little hellion, so boldly pointing out how ironic it is for me to take a seat on the throne of lust when I've never truly got to reap the benefits." I ease her away from me until I surprise her by plopping her seductive ass on the black stone throne that I claimed as my own. "Since that's the case, I must declare you as queen of my kingdom." As much as I want to grab her knees and burn off her clothes to have my way with her, I don't rush or push her. Micah warned me that I must proceed with caution and not overwhelm her. He had made the mistake of showing her more than she could handle, and it left a scar on her soul.

So following his advice, I've decided that I'll make her want to stay. I'll make her crave to come back to me. This will be our paradise.

"I love the sound of that...as long as I don't have to control the masses outside these walls. That was...scary as fuck. I thought I was going to get trapped in a damn orgy." She purses her lips with her words, her face flushing.

I can't hear her thoughts, but whatever it is she's thinking sets her body off again, her aroma not only sending a shockwave through my groin but also to my mouth. I swallow, my hunger growing.

"You are curious," I say, touching her chin, leaning in to lock her in my gaze. "I am curious too. Do you think Kase and Dante would ever invite me to join the three of you?"

She tips her head back and laughs, the musical sound more breathy. Her face reddens even more, and she slides off the throne and in front of me. "What is it with you devils all wanting to ravish me at once? Kase will never let anyone fuck me with their cock around him unless he gets to do the same. At once." She bares her bottom teeth. "And if I let the three of you, what about Micah and Elias? I don't even know how that would work. Two holes, my mouth, and my hands. I won't be able to do anything but lie there."

I moan, imagining her beautiful body lying exposed and quivering in anticipation before me. "You won't know unless you experience it. It might surprise you, like you have surprised me. I still think about you on your knees before me. I've been longing to reciprocate. I want to taste your desire. Just talking about all of the possibilities..." My words trail off. "Let me show you my wing. I need to forget about the world outside us. All I want is to think about you and your beautiful soul. It helps ease the beast within me."

"Whatever you want and need, Andre. You're here because of me, and I'm sorry it took all this bullshit to get me here. I was afraid." Her honesty digs deeply into me, her soul, body, and mind open to me in a world where souls try to remain guarded.

"Let me change that," I say, entering the opened double doors to my suite, still bare because adding things felt too permanent, especially because I hadn't seen Raven apart from visiting through a portal.

Raven nods with a smile, hugging me close as I carry her to the bed fit for an army of devils. The thought of sharing Raven with the others has crossed my mind along with everything I want to experience with her. I've had a lot of time on my hands, just watching those entranced with burning lust from my palace balcony. It's how I spotted her like a beacon of pure ecstasy among the tarnished mass of the damned.

"This place is astounding, Andre. Did you build it? I'm not sure how that works." She caresses her fingers over my shoulders, drawing them over the spot I hide my wings with Hell power.

"Yes, in a way." Setting Raven on the bed, I stand before her and close my eyes, tapping into the invisible energy coursing around us. "Hell power allows me to manipulate the energy around us."

I press my palms together and gather enough power to turn it palpable in my hand until a glowing flower forms in between my fingers. The fire dissipates, leaving behind a delicate, velvety black rose, blooming just for Raven.

Her face lights up as I offer the rose to her, loving her reaction to the pure magic of a mortal soul. "That's incredible."

"You want to try?" I ask, sitting beside her. "You're not just a soul in my kingdom. You're my queen. It will work for you."

Her eyes widen, and she bounces a little in anticipation. "Do I just think about it?"

I nod my head. "Yes. Absorb the power inside of you."

Raven closes her eyes and rubs her palms together, concentrating on something in her mind's eye. Her body bursts into a fiery light, and she gasps and reaches for me. I stare in awe as the Hell power fades. Flipping her midnight hair behind her shoulder, she exposes her breasts now adorned in black and red lace.

She scoots more onto the bed and rests on her elbows, rubbing her smooth thighs together. "What do you think? You gave me a rose, so I thought...I'd give you this."

My breath catches at the sight of her beauty and how she wraps her body like a gift just for me. It sets off my carnal desire, and I can't stop my body from taking control of my mind. A deep groan reverberates up my throat. I need her more than I ever knew, my desire banishing all my hesitation to give her what she wants.

Lunging forward, I surprise her by grabbing her ankles and dragging her to the edge of the bed. She will see me kneel before her and bury my face into the sweet warmth of her pussy. I can almost taste her, her scent more powerful the closer I get. Gasping, she laughs in surprise only to have me steal her voice with a kiss. I taste her mouth, gliding my tongue over hers, enjoying her lips while my hands explore the smoothness of her skin.

"You're so hypnotic," I murmur, breaking from her mouth to kiss her jaw. "I'm going to eat you until I get my fill. I want to hear you scream my name in vain."

Raven moans as I ignite Hell power like a candle on the tip of my finger. I draw it down her clavicle, leaving behind a pink trail in my wake. The front of her bra snaps open, and I bow forward, sucking her breast into my mouth and rolling her tight, pebble-like nipple with my tongue.

Moaning, Raven arches her back and eases her legs open with her desire, silently inviting me to her. She blindly reaches for me. I give her what she wants by undressing with the help of my Hell power. Her small hand laces around my hard-on, the sensation zinging a burst of energy right to my balls. I groan and break from her nipple, working my way down in fast desperation. I want her so badly. It hurts me in a good way. I've been so pent up with this need that all it takes is for Raven to stroke her finger down my shaft and to my balls to send me over the edge.

Another shockwave courses through me, and I grunt as I cum all over Raven's stomach. The release shadows the edges of my vision as ecstasy feeds into me. But it's not enough. It'll never be enough.

"I've been dying, little hellion. Everything about you...I need more. I need your pleasure. That's what will fulfill me."

"Damn," she whispers, but it's not in disappointment. She's amazed with me, her heart picking up pace.

"What's on your mind, little hellion? I'm no good at guessing and don't have the luxury to know what you're thinking." A part of me knows that she might compare me to the other devils or maybe even bastard, unworthy mortals. I won't let it bother me, though. I'm ready to prove why lust is my kingdom. "I'm not a naïve feather-head anymore either."

She laughs breathlessly and grabs the blanket, wiping off the cum on her stomach. "I'm sorry. It was unexpected."

"That's how starved my body is for you. I must warn you, I might be different, but I lack the experience to really let you know." I trace my finger along her hip and over her thigh.

She shifts her knee, giving me a view of her delectable body I want to acquaint myself to. I keep my eyes glued to hers as I quietly memorize every inch with my finger, feeling the dampness of her folds as I spread her pussy lips apart and rub my finger across the pink nub of her clit.

Gasping a moan, she says, "Different doesn't scare me. It

excites me. You excite me. I'm so fucking horny just being close to you. It's unlike anything I've felt. Almost torturous. It's taking all my willpower not to knock you on your back, climb on top of you, and see how much of you I can take."

"I think I'm in love, little hellion. Your words—fuck. You're mine." I slip my finger inside her, the slippery warmth of her excitement making my cock pulse. My mouth water. I want to gorge on every one of her sexual desires. I watch her chest rise and fall, her fingers scrunching the blankets, and then I bring my wet finger to my mouth and suck it, closing my eyes as I savor the sweet nectar of her pussy. "You can live your darkest desires...when I'm through."

A sexy whimper escapes her lips as I spread her legs wide enough to fit my broad shoulders between them. She remains upright on the edge of the bed while I kneel. Starting slow, I familiarize myself with her seductive beauty, gliding my tongue over her knee and licking my way up to her thigh. Her fingers run through my hair in anticipation. She craves me as much as I do her.

"My stunning, delicious soul," I murmur, gliding my tongue over the seam between her legs until I reach the spot I know she favors attention. Her moan strikes me in the balls, and I groan and bury my face, sucking and licking her clit, letting her moans guide me in satisfying her desire.

"Oh, God," she says, arching and yanking my hair.

Her words sting my ears as she unintentionally calls out

to the Higher Power. And I hope It listens now. I yearn for the saviors to know exactly what I have become and what I get with this beautiful soul. She fulfills me unlike anything ever has in my eternity. Her light feeds my darkness, giving me more power than I've ever had. I feel like a god—like her god—as she whimpers in ecstasy, worshipping and praying for the pleasure I arouse in her.

Raven's body tenses, and she thrusts herself back, clutching the bed and lifting her hips as the magic of her bliss showers me in a mist of pure, hot passion. If I could lick myself clean, I would. The taste of her on my lips is better than anything.

"Holy shit," she exclaims, gasping and squirming, extending her arms to me. "I think my soul left my body for a second. It was like I saw Heaven again but it wasn't Heaven. It was you. It was—fuck."

I grin and hook my arm around her, dragging her onto the bed by her waist. She doesn't let me get on top of her but pushes me onto my back with the strength of Hell. I moan, my muscles rippling, my body humming. She straddles my legs and uses both her hands to stroke my cock as she bounces slightly, using my shaft to rub her clit.

"Are you ready to be fucked by your queen?" she says, her voice sultry and breathy. Her incomparable beauty enthralls me as much as her excitement does. She's anxious and needy, and I know I'm the only cure for her unrelenting lust, triggered by my kingdom. "I've been dreaming about corrupting you, Andre. Fucking you how you want."

Fire flickers in her eyes, her newfound dominance so sexy. It's the only reason I want to give in and let her have her way with me. At least this once. Letting her have her way will help guide me into discovering what exactly sets her off. I want to satiate her and then take my fill.

"I'm more than ready," I murmur, groaning as she bows forward to kiss me, aligning her body to mine. "Feed into my desire and take what you may."

Half-squatting, she eases my tip into her hot pussy, slowly at first as her body stretches to accommodate mine. We moan together, the sensation of how tight and wet she is sending electricity through me. She pants, rocking her hips, moaning with every inch she takes in and out.

"You're so fucking big. It feels so good," she says, biting her lip as she picks up her pace. "I thought it would hurt."

"You've been chosen by the devil of lust. There is no pain in your pleasure unless you enjoy it," I murmur, lacing my fingers through her hands. "Your body will bend to our desires. There are no limitations in my kingdom."

Her brows furrow together. "It will?"

I lick my lips and send Hell power burning across my fingers. "Do you want to find out?"

Her eyes widen as the thoughts cross her mind. My skin hums, the energy around us so intoxicating that I can only think about what it'll feel like to enter her in my entirety. My power won't hurt her. I am made of pure pleasure. She will see.

"Whatever you want, but not my ass," she says, smiling. "It's been claimed."

"For now," I tease.

Arching forward, I crash my lips to hers and flip her on her back, using my Hell power to awaken her body in a way that makes her startle and scream in bliss. I thrust into her, knowing how she likes it rough and wild. Her desires run clear and hot through my mind, playing out everything she wants from our passion. I gasp and intake a breath, the energy alone enough to fill the ache in my body.

"Whoa, fuck! Fuck! That feels fucking incredible and strange at the same time," she says, hooking her legs around me. "What is happening, Andre? God."

"Embrace your darkest desires," I whisper. "Shout it to the Heavens. Louder. I want you to scream."

"You're my darkest devil, aren't you, Andre?" she asks, moaning and tipping her head back. "Your need unlike anyone's."

"And you are my light." Grabbing her leg, I stretch it up over her head as I rock hard and fast, stealing her ability to do anything but scream her pleasure. "My eternity. I'll starve without you."

Our gazes lock, and I lose myself in the beautiful depths

of her eyes, my body frantic with need, my cock finding such relief. Heat grows in my balls, the sensation stealing my breath. I've never felt anything like it, and the most thrilling explosion shudders through me as Raven grows even tighter...no, I grow bigger. I can't see my cock, but the sensitivity increases, and I cum so hard that the bed rocks and Raven yells my name, scratching me hard enough to make me bleed.

She screams her moan, her body stiff and arched and trembling. "Fuck, Andre. What's happening? My body. The orgasm." She heaves a breath between each set of words. "It's lasting forever."

"It's my venom," I say, moaning, drowning in both our pleasure. "I didn't realize..."

I ease my hips, starting to slide out of her, but another explosive sensation quakes through me. Shit. It feels so good.

I try to slide out to thrust back into her, wanting to hear her scream in more intense pleasure, but the tightness persists and I can only move a few inches.

"Raven," I murmur, my mind hazy with lust. "The ache in my being hasn't subsided, and...I think I can't let you go."

She pants, her pouty mouth puffing with each of her breaths. "You don't have to. It feels so good. Incredible. I need more of you too. I want you to bend me over."

I groan at the thought of hitting her spankable ass with my hips, and once again try to slide out of her but my cock throbs. Tightening my jaw, I slowly keep trying, ignoring the discomfort. Raven might freak out if I can't figure out how to get my body to release her. I knew I might be different. I can taste lust and desire. Passion fills a void inside me. And Raven? Maybe I really can't truly bear eternity without her.

"Uh, Andre, you okay?" she asks, her eyes still heavy with the pheromones emanating from me. "You stopped."

I shake my head and push deeper, rocking my body until she clings onto me. Adjusting my legs, I get on my knees and reposition her, gripping her knees to pick up my pace again, able to slide in and out of her but not all the way. The sensation sends another round of shudders through me, my nuts tightening, and I grunt and lose myself to her body again, pushing away the fact that I'm stuck. Does it matter? Not until she figures it out.

Thrusting into her over and over, I savor the sensation of her light caressing my skin. The position exposes her clit to me, and I take my time stroking her, hearing her passion sing through the air with every melodious, sexy moan and groan, every pant and gasp. I don't need Heaven anymore, and it's clear why. Raven is my Heaven. My paradise. The only eternity I can imagine.

"Andre," Raven murmurs, stretching her arms out to me. "Cuddle me for a minute. I need to catch my breath. You're insatiable."

"You have no idea." I lie on top of her, resting on my elbows. Brushing my lips to hers, I kiss her softly and sensually, slowing down my passion to just enjoy her.

But then she tries to pull away from me.

I groan, my body throbbing again. It's no use. I have to tell her before she accidentally tries to rip my cock off. She could hurt herself in the process. I'll heal, but her? I need to protect that delectable, sweet, perfect pussy of hers until she can claim her throne in Purgatory when the rest of the sinners jump from grace. Then she'll be able to handle every devilish piece of me.

"Andre, you didn't transform partially or something by accident? I can't seem to move. The pressure increases when I try. It's like you're getting bigger." She releases a light giggle. "That's ridiculous, right?"

I deadpan, meeting her eyes. "I'm not sure."

"You're not sure?" she asks, her voice rising in confusion. She puffs out a breath. "Of course you're not. You've never...damn. This was so fucking amazing that I forgot you were a virgin." Her bubbling laughter rings through the air, slightly maniacal, but she doesn't start whacking me like I expect. "But there must be something."

I close my eyes. "I don't know."

"This can't be our lives now." Her comment comes out a whisper like she's speaking only to herself. "Maybe you just need to cum again."

"Maybe." I don't want to admit how much I've cum in her already. It's the reason she still pants heavy breaths and squirms beneath me. Her mouth says she wanted to rest but her body begs for more.

She laughs again and smiles, cupping my face with her hands. Kissing me, she sucks my bottom lip into her mouth, setting me off again. My body hums and I start again, rocking slowly at first until I can't control my need and thrust hard and fast. Raven gasps her moans, clinging onto me, just whispering my name.

I grunt, my body exploding with the mind-blowing sensation as I cum again.

Fuck. It's all I can think. I worry she's not going to be able to take much more of me. What if this ruins my chance of getting her to return to me? I'll experience eternal torture. All because my damn cock refuses to let her go.

"I'm sorry," I say, gasping breathlessly against her shoulder. "I'm so sorry."

"Andre, it's—"

"The most unsexy thing ever for you to apologize for a poor performance," Kase finishes, putting words in Raven's mouth. "Devil up and keep that ass going." His voice echoes through my vaulted chambers. "Come on. Don't make me show your virgin ass what to do."

"Kase! Fuck, Kase. You came," Raven says, wiggling beneath me.

"What are you talking about, angel-girl? I didn't cum, but if you invite me over..." Kase's teasing voice calms Raven's racing heart.

"You better not fucking leave me out," Dante says, humming. "This kingdom gets me right in the nuts. I mean, shit, Andre. I've had an uncontrollable boner since we arrived."

Raven groans. "Don't you two even think about it. We're stuck. Like fucking dogs." Her exasperation tells me that she's silently freaking out and didn't want to make me feel badly.

Bellowing a laugh, Kase flops on the bed and rolls by our side. "Of-fucking-course. Your cock is huge."

Raven whacks Kase in the shoulder. "No, seriously."

Dante climbs on the other side. "King of Lust is a knotter. Fucking awesome."

"Awesome? Are you serious? You know this means I can't have sex with you, right? He's stuck." Raven purses her lips.

"Aw, come on, angel-girl. You know that bitable ass of yours wants me. Maybe this was destiny." Kase grins, stroking his finger along her jaw. "What do you say?"

"Damn it. You know what? Get your asses out. I accept that this is my life now." Raven flicks Kase's shoulder. She turns back to me and kisses me, purposefully egging the other devils on. "Just ignore them, Andre. They'll get anxious and take this more seriously."

I nod, loving her need to punish Kase and Dante for their flippant attitude. "Anything you want."

"Orgasms," Dante says, his voice gruff. "Give her more orgasms. We all get our power from our sins, and you've been without for too long. You're like an incubus in a way, feeding off her sexual desires. So make her cum."

Determination courses through me, and Raven kisses me again, unfazed by being watched. She enjoys it. I can sense it in her dark desires. She craves the attention Kase and Dante live to give her. Using my hand, I rub Raven's clit until her body tenses with her orgasm. I moan with her, inhaling deep breaths of the incredible scent wafting from her.

"Here, I'm dying to help. Just pound the Hell into her," Dante says, flicking out his forked tongue.

Raven doesn't stop him, so I nod and move my hand, watching him lick her body, not even caring how close my cock is. Arching, Raven screams in pleasure, her ecstasy overpowering my racing thoughts. Kase cheers like a fucking bastard, getting off on watching me devour Raven's sexual appetite along with my own.

My muscles tense and pulse, a wave of the most indescribable pleasure crashing through me sends me bowing forward. Dante swears and manages to move before his head gets caught between us, and I cum so hard that my cock finally releases Raven, and I slide out.

"Spill in the Lust Level," Kase says in amusement. "Damn. I've never seen anything like it."

"Get our soul a towel or some shit. She's not going to want us to watch her drip." Dante summons a blanket with his Hell power and drapes it over Raven. He leans over and kisses her forehead. "I'm going to reward you with the best fucking bath of your life, pretty soul."

Kase slaps my back, chuckling. "And as for you, fucker. I hope you got your fill. It's taken us damn near three days trying to find Raven. I had to fucking barter with Lucian to tell me what level she fell."

"She's been here three days?" I ask in surprise. "Impossible. I didn't feel her until she entered my kingdom not long ago."

"Don't know why. She's different," Dante says.

I know immediately that it's not due to her angel-kissed soul. It was Zade. He was shielding her the whole time if they came from Wrath's Kingdom. Was he trying to keep her hidden on purpose? Protecting her? It doesn't matter.

"So Zade never went to you?" Raven asks, her soft voice drawing everyone's attention to her. "You don't know about Elias?"

"Zade? What the fuck were you doing with him? And Elias?" Kase cocks his head. "He's not with you?"

"Fucking Lucian said he's punishing you both for trying to send him home through a portal." Dante growls under his breath.

"We have to go. Now!" Raven screeches, wrapping the sheet around her.

I don't have a chance to react as Kase opens up a portal to the Mortal World right before me. Anger rushes through me, and I swing my arm, trying to snatch Raven from the bed. She can't go yet. I need her.

Kase lashes his tail, snapping it against my hand, leaving a welt. "Don't start, Andre. She's not yours alone."

"But I need her!" I shout, my skin rippling.

"Get her out of here. I'll keep him back," Kase says, transforming into his true body. He roars, swiping his dagger nails at me. "Go!"

I summon Hell power, letting it rip through my body, revealing the monster I've become. Whipping my tail, I aim my stinger at Kase. He jumps out of the way and through the portal as my stinger sinks into the floor. I was too slow.

Raven is gone, and it's Lucian's fault again.

He thinks he's the most powerful, but he will break.

Hell's mine now. I will make him suffer.

6

ELIAS

SAVING GRACE

I'M GOING TO fucking destroy him. Lucian will pay for doing this to me and stealing my chance to make it up to Raven for how I failed her in our past lives. I was so close to proving myself worthy of our bond as soulmates. But now? Fuck. If I die alone, I won't be able to claim a throne in Hell. I'll...I don't know. I might be reincarnated. I might end up in fucking Heaven. My soul was bound to Hell because of a demon. Because of Vincent.

I'm going to kill his fucking monstrous ass too.

Because fuck this.

I will not die in this damn room. I won't.

I already have my mind, body, and soul set on going out with a fucking bang—banging my damn perfect woman—until I just keel over. There is no other way I want to go. Not now. Not ever.

Strolling to the window, I fling the billowing curtain open and stare at the city lights. I pop the lock and slide it open. I'm on the fourth floor of an apartment building with a demonic guard at the door. I've thought about jumping at least a thousand times. Maybe if I wasn't constantly hacking or if I had the strength to grab onto the ledges of the windows on the way down, I would. Right now, if I jump, I'd probably kill myself. If only three days hadn't passed by.

Something is wrong if Raven and the other devils haven't hunted me down yet.

Fuck. Who knew I could miss living in a mansion with the fucking devils. I honestly don't give a damn as long as Raven remained by my side. I planned to go to Hell for her.

I slam my palms to the window. "Fucking damn it! Piece of shit, son-of-a-bitch bastard! Let me the fuck out!"

My lungs seize, and I bow forward and cough, wheezing and gasping. Pain explodes through my body, sending me to my aching knees, black and blue from getting the shit kicked out of them when I tried to run.

I slump onto my side and groan. "Please, God. I know I shouldn't pray to you after what I've done, but I'm not the same man. I'm begging you to hear my pleas. Raven doesn't deserve this fate because of me. It was never her fault. Not in this life or in the last. God, please give me the strength to survive for her. Please don't let me be the reason her soul gets damned to Hell."

"My fallen brethren. Can you manage to get up? We cannot cross the shield." A soft, masculine voice whispers above me, humming through the glass. It scrapes as it slides open. "If you can get close enough, I can help you the best I can."

I blink and stare at the glowing light trickling in. Opening and closing my mouth, I try to respond, but all I can get out is another wheezing cough. My ribs throb, still tender from getting punched in the side. At least Lucian's burning handprint faded. I was worried I'd be stuck with it until—well, until I die.

"Elias, please. It's Zade. I don't have a lot of time. They'll sense I'm here." Zade's light grows brighter, his silhouette now shadowed on the wall across from the window. "Come on. You can do it. I have faith in your strength."

This asshole. Faith in strength I don't even fucking have. What he asks feels impossible. I can't even catch my breath.

"If you can't do it for yourself, then do it for Raven. She's been in Hell because she stood up to Lucian. I'm here because of her, so I'm begging you. Please try." Zade sends a cool breeze through the cracked window, clearing the agonizing fog from my mind. At least enough to plant my palms to the ground.

With all my remaining strength, I push to my hands and knees and hang my head.

Zade's light grows brighter almost like someone shines a flashlight into the room. "Almost here. If you can kneel—"

"Zade, what are you doing? You were supposed to keep an eye on Dante and Kase. They've been more active in their recruitment with the arrival of Lucifer. The devils' estate was empty." A deep, gruff voice cuts Zade off, and I recognize Cassius's voice from when he interrupted a hot as fuck moment with Raven and Micah, something we hadn't even had a chance to try again because it's hard to get her alone.

A blip of fear tightens my chest, or maybe it's my oncoming coughing fit trying to kill me, either way, I start hacking, my chest rattling. I drop back to my stomach, wishing my body would chill the fuck out. Being here is already torturous enough. I don't need the coughing bullshit.

Cassius intakes a sharp breath. "What are you doing with *him*? Raven made herself clear about where she stands. We cannot intervene. He's not our threat or problem. The blasted devils are what trouble us. Lucian is."

The angelic light illuminating the wall and ceiling fades with Zade's lack of response. I inhale slowly, trying not to cough again as I push to my hands and knees again. Silence hangs in the air, and I fear that the angels left, and I lost my chance for help.

"Saviors, please. Please, I'm begging you. Don't leave," I mutter, forcing the words to come out. "I'm getting up. I can be of use to you if you hear me out."

I groan and struggle, dragging myself to my knees using the windowsill. Cassius and Zade flap their wings, managing to effortlessly hover in place. I envy their brilliant, heavenly wings right now, more than I thought possible. I don't remember the moment I lost mine, and I couldn't give a fuck about such a thought, but I want wings just to be able to get out of here. If what Zade says about Raven is true—fuck.

"Oh, Elias. How pitiful you look. Do you carry any regret for your actions? I don't know what it's like to have been reborn as a mortal, nor do I think you understand the full extent of what you have done, but surely you remember something. Your very essence—your soul, I suppose—would never forget. Not after living amid Heaven's chosen." Cassius thins his lips, giving me a once over. "Such a shame, to be honest. You should have to suffer for all the pain you put so many through."

This fucking dickhead. How am I supposed to ask him for help and to show mercy after I punch him in the face? Because that's what I plan to do. Someone needs to fucking knock his righteous ass down a few notches, and I'll gladly do it.

"You're being unfair, Cass," Zade says quietly, keeping just out of arm's reach of his angelic brethren. "Elias has been through enough. Just give him a moment to speak to you."

I bet Cassius would hit him and call it a smiting for trying to reason with him instead of accepting that he's all knowing. At least in his eyes.

And they say Lucian was the one who fell because of pride. No, Lucian fucking jumped because he was on a damn power trip. Maybe he thought he could do better. Have some fun. I can see how it might be a blast if you're a ruler of Hell and not getting an eternity's worth of punishment fucked into you. Damn. I clench my ass cheeks at the thought. I swear to everything unholy and holy across every plane that Raven better come out of Hell unharmed on every level. If she doesn't, I'll show the other devils what true torture is like for not being there for our girl—for my soulmate. That bond is something no one will ever have, and I won't take it for granted.

Which is why I suppress my deep-seated need to attack Cassius.

As much as a dickhead that he is, he can help me. He can ensure that I don't die without Raven. He just doesn't know it yet.

"Go on, traitor," Cassius says, snapping my attention from my thoughts. "How is it you can be of use to us? You're standing at the edge of your life and mortal existence, still chained to Hell without even having a demonic contract anymore."

I clutch my window frame and swallow my anger. "You admitted that the devils—that Lucian was a problem. I can help with that."

"You keep saying you can help, but I need more than your false hope and assumptions regarding these matters." Cassius's bright wings glow, illuminating the world enough that I have to squint. He does it on purpose to make me uncomfortable. I know it.

"Have you forgotten that I'm one of the sinners to take a throne in Hell...like you?" I flare my nostrils and leer, loving how his smug expression falters. "I might be trapped in the apartment because of Lucian and his hope that I'll die unbound and without Raven or the other devils to help me, but I know that he'll fail because Raven is my soulmate and the fiercest woman I know. She will get to me before that happens."

"I still don't see your point, Elias. If you're so certain that's the case, why ask for a moment of my time?" Cassius glances at Zade as if his brethren might know the answer.

And to be honest, I'm not even sure if I know for myself. What am I doing? I should wait it out the best I can. Raven has a whole lot of Hell on her side that Lucian won't win. It's funny to think where my faith falls. It's not with these angelic bastards, but I need a backup plan. I need to be certain Raven doesn't fail to uphold her end of Lucian's contract.

"The fucking point is that I can help convince Raven to listen to you. You know you wouldn't have to worry about your own ass getting kicked and sent to Hell by Raven if she wasn't determined to save her soul and create Purgatory as its queen." I slowly inhale and exhale, trying to ease the tightness in my chest. "If you help me out of here—"

"You're forgetting that Raven thinks her soul belongs among the other devils. She made it clear that she wouldn't turn her back on Kase and Dante." Cassius glowers, fisting his hands. "I'll take my chances by leaving you here. Come on, Zade."

Fuck. I punch the screen off the window, sending it clattering to the ground. I'll jump on one of their damn backs and ride them down if I have to.

Except an electric shock zings through me, stealing my breath.

Something burns on my back. A mark of some sort. I can see the top of it. I couldn't jump even if I wanted to.

"Wait! Please!" I shout, slapping my hand to the wall. "Don't leave me here to die. My brethren, I'm asking for mercy. I love her. I can't see her fail."

Cassius drops down and hovers in front of the window. Zade remains a few dozen feet up, being useless and silent. I was rather surprised he was the first to show up, considering I've only ever seen him just watching and only getting involved in fighting if he had to. He could stand up to Cassius, but he doesn't. Raven must've did or said something to get him to act.

I heave and cough, my yells setting my body off again. The edges of my vision shadow. My legs shake, threatening to give out on me. Kneeling, I rest my chin on the sill, blinking the fog from my vision. It's all I can do as Cassius glows before me.

He sighs and rubs his palms over his cheeks, turning his gaze toward the night sky as if he can see Heaven among the faint stars, hidden by the light pollution. Closing the space, he rests one hand on the ledge and holds his other one up, testing the invisible barrier without pushing through. My head warms, but it isn't uncomfortable or painful. It's like I'm sinking head first into a heated pool made of something indescribable yet familiar. Heavenly light.

"I can't heal you of your ailments because your human body is too far gone, but I hope this brings you some reprieve." Cassius's voice turns soft with pity.

I open and close my mouth, trying to find my voice. The pain in my side disappears as do the tender bruises on my legs. "Thank you, Cassius." The familiarity of saying his name stirs something inside me, perhaps the feeling caused by a lost memory when we fought together for the Higher Power. "And I'm sorry. I don't know exactly what happened before I gave Raven's soul my angelic light, but I hope you can forgive me."

"I have already, but I cannot let go and forget. I don't know why your declaration of love surprises me, even now, as I heard it before when you were saving Grace. It's rather perplexing knowing that you seem to be stuck in a cycle together, but maybe, just maybe, the Higher Power put me in your path tonight to help break it." Cassius glances toward the sky and stares silently as if he's having a conversation with himself—or someone else I can't see or hear. And maybe he is.

"Break the cycle? What do you mean?" My curiosity gets the best of me. I have to know what the fuck he thinks this is all about.

"I suppose you wouldn't remember how you fought so fiercely to keep her from us. You knew we'd ensure her angel-kissed soul would've found a place bound forever in Heaven and far away from the hands of the devils. How you knew that particular deaths lead to rebirth." Cassius shakes his head. "I guess none of that matters. Not that you two have found each other and we can now break the cycle once and for all...if you do as I say."

A dozen thoughts whirl through my mind. What the fuck is he even talking about? "Breaking the cycle better not fucking mean Raven failing to fulfill her contract." I push up on the windowsill. "I already told you that I can't see her fail."

"I'm not insinuating that. What I'm suggesting is breaking this cycle the Mortal Realm seems to have you in. Unfortunately, I can't force Raven to do the one thing that could help her," Cassius says. "And neither can you. But there is something you can do if you truly want to save her from the grips of Hell."

"What is it?" I ask, locking my gaze to Cassius's. If he knows of something that could help Raven stay far away from Lucian if I should die before I escape, then I'm willing to do it. Her devils will understand, and if they don't, then they can punish me in Hell for the rest of eternity. I don't give a fuck as long as my soulmate doesn't suffer at the hands of a monster.

Cassius smirks, his expression getting under my skin. "Have Lucian void her contract. If you get him to do that, then I will see to it myself that your soulmate finds peace. And who knows? Such an act of selflessness and work for the Higher Power might even sway your soul back to where you belong."

I tip my head back and roar a laugh. "You're fucking out of your mind. Why the fuck would Lucian do that?"

"Because he gets caught up on things that do not go his way and has always been like that. I know Lucifer better than anyone, even after all this time. His pride always gets the best of him, and Raven hurt it by choosing others. She hurt it by denying him the chance to know what it's like to have her willingly share her soul with him. He would rather allow Heaven to obtain her than see the others cherish her. Because his envy and greed consumes him too." Cassius shifts his jaw, his amethyst eyes shining brightly, making him freaky as fuck.

He looks more devil than angel, and if I didn't know any better, I'd think he was about to start spitting fire. "He carries the seven deadliest sins, after all. Now that he is no longer chained to his throne, you can use it against him. All of Heaven can."

Shit. He might be right.

But can I do this? Should I even humor the thought? I know that Raven already has her soul set on a future in Purgatory, and I thought I wanted to claim a throne in Hell to be with her...but if I could save us both?

I don't want to ruin her ideal future. I really, truly fucking don't. But if all else fails, I'd rather her hate me forever than see her burn under Lucian's psychotic form. And this way, Kase and Dante will be safe. This will be my last resort.

"How do I know you'll stay true to your word?" I ask, a part of me hating myself for letting things come to this, but what else am I supposed to do?

"You have to trust me. I will not let you down." Cassius remains expressionless, though his light shines brighter than ever.

Can I trust him? Should I? Fuck. I don't think I have a choice.

"What if Lucian doesn't come here? I won't be able to convince him." It's hard to stay hopeful when nothing is certain. I wish I wasn't in this position at all.

"I will handle that. Convince him to void Raven's contract, and everything will come together how it should be. I know it. The Higher Power has never led me astray with my feelings." Cassius opens his palm and brings it as close as he can without hitting the invisible barrier. "Have faith, my brethren. You'll be set on your rightful path agai—"

The door flings open and clatters on the wall. I whip my head to see Vincent standing in his hellish disgust in the doorway. He snarls at the sight of Cassius near the window and rushes forward. Igniting the room aglow with heavenly light, Cassius stops Vincent in his tracks and disappears.

"Fucking damn it! We have to fucking relocate," Vincent yells, turning his attention to me. "I should just kill you and be done with it."

"Why the fuck haven't you?" I ask, narrowing my eyes.

Grabbing my shirt, he hauls me forward. "Shut the fuck up."

I swing at his boney arm. "You can't, can you?"

Shoving me against the wall, he growls in my face. "I might not be able to kill you, but I can cut out your tongue, so I suggest you shut the fuck up like I asked and be a good mortal. We're leaving."

Shit. I have no choice but to comply.

7

RAVEN

HELLISH EXPECTATIONS

FIVE DAYS. HOW could I have lost five days with Elias? It's all been a blur. Leaving Hell and feeling like it stayed in my soul leaves my mind in a fog. Maybe it's because of Andre and his venom. Dante's never lasted this long, but no one seems to worry about me physically, but Micah, Kase, and Dante have all taken turns remaining by my side as they hunt for Lucian. For Elias.

I haven't even heard from Zade.

"Come on, pretty soul. Please believe me when I say Elias is hanging in there for you. Lucian won't kill him before his time. He enjoys the idea of someone suffering too much to end it so soon. He might even be doing this just to fuck with you. Don't lose hope yet." Dante massages his fingers into the tight muscles of my shoulders, loosening the tension the best he can. "Why don't you let me dress you and take you out? You make great demon bait, and maybe someone can help point us in the coward's direction. I mean, if you feel up to it."

I slowly nod my head. "I'm getting used to the feeling of this hangover from Hell. I think getting some fresh air will help."

Leaning over my shoulder, Dante smiles and kisses my cheek. "Maybe next time you take Andre's king-sized cock, he might give you the proper amount of orgasms, so he can pull out."

I groan and whack him, making him laugh. "You better not tease him about this. Neither of us knew and...I had fun."

"Fun having a monster cock stuck in your pussy?" He lifts an eyebrow in question.

Heat blooms in my cheeks. "You won't understand. His cock isn't just big...I don't know. It felt different."

Dante spins me around and grasps my chin. "Keep describing how good another devil was and I'm going to want to fuck you until you forget. Replicate what you loved about it. I can be creative."

I release an exasperated laugh. "Please don't start. You getting envious over...knotting?" I pause, the memory returning fresh to the front of my mind. It wasn't like it was bad. Just different and unexpected. Shocking. But now I know that I won't be permanently attached to Andre by my vagina, I'd like to experience it again. I could tell when he was cumming, and the sensation...

"You dirty little pretty soul. Are you fantasizing about him now? If I reach under than dress, will you be wet?" Dante purses his lips, trying to hide his smile. "We're never leaving if you are. I—"

I laugh and snatch his wrist, stopping him from even trying. The sound of my voice rings through the air as Dante does more than loosen the tenseness of my muscles. He lightens the heaviness suffocating my soul.

"Mmm I've missed that," he says, grabbing my other hand. Pulling me into him, he lifts me off my feet, letting me hug him with my whole body. "Your laughter, I mean. Not your rejection of my affection."

"Dante..."

"I know, I know. I'm just teasing. And horny as fuck. You're not the only one who Andre's kingdom got to. Feel this fucking thing." Dante drops me a few inches until his hard-on presses through his pants between his legs. "I've given up with it after blowing at least twenty loads since being back."

I crinkle my nose. "I'm surprised you haven't just rubbed it off."

"I may have shed a skin or two."

Grimacing, I close my eyes and shudder at the thought. Dante's laughter bellows through the air as he carries me to our balcony instead of taking me downstairs. The crisp late night air blows my tresses around, and Dante slides a hair tie from his wrist and puts my hair up for me. He's the first man to ever hold my things, so I don't ever need a pocket or purse. I don't even know where he keeps most of the things. I thought I was jealous of the deep pockets of menswear, but damn it. Devilwear is even more accommodating.

"There. Now I can kiss your sweet neck while we fly," he murmurs, adjusting me in his arms. "Also your lips too. I love your gloss but hate having to fight with your hair for access to your mouth."

I laugh again and bat my hand to his shoulder. "You're ridiculous."

"You love it." Bending his knees, Dante launches into the air, cutting off my response.

I snuggle my face into the crook of his neck, shielding my eyes from the icy wind. The soft whooshing of his wings helps calm my racing heart from his quick ascension, and I busy myself with exploring his skin, purposely leaving behind lip prints in his favorite shade of red.

Dante soars over the brightly lit city that sparkles below

like the stars fallen to Earth. I peek over his shoulder, squeezing tightly with my thighs. I know he thinks about fucking me up here. I don't have to ask because I'm thinking about it too, but damn it. We're already descending, and I can't spare another moment. We have shit to do that isn't each other.

Like he reads my mind, Dante mutters, "I swear to fucking Hell that we're going to fuck everywhere and on everything in the Mortal Realm when our kingdom is complete. You name it, we'll fuck either on it, in it, or against it."

I gasp with his freefalling a dozen feet, squeaking as his boots thud on the sidewalk outside of a bar and grill called Risqué. He sets me on my feet, and I smile up at him. "What about on—"

"Ray? No fucking way." A familiar feminine voice echoes through the air. "Raven, what the actual fuck?"

Dante hisses under his breath but doesn't spit venom as two slender arms engulf me from behind and my cousin Tamia rests her chin on my shoulder. "Thank God, you're okay."

"God? Pfft. God had nothing to do with her wellbeing." Dante's low words growl against my forehead.

"I went by Joel's a couple weeks ago after I got your message. I thought something happened to you. The apartment manager said Joel stopped paying rent and when they checked, it was empty." Tamia manages to spin me around, ignoring Dante like he's not even here, but I know she sees him. Her eyes flick to look over my head and back to mine. "You better have a good fucking reason you haven't called me back, and it better not be that you lost your phone. You know where I live."

I rub my lips together, trying to think of a reasonable response. I can't exactly tell her that Joel tried to murder me, and I was saved by the devils themselves.

"Raven has been living through Hell. I suggest you take a step back and control your anger. You are not concerned about her wellbeing. You act as if you've been through turmoil all because of her inability to contact you. What about when she called you and asked for help? What about when she needed you after she lost her job and found herself turning back to a monster of a man because you refused to return her calls?"

Damn. He really did listen to me when I told him about my life.

I touch my fingers to his lips, silencing his words. "Dante, it's okay. She has every right to be mad."

Tamia places her hands on her hips. "I'm not—"

"It's about time you fucking showed up, you bastard." Lucian's smooth voice cuts my cousin off. "It's been, what, a week?"

My blood cools at the sight of Lucian strutting from the side of the building and out of the shadows. How the fuck did he know we were here? Why show himself now? Whatever the reason, it can't be fucking good.

"And who's this?" Lucian has the nerve to give Tamia a

long once-over, making her shift on her feet under his intensity. He offers his hand to her, and she automatically takes it, flushing in her cheeks. "You joining us for the night...Tamia? Beautiful Tamia. I've heard of you."

Fuck me. What kind of game is the bastard playing?

I huff a breath and force my legs to work, stepping between the two of them. Dante grips my hand, turning my fingers numb, but he doesn't loosen his hold. "No, she's not. None of us are, you dick."

Lucian's eyes flash with hellfire, and he tightens his jaw. "Think carefully about how you treat me, Raven. It doesn't take much to give a soul a little push into the pits of Hell." Glancing over my shoulder, he smiles at my cousin. "I suggest you play nice and do as I ask. You don't want to find out what happens if you misbehave again. If you thought a stroll through Wrath's Kingdom was bad..." He lets his words trail off, words quiet enough that only me and Dante hear.

"There you fucking guys are. Come on. I got us a booth." Kase stands in the opened door to the bar and remains expressionless.

Micah stands by his side, flexing his muscles and looking ready to explode into his devil form. His gaze remains locked on mine, and I try to force myself to smile. I have so many questions. How are they here too?

I twist and grab Tamia's hand. "You don't have to join us. We can catch up some other time."

Her eyes shift from me and to each of the devils. She looks ready to run, but then Lucian offers her a handsome smile. One that could pass for angelic. "I have time. I work the afternoon shift tomorrow. I can stay a couple hours."

Shit.

Lucian laughs and drapes his arm over her shoulders, guiding her away from me. In a moment she'd usually scowl and shrug out of a strange bastard's bold infiltration of her personal space, she accepts his fake friendliness with ease and smiles, laughing at something he whispers.

It takes everything in me not to hop on Lucian's back and start pummeling him with my fist. I love Tamia. I know we've had a rough last two years, but we were so close before my engagement with Joel. We moved out here together from across the country in our early twenties and even lived together. I know my decisions revolving around Joel hurt her now. At the time, I was so caught up in his manipulation, I thought she was jealous or something.

That time seems so long ago. My hurt feelings have healed or have been diminished by my current circumstances. Regardless of everything, it never affected how much I cared and still care for my cousin and her wellbeing. She shouldn't be wrapped up in my devilish affairs. I'm afraid that if I don't do something to stop Lucian, she will become collateral damage.

"Just take a breath. He's trying to get to you, Raven,"

Dante whispers, snaking his arm around my waist. "He can try his hardest to charm her, but we will intervene if he tries anything."

I suck my bottom lip into my mouth, stopping it from trembling with worry. Lucian's going to use this against me. I know it deep in my bones.

Kase and Micah surround me alongside Dante when we reach the entrance. I gaze around the place and notice a brightly painted slogan above the bar. Bottoms up for tops down? Classy. The clientele in the place scream skeevy, and I wonder why Tamia was even here.

"Mr. Lucian, what an unpleasant surprise," a man says, materializing a few feet in front of us. "Had I known you'd manage to get out of Hell, I'd have left town."

"You fucking bastard. Come here." Lucian surprises me by stepping forward and shaking the man's hand. I clearly missed the guy's teasing. "It's been far too long."

"Centuries," the guy says, smiling to reveal perfectly straight teeth. "Not long enough."

Tamia laughs in exasperation, her eyes darting to mine in confusion. She's not the only one. Usually demons are bowing and throwing themselves at the devils or trying to test their power. This guy seems just so blasé about everything.

"That's going to change. I've made some new arrangements." Lucian cranes his neck and motions at my devils standing around me. "So why don't you get us a booth and bottle service and let me show this stunning mortal on my arm what it's like to catch the attention of a devil."

Again, Tamia laughs and blushes.

This fucker. I can't believe him.

"As you desire, my liege." The man nods and smiles at Tamia, completely ignoring the rest of us.

He leads the way through the decently crowded bar of nothing but mortals. This isn't a demonic hangout. This is probably the demon's territory where he collects souls on behalf of Lucian.

"I always knew Bart was a fucking traitor," Dante mutters under his breath. "He's going to have fucking Hell to pay."

"We're going to have to re-evaluate our legions." Kase's voice remains low, ensuring that no one outside of the four of us hears. "I knew he'd come here and try to encroach on our territories."

"I suppose what I've offered him isn't good enough." Micah tightens his jaw, speaking for what feels like the first time.

"Nothing ever is," Dante replies, hissing and flicking his tongue.

I gobble up their conversation, unused to how they talk about their demonic affairs in front of me. They usually hide that part—except for Micah, who has let me in on what goes on—and it's strange to grasp.

The demonic bar owner, Bart, stops at a corner booth and swipes a reservation card off the table and pockets it. Tamia follows Lucian into the booth, and my devils wait for me to join her, but I hesitate. I swear I see Lucian's hellfire reflect in her eyes.

It sets me off.

Huffing a breath, I press my hand to Dante's chest. "I can't do this. I'm done with his bullshit. Just keep an eye on me, okay?"

Dante frowns. "Pretty soul, I—"

"Lucian, we need to fucking talk. Now." The words snap from my mouth before Dante can talk me out of facing Lucian. Last time, I was thrown into Hell, but I know better. He's never going to let up, and trying to mess with my family crosses the line.

Lucian offers me a cocky-bastard smile and nods, sliding back out of the booth. He has the nerve to touch Tamia's chin and wink, sending her face flushing even more. Kase, Dante, and Micah tense, all of their muscles clearly flexing through their tight shirts, but none of them try to intervene.

Steeling myself from his darkness the best I can, I don't fight as he laces his fingers around my arm, guiding me toward the back of the bar and into a hallway with the restrooms and another door to the employee-only section.

"We're right here if you need us." Micah's thoughts trickle into my mind, giving me the reassurance I need to face the asshole before me.

Lucian guides me out of everyone's line of sight, and purposefully corners me, pressing his palm against the wall, caging me in. Usually, I'd love this. Dante and Kase do this to me all the time to trap my attention. But with Lucian? I want to knee him in his cock. Too bad I've found out the hard way that he has balls of steel and a love of getting his junk manhandled. He's both a sadist and masochist and a dickhead. I feel almost defenseless facing him alone, but at least now, he's in his mortal form. It's when he goes complete devil with his fire chains that really scares the fuck out of me.

"Lucian, backup a foot. This wasn't an invitation to crowd my personal space." I keep my voice low, stopping it from quivering. If only there was something I could do about my racing heart.

"Is that so? Your soul says otherwise, Ray..." His long inflection of the nickname my cousin uses prods at me. I wish he wouldn't. I never liked being called Ray, because there was a jerk in high school by the same name, and he ruined it for me. Funny how something like that sticks with me.

"You obviously can't really read my soul then. It hates you. I hate you. What you did to me—"

Lucian shoves his hand against my throat, stealing my breath away. Leaning in, his dark eyes blaze with hellfire as he searches my face. I still under his restraint, his fingers shifting to release the constraint on my airway but his strength doesn't ease. He's putting enough pressure on my arteries to slow the blood flow to my brain. I know this. I've learned a lot of kinky shit from Dante.

I open and close my mouth, my fear growing wild yet my body relaxing with the shadows edging my vision.

"Listen, Raven. You were the one who started a fight you couldn't finish. You cannot blame me for your failure." Lucian bows even closer, his breath hot yet minty, and for that, I'm thankful. "All I've wanted this whole time was to show you your worth to be in my presence, and you've done nothing but fight me. Blame me. Think I'm the bad guy."

I inhale slowly, afraid I'll pass out. Still, I can't find my words. He's forcing me to listen to him while he ignores me.

"Things could be so easy, you know. Your soul calls to me." Lucian finally loosens his grip on my throat, and I gasp, sharing my breath with him. "Don't deny it."

His stare breaks away from mine and flicks to my mouth. Something dark crosses his gaze, suppressing the flames glowing from his power. It sets me off, turning my knees weak, my heart ricocheting around my chest. It feels like our first encounter in Hell when he merged his soul with mine.

"I don't give a fuck what you think my soul does," I mutter, my chest heaving with my deep breathing and bumping into his. "I want you to stop trying to torment me. Leave my cousin alone and don't get her involved."

He smirks. "Why not? She's seems so fun."

I claw my nails into his chest, trying to break his skin through his shirt. "Stay away from her."

"Perhaps if you give me something I want." He moves closer, planting his feet between mine where I have to practically straddle his legs and stand on my tiptoes. Sliding his hand into my hair, he locks me in place and licks his lips. "Like I said. Things could be so easy, Ray. A lot of fun."

I tighten my mouth, flaring my nostrils. "Fuck you. Touch my cousin—"

Growling, his hand shocks me by sending a burst of heat through my body. "If your cousin wants me, I'll give her whatever her heart desires. I'll fuck her how she enjoys. She wants me to bend her over and yank her hair. Choke her. She wants to join me in Hell for eternity. All it will take is one little phrase from her."

"Lucian, please." I hate that my anger fizzles out with my fear. I can already see that his wicked smile caught Tamia's attention. I hate it. I want her far away from him. "Don't do this. You've already stolen Elias from me."

His smile widens as he leers. "He's unworthy of one of Hell's thrones. They all are."

I don't respond. I can't.

"But with a little motivation and taking from them the one thing they want most..." Again, he turns his gaze to my mouth. "The choice is simple, Raven. You can either accept defeat and give in to your soul's desire or find out exactly what it's like to fuck with me."

What kind of options are those?

"You know there is only one way any of this will end for you. Let me show you what giving in means. I promise your body and soul will enjoy it." Lucian leans in, his determination to kiss me in a way he thinks will change my mind ignites my Hell strength.

I turn my head as he plants his lips to my cheek, the heat of his body shocking me to my soul. Shoving away from the wall, I push him away and swing my hand. The slap of my palm to his face rings through the air. Pain stings my hand, but I don't attempt to grovel or apologize. I dodge away from him and bolt toward the employees-only door.

Lucian bangs his palms against the walls, sending strange sparks through the air. The world turns wavy around me as if heatwaves blur everything. It reminds me of when Micah would freeze the world. This isn't much different, except I suddenly feel cut off from my devils. I don't hear them. There is no way they didn't hear this, even with the music. At least Micah would decipher my racing thoughts...

"Running is pointless," Lucian calls from behind me. "We're not done talking."

"Take me back!" I call over my shoulder. "You broke your agreement with Kase and Dante. You were not allowed to kiss me without my permission. You're a disgusting creep. I'll never give in to you."

"Raven!" he hollers, his voice deepening.

The ground shakes and something clatters behind me. I

reach the back exit and silently pray the door isn't locked. If it's locked, I'm trapped. I'm already trapped. Fuck his Hell power. Fuck my need to confront him. I knew better. I should've listened to Dante, but I just am so tired of this bullshit and being pushed around.

I ram my palms against the door, and it flies open, the universe or whatever answering my prayer. Blinding light engulfs me as if night turns to day. I stumble and nearly eat shit on the asphalt outside the bar but manage to catch myself.

"Damn it, Raven. Stop! There are angels—" Lucian roars, his voice echoing through the night.

I crane my neck and glance over my shoulder, spotting Cassius touch down on the ground, blocking Lucian from my path. I don't stop, only slowing, and crash into a muscular body that engulfs me in the sweet, gooey scent of roasted marshmallows.

"Get me out of here. Please," I beg, jumping into Zade's arms and hooking my legs around him, not really giving him a choice.

Light engulfs us, the sensation a mixture of pain and pleasure coursing through my very being, and the strange in-between world disappears along with Cassius and Lucian.

Zade flies me into the night and back to the front of the bar. Before I have a chance to say anything, he disappears.

Losing his sudden grace leaves me empty and confused.

What happens now?

8

RAVEN

SOUL TO DREAM

ANDRE SITS IN front of me, his long legs stretching all the way across the summoning circle. Dante brought me home, only to leave again, entrusting me with Andre. Instead of offering to take me to his kingdom, he asked to watch the day break with me like he knew this was what I needed. Just the comfort of his presence and the safety of his protection while the other devils are "handling Lucian," according to Dante.

Whatever that might mean.

Andre reaches out and takes my hands, wrapping his big fingers around mine. "Little Hellion, you're quiet. I wish there was something I could do. If you don't want to visit with me, I understand. I know what happened between us—"

I cut off Andre's words with a kiss, silencing him before he starts filling the air around the summoning circle with assumptions. "I'm sorry, Andre. It's not you. I just have a lot on my mind. Our time together was incredible. Promise."

"You know you can tell me anything, Raven. I'm here for you and not going anywhere...quite literally. Andre chuckles with his comment and tugs my hands a little harder until I crawl closer and sit in his lap.

His huge wings enclose around us, shielding me from the world like he wants complete privacy in the yard. Not like we'd get many disruptions. Tamia doesn't know where I live, and Kase promised she'd get home safely when they called a car service. I just hope Lucian doesn't continue to fuck with me. Ugh.

I shove the thought away. I want to think about anything else but tonight.

Except now that I try to clear my thoughts, Elias falls front and center.

"I just wish I knew if Elias was okay," I murmur, blinking the burning tears from my eyes. "I fucked up tonight, and instead of threatening Lucian over returning Elias to me, I fought with him over my cousin. Now he might do something to her. I just wish...I wish you were here all the time instead of him."

Andre groans and hugs me, his arms feeling like what I'd expect from Heaven and not from one of Hell's rulers. He strokes his fingers up and down the length of my back and just snuggles with me without getting carried away. "Have the others not told you Elias is hanging in there? I can feel his soul through yours. He's not in any abnormal pain."

"So Dante wasn't only trying to make me feel better?" I ask, lifting my gaze to his coffee-dark depths.

The caramel flecks glow with his hellfire, but he still reminds me of what he had been as an angel. His boner for me and all. I don't mention it. I'm sure it's on his mind as much as mine, especially now that I feel the daunting extent of it. And because he ignores it, focusing on me and my need for more than a physical connection, I know things between us will level out. We are capable of more than being locked in his kingdom of Lust.

"I'm nearly certain Dante has other ways to make you feel better than lying to you about your soulmate's condition," Andre says, the corner of his mouth curling up with his smirk. "So much so that I question why his power derives from envy instead of lust."

"Maybe the universe just assumed that he'd become all-powerful if he was. A lifetime of orgasms for all. The masses would idolize him as a false god and worship him." I can't stop the smile from crossing my face. "I also think he'd be incapable of properly punishing those souls in your kingdom. I mean, orgy tornadoes? That's fucking freaky. Poor Zade could barely stand it."

I wince, wishing I hadn't brought up Zade.

Andre surprises me by laughing at my comment, easing away to fill me with the sudden warmth buzzing between our bodies. "Good. Serves him right for thinking he had the right to use you as his guide into Hell."

I scrunch my nose. "I might be overstepping here, and feel free to have Dante spank me later if I am, but Zade...I don't know how to explain it. He cares about you, even still. He didn't go into Hell because of me, Andre. He was there because of you."

Andre sighs and shakes his head. "It doesn't matter. I can hardly stand looking at him in all his divine glory. What's done is done."

"And if I make him jump from grace?" I ask, my desire to know more about what is on Andre's mind to distract me from my own racing thoughts turning all consuming. "What then? Will it change things?"

Andre doesn't respond immediately, falling silent as he thinks about my question. Finally, after another quiet moment, he says, "I'm not sure what you're asking, little hellion. Change things between us or me and him?"

"I guess both. I know he loves you. You were his companion for...forever." I graze my fingers along his cheeks, exploring his handsome features.

"I think you misinterpret that emotion with an angel. It's not the same as with mortals." Andre tilts his head back and stares at the sky. I don't think he does it to watch the stars fade with the coming morning. I think he might be remembering his life on Heaven's path. It would still be fresh in his mind. "I'm not sure how to explain it really. But, one thing I know for certain is that you're mine and I'm yours and no one will ever steal me from you. I've bound myself to Hell for you, Raven. Everything I've done in my existence is what has led me to you, and nothing will change that."

Damn. I don't know what to say, so I kiss him, showing him the affection that matches my feelings for him. He hums and shifts my body, his cock pressing even harder between my legs, threatening the fabric separating our bodies. I wouldn't put it past the king of Lust to be capable of ripping through clothes to get to me. His hungry desire lights his eyes, and I brace for what's to come—surely me, a lot, especially knowing it's my desire and sexual relief that gives him power.

"Raven, I must stop. If I don't, I will take you back to my kingdom and I'm not sure I'll let you go," Andre murmurs, groaning and shifting me again, lessening the pressure of his hard-on. "Denying myself such pleasure will help desensitize me to my need for you."

I pant a breath, my body and mind all out of whack. His coconut scent wafts around me, sending goosebumps over my skin. I'm horny as fuck now. I understand his desire to get better control of himself, but damn. My whole body throbs with an ache that can only be cured by him.

I inhale and exhale slowly, shifting off of him before I start dry humping him and grinding my body to his to prove my theory about his cock's capability to explode through clothing right. "Such torture."

"Perhaps it'll help if you let me cuddle you to sleep. That's where anything can happen." Andre brushes his lips to mine again.

"Anything?" The word comes softly from my mouth, my body cooling as an idea suppresses the urge to have Hell pounded into me.

He nods. "Being so close to your soul has its benefits."

My soul. Fuck. That's it. He mentioned that he could feel Elias through me. What if he can use that with his dream walking? "What about communicating with Elias? We share a soul. Could you use me to reach out to him?"

Andre lowers his brows in thought. "I suppose I could try. You would both have to be asleep."

Like my body and soul have pity on me, I yawn. "We have to try something."

Nodding, he gathers power in his palm, setting the world around us aglow with fiery light. "Close your eyes, little hellion. I can put you to sleep."

Whoa. I've grown used to Andre sneaking into my dreams almost every night, but this is so strange. I feel as if I'm awake. If the world around me didn't look like a new twisted level of Hell, I'd think I was.

"Andre? Where are you?" I ask, finding my voice. Fear snakes through my body, tightening around my chest. He somehow used his Hell power to put me to sleep, yet he's not here.

Silence greets me. What if his power didn't put me to sleep and sent me to Hell instead? Shit. No wonder I feel as if I'm awake.

"Andre, please. Say something." My voice rings through the dark world, only lit by streaks of molten lava flowing through veins in onyx rocks of this freaky cave. Darkness shadows everything on both sides of me.

I'm afraid to move.

I'm alone.

No, wait. Someone else is here.

"Shit, Elias." Like his soul drags me to him by an invisible line, I fly into the darkness and find myself standing over his body.

He curls his knees to his stomach and stares at nothing.

Kneeling beside him, I rest my hand on his shoulder. "Elias."

Electricity zings from me to him, and he whips upright and meets my gaze. Horror crosses his features, his eyes widening and his mouth falling agape. It looks as if he sees a ghost with his reaction. His sudden fear makes me twist to stare behind me to check for demonic monsters.

"Fuck, darlin'. No. No, no, no. This can't be happening. This is my fault." His mouth trembles with his words, and he throws his arms around me, engulfing me in a hug. "Fuck. Please, God. Please. Don't do this to her."

I clutch him, rubbing my hand in circles between his shoulder blades. He feels so real and not like a figment of my imagination in this dark nightmare world. "Elias, hey. Take a breath. We're okay. I'm alive and here with Andre's help. We're dream walking in your nightmare."

Elias heaves a few deep breaths. "What? Fuck really? Why does it feel so real?"

"Because it is real in a way," Andre says, materializing beside us.

Andre's presence startles Elias, and he throws himself onto me protectively, using himself to shield my body. Clapping his hands together, Andre transforms the world around us, destroying Elias's nightmare of Hell and turning it into a field of endless rainbow flowers with pink clouds hanging in an indigo sky. He still hasn't lost his romantic touch being a devil, and I manage to ease Elias upright to glance around.

"I'm using my power to manipulate Raven's soul. We're

all on what I can only describe as an alternate plane as if you project from your bodies and merge as one entity." Andre smirks and ruffles his hand through Elias's hair as if he's a scared child. I can't help but smile. "Your captor can't keep me out. Never could. Never will be able to now that I've got to connect with you on such an intimate level."

"I swear to fucking Hell, Andre. That better not mean what I think it means with that cock of ass destruction looking like it's going to swing at me, knock me out, and have its way with my butthole. Raven's either. We're not capable of handling that thing in this life." Elias furrows his brows with his words, looking like he wants to take a swing at Andre's groin.

I whack Elias with a laugh. "Haven't you heard? Anything is possible in a dream. What happened to my sexy, brave hunter?"

Andre bellows a laugh at my teasing of Elias. "Anything is possible with the power of lust at my fingertips." Purposefully leaning closer, Andre grabs Elias's hair to hold him still to whisper in his ear. "And for the sake of your knowledge, Raven rather enjoyed her time in Hell with me. I've officially been corrupted by that mouthwatering pussy of hers."

Fuck me.

I throw myself between the two of them as Andre's devilish side peeks through. I both love it and hate it, because he didn't need to go there and announce our intimate affairs, though I know it was only because he wanted to prove Elias wrong.

"Okay, stop it. No more talking about sex, anal, dream threesomes, or whatever else the fuck Mr. Lust's power ignites between the three of us." I turn to Andre. "Please, chill. He's fragile, even in this dream state."

"I'm not fragile," Elias snaps. "I'm trying to protect our assholes."

Andre massages his fingers into my shoulder like he can't help touching me anyway he can as all these dirty thoughts cross his mind. "I think he's more afraid of the pleasure that will occur. Mortality has done a number on him. He just needs—"

"Stop. Seriously. Both of you. I just wanted to come here and see for myself that my soul mate hasn't keeled over before I could put him out with a bang." I grab Elias's face, forcing him to stop glaring at Andre. "Can you tell us where you are? Anything that can help us find you?"

Elias sighs a breath and rests his forehead to mine, enjoying the closeness of my soul while he processes my words. "I was locked in a fourth floor apartment with a view of a city, but Zade and Cassius...I've been relocated because they found me. I don't know where I am now. I was blindfolded and moved into a bathroom with no window."

I inhale a small breath. "Zade and Cassius? They found you?"

"Days ago, I think. I'm struggling to keep track of time."

Elias shifts his head, closing the space to my lips. He kisses me softly like he was waiting for me to make the move and couldn't stand that I hadn't. "It doesn't really matter. They said they couldn't help me."

"Fuck. Zade didn't tell me any of this. He's been non-existent until tonight, and even then, he didn't stay." I sigh and tilt my head, glancing at Andre. "Why doesn't he ever do anything? It's like he wants to but then he doesn't."

It's now that I realize what sin will be his downfall.

Sloth.

Shit.

Now that I realize it, I can piece things together. He struggles with not acting. With blatantly choosing not to do something such as help Elias and me. Sure, he thinks it goes against his divine purpose, and it might, but I can use this information. I need to turn his behavior into not doing things. If I can get him to ignore his duties or neglect them, he could eventually abandon them.

But in this moment, Zade's jump from grace isn't important.

Elias is.

"He's an angel, darlin'. He said he was doing you a favor," Elias says, pulling me from my thoughts. "I'm sure his dickhead superior who caught him was ensuring he couldn't get word to you. They couldn't care less about me. I'm a traitor to them. If I die, it solves their problems."

I hate that he's right.

"They're fucking bastards." I clench my fingers into fists. "I'm going to tie Zade up and hold him hostage in Dante's room. Then I'm going to—"

The world quivers around us, stopping me from finishing the start of my torturous plan...though it also could be the start of a good time. Fuck. I need to get my shit together. Andre's lust seeps into me, making it hard to not turn everything into a fantasy. Usually I'd appreciate it, but something prods at my very being.

"Uh, Andre?" I question, peering around. "What's happening?"

Andre flickers in and out of existence without responding.

"Raven?" Elias clutches my cheeks and kisses me again. "You keep disappearing. Please don't leave me. I'm not ready to let you go."

My heart slides into my stomach at his pleas. Andre materializes again and rests his hands on my shoulders. Elias pulls me closer and hugs me, burying his face into the crook of my neck. His body shudders around me, and I gasp at the heartache suddenly stealing my breath.

"We have to go, little hellion," Andre says softly. "I'm sorry."

"Please, stay with me." Clutching me tighter, Elias tries to keep me with him. "I'm afraid. I'm fucking scared that if you go, I'll never see you again."

But I don't have a choice.

The world fades.

With one more kiss, I pull away and capture Elias's watery gaze. "You better fucking hang on for me. I mean it. I will find you."

"Raven, I—I love you, darlin'. More than anything. I'll do whatever it takes to save you." Elias fades away with his words.

I open my eyes to a world of flames.

9

RAVEN

DEVILISH CONSEQUENCES

I LIE FROZEN on the couch, staring up at the vaulted ceiling. I don't know exactly how long I've been here, a couple hours, but it's taking my body a helluva long time to find the will to wake up. I'm exhausted. My heart hurts. It doesn't help that every time I open my eyes, I see the devils in their true bodies in the middle of the living room and the place is trashed. The coffee table lies in shambles, and the wall painting I picked out hangs crooked with a burned hole in the middle of the canvas.

No one yells, but everyone seems to radiate with Hell power, and my head spins because of it. I've been through so much the last couple days that whatever Andre did to put me to sleep doesn't want to release me. It wants me to remain in the same circle of flames, surrounded by darkness, that Andre left me in before I woke up the first time here. Not to mention, I feel as if I've been drinking all night and now have a killer hangover, yet I was dosed with a shot of Hell and not a yummy margarita. Fuck, I could use one right about now. I'd rather be shitfaced than finally gather the strength to face my angry devils and the fuckhead who wants to be a pain in not only my ass but my soul.

"Why the fuck do you even care if the fucker dies? We'll be nice enough to let you get your fill of her soul every once and a while. Whatever keeps you in line." Lucian crosses his arms over his broad chest, the velvety dark skin of his beast looking almost unreal in the soft light of day peeking in through the window. If he didn't currently stand ten feet tall on hooves with two massive horns, a glower on his face, while holding a fire whip, I'd even say he was ethereal and beautiful. He just looks scary.

Kase growls and sits back on his haunches. Red power zaps across his devil form like he can barely contain his wrath. "Are you fucking stupid? You just don't get it. Elias is her soulmate. He is intended to take a throne no matter what you think. You've already let this realm get to your head. We have a contract."

"Fuck the contract. What you want is Raven, and I'm offering to share her damn soul like we had originally worked out." Lucian wraps his fire chain around his hand but doesn't act on it.

Swinging his fist, Dante punches Lucian in the face hard enough to send him reeling. I suck in a breath, expecting Lucian to retaliate, but he doesn't.

And then everyone looks at me.

"It's about damn time, angel-girl. You sleep like a fucking rock." Kase bounds toward me in his feline form and bows next to the couch, lowering his big head to my eye level. "Andre said you were exhausted, but damn. Remind me not to allow him to Raven-sit when there are punishments to give."

Punishments? What the fuck is he talking about?

"You fuckers have wasted all of our time. She doesn't have it in her to summon the nerve of a devil," Lucian snaps, transforming from his hellish form into a man. "Just fucking accept that there is nothing to do and move on. Stop letting her tug you around by your damn cocks."

Micah sighs, transforming into his human self next. "Stop coming up with excuses and accept the consequences for your actions. You wouldn't want us to assume that you're afraid, now would you?"

I tense at his comment, expecting for Lucian to blow up and attack, all he does is glower.

"The last thing I'm afraid of is Raven. Let's just get this over with, so I can get back to cleaning up the shitshow of a world you two have created. It's no wonder the legions so easily turn to me. You're more fitting for the pits than managing the contracted souls here." Lucian smirks, trying to get under Kase and Dante's skin.

I get the nerve to clutch onto Kase's muscular devil form and pull myself to my feet. My knees shake for a moment, but with his support, I remain tall. "Shut up, Lucian. You obviously don't care about what's truly important, and I'm tired as fuck over having to constantly deal with your self-centered, idiotic, dumbass. I thought I was scared of you, but now you're just annoying the shit out of me."

Lucian glowers and steps forward, acting like he might rush me. Spreading his black-feathered wings, Dante creates a protective wall and hisses. The two of them stand off, testing each other and seeing who's going to make the first move, but Kase wraps his tail around Dante and Micah locks his fingers onto Lucian's shoulder.

"There is no need to fight. We're all on the same side, and if everyone would settle down, we can carry on. We have bigger things to deal with than this power struggle you insist on always having with each other. Like the saviors. Cassius grows bolder with his confrontations. You saw his army tonight. I haven't seen him summon the guardians in centuries. Not since...not since Elias fell."

Something inside me explodes at the mention of Elias, and I charge across the room, duck under Dante's wing, and launch at Lucian. He reflexively catches me instead of knocking me away, and I slap him in his smug face.

"You're such a fucking bastard!" I scream, swinging my hand at him again. "Tell me where you're keeping Elias!"

Strong hands hook to my waist, yanking me away. Kase's familiar vanilla vetiver scent wraps around me, snuffing out the Hell threatening to ignite and set the room ablaze.

It's not enough to chill me out completely. I thrash and try to break free. "Put me down. I'm going to beat the fucking answer out of him."

"Easy now, pretty soul. You need the proper weapon for that kind of torment. Plus, I don't want your hands all over him." Dante ruffles his feathers, closing his wings. "I have the perfect thing."

I tighten my jaw, glaring at Lucian. "You better bring the Andre 3000 dildo for the strap on because I'm going to fucking beat him with it before pegging him until he calls me master."

Dante howls a laugh. "Shit no. It's supposed to be punishment for trying to steal a kiss and not open a damn door for him thinking he can have you in any way he pleases."

Lucian's stone face breaks, his jaw twitching. Shit. That's

not a threat to him. He loves the idea. And I might like it a teensy bit too. The power in dominating him and proving that he might be the most notorious devil, but when it comes to him fucking with me and my life, he's going to learn that I will fuck back harder, more viciously, and with the biggest fucking spirit dick in the universe. He might think he is the rightful controller of Hell, but I know I'm its rightful queen and the Seven Sinners are intended to be my kings.

"Your affection isn't free to take, and there are consequences," Dante continues, ripping me from my thoughts. "We've made it damn clear that he can't bully you into it either, which is why it's time you teach him as much. He's to kneel before you and apologize and accept getting whipped by his own chains."

"Only if she wants to." Lucian folds his arms over his chest. "She could decide that her rejection is enough."

I blink a few times. "Wait. I'm whipping him with his chains?"

Micah grabs the fire whip from Lucian and dangles it in front of me, proving that they're serious. "As many times as you feel is necessary. We don't take these breaches lightly, heathen. It's important in maintaining a semblance of peace between us."

I hesitate, nervous to touch the glowing chain. I'm afraid it might burn me.

Lucian mistakes my reluctance for something else and

grins. "I told you she didn't have it in her to follow through."

Kase and Dante both chuckle at the same time, knowing exactly what Lucian's words just did. I summon my strength and bravery to snatch the glowing chain from Micah and narrow my eyes at Lucian.

His nostrils flare, and a wave of sweet, sweet smugness crashes over me. I just proved him wrong, and he knows it. We all know it.

I step forward and meet his eyes, hoping that I can summon even an ounce of intimidation. "Why don't you make things easier on yourself?" I say, using his own words against him. "Tell me where the fuck you have Vincent imprisoning Elias, or face my wrath."

Huffing a breath, he grabs the hem on his shirt and yanks it over his head, tossing it at Micah. His muscles bulge and flex with his movements. Lucian locks his dark eyes to mine and proceeds to unbutton his pants, kicking them off too, showing off the fact that he goes commando.

It takes everything in me to keep a straight face and not look down at his cock—big even soft—though I expect it to rise and harden at any second.

"Why don't you make this fucking easy and get on your damn knees, suck my cock, and beg me not to throw your soulmate's soul to my hellhounds." His jaw twitches as he smirks. "I'm sure they'd eat it faster than the glutton over there."

Micah scowls at Lucian's words but doesn't respond. None of my devils do. A part of me wishes they'd stand up to his comments, but I know if they do, Lucian will never take me seriously. He will never consider me worthy of a throne in Hell. I'll always be a lowly mortal in his eyes.

I tighten my grip around the chain, strangely hot but not painful. "Turn the fuck around, you asshole. I'm done with your bullshit. You think you're some badass, but all you really are is a weak, rejected bastard who thinks he's a king. In my eyes, you're a fucking peasant. Now bow, Lucian. Bow and feel my punishment."

Lucian growls and fists his hands. He opens his mouth to say something, but Dante surprises me by kicking his legs out from under him. Grabbing Lucian's hair, he yanks his head back and places his leather belt in his mouth. Silence fills the room apart from Lucian's boiling anger, his resolve tested by the fact that Kase, Dante, and Micah all surround him, ensuring he remains before me.

My heart raps against my ribs, the discordant beats twisting my soul. On his knees, naked, and hunched forward in his human form, Lucian no longer embodies the fierce ruler of Hell. He embodies the bastard who deserved more wrath than even Kase can offer. He deserves the wrath of a woman like me, scorned, put through Hell, and thrown to the demons over and over again. And I'm done. I have one job, and I will complete it. Lucian will not stand in my way. If he can't accept that the rulers of Hell are intended to be by my sides, not above me, then he can fuck off and live eternity with a wounded ego in the farthest corner of our rising kingdom.

"Just fucking do it," Lucian snaps, his voice rumbling with annoyance by my prolonging his punishment.

"You know, if you'd just tell me where the fuck Elias is so we can bring him home, I might grant you mercy this time." I flick my attention to my devils, but they remain expressionless. Again, they've put this punishment and Lucian in my hands.

"Mercy is for bastard angels," Lucian snaps. "Now do it or don't. I have things to do."

I heave a few breaths. "I just don't understand what the fuck goes on in that head of yours. You keep telling me things could be easy if I give in, but have you ever thought that it's your ass making things difficult? This could be easy if you'd just devil the fuck up, stop acting like a dickhead brat, and accept that my eternity belongs to those who see me as what I'm intended."

"Because your soul should be mine! Mine and no one else's. You will be the reason I rise and change Hell. I'm taking control of the damn Mortal Realm and then Heaven. This universe will be mine." Lucian's horns poke through his forehead, startling me.

Fury explodes in my very being, and I swing the chain, lashing it across his back, stopping him from transforming into his devil form. "Fuck that! You're not. You're going to follow through with what you originally had planned."

Lucian tenses as a thick, molten line ravages across his back. "Not when you fail, Raven."

"Shut up!" Something insanely dark steals my vision, shadowing everything in red. Like my soul separates from my body, I stand beside myself and watch as fire lights my eyes as I whip the fire chain over and over across Lucian's back, screaming and yelling at him incoherently.

Lucian falls to his stomach, heaving and clutching the floor, but I can't stop. Hell consumes me. I want him to suffer like he made me suffer. Like I'm sure he's made tons of other people suffer.

And then the world stops. The fiery chain disappears from my fingers, and I shudder and gasp, trying to figure out what the Hell is going on. Bright light shines in from the living room window, and I stumble toward it and away from Lucian's body and the three dark figures huddled around him.

I yank the curtains open and meet Zade's blue eyes, his features so soft and ethereal, glowing with his heavenly light. His eyes widen as his gaze darts past mine to peer at the mess frozen behind me, and he opens and closes his mouth, but no words come out.

Zade slowly shakes his head and frowns.

I reach out and press my palm to the glass. "Zade, I—"

He vanishes, kicking on the world around me. My body and soul collide back together, winding me, and I drop to my knees. Anger and despair course through my body. Zade's expression screamed everything. He now thinks I'm a monster. He was afraid of me.

And angels? They don't help people like me.

Especially because Lucian's darkness feels heavy in my soul.

"Damn, angel-girl," Kase murmurs, touching my shoulder. "Let me—"

I cry out and shake my head, afraid that whatever light within my soul that attracted him might be in jeopardy. I can't control my racing thoughts and mind. It doesn't help that Lucian remains stiff on the floor in silence.

I just don't understand him. I don't understand what the Hell was the point of this.

I hurt on every level. My body, mind, and soul. I never wanted to be this person, but here I am, scaring angels and whipping Lucian. He did this to me. He got too far under my skin, and I don't know how to move forward. What if this moment cemented my eternity? What if I can never get Zade to join us? My actions and fury toward Lucian might've just changed everything. Maybe this is what he wanted all along.

"Leave us." Lucian's sharp voice rings through the air. "I would like a moment with Raven."

Dante fists his hand. "The fuck we're going to let you. She—"

"It's okay, Dante. I want to hear him out. I know you

won't be far, and I'll try to stay open for Micah if I need him." I open and close my hand, Lucian's mark on my palm glowing from using the fire chain.

Dante hisses and shoves his boot into Lucian's side, flipping him over onto his bleeding back. I wince, the lashes cutting across his formerly smooth skin bad enough that I can imagine how painful they are. Lucian's soft grunt proves as much.

"Try anything stupid and it'll be me who holds the whip." Dante knocks Lucian with his boot again for good measure. Maybe now Lucian will learn just how psychotically protective my devils can be.

Micah and Dante have to pull Kase with them, because he gathers his red Hell power, ready to chuck it at Lucian, even injured on the floor.

Groaning, Lucian trembles as he rolls back to his side, leaving small bloodstains on the floor. "You proved me wrong, Raven," he mutters, propping himself up on his elbow. "I didn't think you had that much Hell in you. Your light is as deceptive as I am. We're more alike than I realized."

Ugh. The last person I want to be compared with is Lucian. "We're nothing alike. You pushed me into this. I don't get off on punishing people relentlessly like you. I just want you to stop being—well, you. Being a dick to me is one thing, but when you threaten the people I care about—I will figure out how to make you stop."

"We're going to continue to go round and round until I wear your soul out. You feel that darkness inside you, darkness that everyone thinks belongs to me, but it's all you. Soon enough, you will realize and accept it. I saw it last night. I saw it today. That darkness is what makes us alike. You haven't lived long enough to truly embrace it." Lucian turns his head and finally meets my gaze instead of staring at the ceiling. "You could be the ruler of Purgatory, but you could also be so much more."

"I'm not on a power trip. Why can't you understand that? You think you can manipulate me to do whatever you want. You think you could come here and suddenly steal control from Kase and Dante, who've been trying to finish what you all started together. I want to know why. It's more than what you say it is, and I know it. If you wanted my soul so badly, you should've just listened to everyone. Now instead of having your brethren surrounding you like you originally wanted, you have enemies." I rest my chin on my knees. "You're just as alone as you were bound to Hell."

"You say that as if I don't enjoy being alone." His eyes flicker with fire. He's lying, and we both know it.

"I don't even know why I bothered giving you an extra moment of my time after this. Why you would want it? I just beat the fuck out of you. If I were you, I'd leave and never want to see me again. You really are twisted." I start to push to me feet, and Lucian jerks out his hand and grabs me by the wrist.

Panic squeezes my chest at his strength, but then he loosens his fingers and surprises me by twining our hands together. I'm too shocked to do anything. I shouldn't allow him to. I mean, it's in the contract that he can't steal my affection which is why it came to this. But for the first time ever, his features soften and the Hell vanishes from his eyes. He looks mortal—no, he looks angelic.

"I know I'm fucked up. That's what happens when you're bound to the place where the darkest souls end up. In Hell, humanity is gone. Humanity only lies in this realm." Lucian scrunches his brows, sitting up. "And even then, it's hard to find light. I tend to swallow it up and destroy it."

"You're a black hole," I murmur.

"I was once known as the Morningstar." His dark eyes soften in the corners, and he offers me a smirk. His handsome features hold my attention. I haven't had much time to truly study Lucian. Now that I do, I can't help myself from taking advantage of it. It's like all those times I've watched documentaries about serial killers. My fascination as to why they do what they do and how they manage to act as if their lives are normal...fuck. This has to be unhealthy, wanting to know Lucian in hopes to figure this out. He doesn't deserve my brain space like those monsters on TV. Yet here I am...

I sigh. "Lucian, what am I really doing here? What is it you hope to gain by this conversation? I'll never forgive you or do what you want because of what you've done. Elias is alone and sick. He's dying. I don't care if you did it to make me fail. What I care about is him and how he deserves better than to die like that. He's my soulmate."

"He's also the reason you're in this position. Had I known you were his Grace, I'd have done things differently. I assumed he'd have done better than force you to relive the same sort of torturous life you had before." Lucian grazes his thumb over mine.

My skin cools as his words sink in. "Wait, you knew me as Grace?"

"I knew of you but never got the honor of meeting the woman whose love could get one of my former brethren to turn his back on his purpose. We were negotiating a contract that never was completed. I assumed the saviors got to you and he was put back on his righteous path. It's not like I was free to find out those things." Whoa. Things are starting to make sense.

Damn it. I hate how many questions I have. "When did you know I was the soul? Is that why you're being such a dick? More so now than before? You're holding a grudge because—"

Lucian covers my mouth with his hand. "Answers come at a cost, Raven, and right now, there is only one way for you to pay."

Anger rushes through me. "I'm not fucking you, Lucian."

He licks his lips. "I'll save that one for when you truly become desperate."

Frowning, I search his gaze. Should I even ask him what he wants? He's probably just toying with me. What I should do is run to my devils and tell them what I know so far. Maybe they can find out the answers.

"I want you to let me touch your soul again," Lucian says, not waiting for me to ask him. "Help heal me from your punishment."

Damn. He'll give me some answers if I let him touch my soul?

I turn my gaze away from him, afraid that the new softness in his eyes will persuade me without giving me a chance to weigh the worth of such a deal. On one hand, I find a little soul touching not as intimate as fucking. But then again, shouldn't I force him to suffer at least a little bit of pain for his actions?

"I...I gue—" A bright light at the front window steals my attention away from Lucian, and my heart skips a beat. It's Zade. I know it. The sudden urge to go to him consumes me more so than getting answers from Lucian. Maybe this is a sign. Obviously it's divine intervention, and I can't ignore it. Not after seeing Zade's expression while watching me beat the shit out of Lucian with his own chain. "I'll think about it. I'm sorry. Maybe had you just asked me instead of withholding something I want to know, I would've. But right now? I want you to think about everything. Like I said, you're the one making things difficult."

I hop to my feet, not waiting for him to respond. Dashing away, I run through an entertainment room and head toward the back door. I don't want Lucian to chase me out front. This will get me a bit of time to put some space between us to clear my head.

I hesitate near the back door for a moment, listening for Kase, Dante, or Micah, but I think they've gone upstairs or have moved to the huge office where the three of them like to discuss demonic affairs. I know Micah will be listening to ensure I'm safe and will only come if I'm not. Lucian will have to get to his feet to get them, and I'm not so sure he can.

I shudder at the reminder, forcing the darkness clinging to me away.

Right now, I need a bit of angelic light.

So I race out the door and call Zade's name.

But he doesn't come. It's not him. It's not Cassius either.

A tall angel with golden wings scowls at me, raising his flaming sword.

10

RAVEN

BASTARD SAVIOR

"RAVEN ROSE! YOU are an abomination to Heaven's order. You must accept your eternal damnation." Expanding his wings, he pushes off the ground and flies at me, aiming his sword.

I jump out of the way. The fucker stumbles and stabs his blade into the ornate frame around the glass door. If the devils don't know he's here, they do now. An earsplitting pop sends bursts of fire and electricity through the air as the unfamiliar savior sets off the protective barrier created by Hell power.

"You better fucking get out of here or the devils themselves will pluck every weird-ass feather from your wings." I dodge out of his line of sight, running behind one of the wide pillars, holding up the balcony overhead. Heavenly light illuminates the porch, and I squint at its intensity.

"I will not fail the task given to me. It is my duty and honor to exterminate the forsaken soul from the Mortal Realm." The angel launches toward me again, flapping his wings to increase his speed.

And fuck.

I screech at the sight of his blade impaling through the pillar, cracking it enough to shake the balcony overhead. Swinging his free hand at me, he grabs onto my arm and yanks me closer. It takes a burst of Hell strength to brace against the pillar, stopping him from pulling me into his still flaming blade.

"Let me go!" I yell, ripping myself away. I flail my arms, trying to catch myself, but fall hard on my ass.

"Never. It is my duty, and with its completion, I can ascend to fill one of the positions among the arch angels. I will not fail." The angel plants his boots at the sides of my hips and towers over me.

His golden wings glow with enough intensity that they could very well embody the sun, bringing the morning early. I refuse to cower beneath this bastard, begging for mercy, so I jerk my leg up and kick him between his legs. He reacts by jabbing his sword at me, and I scream, unable to move. This is it. Out of everyone in the universe, it's going to be some stranger trying to gain power in Heaven to end my mortal life.

Damn it.

A roar explodes through the night at the same time fire engulfs the angel, knocking him away from me. I dig my fingers into the grass and crabwalk backwards until my back hits against one of the patio chairs around a seating area near the flower garden.

My body aches as my mind reels, and I crawl around the loveseat and peek my head over the cushion. I stare in surprise at Lucian whipping his fire chain at the angelic warrior, knocking his legs out from under him. His golden wings prevent his back from hitting the ground, and he uses them to propel forward. Jabbing his sword, he stabs Lucian in his side. Glowing blood pours like molten lava from his wound, but it doesn't stop him from charging. I don't know who this angel thinks he is, but he's obviously no match for Lucian, especially in his towering true body.

A warm hand grabs my shoulder, startling me, and I nearly punch Micah in the balls. He catches my fist and drags me into his arms, searching my face for signs of injury.

"You need to go back inside and stay there. Looks like the warriors are ready to rise in rank and fill the spots Andre and I left behind. There are at least six guardians circling. Dante's taken flight with Kase. I need to fight them as they fall from the sky, but I can't focus worrying about you." Micah jogs his way toward the back door, ducking and spinning with me, taking a burst of heavenly light to his back as a righteous guardian swoops down.

"What the fuck. Don't they know who you are?" I ask, gripping Micah, stopping him from tossing me inside and bolting.

"They're willing to sacrifice themselves to try for the Higher Power," Micah replies, forcing me to let him go. "Now stay inside, heathen. I'll gladly punish you if you don't."

Micah slams the door in my face, and I stare in shock, watching him transform into his giant boar-like body with his massive tusks, ready to gut any angel within reach. The ground quakes as he charges away on all fours. Clutching the doorframe, I remain plastered to the glass, practically pressing my nose against it. From the safety of our mansion, no angel can hurt me. Hell will blow them away. But damn it, if I'm not still a bit scared. It's worse than my fear with Cassius. At least he changed his tactic and stopped treating me like a worthless piece of shit for not wanting to sacrifice myself for the greater good. These guardians or whatever seem to have the sole purpose of destroying me.

Which makes me wonder. Why did Lucian rescue my ass? Things could've been easy for him had he let the angel take my life.

Why the sudden change from being a difficult twit to this?

Fire explodes in front of me, billowing toward the sky. I watch in fearful awe as Lucian stomps his giant hoof into the concrete where the devils do their usual summoning circle to bring Andre here. But this is different. Andre doesn't appear within it—no, someone is already in the center of the fire ring.

It's the angel.

I gasp a breath, wide eyed and shocked, as I watch the portal open with a rumble. The putrid scent of Hell sneaks in through the seal of the door, but I'm no longer fazed by it. But what jabs at my soul is watching the angel's golden wings smolder and burn within the summoning circle. Lucian roars and snarls, whipping his chain again, and the angel hollers and disappears, the fiery ground swallowing him whole and taking him to Hell.

Oh-fucking-shit.

The pure shock of watching Hell consume an angel rattles me to my core. I warned the bastard. He didn't listen. So many of these fuckers don't listen.

Lucian stomps his hoof into the ground, shaking the world around me. The fire vanishes in a cloud of smoke, and he slowly twists, clutching his side. Stumbling toward the door, he transforms back into his human façade and hits his hands to the glass before dropping to his knees.

"Fuck, Lucian." Without thinking, I shove the door open, getting him to move a bit, and stretch out my hand.

Locking my fingers around his thick wrist, I use my Hell strength to drag him inside. He groans, his naked body bruised and bleeding, scratches and cut, and he trembles on the floor, just lying there. Oh how sweet should it be that Lucian himself seems to have fallen. How he seems to have weakened coming to the Mortal Realm. I should laugh and gloat. I should be thrilled.

But un-fucking-fortunately, all I feel is pity.

I might be a bit twisted and can have a psychotic streak with my devils, but I'm still human. I still have angelic light glowing within my soul and a heart that aches the longer I look at the pathetic sight before me.

I squat beside him and touch his shoulder. "Lucian—"

"Leave me," he snaps, pressing his hands into his side, his strange blood thick and glowing across the surfaces it touches. "I don't need your pity."

I sigh and shove him over, shrugging out of my shirt. Pressing the fabric to the wound on his side from the angel blade, I try to staunch the bleeding. "Too bad. It is in my very being to see that you never get anything you want from me and everything you don't. So suck it up, Satan. You're going to drown in the pity I have for you."

Surprising me, he chuckles and glances up, meeting my gaze. "Careful, Raven. I like when you call me that."

The fucker proves as much, motioning toward his hardening cock. Heat flushes through me, and I avert my eyes. He does not need to watch me appreciate his devilish dick. Why I always fall for such a sight on every devil is beyond me. Kase was right about me. Satanic cocks do in fact compel me into thinking things I shouldn't. Lucian might be on the verge of drowning in my pity, but I'm about to drown in his sin.

I must resist.

"All right, Lucifer. Calm your cock or I'm not going to help you." I scoot closer and kneel beside his head. His eyes follow my every move and light up under the use of his angelic name. I press my hand over his lips, shutting him up before he can even think to speak. "Let's get one thing straight. This is not an invitation to try to force your affection on me. This is a thank you for protecting me outside instead of letting the savior send me to Hell."

"I couldn't give the fucker the satisfaction. Your contract belongs to Hell. I'm having too much fun on this plane to give it up to torture you in my kingdom." Lucian's words vibrate against my palm. He licks my hand, shocking me, and I jerk it away and plant it on his chest. His heart thrums in quick beats, set off by my sudden touch.

I try not to react, tightening my mouth. "Okay, whatever. Maybe I should've let him send me to Hell to get a break from you. You're welcome to stay here when I go."

Lucian laughs again, the sound so fucking weird but nice.

I might prefer it over his rumbly growls. "You'd miss me. I promise."

Narrowing my eyes, I decide against giving in and denying his comment. He's gone from asshole to cocky to charming seemingly overnight, and I won't let myself get distracted by it. It changes nothing. He's still one of my worst enemies until he returns Elias to me.

"All right, asshole. Do your thing quickly, so I can wait by the door for my favorite devils to return. They're going to need a reward for everything they're putting up with because of you." I hover over Lucian, letting my hair spill around my face, blocking the world with its veil of midnight color.

"Quick isn't something I do, Raven. Not with you." Rolling over, Lucian lands on top of me and grins, loving the shocked state his sudden gesture leaves me in. "Never with you."

Our eyes meet and I stare up at him like the wide-eyed prey his predatory side sees me as. Regret blooms inside me the closer he leans until the world fades away and a strange warmth washes it away. I gasp against his mouth only an inch from mine and tip my head slightly so our lips aren't aligned. The room shifts into a brilliant nothingness of pure white as Lucian now stands before me, naked and rippling, his body free of injury.

He truly is achingly beautiful bathed in the light of my soul, his velvety skin radiating with a new kind of glow. His hard features soften, and a smile curls the corners of his lips. He graces me with a bright smile, his whole face lighting up. I can't stop my feet from taking me closer until I'm only a foot away.

"You enjoy seeing this side of me," he murmurs, gently reaching up to caress my cheek and push my hair behind my ear. "This is what your soul does to me, you know. I no longer have the capability to shine with angelic glory. But you make it so."

"Don't get too comfortable, Satan," I tease, my worry, fear, and pain melting away in this world of light. "This is a one-time thing."

He lifts an eyebrow and rubs his hand over his dark beard. "I love when you lie to yourself."

I glower, pressing my hand to his chest. "I'm not lying. You stole Elias from me and won't return him. I will make sure I'm never in the position of needing your help again. Now hurry up."

"A kiss is in order if that's what you truly want. You have to accept my darkness into your light, and with how hard you resist, that's the second best way." His eyes sparkle with the light of the world around us.

"What's the best way?" I ask, regretting my question immediately. His expression says it all before he even says anything. "Never mind. Fucking my soul isn't happening."

"What if I make you a deal? You seem to have caught me

in a rather giving mood, Raven, and feeling your soul like this...it's hard resisting doing what I want." Lucian steps so close that his cock grazes my stomach with still an intimidating amount of space between us. "What if I manage to get Vincent to change the terms of our contract to bring you Elias?"

My heart skips a beat at his words. "You'll bring him back if I let you fuck my soul? Seriously?"

He glides his fingers along my shoulder, pushing my hair to my back. "I said I'd get Vincent to change the terms. Right now, he will not comply to any of my requests. I can't break our agreement without...giving a throne away. Unless that's something you're okay with."

Fuck no. The thought of Vincent taking a throne in Hell skeeves me out more than anything in the universe. He threatened to yank out my teeth for biting him. The fear of that moment still lingers with me.

"How do I know you'll actually follow through? What if he doesn't agree?" I tighten my lips, twisting them to the side with my questions.

Lucian bows closer, his mouth so close that his lips brush mine when he says, "Our contract will be binding. If I fail, your soul will be free."

What? He can't be serious. "You're lying. You wouldn't do that."

"I would, but I won't have to. I will uphold my end." Lucian's hand slides down my arm and travels to my back as he pulls me flush against him. My soul explodes with tingles, the electric sensation traveling through me and landing right between my legs. "Do we have a deal? Let me fuck your soul and you'll get your soulmate back. If I fail, your soul is free."

My thoughts whirl with his words. Can I do this? Fuck yeah. I've done worse with Joel. It's probably one of the better deals a mortal has gotten. Either way, I win. I'll get Elias back or my soul will be free and I will still have a chance to find him. Who cares if I have to give into Lucian? I'm nearly certain my devils would agree with me. They've already come to accept sharing me, and if this cements our eternity ruling Hell? I'll take this for the team.

I slowly nod my head. "Deal."

Lucian's lips crash into mine with my words, and I groan against his mouth, tasting the spicy cinnamon of his kiss deep in my soul. I don't even have a chance to react before my clothes vanish, and Lucian's warm hand drags across my stomach, traveling to touch between my legs. And damn. I love and hate how good it feels, giving in to his dark temptation.

If only something didn't snap through me, stealing my breath. The light blinks out, leaving my vision dark, and Lucian snarls above me.

"Micah! Raven and I made a deal. Stay the fuck back," Lucian yells, his devil voice vibrating across my skin, pulling me from my haze. His monstrous devil form hovers above me, his horns jutting from his forehead.

Micah responds with a roar, shaking the ground. He rams his big head into Lucian, knocking him off me. One second I'm on the floor, and in the next, I'm cradled in Micah's arms. "You cannot bully her into deals like that. I won't allow it."

I open my mouth to argue with Micah, but his face contorts into his hellish façade, stealing my words. He carries me away.

"Micah, come on. Lucian and I made a deal where I win either way. What's a little soul fucking? It's my soul, my soulmate, and my decision. I'm trying to not only do my job but also ensure an amazing future for us." I sit beside him on the edge of the bed, unable to stop my frown. "Please, I need you to be okay with this."

Sighing, Micah laces his fingers through mine and pulls my hand to his chest. "It's not that I'm not okay with you being with someone else. I've accepted that to enjoy you, I must share you. What bothers me is that I know you wouldn't do this if Elias were here. You'd never resort to such intimacy with Lucian. He's no different than before, but he's adapting. He's studying you and trying to use his new awareness to get to you."

I huff a breath. "Micah, that's nothing new. You were the one to suggest that I give Lucian a chance. You told me that he was acting like this because he was lonely. Now what? I finally found a reason to play nice and you don't want me to? Is this about you? Are you annoyed I haven't fucked you yet?"

Orange fire heats up his wicked gaze, and he flares his nostrils. "I've told you it was never about sex with me. This is about Elias. He wouldn't want you to resort to bartering your body for his life."

I shake my head and tug my hand away from him. "Yeah-fucking-right. I know Elias—"

Growling, he says, "I know him too, Raven. I've known him all my existence. Please, give me a chance to figure this out. I have an idea that might work to bring him back and keep your soul away from Lucian."

I close my eyes for a moment, settling my nerves. If Micah has come up with another way, I will let it play out despite how scared I am of failure. Failing doesn't just mean Elias dies alone. It means so much more, and I've been so used to fighting for my own soul that it's hard even now to let someone else handle it.

"I can't allow you more than a day, Micah," I say, my voice growing soft. "He's running out of time. This can be easy. And if you're worried about me falling for Lucian's manipulation, don't be. He hasn't earned his right to be with me. Not like Dante and Kase. Not like Andre and Elias. And especially not like you. You've done everything in your power to try to help me, Micah. You care about my soul in a way no one else does, and I know this. I appreciate it."

Holding up my hand, I show off the glittering ring with the soul he trapped within just for me, still the only jewelry I wear from my devils, though Kase is wearing me down with his desire to bling my body with a hood piercing. "This ring proves it. I wear this in your honor."

His sharp features soften and he pulls my hand to his lips, kissing my knuckles. I get caught in his fiery gaze, my body still buzzing from my strange-ass moment with Lucian. Micah studies me as if he peers right at my soul and plans to touch it how Lucian had. It's like he wants to make me forget that it ever happened. And suddenly, I want that too.

"Your thoughts, Raven," Micah murmurs. His eyes break from mine, and he drinks in the rest of me. "You want me. You crave me. I can sense it in your being."

Heat warms my face as our minds open completely to each other and a wave of Micah's lust crashes over me, and I let it wash away the craziness of the night. It leaves me wanting to bare more than my soul to him. He's been far more patient with me than the others, and while he claims our relationship isn't about sex, I know he desires to experience it. He wants to know me on every level. And I plan to give him what he wants. Take what I desire. Corrupting devils is far more fun than corrupting angels. All it takes is a small stroke of my hand to unleash Micah's wild side.

I link my fingers to his shirt and tug it over his head the same moment I slide onto his lap and straddle him on the edge of the bed. He moans and braces his body with one hand to stop me from pushing him back. With his other hand, he ignites orange Hell power in his palm and smolders the front of my shirt, the flames leaving me topless for him. He lifts me higher, using only his leg, the pressure of his knee between my legs feeling intense and incredible. He bounces me slightly, sucking my nipple into his mouth. I clutch his hair, grinding against the pressure of his body. Fuck, it feels good.

Giving in to lying on his back, Micah drags me up his chest until my knees hit the bed above his shoulders. He spreads my legs wider and singes the seam of my pants, burning right through them. And then he half transforms, his long tusks caging me in place and holding me still as he drags his tongue across my body, the sensation hot and tingling and so fucking amazing that my whole body trembles.

I stiffen and brace myself, clutching his tusks as an orgasm rips a scream of pleasure from me. Micah falls to his gluttony, only stopping long enough to smile and lick his lips. His tusks vanish as he shifts completely back into his human form only to get me to turn around. And then he starts all over again, eating me out even more desperately. I groan as he slides his tongue from my clit and back and pays extra attention to my ass. I gasp and bow forward, enjoying his gluttonous need for my body.

I can't reach his cock with my mouth from this position, so I pop the button of his pants open and spit in my hand for extra slipperiness. My touch sets off his devil side, and I'm so fucking glad he can't see me because damn. His devil cock curves in a way that fascinates me. I want to know what it feels like, the sensations it'll create, how the curve gives it a grooved texture.

"You want me in my devil form, heathen?" Micah asks, hearing my thoughts. "Are you sure?"

"I love you in every form you take, Micah. You're my perfect gluttonous sinner. Fuck me however you desire—except my ass. That's been claimed." I laugh breathlessly with my words, letting Micah shift me onto the bed.

I expect him to flip me around, but he comes up behind me and flogs me with his long, tough tail, letting me feel the sensation of his Hell form without seeing him. He's nervous yet excited. I can feel it deep in my being.

"We'll see about that," he murmurs, shifting my legs together a bit more as he rests his hulking legs on the outside, though his hands remain the same as he grabs my hair and arches my back to kiss me. "Unlike the other devils, I stretch to fit however you please."

I don't get a chance to satiate my curiosity, because Micah thrusts into me, unable to control his wild beast side, dying to claim me. The sensation arouses my very soul, the sensation of his curved, ribbed cock stroking against my G-spot.

"Oh, fuck!" I scream out, the pleasure so intense that I feel myself squirt with my orgasm, his quick, rhythmic thrusts hitting me perfectly in all the right spots. "Micah, your cock. It's indescribable. I—" Holy shit. I scream out again, my body tensing with another orgasm. I didn't think this was possible, but Micah's passion does something crazy good to my body.

"You're like Heaven and Hell combined in an unfathomable wave of ecstasy," Micah murmurs, hitting his rock-hard body to my ass, ravishing me with his gluttonous need for our passion.

My arms give out on me, and I bow forward, moaning and gasping, losing myself to the intense waterfall of bliss. I savor every second of getting fucked in such a way that I feel deep in my being with every damn quaking orgasm.

"My beautiful heathen. This will be our eternity regardless of whether you succeed in fulfilling your contract. I've ensured it. I never want you to worry. Your soul is mine." With his words, he moans shockingly loud, almost roaring, and I clutch the blankets as he thrusts a few more times. He digs his fingers into my hips with his orgasm, the sensation strangely exciting like a small explosion that shocks every one of my nerve endings in a good way.

Micah slumps onto me only to roll me over and into his chest. "I want more of you. I can't seem to get enough. Why don't you forget about everything and let me take care of things? You will never have to worry about being mistreated by Lucian. Not with my name on your contract too."

"Wait, what? How could you even suggest a thing, Micah?" I can't stop my mind from whirling.

I had been worried about Dante's envy and possessiveness, but maybe it should've been Micah I needed to keep cautious with. He is a glutton after all. He will never feel like he gets enough of me, my soul, or whatever else he sets his sights on. And bringing up the fact that his name is on my contract? I didn't realize how serious he was when he'd make promises about our future. I had assumed he just felt entitled and thought since Kase and Dante weren't exactly getting along with Lucian that he was going to be there if things fall apart. Now it sounds like he wants them to.

Micah props himself up on his elbow. "How can I not? I know you worry about everything. I don't want you to always wonder about what will happen. This way we can ensure it."

I gather the blanket and scoot to the edge of the bed. "That's very thoughtful, but you know I'm set on getting this shit done."

He sighs and arches forward, his body still hard and flexing in all the right places. "Raven, come on. Don't run. I can hear your thoughts racing. Your fears are unwarranted. I won't be overly possessive. I'm sure I can work things out with the others. Contracts can be re-negotiated once you're mine. We—"

"Micah, I think this was a mistake. I thought it would help you, showing you that I care about you, but you're speaking as if you're my soul keeper and not a man who wants me as his queen." I tighten the blanket around me. "I'm sorry."

"I am your soul keeper. You're my purpose," Micah argues, standing up.

I wave my hand getting him to stop. "I think you need some space to get your shit together. You're letting your gluttony consume your rationale. Please, just stay here and try to find your good sense. I'm going to take a bath in Dante's room and wait for them to return."

Micah throws his arms out, his features sharpening in annoyance. "I have a shower we can wash in together."

Fucking Hell. And I really mean it. It's hard to know what's going to happen when you let it inside of you.

"Next time, okay? Just...I have to go. I'm sorry." I rush from the room and bolt down the hallway to Dante's room. I never expected to be a hit it and quit it type of person, especially after taking the virginity of the ruler of Gluttony, but damn it. I wasn't prepared for him to start planning an eternity for if I fail.

Or asking me to purposely do so.

I don't spend long cleaning up in the bathroom I share with Dante. After a quick shower and using the damn cum sponges I never knew existed until Dante set a box in full view on the counter, I throw on some panties and one of his shirts, just wanting to hide in the massive closet until he returns.

But ethereal light on the balcony catches my attention. My heart slides into my stomach, and I grab onto his biggest dildo on the shelf, getting ready to clobber a guardian savior with it if I have to. I will show no mercy after their bullshit.

Zade stands frozen on the other side of the door, his eyes darting from mine and to the heavy silicone monstrosity resting on my shoulder.

I automatically drop it to the floor with a thud and stride to the glass. "You're here. I thought you sent an army to murder me because of what you saw earlier."

His brows pucker and he shakes his head. "I'd never. I know how much you mean to Andre."

"Then what are you doing here?" I ask, hugging my arms across my chest.

"Can we talk? Somewhere I don't have to worry about getting attacked by one of your devils?" He peers past me. "I won't take you far. Across the yard."

I open the door completely and step out into the cool night. "I'd like that. I wanted to explain myself. What you saw—"

Shaking his head, he covers my mouth and hooks his arm around my waist, lifting me off my feet. "Not here. Come on. Don't worry about the guardians or anyone else. I promise to keep you safe."

I stare into his vivid blue eyes. For once, I might actually believe him.

11

KASE

FOR HELL'S SAKE

"SHOULD YOU FOLLOW them or should I?" Dante drapes his arm over my shoulder as we watch Zade fly a few dozen feet away with Raven, trying to hide the two of them under one of the magnolia trees along the perimeter on the vast property.

"Me. If I confront Micah, he'll be back in Hell taking Andre's place. The fucking bastard knew better than to bring that shit up with the contract." I growl with my words, pissed the fuck off that Micah ruined what should've been one helluva good time with Raven. He should've just kept his face buried between her legs instead of opening his goddamned mouth.

Should I have been peeking in on them? Probably not. But with how loud the two of them were, I couldn't help crossing the line. It's not like Micah hasn't spied on us before, and Raven is so open and accepting of my nature that she'll only be annoyed because she didn't know. She gets off on being watched in all her sexy perfection, and she knows it.

As for Micah? Fuck him. He knew he needed to earn that sweet pussy of hers, and I don't think he has. Or maybe he just lost the right.

I growl again. "Damn it. Maybe I should. He'd deserve it." Am I still holding a grudge since he took my wings? Fuck yeah.

Dante chuckles, unfazed by my comment and anger boiling from my hands in a red orb. "That could be a lot of fun with Andre. We could fucking bet on how many orgasms it takes for him to release her. Maybe it'll give our pretty soul the little nudge she needs for more ass play. I'm getting hungry for a Raven sandwich with you, especially after seeing Micah with her."

I can't stop the smirk from stealing my glower. It was a damn glorious sight. "It was practically raining pussy juice. I might have to put a kink in my tail and recreate that."

Like the asshole he is, Dante slides his arm down my back and grabs my tail, tightening his hands around it. I startle at the pressure and tighten my jaw, trying not to react. It's been a while since he played with me like this. It's become Raven's thing.

"I'll help," he teases, stroking the length and making my damn nuts ache with my boner. He drops it and gives me a push, knowing I might not move if he doesn't. "But later. Maybe I'll test it first and she can watch."

"Are you offering to be the meat in our sandwich then?" I laugh and flick his cock through his pants, getting him to jump out of the way of the door to my balcony. "She'd love that."

A rumble escapes his throat. "Don't get me started, Kase. I'm fucking horny, and I know she might not be in the mood. Now go do what you do best and cock-block another bastard. I want her back here and in my arms. She deserves proper after care, which I'll fucking make sure Micah knows how to do."

I step onto the balcony. "You fucking better beat that into him."

"Or bring Raven back and she can do it for us." His eyes flash green with his words, the energy of watching Raven whip the Hell into Lucian still fresh on everyone's mind. I knew she had it in her, but damn. Watching her devour his darkness and use it has me anxious and excited.

"Beatings from Raven all around." I laugh and swat him with my tail, running and jumping from the balcony to avoid his retaliation.

The cool night air steams against the heat of my skin, and I catch sight of the faint glow in the distance. Instead of transforming, I stroll across the lawn, swinging my tail with my movements. Dante fucking has me all riled up now. If I were in my devil form, I'm not sure I could sneak up on Raven and Zade. Startling angels and catching them on the verge of losing themselves to Raven's mortal allure is my fifth favorite thing in life.

"Can I kiss you for a moment?" Zade asks, his soft voice trickling to me. "I want to help set your light aglow and push away the darkness clinging to you. What you were forced to do—"

Raven and Zade come into view as she cuts him off with a kiss, placing her hands against his chest while she pushes him against the tree trunk. That naughty soul. She sure loves dominating the angels every chance she gets. I'll have to remind Dante to truly reward her with some role swapping power play. I can't get my controlling ass to submit, but I know he can.

"Raven," Zade murmurs, easing away from her mouth. What a fucking dumbass. He shouldn't pull away from her affection. He should give in until she's good and ready to release him. "I want to kiss you all night but I must hurry and tell you why I've come."

Anger rises through me, my wrath heating my body enough to feel as if the temperature drops. With all the new dicks around, I can't help getting pissed off at seeing the shortcomings of others. Raven deserves the fucking best. She doesn't deserve to feel like you want even a moment less of what her pouty mouth has to offer.

"Oh, right. I'm sorry." That perfect angel-girl should not be apologizing to this bastard. He should apologize to her.

My rage gets the best of me, and I storm forward, giving away that I'm watching the two of them. Raven's eyes widen, and she spins toward me, closing the space. She expects me to dodge around her and extends her arms out. I try anyways, but the sexy little Hell raiser she is tackles me.

I let her, landing on my back with a grunt. She straddles my waist and tries to grab my cheeks to draw my focus from Zade. I must be losing my touch, because he stands there without fluttering away like a scared pigeon. I growl deep in my throat until Raven yanks the big shirt she wears up, shows me a view of her naked body, and then smothers my face with her tits.

My growl turns into a purr, and I can't stop from blowing between her cleavage, making her laugh. I trap her, not allowing her to scramble off me and teach her a lesson by sucking her hard nipple into my mouth.

I sense Zade staring at the two of us and shift Raven, giving him a show he can't avert his eyes from. For good measure, I roll her off me and use my knee to keep her shirt up. "When you deny my beautiful soul your affection, I must complete the task. Look how happy she is exposed for us."

Raven groans and blindly reaches for my tail, managing to snatch it. She winds it around her palm, silently threatening me to tone it down, but it's hard. I'm fucking hard. Zade's hard. Maybe it was a damn terrible idea to come out here and poke her dark nature after she was just pounded by Micah.

"He's not ready, Kase. You know I don't like to push them." Raven snags her shirt out from under my weight and adjusts it, hiding her hypnotic tits, the bounce with her movements driving me wild, especially watching them jiggle and swing as Micah mounted her like a fucking animal from behind.

"But I do," I tease, lifting her shirt again as she tries to get to her feet. "I'd push him right off his damn angelic pedestal if I could for you. Though, you might consider letting him get his cock wet as an angel. I'm tired of virgin devils thinking that they can keep you to themselves."

"You heard?" she asks quietly, her teasing smile faltering.

I wag my eyebrows at her, watching her surprise shift into something darker, sexier. I knew she would like the thought. "Not only heard. Dante and I fucking watched. And let me tell you, I—"

She slaps her hand across my lips. "You little perv. How

the Hell did you manage to stay quiet?"

"It's easy when you're so loud that the whole neighborhood could hear." I lick her palm, thankful that she cleaned up. Micah already gets on my nerves. If I had to taste him...I shudder. Never fucking happening.

A heavy sigh sounds from beside us, and I whip my attention away from Raven to glower at Zade. He straightens his shoulders, his annoyance tightening his mouth. It makes me want to continue to ignore him and get Raven riled up, but her naughty ass untangles my tail from her hand and strides back to Zade.

"I'm so sorry. It's been a crazy-ass night. What is it you needed to tell me?" Raven glances at me from over her shoulder. "You can whisper it if you want."

I smirk, lifting an eyebrow at her. She damn-well knows that she's going to tell me the second his feather-head vanishes.

Zade clears his throat and shakes his head. Good angel. Maybe he won't be as hard to tolerate if he's obedient now. "That won't be necessary. It's about Elias. I've located him."

Raven gasps in surprise and throws her arms around Zade, practically climbing him like a tree to get in his face. I glower as I watch her kiss him, and once again, the unappreciative dickhole pulls away. A soft smile curves his lips, one that makes Raven smile too, and I fist my hand, wondering if I can distract her and punch his fucking face.

Must. Control. Wrath. But damn it. I want to dish punishment to every-fucking-asshole who does anything that can possibly hurt Raven tonight or make her feel anything less than the beautiful fierce queen she is.

"You've located him, huh?" I ask, strolling closer, the heat of my Hell power warming my tight fists. "Now why would you do that?"

My eyes dart to Zade's hands tightening around Raven. He fears me and he instinctually desires to unnecessarily protect her. I'll give him a point for that. Overprotective I can live eternity with. Asshole possessive bastards, on the other hand? I'll have to teach everyone the same damn lesson I taught Dante. Raven chooses who she wants to give her affection to and if she wants to give it to every damn devil she creates, then I will stand by her side and work out the logistics of the massive orgies I know will be in store.

"I had an agreement with Raven. I messed up the first time and felt like I should keep trying. I would have gotten her soulmate and brought him here, but Cassius intervened and stopped me." Zade remains expressionless, guarding himself from the sudden sadness crossing Raven's face. "I'm sorry there was nothing more I could do. Cass is afraid of what you're capable of despite knowing that I won't leave my righteous path."

That's what he fucking thinks. I'll prove it. I'll help Raven get him to turn his back here and now. I know he's curious and wants to experience some of the pleasure that comes with her attention. His surprisingly magnificent cock outline proves it. He's no Andre, but he's no blasted mortal either.

"It's fine, Zade. Anything helps. I'm sure Andre will appreciate that you've already done so much." Raven hugs him close again and plays with his blond hair.

That sneaky sexy angel-girl. I see exactly what she's doing. And now that her comment sinks in, I can tell what she's planning. She's using Zade's connection to Andre to get him to sway. The bastard's probably broken up about Andre leaving him. And who fucking knows? It might be even more than that.

"Maybe after we pick up Elias, I can arrange something? I'm not sure I want to travel to Lust's Kingdom, but we could summon him." Raven strokes her fingers along Zade's cheek.

"That is probably no longer a good idea." Zade frowns with his words. "He made it clear that I was no longer accepted in his life."

"You could always just fucking jump and join us, asshole," I say, butting in. "I bet Andre would give you some extra attention if you just bent over and dropped your pants. It's the best way to get to the ruler of Lust...if you think you can handle that massive ass-annihilator of a cock. Prove to Raven that anything's possible with some prep."

Her eyes widen and she scrunches her nose. Zade finally breaks his stern expression and raises his eyebrows. He's fucking thinking about it. And damn. At this point, I don't give a damn whose ass it is, I can't wait to see the champion of desire slide his megaladick into the hole of assland.

Raven shivers and snaps out of her sudden fascination at Zade's expression. Oh, damn. I think she just realized she might have an ass play fetish watching someone else. I'm going to fucking have to test the theory now.

Zade groans and slides Raven from his arms, scrubbing his face with his palms. "Give me strength," he whispers under his breath.

Raven hears him too and touches his shoulder. "I'm sorr—"

I grumble and toss a ball of red power at the ground, startling her. "Stop with the fucking apologies to him. You have nothing to be sorry about. This dickwad needs to tell us where Elias is so we can hustle and grab his ass, come back here, and do some experimenting."

Zade unfurls his wings, his shining light stinging my eyes. "He's being held at the Canyon View apartments downtown. On Sixth."

Raven grabs his hand and squeezes it. "Thank you."

"If you really want to thank him, why don't you give him a quick blowie? He looks ready to bust a nut anyway. Maybe it'll push him to join us." I drape my arm over Raven's shoulder, meeting Zade's eyes but talking to angel-girl. "Remember Andre? His cum gave you a peek into Heaven."

Raven glances at me in her peripheral vision. I fucking love teaming up with her for this shit. "Oh, I guess that would be okay. If he wants one." Her naughty mouth and willingness makes me want to bend her over and fuck her as she does so.

I touch Zade's cheek with my tail. "You want one, angel-boy? You and angel-girl could—"

Batting his hand, he tries to knock my tail away but I'm far too fast for that kind of bullshit. Zade ruffles his feathers. "Perhaps some other time. I must go."

Damn. I want to punch him for his rejection.

Raven stands on her tiptoes and kisses his cheek. She whispers something into his ear, making the fucker glow brighter, and I wind my tail around her waist, ensuring he doesn't try to steal her away from me at the last second.

With one more look at me, Zade shakes his head and backs out from under the tree. He flaps his wings and launches into the air, circling once before disappearing. Raven tilts her head toward the sky and watches the world above us longer than necessary like she expects him to return at any moment. Maybe come falling from above with a change of mind with his hopefully throbbing balls.

"Keep staring at the stars like that and I'll start to think you want him to sweep you away to the land of flaccid cocks and desert dry pussies from the lack of anything fun." I nudge her with my shoulder. "You love things way too wet and slippery for that bullshit. It doesn't mist from the heavens because everyone's banging, you know."

She turns and whacks me. "Ew stop. You're going to ruin the rain for me because now I'm going to think about heavenly cum. That's weird."

I roar a laugh and scoop her up, getting her to wrap her legs around me. She squirms, feeling my tail shift her shirt out of the way as I blindly follow the line of her ass crack. I'm so damn horny that I'll accept fucking her with my tail for even just a minute. Her hands slide up and around my neck and she wiggles like crazy, testing my ability to hold her, making me work for it.

She clenches, puckering that tight asshole of hers. "Kase, I want you to fuck me as much as you do, but if we start, you know neither of us will stop. Then Dante will come and join us, and the next thing we'll know it's a week later. Elias might not manage that long. Save your horny sex frenzy as celebration."

"There's only one way I want to celebrate," I mumble, testing her ass again to see if she relaxes. She does only to pinch the tip of my tail between her butt cheeks, making me grunt with an unexpected moan.

"Fine. If you can manage to behave and help me get Elias, I'll let you fuck me in the ass," she says, grazing her lips to my ear. "With your cock."

"Hell-fucking-yes. Fucking finally." I wind my tail back up and hide it with Hell power. I drop her a few inches and playfully hump her just to show how fucking excited I am. She feels so fucking good already. I can't wait.

She bonks her head to my shoulder. "Just remember, the future of all ass-play now rests on you. If it's not fun, you will ruin it for Dante."

I sigh. "Damn."

"You should feel the pressure of your decision if I'm going to take the pressure of your majestic satanic cock." She smiles with her comment, using my own words against me.

"You're so evil," I mutter. "I love you. My cock loves you."

She laughs and shakes her head. "Who knew a little ass agreement would turn you into such a romantic."

"You hear that, Micah? That's how you romance our soul. Keep it short and dirty or just show her in other ways. Don't make her regret wetting your dick by making her think you've turned into a selfish prick who will deny her all the love she deserves, which is why her soul calls to all of us. You should realize it by now." Dante hangs his hand over Micah's shoulder as the two of them stand on his balcony and watch us from above.

I was too wrapped up with Raven to notice them. "Yeah, you fucker. This is your one free pass just because you haven't learned to think under the influence of everything angel-girl embodies. Next time, if we catch her running from you to bathe alone and all confused and emotional without the proper affection she deserves after pounding your Hell into her, I will hang you up by your nuts and force you to balance with your ass on a broom."

Raven's eyebrows shoot up on her forehead and she sucks in a breath. "Kase, that's fucking—"

"A promise," I say, cutting her off. "But I won't have to keep it now, will I Micah?"

He flares his nostrils and nods. "I am truly sorry for tonight, Raven. You gave me such a gift, and I wronged you. I hope you forgive me."

Raven rubs her lips together. "I do, Micah, but I hope you know how serious I was. I will not stand around and accept failure. You having your name on my contract doesn't make me feel better. It makes me feel like you don't care if we succeed."

He blinks a few times. I think the bastard finally gets it. It's a good thing, because I was fully prepared to beat it into him. "We will succeed. I promise. We'll do what I told you and get Elias back."

She smiles, her worry in her eyes vanishing. "We won't have to resort to that. We have Elias's location. We're getting him tonight."

Dante grabs onto Micah and launches with him off the balcony and beside us. "Hell yeah," Dante says, hugging his arms around me and Raven. "I thought there was a reason you two were in a good mood. Thank fucking fuck it wasn't because you chose to have a threesome with blondie. It better be a fucking foursome if that happens.

Raven rolls her eyes and pats his cheek. "Only if you help me handle all the cock."

He licks his lips and presses his tongue to the inside of his cheek, holding his curled fingers in front of his mouth. "Gladly."

"Damn, angel-girl. You're testing me on purpose, and I swear to fuck, I'm not going to fail because of it. That ass is mine." I spank her, making her jump. "Now everyone get their shit together. We have a soulmate to find."

"Finally," Dante says. "Who's telling Lucian?"

Micah shakes his head. "No one. Let him learn that his behavior will ensure he never gets a taste of Raven's light."

"Unless she asks," I remind him. "Remember that. Whatever Raven wants, Raven gets."

"Hell and all its rulers," she says, smiling.

Damn. I bet she could get the universe if she wanted. She can make anyone fall to their knees.

12

DANTE

AS THE WORLD BURNS

I ACHE FOR Raven. And for once, it's not my fucking nuts. The light of her soul remains dim, letting the darkness both Micah and Lucian left behind consume her. I despise their darkness and want nothing more than to annihilate it with my own. Raven knows that within the fiery pits of my being lies everything she craves—protectiveness. Obsession. The innate need to destroy anything that dares mess with her light in a way she doesn't approve, want, or can't handle. It's my job as her future king to lift her up and hold her high above us all as our queen.

"We're almost there, pretty soul," I murmur, combing her billowing hair from her throat to kiss her cold, goose-bump ridden skin. I had planned to fly alone, watching Kase speed down the highway with her and Micah, but Raven quietly stepped into my arms, and I couldn't deny her.

She whispers her response, her soft voice lost on the wind. Wiggling a bit, she adjusts herself and presses her face to the crook of my neck. Her body trembles, and I squeeze her tighter, rubbing my hot hand over her arm, trying to warm her up. Except she's not shivering from cold. The cool trickle of her wind-kissed tears splash on my neck. And fuck. She's crying.

I growl in annoyance but not at her. I'm fucking ballistic that Micah and Lucian have fucked up her mental state enough that she's hurting. She's experiencing the turmoil only the damned should ever feel. I don't give a flying fuck if Micah apologized. He should've never put her in a position to ever doubt his intentions. And Lucian? That asshole just needs to return to Hell. He gave up his right to be graced by Raven's presence when he tried to break her contract and proceeded to put us in this position in the first place.

Except doing anything other than being here for my pretty soul is all I can do besides punch some sense into the others when Raven's not looking. It is her will to decide whether or not she allows anyone else into the light of her radiant being despite my opinion about them.

I hate to admit it, but I see the attraction kindling between Raven and Lucian the same as I see when she puts her sights on a savior. Her ability to shrug off the bad and see the good makes her so entrancing to a fault. I just hope Lucian quits being a monstrous devil, treating her as if she isn't the brilliant, angel-kissed woman we need. He wasn't always such a manipulative dick. He hadn't let the sins of his making consume him before mingling his darkness with her soul. I used to suck Lucian's cock for fuck's sake, and not because he demanded it. It's as sexy as his damn horns, and if he'd just get the burning stick of Hell out of his ass, we could resurrect our friendship that had us jumping from grace with the intent to bring balance to the universe. Before we created Hell, most souls were purely recycled—even the worst of them—and all that did was send humanity on a path of destruction.

"Dante, can you distract me? Make me a member of the Mile High Club or whatever the equivalent is to getting fucked by a devil midflight?" Raven clears her throat and tips her head back, capturing me with her glassy eyes.

I swipe my fingers across her cheeks, smearing the blasted tears for caressing her skin in a way only I should. "Oh, pretty soul. How I want to warm my dick inside your hot pussy right about now, but five minutes isn't enough time. I doubt you want to soar around for at least fifteen minutes for a quickie that will only leave us both sexually agitated. One orgasm is not good enough."

Her eyebrows shoot up on her forehead, and she laughs in exasperation. And fucking damn it, if it's not the most melodious sound I've ever heard. "One orgasm is better than none."

"Now it's that kind of standard I need to continue working on fucking out of you," I tease, bowing forward to brush my lips to hers, tasting the salt of her tears. "You will accept neither option. From now on, I'm putting a fucking five minimum orgasm rule in place."

The smile she graces me with lights a fire right in my balls, and I consider how quickly I can stay true to my words during the descent to the apartment tower below. Kase's red Ferrari's brakes squeal as he drifts into the spot between two beater cars, his parallel parking absolute perfection.

"I expect ten when we get home, but only after I have a moment to love up on my soulmate. Maybe you can help me cuddle him up. He'll never admit it, but he enjoys your bite as much as I do." Raven blows out a breath, the sadness that was clinging to her now melting away with the heat of her rising happiness, knowing that Elias is finally coming home.

"You sure have a thing for pathetic, you know," I quip, grinning with my words. "Do I need to stop putting in my best and get the shit beat out of me more often? Will that ensure your luscious lips caress every inch of me and you attempt to heal me with the power of your pussy? Because your light is truly addictive magic, and it'll be worth the pain."

"Don't you dare get hurt on purpose. Elias is sick, and he's been through a lot. I love you all psycho and possessive. It makes me want to sometimes challenge you for power and really discover how to get you on your knees." She reaches between us and grabs my cock, rubbing the length of my shaft. "Do me dirty and take care of me after. That's what I like best from you."

I hum my contentment, flexing my boner in her fingers. "I accept your challenge. If you manage to dominate me and make me call out for your mercy, you can do as you please. I have a nice fucking strap-on for you that'll give you pleasure as you bang me, channeling your spirit dick into real life."

I chuckle, loving the fuck out of her expression. The idea excites her and we both know it. I've felt for myself how wet she gets watching me submit to Kase. She's really coming out of her sexual oppression stemming from her relationship with the bastard Joel. He really fucked with her, making her accept that pleasure wasn't intended for her.

Fuck that. Raven is the mother-fucking queen of my Kinky Kingdom.

"You know what?" she says, her smile widening. "It's on. If you want me to gear up and show you what it's like to be fucked by me, then I'm ready. I'm going to fuck you so hard that my light will make you see Heaven again. You're going to take my spirit dick like the sexy beast you are until it's you cumming across the damn walls."

Oh fucking shit.

That dirty mouth is ensuring an eternal boner.

"My pretty soul," I murmur, crashing my mouth to hers. "I am at your mercy already. Now let's get your damn soulmate, so we can give him one helluva show. Maybe one fucking final bang to bring him to our kingdom."

"Who knew I'd want that? Your kind of psycho has officially become my brand of pleasure. It really gives a new meaning of going out with a bang." She clutches onto me, speaking against my mouth as I dive down, zooming toward Earth.

"I love you for it. Even pathetic bastards like him deserve to have a hot, sexy, beautiful woman fuck him to death. You truly are an angel for agreeing to it." I slide my tongue into her mouth, letting her grind her body against mine through our clothes.

I land with a thud but refuse to stop until she's had enough of me. With the way she sucks my lips and practically unscrews my barbells with her tongue in her desperation, I'm nearly certain it'll never happen. I don't fucking care if she wants to kiss me like this for the rest of eternity. I'll adapt.

"Keep it up, and I'll act on our deal right now, angelgirl," Kase says, his hot presence warming Raven between us. "Spread those spankable ass cheeks open for me, Dante."

I chuckle and do as he says, clutching her ass and spreading her wide open. “Sounds like a plan.”

Raven gasps and yanks my hair, pulling herself away. “Try it and see what happens if you dare try to enter without lube.”

“Back pocket,” I say, closing the space to her lips again. “I’m always fucking prepared.”

Her peal of exasperated laughter vibrates across my lips, and she throws herself away from me, landing in Kase’s arms. I fall in love with her even more than I already am with the way she grins at Kase while wagging her finger at me. I never knew such a thing was possible. I knew from the moment I saw her soul that I was obsessed with her. But love? Devils shouldn’t love anything besides torture and punishing people—getting justice for a soul’s bad decisions in life—yet here I am, psychotically, deeply, unfathomably in love with the woman in my best friend’s arms.

And then the current boner killer of our night growls, killing Raven’s excitement, knowing how close we are to bringing back the Jizz Master into her life. At least with Elias’s poor aim, Raven’s hair won’t constantly fall in her face or get in the way—natural gel. Fucking hilarious. I plan to throw his cock off course to ensure he never lives his nickname down for all of eternity.

“They’re coming for us. Zade was right. He’s here.” Micah explodes into his devil form, his monstrosity of a body towering above us. “Protect Raven.”

"He did not just command us to do the fucking obvious," Kase mutters, tossing Raven in my direction.

She squeaks and heaves a breath near my ear, fear tensing her nerves. "Try not to—"

Micah launches at a man exiting the apartment building, smashing him under his massive hooved feet. She sucks in a breath at the sight of the man screaming as his legs and pelvis are crushed and his insides explode from the weight. And damn, he's still ali—

Micah stomps on the man's head, silencing his ear-piecing screams. "Those who defy the rulers of Hell will perish," he says, his threat ringing through the air as two more jackasses exit the building and aim their puny weapons at him.

"I'm going to be sick," Raven murmurs, gagging as her stomach heaves.

"Fly up and check the windows for wards. That'll be the one Elias is in," Kase says, whipping his tail at a man and dragging him toward him.

"God, please," Raven murmurs, using one of her hands to cover her ear as she presses her head to my shoulder, trying to block the noise. "This is fucking brutal."

"These assholes are our enemies, filthy-evil souls, and trying to block you from finding your soulmate. They deserve nothing short of ruthless punishment," I say, adjusting her in my arms to take flight.

"Still nasty as fuck," she mutters.

I don't disagree. I've never truly studied Micah unleash Hell on a mortal and damn. He really doesn't have an ounce of mercy left, slaughtering these bastards in painful ways to hear them suffer. Like sure, I'll cut a cock off and shove it down a rapist's throat and out his ass to repeat the process, but turning these flesh bags into gut pancakes one foot at a time? Eh, whatever. I don't actually give a shit but will play along with Raven so she doesn't think she has to suck it up.

I shift, blocking Raven's view. "Messy too. Good fucking thing it'll be Vincent's job cleaning their remains since the wannabe ruler of this plane was too chicken shit to come out and fight himself."

She gags again. "Ugh, hurry. It smells worse than Hell."

I chuckle, watching an asshole flail his burning arms like an idiot, setting himself aglow with Kase's power. "It's because they're burning before heading to the—"

Raven slaps her hand over my mouth. "Hurry up and fly Dante. I know you're hesitating, so that you can fight at least one contracted soul. Stop it with your envy over this shitshow because Kase and Micah are having fun. We'll have our own fun. But you have to get Elias first."

She knows me so well.

With a sigh, I expand my wings and launch us into the air, soaring straight up to the top of the five-story apartment building. Most of the blinds are closed, disallowing us a view inside, so I have to rely on my Hell-senses.

"I need you to hold on as tightly as you can. We're going to freefall along the building to test them for warding. It's the fastest way." I reposition her arms to encircle my neck and get her to lock her ankles across my lower back. "I need both my hands."

She swallows her nerves, her body trembling as she squeezes me in a death grip. "Ah, hell. I hate these kinds of rides."

I laugh. I can't help it. She just equated me to a fucking ride at a theme park. "Should I count down?"

She gasps. "I don't—"

I close my wings, the sudden drop stealing away her ability to even scream. My fingers graze the first five windows down, and I swoop my wings out and propel us back to the top. None of the corner apartments have been touched by Hell.

"Fuck," she says, gulping a breath. "Fuck."

I think the motion has stolen her ability to articulate anything. A smile crosses my face in amusement. I might enjoy her reaction a bit too much, because she sounds the same as she does during a good fucking.

Without waiting for her to get her mind to function, I drop down again, closing my eyes to sense for warding and Hell power. Even if it's not used on a window, I'll still be able to feel it from a short distance.

Nothing triggers my devil nature.

I catapult back to the top. "Three more rows on this side."

Raven only groans and pierces my neck with her nails, leaving what I'm sure will be a hot mark along with scratches. If only they were from her getting banged by me.

I fly from the ground level and back to the top. Raven swears in my ear, bracing for the drop again, but one touch of my hand on the top floor window makes me hesitate. The hot sensation of Hell power rises from somewhere beneath us—the apartment a level below.

"Found it," I say, spreading my wings to float a few feet down to the next window. "It's this one. Get ready."

Raven twists her torso, glancing at the window with a small etching of Lucian's mark in the corner. I hiss and flick my tongue, extending my fangs. I nudge Raven out of the way a bit more until she clings to my side. I don't want to accidentally get the heat of my venom mixed with Hell power on her—the combination capable of eating all organic materials.

Swinging my fist, I shatter the window with one punch and use my arm to clear away the glass. I ignore the few cuts from the shards managing to pierce through my sleeve. Raven reaches out and snags the blinds for me, ripping them from the window frame. A man hollers from the other side, preparing to shoot at us. But I'm too quick.

I hiss and spit my venom into his face, turning his angry holler into pure, torturous screams. He flails away, clutching his face, but there is nothing he can do as my power devours him. His body thuds to the carpet, the scent putrid enough to make even me hold my breath. I carefully help Raven inside and climb in myself, listening for any other threats, but the place is quiet.

"Let me lead the way, Raven," I say, grabbing her by the wrist before she makes a run for the hallway.

She sighs and nods. I know she just wants to hurry and get to her soulmate. I can see her annoyance that I slow down even more before we get to the first bedroom. I can't help it. This apartment may have been warded to imprison Elias, but he's no longer here. I know it deep in the darkness of my power. No living soul inhabits the place—which means one of two things. He's either been relocated again or we're too late.

I clear my throat, trying to think of the best way to handle Raven. This could destroy her on a level I can't fix.

"Dante, come on. I bet he's in the master bedroom," Raven says, allowing her voice to echo through the room. "Elias?" she calls. "You here?"

Silence greets her, and she tips her head to look at me. I'm too slow to control my expression, and she realizes something is wrong.

"Raven, I don't sense him," I finally mutter. "I—"

Using her Hell strength, she breaks away from me and bolts toward the end of the hall. Thrusting the door open, she smacks it against the wall and freezes. A strangled cry escapes from her throat. She stumbles into the hallway and hits her back on the hallway wall.

"Dante," she says, clutching her chest. "Dante, is it him? Is it fucking him?"

I stride forward and past her, entering the filthy bedroom. Most of the furniture has been trashed, and garbage litters the floor like whoever was guarding the place ate in here. Slept in here, too. Showered in the bathroom? Nope. That's where the body of a man lies, his hoodie yanked up, hiding his head. I haven't memorized Elias's body like I have Raven's, so I can't tell if it's him from here. The build is similar, but long sleeves prevent me from seeing any recognizable tattoos.

"Dante, is it?" Raven asks again from behind me.

I steel myself for whatever the outcome may be. This could be it. This could be the moment that destroys an eternity of hard work and a future of paradise alongside the most spectacular soul in existence.

Grabbing the back of the dead man's hoodie, I lift him up and arch his back to look at his face.

Guts spill out from a long cut from his waist band to his ribs. Raven gasps and whimpers, her shock over the monstrosity left behind by Vincent, his mark clearly branded on the guy's forehead, stopping Raven from grasping anything apart from how disgusting this is.

I drop the guy and kick him, rolling him to his back. "It's not Elias."

She blows out a breath in relief, a cross between a cry and laugh escaping her mouth. "Thank-fucking-Hell. I was so scared." Strutting into the room, she closes the space between us and covers her mouth and nose, peering down at the body. "But where is he? How did they know we were coming?"

I comb my fingers through my hair and shift on my feet, getting a better look around.

There was definitely a fight with the scorch marks across the carpet and broken furniture. "I'm not so sure anyone knew. This guy didn't get slaughtered because they were hustling to relocate. He was gutted. There must have been an invasion."

She purses her lips. "Another demon?"

I shrug. "I think human."

Raven tugs at the ends of her hair and swivels around, searching the room.

She shuffles a few feet forward and touches one of the scorch marks on the floor, pinching the remnants of ash between her fingers.

"Hunters," she says, tilting her head to gaze at me. Her stare whips to something on the floor behind me. "They came for him. Look."

Following her point, I spot the bloody dagger of a knife and pick it up only to scorch my fingers. I chuck the damn thing at the wall, sinking the blade into the plaster. My fingers sting, the sensation of heavenly power from touching a blessed knife annoying as fuck.

Swinging my fist, I punch the wall. "Fucking bastards!"

"I'm going to kill them all," Raven says, baring her teeth in anger. "I swear to fucking God, the saviors, the universe, and every damned soul in existence. These bastards will suffer for this."

Damn, she sounds so hot. My psychotic pretty soul.

"Fuck yeah, they will. At least we have an idea where to find them." I stride toward her and snatch her off her feet and into my arms. Going to the window, I smash through it and launch into the air to fly to Kase and Micah.

The two of them tag-team, ripping an asshole in half before kicking him into a portal, finishing off the contracted souls.

"He's not here," I say. "He was taken by hunters."

Micah's eyes flash orange. "Hunters?"

"Fuck." Kase summons red power between his palms, thrusting it at Vincent's apartment building and home to his shitty, useless minions. It sparks across the siding and sets it on fire.

Micah follows his lead and thrusts a wave of Hell power at the building, adding to the destructions. "Let this be a message to Vincent and anyone who stands against us."

"They will pay, and so will the hunters. I'm out of mercy," Raven says, clenching her fingers. "I'm done."

Me-fucking-too. I've had enough of these high and

mighty hunters trying to mess with our plans. I've had it with lowly demons thinking they can create their own hellish kingdoms.

I will prove as much.

Their fucking world will burn.

13

CASSIUS

REPENTANCE

DEAR ALL THINGS holy and good in the world, please have them show. Its divine grace blessed me with this task, and if Lucifer doesn't show with Elias, I will have failed. The Mortal Realm and all of Heaven rely on me. It is my sole purpose in life to ensure my brother's unfathomable plans don't come to fruition. My deal with a demon cannot be in vain. It can't. I feel it deep in my being that this is the right path to take.

I never expected my fallen brethren to ask me to show him mercy by saving the mortal soul that ruined his grace. That moment he told me what was deep in the dark abyss of his tainted soul, I knew exactly what to do. It was the sign I needed after facing the hurdles the devils put forth. And now, things will be right with the universe and return to as they should.

I mean, as long as my forsaken brother shows. It wouldn't be the first time he's disappointed me. From the moment I saw him start to drift from the light of the Higher Power to watching him slice his own wings off his back to plunge from Heaven, taking his light with him, I knew that our bond was lost. He blames me for not sticking by his side. I don't have it in my essence to return the same blame, but I will not stand by and watch him try to destroy everything our creator has done. I won't.

It is my duty and obligation to see to it that these shifts in power don't occur. I'll do anything to keep Hell where it should be—beneath Heaven and the Higher Power—which is why mortals were engrained with the idea to look down at the dark masses jeopardizing the foundation of power souls bring to our existence. Hell will be and should be always beneath the greater good. I will do whatever it takes, even if it means making deals with my brother. Heaven must remain above all. It is where it belongs.

A rumbling engine drags my attention away from the

desolate road in front of me, and I spin to catch sight of a sleek, black vehicle squealing as it turns sharply onto the street. I'd recognize Lucifer's darkness anywhere as it radiates around him like ever-present smoke billowing from the depths of his evil.

The fucking abomination, twisted fool of a monstrous bastard, piece of shit, staining everything he ever encounters with his inky, vile, existence. Just watching his eyes glow with Hell power and the cocky grin cutting his sharp features ignites a wave of vengeance through my heart. If I could jab my flaming sword through his hideous, blasphemous fake human façade and cut his horns free, I would use them to gouge his eyes out so he can never see the exceptional beauty and life the Higher Power has gifted to us in this universe.

Damn. The profanity whirling through my mind is nothing short of glorious perfection. It was Lucifer whose mere existence as a devil that has given me such a gift that I protect within my being. There is no need to speak the words out loud. They are far more powerful to contain within the light of power I'll use to avenge my lost brethren for what Lucian has used Raven to accomplish.

"Hey bitch-face, pay attention or I'll stomp the throttle." Lucifer hangs his head out the window of his vehicle and revs the engine. "You're lucky as Hell that I need you to be able to fly this little shit out of here or you'd see the underside of this Porsche. It's a fun fucking drive."

I turn my gaze toward the inch of space between my legs and the bumper. Unsheathing my sword, I set it aflame with heavenly fire and drag it across the hood. Lucifer flings the door open and transforms into his disgusting Hell form, trying to intimidate me as if he is ever truly a threat. He's already tried to push his power at me once before at the mortal establishment I managed to grab his attention at during his obnoxious use of thinning the veil between planes—something he should've lost with his disgraced jump. He knows that to be a true match to me, he must bind himself to the pits of Hell. All he can merely do is prove how far he's fallen.

I am and will always be above him. My wings and grace prove it.

I raise my palm, gathering heavenly light to stop him in his tracks. "Now, Lucifer. Is that really necessary? It is merely a material object with no true value in the grand picture."

He flares his nostrils and chucks a stream of Hell power at me, which I easily deflect with my light. "Always the righteous, mightier than thou fucker, I see." At least he knows his place.

The fact that he agreed to give me Elias for the sole purpose of keeping Raven out of the hands of the other rulers of Hell also proves it. He made it rather easy by being caught up in his need to run Hell in its entirety and withhold power from the other devils and Raven. His inability to see beyond himself has finally benefited me. His pride has gotten so much in the way that he's willing to void Raven's contract to ensure if he can't have her at his mercy, then no one can.

Love truly can change the universe. It's Elias's need to protect Raven from Lucian that made this possible. His sacrifice will be everything Heaven needs.

"Brother, cool your fires. I don't want to be here with you as much as you don't want to be here with me. Now please, let's call a momentary truce and get things settled. I'm sure you'd like to get back to your...hellish life." I tighten my jaw, offering a smirk. I wave to Elias in the front seat. "Come now, Elias. I'm sure you would like to enjoy the rest of your mortal life in peace."

Elias quietly slides from the passenger's seat and strolls closer. "I need to see him hold up his end of the bargain before we go."

Sighing, I stretch my wings and use them to propel me to Lucifer. Fire burns his dark eyes, his features frustratingly similar to my own. Why were we created this way? It will always be a mystery. It's been so long since he was my companion and not my counterpart. I can't remember what it was like sharing such a bond. Well, except for the ease I have doing what is necessary for the greater good. Things many of my brethren cannot fathom.

I suppose because even fallen and disgraced, a part of him will always stain my existence. His mark is my mark, though I use my light to disguise it. I used to not always, but some mortals have tainted the true meaning of my mark, associating it with Lucifer over me, the protector against evil.

The fucking bastard. His closeness in this moment prods at my core. I can't silence my whirling thoughts, speaking the words my tongue wouldn't dare say aloud.

Lucifer shoves his door open and growls, summoning a Hell contract from a plane I would never dare enter. He holds it out to Elias but doesn't release it right away. "Remember the stipulation. You must die unbound and not by Raven's hands. Once that happens, her contract will void and this fuckhead can take her soul."

Elias yanks the contract away from Lucifer and unrolls it, looking it over in silence. I fidget, waiting for him to finish reading everything unlike most mortals. Lucian's eyes bore into the side of my head as he watches me gaze at Elias. It takes everything in me not to give Lucifer the attention he wants.

"As you can see, upon your death, you will be given a portion of my kingdom. You will help overlook my affairs and control my armies." Lucifer reaches out and jabs at the contract.

"If I'm Hell-bound," Elias says, finally finishing. He rolls up the contract and hands it to me. "Right, Cassius?"

"Oh, you will be," Lucifer says, not giving me the chance to respond. "Just remember where you belong when you descend and remain loyal to me and you won't have a problem with the other devils. I will keep them in control and on their paths."

My jaw twitches, and I refrain from smiling. Because one of the things I'm certain about is that the other devils will rise and challenge Lucifer. They will stand together and shove him back where he belongs. It's what I'm counting on. It's one thing for Kase and Dante to remain on this plane. But my wayward brother? He's done far too much damage already. I'd hate to think what he plans to do once I take Raven's soul to the one place no devil is welcome and the place her light will forever be protected. Once she's torn from the darkness and into the light, she will finally see that her true purpose is not intended to help Hell rise but insure it remains beneath us.

I rest my hand on Elias's shoulder. "Your sacrifice will be worth it to keep your soulmate out of the devils' clutches. She might be content now, but the devils will grow bored of her. When that happens...it's best we do not find out."

They would most likely suck the light from her until Raven's soul is nothing but an overused casing of a wasted gift. If that happens, her eternal suffering will surely far exceed any entity in this universe.

"Yeah, yeah. You know my feelings about all this, Cassius. Don't forget this deal was born from my desperation. Had I not have been railed in my metaphorical ass by this douchebag, I'd be soaking my cock in the magical warmth of Raven's pussy as she creates paradise for me and my devil comrades, something you and your dry, limp, embarrassingly useless dick will never truly be able to grasp or appreciate." Elias glowers at me and swats my hand away from his shoulder.

I purse my lips and ruffle my feathers. I hadn't thought much about his feelings apart from his desire to keep Raven from finding her soul a slave to my brother. He might be right about my naivety over mortal activities, but I couldn't care less. I find great pleasure in the good work I do for the divine. I don't need to "soak my dick" in anything but the mighty light of Heaven. That is paradise.

I scrunch my nose at my thoughts. Perhaps my faith and purpose are a bit strong, and I see the accidental innuendo—but no matter. I stand by my convictions that fighting and protecting the sacred is all I'll ever need.

"What is the phrase...different strokes for different folks, Elias?" I square my shoulders and flick my attention to Lucifer. I can see his judgement blooming across his hard expression. He thinks I might act high and mighty or perhaps am hypocritical, but how could I be when I speak from the truth of my essence? I am above him. He will never rise as high as I can fly without falling and crashing to the ground. But me? I can soar.

"You are one fucking contradictive asshat," Elias mutters under his breath.

I remain expressionless. "Some things are just impossible for a mortal to understand. Perhaps if you never let things come to—"

Lucifer throws a burst of hellfire at my feet, startling me. I grab Elias and drag him with me the few feet I fly.

"Just get the fuck out of here before someone tracks me down. Raven is on the verge of letting me fuck her hard enough to rearrange her insides if I help her 'find' this asshole, which doesn't fucking matter to me because failing results in the same damn outcome. Raven's contract will be void." Lucifer strides forward and jabs me in the chest. "Don't let the bastards get word of this, got it?" Turning to Elias, he adds, "See you in Hell, fuckhead."

Lucifer once again tosses hellfire at us, forcing me to carry Elias out of the road. My forsaken brother squeals his tires and leaves us in a cloud of burned rubber as he zooms away. Releasing a breath, I shake off the presence of his lingering darkness and summon heavenly light between my fingers to help push it away. Elias studies me in silence, his pallor washed out with his sickness.

I reach out and press my palms to his cheeks, bathing him in my light, hoping to ease his aching body the best I can. A mortal in his condition in this state of his cancer usually would struggle to stand, but he somehow keeps his strength, fighting everything against him, even his own body. I'd call it miraculous, but it's not. Some things just happen like this without an explanation from the Higher Power.

For all I know, Elias could live for another month...or he

could die tonight. Even angels of high esteem like myself aren't privy to all of the universe's answers. All we can do is keep going to see where the Higher Power sets things in motion. And Elias's path in his existence is winding, rough, offbeaten, and completely unfollowable to most.

Except Raven.

She might now be guiding his way and helping him through the obstacles, but it's not her job. It should've never been her purpose. Her soul should've moved on and found peace nearly two centuries ago.

"All right, man. Are you fucking crying? You're starting to freak me out. Why are you staring at me like that? I've had enough of your angelic molestation. I didn't ask you to help me. Your light doesn't energize me." Elias flicks my shoulder and steps back even more, putting space between us. "It's just creepy."

I blink my watery eyes and pull myself together. I know he has few memories of his eternity before he fell for Grace, but deep in his mortal soul lies the angelic brethren who fought so fiercely in honor of the Higher Power. I can bring that back if I can just give his soul a little extra push...

Lucifer has stolen too many of my companions already.

It's in this moment I realize that I will do whatever it takes to ensure Elias returns to Heaven instead of falling into Hell. I know it is what the Higher Power would want.

"Pardon me, Eli. I'm merely helping you. With enough of

my light, we can destroy Hell's darkness around you completely. Your eternity is not lost yet. I'd like you to see as I do and have faith that you and Raven will be together for eternity in the light of Heaven. Hell will never touch either of you again." I expand my brilliant white wings, setting the dark world around us aglow. "What do you think? You've repented enough. I wouldn't have these thoughts if it wasn't possible."

Elias's frown softens. "What? I'm not sure I understand."

A wave of soothing warmth washes over me, and for a moment, I glimpse the divine world of my beloved home. I knew I was right. This is the sign I need to push harder at Hell's darkness. Lucifer thinks Elias will fall to Hell but it seems he's been granted a miracle for putting Raven before himself and choosing rightly, his actions swaying him toward Heaven.

I smile and close the space again, clutching his cheeks. "Elias, my friend, this sacrifice you've made has blessed you. The darkness fades. If you accept my light, the universe will fall back in order."

Opening my arms, I surprise him with a hug and kiss the top of his head, a rush of relief leaving my whole body zinging. I knew my hard work for the Higher Power would benefit us all. I knew I could do this far better than anyone else. Micah might have been given the task, and then Andre. Zade was too hesitant to carry such a burden, so the job of keeping the devils at bay fell in my capable hands, where it should've been all along.

"Feel the power of Heaven. Let it wash you free of your mistakes and sins," I murmur, smiling wider at the confusion, surprise, and then finally acceptance crossing Elias's expression. "We've done well. You're rather lucky that the Higher Power led me to you."

Elias grimaces. "Dude, what the fuck? Are you having a breakdown? You're glowing so brightly I think I'm getting a sunburn. Chill."

"Embrace the glory of a new day," I say, stretching my arms toward the sky. "You and your soulmate will have the peace you want. Now, come on. It's time to take you somewhere safe to wait out the remainder of your mortal life. Just imagine how indescribable it will be when your soulmate joins you and you can return as one and be whole again."

Elias groans. "Fuck that shit. I only agreed to Lucian's deal to get the fuck out and return to Raven. Knock that shit off with your light. I'm going to Hell, and Raven's going with me."

The amazing feeling of touching home vanishes with his words. Ice crashes on my head, stealing the glory of the Higher Power away with one comment.

I tense and clench my fingers into fists. "You can't back out. We had a deal. You are to come with me to die in peace. I've already told you that you will join Raven in Heaven."

"Are you a dumbass or what?" Elias says, meeting my gaze

with a stare comparable to that of a devils. "You can't make a deal with a mortal. You said it yourself that it was Raven's choice, and I plan to keep it as such."

My chest heaves, my shock and anger leaving me unsheathing my flaming sword. "Don't make this mistake, Elias. We have an agreement. You and Raven are to ascend into the Higher Power's grace. Heaven depends on you."

Shaking his head, he smirks in amusement. "Why can't you get that I fucking played you, Cass? You were my last resort, but Lucian said it himself; Raven's soul is free regardless. If I die unbound—which I will. Or if he fails to help her find me—which he will, because I'm finding Raven first. I agreed to let her take me out with a bang, and I intend to keep my promise. I will take my throne so she can take hers. Now fucking leave, you crazy bastard. It's over."

Something strange runs hotly through me only to be pushed away at the sight of headlights coming down the road. And fucking-fuck. Fuck, fuck, fuck. Motherfucking Hell. Elias can't get away with this. I won't allow him to jeopardize everything. He will not play me like a fool.

Flapping my wings, I launch forward, preparing to fly away with him. He doesn't have a choice anymore because he's incapable of making the right one. Always has, and now obviously always will.

The glint of something glass sparkles in Elias's hand, but I'm moving too fast to avoid him. Swiping his hand across my wing, he drags a shard of mirrored glass deep into my flesh. I knock him onto his back, only to feel the force of his fist punch me in my supposedly blasted useless dick—and it hurts, surely as much as Hell does. I holler and stumble, the pain in my groin and the injury to my wing, forcing me to land.

A horn blares, the ear-splitting sound startling me. I don't have a chance to brace for the impact of a sedan as it plows into me and sends me crashing to the ground. The heavy weight of its tires crushes both of my outspread wings, and I howl in agony.

"Elias! You can't run! You belong to Heaven. You were created there and will come home whether I have to drag you there or send your soul myself." I push up and watch Elias drag a frightened woman from her vehicle. She screams and hits the window, but there is nothing she—or I—can do for that matter.

Fucking Hell.

Fucking treacherous greedy bastard, putting himself before everyone.

He and all the devils are going to pay. I'm through trying to nudge people onto their rightful paths. Heaven needs me as their powerful leader.

This is war.

14

RAVEN

GREED

"IT'S BEEN SIX days now. How important is your soul to you, Raven? Come on, look at me. I got you a present." Lucian hovers in the doorway to the bathroom. "It sparkles as much as the diamond on your ring, but this one is special. Just take one look. If you don't like it...the fuck you won't. Don't make me have to go over there and put it in your hand."

I keep my eyes trained on the window, watching the dark

sky fade to indigo with the oncoming sunrise. I've stayed up all night, watching and waiting for either Kase, Dante, or Micah to return or for Andre to arrive. I'd gladly spend my day sleeping in the grass beside him to avoid Lucian from wearing me down. I promised myself one week to get things in order and only because Zade told me that he believed Elias would be okay since he's not with a demon.

He doesn't know exactly where he was taken by demon hunters, but if he thinks Elias is safe enough for me to wait a bit longer for my devils to search every damn inch of this town, then I'll allow it.

Lucian whistles, trying to get my attention. "Ray, you have five seconds."

I stretch out my arm. "Just fucking hand it to me and leave me alone. Can't you see I'm..." This pervy bastard.

Lucian slaps my palm with his heavy boner, grinning as I whip my attention away from the window and toward him. I'm too shocked by his gesture that I don't move, gazing at his dick piercing with what looks like a glowing red stone on the ring, glittering with the thumps against my hand. I don't know what comes over me, but instead of whacking him in his freshly shaved balls, I lock my fingers around his shaft and tug him closer, getting a better look.

"Are you ready to give it a try? The ring will set your body and soul on one helluva ride. It contains my power, so you can really feel it deep inside you." Lucian arches his back a bit, forcing me to lean away before he pokes me in the face.

"Uh...thanks, but no. I don't need any part of you inside me yet." I release him and nudge him away with my knuckles.

"Yet. Why wait? It's pointless. I could find Elias in twenty minutes if you'd give in and allow it. You know how good I'll make you feel." He shifts to get into my line of sight, taking a minute to stroke himself.

And damn my eyes. I can't get myself to look away. The faster he does it, the more intense the bead on the ring glows. Shit. Is it vibrating? I think it is. Hell power operated.

I squirm and squeeze my legs together, annoyingly getting turned on. "Enough, Satan. I get it. Your piercing will probably give me a soul-gasm. The answer is still not yet. If I want to experience a blinged out, Hell power-infused dick, I will ask Kase to swap his jewelry, though it's unnecessary for him. He doesn't have to compensate for anything."

Lucian growls and ignores me, totally turned on and enjoying the fact that I can't seem to avert my eyes. "Say what you want. You can lie to yourself but you can't lie to me. You want me. Bad. I can see it in your face. I can smell it all over you. You're wet. Excited. I bet you're even fantasizing about what it would be like to deep throat me. How my cum tastes."

I groan and cover my face, forcing myself to stop looking. "That's all you."

"Prove it. Spread those trembling thighs for me and let me see your panties. If I'm wrong, I'll stop. But if I'm right, you'll let me aim at your face." Lucian moans, quickening the pace of his strokes, totally serious.

"No fucking way," I mutter, crossing my legs.

"Because you know I'm right," he murmurs, really going to fucking town. I've seen Dante masturbate but it's nothing like this. Lucian looks like he's going to yank his damn cock off in his race to cum.

"Because it's a shitty deal. I get nothing out of spreading my legs for..." This fucker. He totally threw me right into this innuendo.

"What the fuck are you talking about? You get everything. My power fucked into you. Orgasms. Look at my girth. Imagine how you'll stretch that tight pussy to welcome me. I'll bend you over the bed, so you can get a good feel of my gift to you. It'll work your g-spot until you can't think of anything but me." Lucian hums and closes his eyes, his fantasy totally helping him get off. "And then when I cum inside you...we'll both feel it in our beings. You'll want me again and again. You'll love it so much that you'll even beg me to fuck you in your ass. Maybe then I'll let you get on top of me while you scream in ecstasy. You can hold my horns and bounce that big ass up and down. I'll finger you while you do, play with your clit..."

Oh, shit.

I nearly lose myself in his dirty-ass fantasy of thinking I'm going to ride him cowgirl style with his cock in my ass. My body tingles, loving the idea against my mind's pleas to protect my poor ass from a devil who probably thinks he can treat every hole on my body the same. It's enough to get me to clench my ass cheeks.

Lucian moans again, getting awfully close. I don't like where he's blindly aiming, especially with his panting and heavy groans. "Raven, it's going to feel so fucking fantastic. You will fuck your soul free of the contract but you'll never want to leave me. Every second of every day you'll whimper and beg for me. You'll feel—"

I gasp as his eyes snap open and his whole body ripples, flashing his Hell form. I scramble out of the way, bracing for him to try to cum on me, but he swivels his hips and moans so incredibly loud, his deep voice far sexier than I want it to be, and explodes with his orgasm all across the bed. He blows out a long breath and captures me with his gaze, watching me watch him. That was one helluva finish, and something dark inside me is annoyed that I didn't join him in the fun. It's like he knew exactly how to mess with me. I could've told him to stop. I could've left him. Instead, my ass wanted to stay for the whole show. Now he's going to be cockier than ever.

My stupid curiosity might lead me right onto his cock just to discover what it's like to fuck the most notorious, evil devil.

"You dirty girl. You loved that, didn't you?" Lucian whispers, grazing his hand over my cheek to tuck my hair behind my ear. "You're only resisting me because you're a stubborn brat. Isn't that right?"

"Yes." What the actual fuck? My mouth did not just say that damn word before my brain had time to process.

He obviously didn't expect it either because fire lights his eyes and a smile turns his hard features soft and handsome. He loved my response and looks ready to push me harder. And I'm on the verge of breaking. His dark allure is hypnotizing me. His asshole attitude is turning endearing. As for his dirty talk? I'm now horny as fuck and suffering a serious case of blue bean.

"Raven," Lucian whispers, bowing to get on my level. "Say yes to me. Say yes and let's learn how to move forward together. I can show you the true extent of my power and how you'll want and crave me—to obey me and let me take care of you forever. You can be my beautiful, insatiable woman without having to worry about anything but our pleasure and power. Just imagine—"

The glow of hellfire lights the dim room around us, and the scent of a portal opening snaps me from considering his idea of my possible future with him. And thank fucking Hell. I don't know if it's because I'm horny, lonely without the rest of my devils, or just becoming desperate, but I nearly do say yes to him. It even hurts me a little that I don't.

"I'm sorry. No. Andre's here, and I won't keep him waiting. It's been days." I pull my wild thoughts together and stand up, tipping my head back to look into Lucian's dark eyes. "If you really want me to consider any of those things, you have to accept that my soul isn't intended for only one devil. You have to accept that it's going to take more than getting hot and bothered for me to do anything you want."

"Raven, I—"

I shake my head. "I'm giving my devils a bit more time to find Elias. You know, if you would help them, I might reconsider everything."

Lucian doesn't speak. He doesn't do anything except watch me leave. And for once, he just lets me go.

I've never been so thankful for the stench of Hell as I open the backdoor and spot Andre in the center of the summoning circle.

His face doesn't light with a smile though. My heart sinks into my stomach. Something's wrong.

"Little hellion, I know you don't like going to Hell, but I need you trust me and let me take you there." Andre extends his hand to me. "It's important."

I inhale a sharp breath. "What is it, Andre?"

"I can't speak here. Please, come to me." Andre waves his hand again, keeping his voice low.

Fuck. I shuffle across the flaming barrier and into Andre's arms.

He lifts me up. "Hold on, Raven. It's going to be an uncomfortable ride."

"Oh, my God! Elias!" I throw myself from Andre's arms and abandon the summoning circle.

I kept my eyes closed through the journey through Hell in Andre's arms, thinking the absolute worst. The fact that Andre wouldn't say anything only made it worse. I expected him to take me to Lucian's kingdom or some shit because Elias died. I never expected Andre of all devils to reunite me with my mate.

"I don't understand. Why didn't you tell me where we were going, Andre? And Elias, how the fuck? How long have you been here? Why didn't you call me?" My questions tumble through the air as I speak to the both of them. I grab the front of Elias's shirt and shake him. "God, damn it. I've been freaked out, so fucking kiss me first."

Elias groans against my lips, kissing me as if it could possibly be our last time. He lifts me off my feet and sets me on the rickety table of his old house, now completely trashed with strange graffiti spray painted on the walls. I'm so horny from Lucian's attempt to seduce me, and I pull his hips between my legs, locking him in place. Tangling his fingers into my hair, he deepens our kiss, sliding his tongue into my mouth.

Andre moans from behind me, the soft raspy sound as sexy as Elias's desperation to devour my affection. I don't even remember the questions on my mind or what the fuck is happening anymore. All that matters is Elias is here with me, alive, and so fucking hard that all I can think about is getting what I want.

"I missed you," I murmur, continuing to kiss him. "Andre, how can I ever thank you for bringing me here."

"Just don't stop. Your emotions...I can taste them. I'm famished." Andre's words light me up, burning me from the inside out with explosive passion. I realize why my need to be with Elias is so strong. It's Andre. His scent alone sets us off like an aphrodisiac.

I gasp, breaking away from Elias's mouth. He only shifts to kiss my jaw and lick down my throat, sucking the base of my neck.

"Elias, carry me to the summoning circle. I can't leave Andre out," I say, combing my fingers through Elias's hair.

Andre flaps his wings, his eyes lit with his desire. "Don't come into the circle. Just next to me. That's good enough. I just want to watch."

I furrow my brows, but Andre's soft smile of encouragement stops me from asking him why or arguing. If he didn't have a reason not to, I know we'd all get swept away on this river of lust.

"She's so sexy, isn't she Andre?" Elias asks, sensing the same thing I do. But I'm certain he won't question it. I can see and feel his excitement over getting me to himself in the presence of a devil, something I'm sure Kase, Dante, and Micah wouldn't allow.

"So stunning. Undress her for me, so I can see all of her." Andre stands within the hellfire, his muscles flexing and his eyes drinking in every inch of me sitting on the table. "You too. I want to feel and taste her desire for you, Elias."

A smile crosses Elias's face and he chuckles. "Whatever you want, man. You brought my soulmate to me. If Raven is cool, I'm fucking perfect."

I stretch my arms over my head, biting my lip. "This will be our thanks."

"And mean so much more than you know." Andre watches me with such a fiery intensity that heat crawls up my body to set me ablaze.

Elias grabs the hem of my shirt and pulls it over my head, exposing my boobs and the fact that I wasn't wearing a bra. Andre's lustful gasp mirrors Elias's, and I squirm and slide from the table, nudging Elias to walk back until we're only a foot away from Andre.

His nostrils flare and he licks his lips. "Describe how she feels. Help me imagine."

Elias brushes my hair over my shoulder and cups my boob, stroking his thumb over my hard nipple, making me moan. "Tight. Hard. Her tits are soft until you strum her right here." He rubs my nipple again. "Then they're like perfect, smooth pebbles." Bowing forward, Elias sucks my boob into his mouth. "She tastes subtly sweet too."

I grab Elias's shirt and yank it over his head, wanting to

touch him back and feel the heat of his body. Andre groans and rubs himself through his pants, never taking his eyes off the two of us.

"Get on your knees for her. She wants you to taste every inch of her delectable body," Andre says, lowering himself to the ground at the same time Elias does, following Andre's command without hesitation. "I want to see her so badly."

"Me fucking too. She's so hot. Just look at her hands trembling in anticipation." Elias links his fingers through one of my hands and manages to tug my pants down with the other. "Blue lace," he murmurs, snapping the string of my panties on my hip. "My favorite color. Why don't you turn around and let Andre see?"

I nearly say, yes sir, but instead sway my hips as I turn and arch my lower back to pop my butt out more. Elias slaps my ass with both of his hands and massages my body, spreading my butt cheeks open and closed with his gesture as I bend down, feeling Andre's scorching attention.

"Kissable, lickable, bitable, fuckable," Elias murmurs, hooking his fingers to my panties and pulling them down. He nips my ass cheek with his teeth, proving as much.

I gasp, my knees weakening.

"She loved that," Andre comments, a moan vibrating through the air. "I want a taste of her."

Oh, my fucking devils. Elias grins at my expression, and I pant as he stretches my leg to rest my knee on his shoulder. He trails his fingers up my thigh and slides two into me, fingering me slowly and sensually, managing to rub my G-spot enough to make my whole body quiver. Extending his arm past the hellfire barrier, Elias offers his hand to Andre. The sight of Andre sucking Elias's fingers into his mouth, tasting my excitement should weird me out. But damn. He looks so sexy doing it. Elias has made his boundaries clear before, and I had assumed this could be one of them, but it's as if he now fully embraces that life with me will always include others and he wants to be a part of our eternity and will be a team player. He does it because I like it.

Maybe he'd be different with Micah and the faint memory of their companionship as angels, but right now, none of that matters. I want everyone to get something out of this that they enjoy and to ensure they're content and taken care of how they need. Right now, Andre's starving for our lust. And Elias? He's in desperate need of my affection and intimacy as much as I need his. I thought I lost him, and even thinking about going another minute without bonding the way we desire in this lifetime feels torturous.

"She tastes like paradise," Andre mumbles, his eyes half-closed and heavy with our lust.

Elias teases me by gliding his tongue across his bottom lip. "It's better than anything. I plan to bury my face right between her thighs and survive on her body."

I grin and play with his hair, knowing he says the words

just for Andre. "Would you like to see him try, Andre?"

Using two fingers, Elias spreads my body wider, exposing my clit. He gently blows a cool breath, the sensation making me suck in a breath. "See how she squirms?" Elias bends forward and licks my clit before sucking me into his mouth and rolling his tongue.

I clutch onto him, my whole body shaking. I stretch out my arm and reach for Andre, silently begging him to help support me. My body hums with pleasure. Tingles burst through me, and if Andre wasn't supporting me, my weak knees would give out.

Like Elias senses it, he adjusts his legs and pulls me down with him, lying on his back with me sitting on his face. Andre watches with his alluring intensity, breathing deeply and stroking himself through his pants as he enjoys our show.

"She's going to orgasm. I can sense it," Andre says, the fire surrounding the summoning circle glowing brighter, more powerful.

Elias dips his finger into me as he kisses, licks, and sucks my clit until every nerve-ending in my body explodes at once, sending me bowing forward to plant my palms on the floor. The room bursts with Hell power, and Andre shifts into his true body for a few seconds before turning back. Elias smiles, easing my legs open to escape the cage my body traps him in.

"You like that, Lust King? You want more?" Elias asks, not missing a beat. "I bet you'd love watching our woman get plowed by me from behind. I'll give you the perfect view. Just wait."

I giggle and crawl forward, staying on my hands and knees. I shake my ass, teasing the two of them. Peeking over my shoulder, I meet Andre's glowing eyes devouring the sight of me. Elias drags over some couch cushions, surprising me, and I wait in anticipation, watching him kick out of his pants and stroke his hard-on. He gets me to rest my knees on one of the cushions, lifting my body up a bit. I shift in anticipation, following his silent instructions as he gets me to face away from him and Andre completely. It's now that I see the cracked mirror leaning against the wall.

"Get low for the best view," Elias says, returning to kneel behind me. He massages his fingers into my ass cheeks again, giving Andre a tease of every inch of my body.

"Look at her pucker. Kase and Dante love to tease about anal. Is that what you're thinking about, little hellion? Should he tease you with his finger?" Andre settles onto the ground, lying on his back. It's now that I see he's released his colossal cock from his pants and uses both hands to rub it, one of his own big hands unable to close completely around it.

"I'll do whatever the hell you want, darlin'," Elias says, fingering me again, wetting his finger until its slick. "You're extra wet. I love it. I'm at your mercy with your perfect pussy and tight ass."

Well, why the hell not? "Give Andre the show he wants,"

I say, biting my bottom lip. "But only a finger."

Elias fingers me again, stroking himself at the same time until I can barely take it. Andre watches our every move, his face so serious, his bottom lip puffing with his deep breaths. The two of them love every second of this—and I do too—especially when Elias aligns our bodies, slipping his thumb into my ass at the same time he rocks into me with one leg elevated on the stack of cushions. He wasn't joking about giving Andre one helluva view. I kind of wish I could watch through his eyes. The way Andre watches us, stroking himself, is so fucking hot. I want more.

Elias moans, locking one of his hands into my hair while resting the other on my shoulder. He fucks me hard and deep, wild and feral, more carnal than the other devils have. His hips bump against my ass with his quick thrusts that slap his balls against my clit like they know how much it wants their kind of spanking. I scream in pleasure, the short bursting sound echoing through the air. My whole body lights with electricity, the hot bolts zinging in all the right places. My emotions swell and steal my breath, my body and soul aligning with Elias's until it feels as if we merge as one.

"So incredible," Andre murmurs. "You two are exactly what I've been craving. Such unashamed attraction and need. Two souls shining so brightly and mingling as one. A cock fit for my queen and a man willing to do whatever it takes."

Elias groans, picking up his pace as he reaches under and

plays with my clit. The bliss building inside my body grows and grows until I can no longer contain the explosive sensation begging to burst free.

I scream in pure ecstasy, my muscles tensing and sending a shock wave through me. Andre grunts and cums, setting the summoning ring billowing toward the ceiling. My mind turns to mush as Elias keeps up his exhilarating, mind-numbing thrusts until he bumps his body a few times to mine as he cums.

"Delectable," Andre mutters, his voice husky and deep. "I'm so grateful and in love. You have given me everything I need to maintain power."

Elias slides out of me and pulls me into his arms, breathing deeply until both of our racing hearts slow. He strokes my arm with his fingers, not saying a word as we cuddle beside Andre, using the cushions as a bed. The summoning circle dims as we relax and my unending wave of lust tames.

Everything snaps into place as I suppress my desire and remember what happened. Andre's power and pheromones really got to my head, though I don't regret it. He only gave the little push I needed to do what I desperately wanted to with Elias.

"Fuck," I mumble, propping myself on my elbow. "This was so wild and so good, but now that you banged some sense into me...tell me everything. How are you here?"

Elias stretches his arms over his head with a groan, drawing my attention to his nipple piercing. I can't stop from gliding my finger over it, wanting to memorize him in this moment while saying a silent thanks to the universe that he's here and alive and real.

"Short version...I played fucking Lucian and Cassius. Darlin', when you feel like you're on your death bed and feel like a failure, you get desperate." Elias tightens his jaw and meets my gaze. "I almost don't want to tell you everything that went through my mind, thinking that I failed you. The last fucking place in the universe I ever want you to be is a goddamn slave to Lucian."

I frown, unsure of what he's getting at and why he feels the need to explain himself. "Just spit it out. You made a deal, didn't you? But Cassius? He's working with Lucian? What the actual fuck?"

"Take a breath, little hellion. It's not the kind of deal you think. They are not working together, and neither of them knows that Elias is here, and we must keep it that way. It's why I waited so long to bring you here. We couldn't allow Lucian to figure out that Elias isn't as selfish as he thought." Andre sits up and expands his wings. "Lucian and Cassius both yearn for a future where you don't succeed, no matter what happens to your soul."

I search his eyes and turn to Elias. "I still don't think I'm following. Lucian wants my soul. He's made it clear."

"At first he wanted it regardless. Now, he wants you to

give it to him and only him without you taking a throne. He's more concerned about rising above everyone and is willing to give you to Heaven to ensure it. Cassius encouraged it. That fucker tried to use me to manipulate Lucian and send our souls to Heaven. You're the most important woman and soul in the universe, Raven. You will change everything, and now, you can without the chains of Lucian binding you." Elias pulls me closer until I sit on his lap. "And unfortunately, my life and death helps determine whether you take your throne."

I blink a few times, studying my hands and staring at the ring Micah gave me. "So those bastards had tried to arrange things to send my soul to Heaven just to prevent me from completing our mission? And you went along with it to get away? How did you escape?"

"Cassius is so full of himself that he didn't think that I'd do anything for you—he has it in his head that Heaven is the only thing you could want and not the devils. I stabbed his wing, punched him in the nuts, and stole a car." His face lights up with his words. "And Lucian now thinks I'm being protected by the bastard to die in peace. When I die, your contract with him ends."

My eyes widen. "That fucker. We have an impending deal as well. If I fuck him, he'll help me find you or void my contract if he fails."

But why? Why would Lucian go through all this trouble with making deals to guarantee my contract ends? I don't understand.

"I don't know, darlin'," Elias says, sighing.

"We will figure it all out, but until then, Elias must be kept safe. Lucian will end his life for that reason." Andre rubs his chin. "And it seems Heaven wants to do the same thing, considering it looks as if Elias's soul might fall into grace. His binds to Hell are weak."

"Shit," I mutter. "He has to be Hell-bound and unclaimed by a devil for me to take. If he's not—"

A crash outside the house startles me, cutting my words off. Bright light shines through the window, and Elias rushes to grab my clothes.

Andre growls, the threatening noise reverberating through my bones.

The front door flings open, and I squint at the shining light.

"Zade?" I ask, seeing the familiar angel. "What the fuck?"

He stands silently, his flaming sword drawn. "You have to go. They're coming."

Andre roars.

15

RAVEN

HEAVEN'S ARMY

I SCRAMBLE TO my feet, stealing Elias's shirt to shrug on, which is faster than dressing in my own clothes. The hem reaches my thighs, covering my body. I beat Elias to Zade and extend my palm to Andre, now trying to do the impossible by crossing the barrier.

"Calm down, Andre. I'm not here as your enemy. I've come with a message that the guardians have sensed your portal. You must leave." Zade flexes his muscles and peers at the dark yard behind him. "They come with vengeance in their hearts and righteousness in their minds."

I tug at the ends of my hair. "Can't you do something? Tell them that you took care of the problem?"

Zade shakes his head, his frown deepening. "I'm sorry. There's nothing I can do."

"You mean there is nothing you will do," I snap, digging my nails into my palms. "Why do you even bother? Just go before they catch you here. It'll be me and only me that takes your fucking wings." Anger explodes through me. I don't mean to be a bitch, but after everything I've gone through, I'm not messing around anymore. I'm not going to deal with Zade at his own pace, because he will jump from grace for me. I'll not have him ruin my already shaky eternity because he's not brave enough to act.

Zade's eyes sparkle, glassing over with his hurt. "Raven, I'm—"

"Either stay and help or just go!" I yell, spinning on my feet, looking around for anything I can use to protect Elias. "I don't have time to deal with you."

And like that, Zade disappears, the door slamming shut with his exit.

"Fuck!" I yell, swinging my arms through the air. "I thought that Heaven would only ever send fucking righteous Cassius to try to get in our way. But this angelic army? Bullshit. How do we deal, Andre? You're stuck in a circle."

Andre half transforms, his features turning monstrous with his giant curved tail swinging over his back like he plans to impale someone or something. "We don't do anything. You're going to cross the barrier and let me take you to Hell."

I heave a couple breaths and nod. "Fuck. You're right." I jog the space to Elias, silently standing with only his jeans slung over his hips. "That's what we'll do." I take Elias's hand and tug him with me to enter the summoning circle.

Andre's tail penetrates the floor in front of me, blocking our way. "I said you, Raven. Elias can't come. He can't enter Hell like you can, and even if he could, I wouldn't allow it. It'll alert every fucking demon that he's here and they'll come. Lucian will come."

I sigh. "I'm not leaving without him."

Andre growls. "I can't protect you unless you do, Raven."

Stepping away even more, I clutch onto Elias and whip my hair back and forth with my rejection. "Then go get someone who can, Andre. I'm not leaving. Don't ask me again. Just hurry."

Andre roars in anger and transforms completely into his devil form. The hellfire of the summoning circle crackles and explodes, reaching the ceiling. It vanishes along with Andre, only some ashes and scorch marks remaining behind. I comb my fingers through my hair, fear tightening my chest. What if Andre doesn't get to the others in time? Elias and I are mortal.

We're powerless.

"Raven? Hey, focus. I need you to listen to me. You're faster and stronger than me, so I want you to barricade the window and door of the bedroom. We're too open out here." Elias tugs my hand, getting me to pull myself from my panic. He smacks my ass, getting me to rush toward the bedroom first. "Flip the mattress up on the window, then the frame. I'm going to see if I left any weapons behind."

I do as he says, running to his old bedroom, riddled with scattered moving boxes, books, empty cartons of cigarettes, takeout containers, clothes, and some old electronics that have to be two decades old. I haven't seen a VCR since my mom sold ours at a yard sale when I was a tween.

Grabbing the pillow and blankets, I drag them off the bed and prop up the mattress, finagling it on its side as I carefully step between the wooden slats of the frame. And looking at them, I think they could be useful. I can't stab an angel with them but I can swing it like a bat and keep some distance.

"Next time Micah creates an angel ward, make sure I pay fucking attention." Elias drops a duffle bag in the middle of the room and leans forward, coughing and out of breath. He sounds utterly awful, and I wish I could close the space and rub his back, but keeping the angelic army out is far more important. If we can't, we might not make it.

"We'll learn together, okay? By the time this shit is behind us, we won't even have to know. Those bastards will be too afraid." I manage to lean the mattress against the window and then prop the metal and wood frame against it. I know it won't keep anyone out, but it will at least slow them down.

"Damn straight, darlin'. They'll regret ever thinking they could get in our way from our eternity together. We've been through Hell, Heaven, and every damn thing in between to get to where we are, and I'm not letting anything screw us over." Elias digs into the duffle bag and pulls out a curved blade. "Now help me take care of the door to ensure it."

His words fill me with hope. Rushing across the room, I do what he says and shove the dresser in front of the door, blocking it. Elias motions to the night stand, and I haul it over. He helps me arrange the barricades until there is nothing left.

Elias scoops up the bag and takes my hand, tugging me along to the closet. The broken rod lies on the floor, reminding me of how we first met in this lifetime and he tied me up in here like a fucking bastard. Picking it up, I add it to my arsenal along with the wood slats from the bed frame.

"Remind me when this is over that I need to repay you for this," I murmur, waving the broken rod. If I don't joke or concentrate on something else, I might panic. It's too quiet. The world is too still. It makes me wonder what kind of powers the guardians have and if they can transport us to a different plane to ensure no one finds us.

He hums under his breath, lifting an eyebrow. "Careful,

darlin'. I'm still horny as fuck. When this is over, it won't be you repaying me. I'll tie you up all over again and make up for leaving you hanging without a good time."

"You better." I lean in and kiss him, trying to distract myself from the building anticipation.

My whole body buzzes as goosebumps prickle over my skin. It's the strangest thing—almost like a sixth sense. I don't have to see the angelic army to know they're coming and close.

Elias's muscles ripple as he tightens his hand around the knife. "Shit. They're close."

"You sense them too?" I whisper, flicking my gaze from the blocked window to the barricaded door.

Elias shifts, nudging me to press my back against the closet wall. "Just stay behind me, okay? If you get hurt—"

"I don't fucking think so." I surprise the hell out of him and yank him back by his shoulder, shuffling around to plant my body in front of him. "If I get hurt, I'll survive. You're crazy if you think you're going to fight. It's my job to protect you, Elias. If you die...you're not fucking dying like this. Now don't even try to argue."

Elias groans and dangles his curved blade in front of me. "My sexy, infuriating woman. It goes against my instincts as a hunter to let you but damn it if your protectiveness isn't fantastic for my ego. I love it that you're ready to channel Hell and be a psycho badass for me. Micah was right about it being a boner trigger."

I can't help my exasperated laugh. Most men would get a bruised ego if I made it seem like I was more powerful and stronger than them. Elias knows his limitations and melts into me, silently thanking me that I'm not forcing him into a position he knows he might not be able to handle as well. Like with the furniture. He knew I was capable of taking care of shit and didn't have a problem letting me do something for him instead of cry and ask him to save me.

"I will gladly be your warrior queen in shining armor, my dame in distress. Your assurance and faith in me gives me the power of a spirit devil boner." I adjust the blade in my hand and glare at the window. Faint light trickles in from the crack around the mattress.

He rests his hands on my sides, letting me support his weight some. "Nah, darlin'. The devils think they have these almighty cocks, but you have the power and strength of your pussy that keeps them all in line. Your power is all you and your ability to withstand Hell, no matter if it's fucking you or trying to break you. Don't ever forget that. No one wants you against them—Heaven or Hell."

I crane my neck to meet his gaze. "I love y—"

A loud crack cuts off my words, startling me. My scared-ass nearly drops the blade, taken off guard by how the furniture crashes together as the heavenly forces blast them away from the window and door at once. And shit. Elias might've made me a bit full of myself for a second, because my confidence vanishes at the sight of two fearsome angels—a man and a woman—in black clothes and leather with gold wings bright enough to radiate their heavenly glow like a halo around their whole bodies.

"Raven Rose, you are an abomination. Come forth and kneel before me. I will not ask twice. If you do not, you will not receive mercy." The female angel flaps her wings and soundlessly strolls over the fallen dresser.

"I'm used to that bullshit, so no. Just stay the fuck back. I won't hesitate to cut your wings off and give them to my devils' hellhounds as chew toys." I straighten my back, wishing I could slap the bitch in her righteous face. She stares at me like a shit on her boots.

"Elias, my fallen brethren, if your mortal undoing can't see reason, perhaps you can." This comes from the male angel remaining outside. "You are ill and dying because of your treachery. You will find peace if you make the right choice. Bring the abomination forward and accept that this is your rightful path."

"Fuck off, dickhole. Raven is my only path." Elias grips my hips tighter, leaning into me. His lips touch my ear. "Get ready, darlin'. Aim for their hands first. Wings second."

"You've given us no choice. You have nowhere to run. Our army surrounds you." The woman strides toward us, unsheathing her sword, setting it aflame in angel fire. It glows blue instead of bright yellow-white like Cassius's.

"Duck and charge. I'll swing." Elias shoves me, getting me to attack first.

I bend low and run at the woman as Elias swings the clothes rod at her head. She instinctively lifts her arms to protect her face, and I ram my shoulder into her stomach. My Hell power knocks the both of us off our feet, but the angel uses her wings to propel us up, causing me to lose my balance. I screech and blindly slash the blade at her, slicing her palm as she tries to gather heavenly light.

"Meri!" the male angel shouts, shooting angel power at us.

I keep swinging the blade, not giving the woman, Meri, a chance to do anything except block herself. My vision shadows with my fury and the heavenly light spilling into the room from her body as if her light tries to protect and heal her but can't keep up.

"Raven, her hands!" Elias shouts, swinging the clothes rod at the guy angel. Elias clocks the angel's wing, only to have the guy snatch the rod and drag him closer.

All it takes is that tiny distraction for Meri to get in a jab. Pain explodes in my middle like fire and ice and sheer agony. Meri didn't punch me with her fist. She fucking stabbed me with her angel sword.

My legs buckle, sending me crashing to the floor. I try to suck in a breath of air to scream Elias's name, but the words won't come.

And then the male angel elbows Elias in the ribs. He gasps, his face paling and losing color. Commotion echoes outside. I clutch my bloody stomach, trying to think of something, anything, I can do to save us. I can't pray for mercy. Begging to spare us won't work either.

Meri abandons me, leaving me bleeding on the floor as the pain of her blade sears me to my very soul. Her golden wings glow, tiny pinpricks of light shine brighter where I managed to stab her with Elias's knife. She remains unfazed and expressionless as she joins her companion, and the two of them stand above Elias, looking down at him.

"Your sacrifice will right the paths of many, Elias," the male angel says, flexing his muscular arms.

"Fuck...off." Elias can barely spit the words out through his coughing.

"Meri, Mikail, you must hurry," another angel says, the blond man crossing his arms on the other side of the window. We cannot distract and mislead the devils much longer. Our shields weaken."

The angel, Mikail, nods and unsheathes his flaming sword, longer and brighter than Meri's shorter blade. Heat burns over my skin, and I blink a few times, watching as sudden flames eat the world around me, separating me from the angels and Elias.

"May your cycle finally complete and your bond to this mortal break." Mikail aims his sword at Elias.

"Raven, Raven! This isn't over! I'll find you. I'll destroy the universe if I have to." Elias's words rip me from the burning world and back to his old bedroom.

"Blessed be the Higher Power," Meri says. "Blessed be our armies. For this finally ends here."

I gasp and scream, staring in horror as Mikail slams his sword at Elias, unable to do anything but lie placidly and weak beneath him. Molten power burns over my hand, the mark of my contract with Lucian igniting, unleashing Hell through my palm. The angels yell and scream as the hot power whips over them, burning the wings of their feathers and smoldering their skin.

With the burst of energy from Hell, I scramble to my feet and charge them, slapping my hand to Mikail's arm, branding him with Lucian's mark the same way I had branded Zade. The angel outside the window yanks Meri through but not without the shock of power burning him too. It lights the whole room in strange flames, the heat painful but nothing like the agony still coursing through me.

"Raven, let it go!" Elias shouts, struggling to get to his feet. "You have to let it go!"

My body acts as a vessel for the power of Hell and it simmers like a boiling pot about to overflow. Elias's words knock sense back into me, spilling the darkness from my being until the fiery world fades. My knees buckle as I try to step toward him, and I fall flat on my stomach. Shadows steal the world from me, leaving me in a strange abyss of darkness, though the pain of my body doesn't release me. I focus on trying to move, trying to speak, trying to do anything to drag me from this strange state.

"Darlin', hey. Hey, it's over. You fucking did some strange-ass Hell power shit. You saved me." Elias drags me into his arms and cradles me, running his hand over my beaten and bloody body. "Now let me look at you. I'll destroy those bastards for hurting you." Carefully, Elias tugs up the hem of my shirt and intakes a sharp breath.

"Shit, this is bad, isn't it?" I ask, whacking his hand away from my burned yet still slightly bleeding stab wound. "It hurts like a mother fucker."

Elias locks his hand around mine, restraining me the best he can while he looks at my stomach. "It seems that most of the wound has been cauterized. Do you think you'll be able to walk? I don't think we should stay here."

I groan and rub my hands against my eyes. "Do you have a phone or something here? I can call—"

Light glows from the broken window, startling me. Elias drags me to my feet and helps me walk toward the hallway. This isn't over. One of the angels said they were blocking my devils.

"I don't think they'll be able to get to us if they wanted to, but I know somewhere we can go, but you have to trust me." Elias tightens his jaw, guiding me toward a side door that leads to an empty one-car garage. He snags the single helmet off a work bench and doesn't give me a chance to argue before locking the strap in place.

"You have a motorcycle?" I ask in surprise.

"Did you really think I was going to surrender all of my human possessions when I moved in with you guys? This is my house. I wasn't just going to sell it and risk not having a backup plan. It's no secret."

"I hate that I didn't know," I mutter, trying to suppress my fear. I've never been on a motorcycle before, and this one looks...like it's been through as much as his beater of a car.

He takes my hands in his for a moment. "We'll amend that, okay? The not knowing. I swear when we get home, you're going to know everything there is to know about me. Things you won't even want to know."

I force myself to smile. "Good. Because unlike what those bastard angels think, our bond can never be broken. If anything, they just proved to the universe that we're strong as fucking Hell."

"Hot, too," he murmurs, kissing my nose. He flicks the visor of the helmet down. "Hold on tight. We're going to need to outrun the angels."

Shit.

Hell help us.

16

RAVEN

HUNTED

"ARE YOU FUCKING kidding me? We can't stay here." I follow behind Elias, trying to ignore the fear tightening my chest. "The angels have a deal with the hunters."

Elias grabs my hand and forces me to keep up with his brisk pace. "Neither a strong one nor one to the guardians. Some of the Hell-bound were afraid of an angelic smiting after the shit they pulled despite Cass-hole forgiving them. He's the one who arranged for the hunters to get me from Vincent and to Lucian."

"That's why we found one of the holy weapons." It's not a question. I just assumed maybe Lucian made the deal since Vincent wasn't going to give Elias up.

"That's right. When it comes down to it, all these fuckers really want is to survive and kick some ass no matter the consequences. They also still have the banishing room. We can use it to open a portal for access to the devils." He sounds so confident in his plan that it settles my nerves, especially seeing a guard wave at us instead of trying to kill us on sight.

"Okay, if this is what you think will work, but if anyone tries anything...I'm cutting their dicks off to offer Dante and Kase a cock bouquet. They like that kind of thing and it'll stop them from trying to disembowel everyone here." Twisted? Most definitely. It's not something I want, but these fuckers would deserve it.

Elias raises his eyebrows, but doesn't call me out on my psychotic thoughts. "I'll restrain them."

I smirk without comment.

Elias slides his arm around my waist and pulls me close, adding, "Preston might be a bastard and can't grasp the concept of me being anything other than a hunter and his best friend, but he won't hurt you, so you won't have to resort to it. I have a plan to keep everyone calm. You just have to trust me."

I unfasten the strap on the helmet but don't take it off in case. The fuckers here might not try to kill Elias, but they think I'm Hell's whore for loving the devils beyond their narrow scope of thought. "I do trust you. It's just—I fucking hate them all. I can't promise to be nice. They arranged a ghost to possess me. That shit lingers with me, you know?"

A frown pouts his lips and he subtly nods. "I hate them for that too. We're only here out of desperation. Don't think my nicety toward Preston is real, okay? He will pay for what he did. When I take my throne, I'll guarantee it. I traded my life for his, and he fucking shit on me."

I bob my head, hugging his side. I don't want even an inch of space to get between us. "I want him to regret his actions for the rest of eternity. The selfish prick."

Elias digs his fingers into my hip, slowing down outside the warehouse door to the hunter's compound. Different marks glow around the frame in both red and white light. I don't recognize any of them, but they must be the wards. It's still strange to me how they know how to create them—learning from who knows where. A ghost, for one. Maybe even angels from long ago.

"Elias! What the actual fuck? You're supposed to be on your deathbed in the arms of the saviors." Preston's familiar voice cuts through the room in a part of the building I've never seen. The open warehouse has been converted into a huge living space partitioned off into rooms to create more privacy.

Elias lugs me along, half carrying me as I drag my feet. "What? You want to get rid of me so easily? I'm dying but I still have some life left. And so you know, I never made it to Cassius. Fucking Lucifer had other plans in store. We barely escaped those devil monsters."

Preston's brows pinch together. "Shit, I knew it. I fucking warned that angel that he has too much faith for this to work out. He swore to me that you'd be safe."

Elias rubs his hand up and down my arm. "Raven saved my ass, but now we're in trouble. They're after us and Cassius has vanished. We need somewhere to crash until I can get him to show up."

"We won't stay long. We would hate to put you in the line of Hell after everything you've done for Elias." It hurts me to my core to say the words and play along, but I can tell it's what Preston needs to believe us. "I have some family we can stay with, but I need to use your phone."

"I get that, but it's not necessary," Preston says, tightening his jaw. "We can handle ourselves. Your family? Why would you risk it?"

Wow. This asshole. What a way to twist my good intent and make me feel like shit.

Elias tightens his hold on me. "Raven's just worried about them and wants to protect them too."

I force my lip to pout instead of scowl. "Lucian—Lucifer brought my cousin into this bullshit. I'm scared for her."

"Oh, shit. You should still stay here. I can send some guys to her place to keep a lookout until things settle down." Preston's eyes lock on mine as he tries to figure me out. He reaches into his jacket, and I take an automatic step back. But he only tugs out his phone. "Why don't you call her? It might make you feel better."

It takes all my will not to snatch the phone and to accept it politely. I just want to call my devils and get out of here.

"Thank you," I mutter, flipping the old-ass phone open. I haven't seen one like this since high school. Good fucking thing I have Kase's number memorized. "I appreciate it."

Breaking away from Elias, I finally tug the helmet off and hand it to him, feeling a bit vulnerable. I don't stroll away for privacy as much as I want to and instead just turn my back and dial the number.

The line clicks but no one speaks. I peer at the tiny screen to make sure I've connected.

"Tamia?" I ask, trying not to sound as if I'm on the verge of crying. "Tamia, it's Raven."

"Angel-girl, fuck. You're in so much trouble for scaring the hell out of us. Where are you, so I can disembowel anyone who dared lay a finger on you. Andre said you refused to leave the Jizz-Master alone." Kase's voice growls with his words. "Do you know how badly I want to spank and then fuck that ass of yours for being a disobedient soul? They want you, not Elias."

I want so badly to tell him to shut the fuck up and focus, because the guardians definitely have a boner for killing Elias too. If only I couldn't feel the weight of Preston's stare on the back of my head as he murmurs quietly to Elias while trying to discretely listen.

"I know. I'm sorry for that. I'll make it up to you as soon as I can. I have some things I need to take care of first. I'm staying with Elias's family for a bit." I try my best to sound inconspicuous. "They want to spend as much time as they can because..." Stupid eyes. Everything suddenly gets to me, and I have to wipe my cheeks.

"The smart bastard. He's going to get one helluva reward for this. We'll wait for your summons, okay? I swear we'll be there faster than a virgin angel getting a blow job." Kase sighs with his words. "Just hang tight."

"I love you," I whisper.

"And we more than love you, pretty-soul. Obsessed," Dante says, his comment making me smile.

The line clicks, and I swivel and hold out Preston's phone, keeping my gaze on the shiny concrete floor. Tears burn my cheeks, not helping me any. I shouldn't be crying. I'm tough enough to handle this, but sometimes I just don't want to. I'm going to need a good cuddle session and a round of letting Dante have his way, so I don't even have to think or decide on something as simple as which color panties to wear. I love this about my devils. They don't ever judge me when I want to be tough or to just be coddled. They taught me that wanting to put control in their hands isn't a sign of weakness. It's a sign of complete trust, which is what I'm doing now with Elias. What I want to get to with Micah and Andre. What I'll fight like hell to maintain with Kase and Dante.

"Why don't you take her to the showers and help her get cleaned up? Whoever you two fought to escape looks to have suffered some wrath. I'll ask Dolly to fix her something to eat." Preston pats Elias on the shoulder. He thinks the blood on my clothes belongs to someone else.

Elias doesn't correct him and only nods. "Same room?"

Preston nods. "Same room. I'll grab a couch until we can arrange things to give you a room."

Preston doesn't say anything to me, letting Elias guide me deeper into the warehouse and down a hall made from plywood, partitioning things off. It's now that I spot a platform above with a lookout in front of what probably used to be an office. There really isn't much privacy with someone watching. I bet they get a fucking eyeful of all these dudes jerking off at night.

I shudder, pushing away the thought.

"You okay?" Elias whispers, keeping his voice low. "You got ahold of them?"

"They're ready. Apparently you get a reward for your smart thinking and I'm going to get punished for being naughty and not leaving you." I smirk at him, already feeling better with the space we put between us and Preston.

"Hopefully not by Andre's cock in your ass. I don't think I can handle knowing that you'd agree to doing that for the sake of making them happy." Elias tightens his lips and tries not to react. "I don't care how wide they claim an asshole can stretch."

I laugh in exasperation. "That's definitely a hell no to Andre. Technically, my deal is with Kase, but maybe he's planning to give it up as a reward to you."

The look he gives me speaks volumes. He loves the sound of it. And shit. They can't all want a piece of my ass, can they?

He clears his throat, his cheeks reddening. "I'm good with whatever you want from me. I'll never ask. You get that enough from them."

I giggle and lean into him. "I love you, you know. Maybe I want you to ask me."

"Damn," he mutters under his breath. "You're so fucking bad. The devils are going to be pissed because now I plan to join you in the shower. Fuck you for as long as I can. I can't get enough of you and those asshole angels ruined everything."

"Or we could summon them now and go home, take a hot bubble bath, let Kase make us some sandwiches and Dante wash our hair. Light some candles. Each get a little venom bite..." I grin like crazy, watching his expression morph into full-blown lust. I knew he liked Dante biting him, though he'd never admit it.

"Shit, darlin'. I shouldn't like the sound of that, but damn. I'll fucking let the devils pamper us until the day I die. But I want you to wash my hair." He winks and picks up his pace. "No fucking way I'm getting between Dante's legs."

"Could be worse. I swear Kase's tail has a mind of its own." I crack up as he scrunches his nose, his gray eyes sparkling in the harsh lighting overhead.

Elias leans in and kisses the laughter from my mouth, quieting me down as we sneak past what looks like communal showers and along the back wall. I suck up the fear tightening my chest, remembering exactly what went down in this back room the last time I was here. People died. It's where I saw Elias's angel wings from after his fall.

Closing the door quietly, Elias peers around the room with scorch marks on the floor. The faint smell of Hell lingers in the air. It probably wasn't long ago that the hunters sent a demon to Hell. Maybe even one of Vincent's associates if they were the ones to get Elias.

"Grab the salt over there. I'll get the other supplies. I want you to draw the circle. Your hands are steadier." Elias motions to giant bags of salt on a shelf. These guys really are prepared. "We have to move fast."

I race across the room and heave a twenty pound bag of salt from a stack under the shelves of holy water. Elias points to the ash ring from the last time these hunters opened Hell, and I use the line to dump the salt in a ring, ensuring there aren't any breaks. Elias sets a couple candles within the ring and surprises the hell out of me by cutting his finger and drawing some weird ass symbol. This isn't the same as what he taught me about sending demons to Hell. This portal is intended to bring one out.

Elias pulls a lighter from his pocket. I haven't seen him smoke in a while, but he must carry one out of habit. "Stand within it, darlin'. It'll help with your contract still in place. It took me a long ass time to get it right for Andre. We need this perfect now—"

A gunshot rings through the air, startling me and Elias. He jumps forward and crashes into me protectively, instinctually. If I thought Preston would try to kill him, I'd flip Elias onto his back and take the bullet.

"What the fuck, Elias? You're trying to unleash Hell after everything you have been through? I don't understand. I thought you were coming around." Preston waves his gun, pointing it at the ceiling. "This is her doing, isn't it? What were you planning? You were trying to end us, weren't you?"

Shit. Shit. Shit.

Elias raises his hands in surrender, slowly easing off of me to get up. "I wouldn't do that to you. It's just—it's not what you think. I'm trying to—"

Aiming the gun in my direction, Preston fires, sending a bullet ricocheting from the concrete floor to the drywall behind me. "Shut up! I knew this was too good to be true. I knew she was too far into your head for you to make the right decision." Preston glowers and points the gun again. "I damn fucking knew that she let Hell get too deep inside her. She's the fucking slut of Satan. She's dragging you down with her."

Hey now. I haven't even slept with Lucian yet.

Preston glowers at me. "I won't let her. This ends here."

I brace to be shot. I brace for my life to end. What I don't expect is for Elias to flick his lighter, drawing Preston's murderous glare away from me. It's all I need to launch forward. I crash into the bastard at the same time Elias ignites the candle wick, sending billowing flames around the circle as a portal to Hell opens up.

Swinging his fist, Preston punches me in the cheek. Pain explodes through my head, and my eyes burn with tears. I haven't been hit like this since Joel. The action sets me off, shadowing my vision. I flail my hands, smacking Preston over and over again. Elias shouts something I can't decipher, my anger stealing the world around me away.

Preston manages to get an opening in between my hands and shoves me off. I hit my back on the floor with a gasp, the air exiting my lungs in a painful breath. I can't roll away fast enough. Tackling me with his heavy body, Preston grabs my head between his hands. His nails bite into my cheeks as he prepares to break my neck.

"Preston, no!" Elias shouts, rushing toward us. "Stop!"

I scratch at Preston's arms, trying to get him to stop.

"This must be done, brother." Preston snatches a knife from his belt and swipes it at Elias, cutting the fabric of his pants. "Stay back or I'll make it painful. You have to let her go. God will bless us for following his will."

"You don't even know what the hell God's will is that you're truly following. Now let her go. This is your last chance." Elias stands nearby, his voice deepening with his warning.

"You'll have to make me. I won't let her drag you down with her. Not after everything you've done." Preston flares his nostrils, fighting against my Hell strength. His determination and position stops me from getting leverage. I'm trapped.

"Preston, please. Please." Elias's voice cracks.

Preston doesn't listen. He doesn't respond.

I squeeze my eyes shut at the tightness of my muscles in my neck. Preston keeps twisting, turning my head in an agonizing position. I can't scream or concentrate on anything but trying to scratch him. He doesn't even flinch as his flesh gathers under my nails.

Gunfire rings through the air and blood and brain matter splatter across my face. I stare in shock, my hearing muffled from the pop. Preston's dead body slumps on top of mine, still trying to trap me even with his death.

I screech and fling him off with all my Hell strength, the pain and exhaustion of the last few hours wearing heavily on both my body and soul. Haze turns my vision fuzzy as Elias stands above me. hellfire leaps toward the roof behind him, haloing him in fiery light. One second I stare into his glassy, steel-gray eyes as a man, and in the next, a huge foxlike beast with a coat the same color as hellfire towers in front of me. Long canines jut from its elongated mouth and two horns stretch toward the ceiling next to triangular ears.

I open and close my mouth, trying to form words, but nothing comes.

And with a blink of my eyes, the strange demonic apparition disappears and Elias stands before me once again.

Another figure joins him, and then another and another until five silhouettes hover around me, the world still glowing with the fire of Hell.

"Raven, shit," Micah says, stepping closer.

"Fucking stay back. Dante will look at her and heal her if needed. You take care of the hunters." Kase growls and locks his tail around Micah's neck, pulling him back. "I'll handle Elias. We'll meet where we discussed. Make sure no one follows."

"Don't kill anyone else," I murmur, stretching my arms up, waiting for any of them to pick me up. "It was all Preston."

"You heard her. Lock them up, and we'll deal with them later. We have more important things to do." Dante scoops me up into his arms and buries his face in my hair. "Like taking care of our soul first."

"And fucking taking out the guardians after," Kase adds, picking up Elias without even asking him. He turns to Andre and kicks Preston's body. "Take this fucker with you."

"Gladly," Andre says. "I have a special place for him. He will pay."

17

RAVEN

HOW TO SAVE A LIFE

"ONE OF US has to go appease Lucian. He believes we're plotting against him." Micah's voice tugs me from the dark recesses of my mind. "He's asking about Raven. I told him that until he shares his business in regards to her on his days that I won't be humoring such demands of information."

"The bastard will grow suspicious if we don't take her home." Dante hisses under his breath. "It's supposed to be my day, so I'll take her."

Micah sighs. "She's not going to willingly leave Elias."

I groan and stretch my arms over my head. My body feels as if Joel nearly beat me to death all over again. It takes a lot of effort to open my eyes, my mind still in a state of bliss from Dante injecting me with his venom. Everything over the last day has been a blur, and I barely remember where I am—a new apartment outside of Angel Canyon and toward Lake Hills. It's far ritzier than the apartment complex I lived at before, this one having a wall around the complex and a security guard at the entrance. Plus the view of the valley and a nearby lake is breathtaking. This could be the perfect getaway spot if it had more than one bedroom.

A big body shifts on the couch and helps ease me up. Dante snuggles his arms around me, letting me rest against his chest. I can't stop the heat warming my skin. Everyone sits so close in a protective wall around me, even Andre, sitting within his summoning circle.

"Fucking finally, angel-girl. How you feeling? You're so lucky that all I have the urge to do is love up on you instead of punishing your bubble butt like I had planned." Kase gets in my face and clutches my cheeks. He ever so gently brushes his lips to mine, kissing me softly. "And it makes me ragey as fuck. I want to murder everyone in the vicinity of that damn compound for your pain. That bastard is going to be planted right beside Joel in my fucking kingdom with his asshole out instead of his face. My legion will enjoy—"

"Kase, that was Elias's friend." I cringe at the thought of Kase's eternal punishment, remembering the weird ass trees in the forest of wrath. "Maybe leave his asshole out of it. I don't know why you're so obsessed."

Red light glows in his smoldering gaze. "It's an expectation mortals have, and I can't disappoint if they think Hell wants a piece of the shittiest part of them."

"Yeah, but like I said, Preston was Elias's friend. They were close like brothers. He might've been a fucking bastard but so are you all sometimes. Do I have to remind you of the dumpster plan?" I ask, trying to remain serious. Turning to Micah, I add, "Or the whole, I should only belong to you bullshit."

Dante hisses, sitting up straighter. "You naughty soul, holding stuff against us. Maybe ask Jizz Master what he wants to happen. Souls don't go to Hell for a good time...at least not the truly bad ones. Occasionally, we get ones that just reject the Higher Power and all the mortal rules around it to scare souls. Those ones we have a soft spot for."

I tip my head back. "What? Are you for real? Even good people can go to Hell? You guys never mentioned it."

"How do you think demons have come to be? We're not creators and not many angels abandon grace, as you know. Call it a perk." Kase grins at me. "Of course, unless you contracted your soul, then that's another story."

Andre groans and rubs his fingers through this hair. "I'm sorry, little hellion. I know you have an insatiable curiosity but Lucian keeps tapping into Hell. I need to leave, but I need to know what we're planning and what I need to do." He looks to Dante. "Perhaps I can take her to my kingdom and feign another...incident. It would better explain Raven's absence and why I never brought her back."

Kase chuckles. "You're just ready to recreate it, so no. Her pussy is closed for knotting until we figure out what to do and how to handle Lucian."

Heat warms my cheeks. "Kase."

Elias's eyes widen. I don't think he knows what had happened, but by his expression, he obviously has an idea. "Shit, darlin'. That would be one helluva..." His words trail off and he snaps his mouth shut. "Why don't you let Dante and Kase take you home? Appease Lucian for a moment so he doesn't come searching. Micah will watch out for me and make sure I don't keel the fuck over without one last bang."

I want to argue so badly with his suggestion. How can I leave him after everything? Not only is my fate tied to his, but I also just got him back. I had no idea how hard being away from my soulmate would be. We re-bonded quickly. I know I have my other devils to keep me occupied, but...I want them all. I love this moment with us all working together.

I press my lips together and turn to Micah. "Is that okay with you?"

He nods. "I will protect him with my very being as if he is you. Go home with Kase and Dante and perhaps use your light to set him aglow. Whatever happened between you recently has him...acting anxious."

Sighing, I palm my forehead. I'd already forgotten how I ran out on Lucian after his crazy jerking off session right in front of me and how we both knew I liked it. "Oh, jeez."

"This is Micah's way of asking what the fuck went down without flat out asking," Kase says, lifting an eyebrow. "Because he's right. He's a bit more obsessed. You show him your tits? Stroked his horns? We know he's hot."

"And you're our perfect kinky soul. We won't blame you. Hell, whatever gets him in a good mood...if that's what you want. I'm happy whipping the Hell out of him." Dante nuzzles his nose to the crook of my neck.

I throw my hands up. "I don't know what the fuck is really going on. He infuriates me yet he turns me on. I just—I don't want to go there with him because he hasn't accepted that I'm officially a devil cock collector. I'm greedy, envious, wrathful, lusty, and a damn glutton because of all of you...and I like it."

"I fucking love it," Dante teases. "Whatever makes you happy."

His words stretch a smile across my face. I had no idea how amazing it would feel to know that there are others who want me to have my way and create a life I can happily live eternity in. And the feeling is mutual.

"You all make me happy," I say, smiling. "Enough to deal with Lucian and the saviors. Because I want this forever." I motion to all of us. "This is my idea of the perfect eternity."

"Then let's get the fuck to it." Kase stretches out his arms. "Time to show these bastards what you're truly capable of."

I knock on the doorframe of Lucian's room, catching sight of him just sitting on the edge of the bed. He looks so incredibly angelic as he stares off into space. Turning his head, he meets my gaze, and for a split second, I realize that Micah was right. Something has changed. Unfortunately, he summons his dickwad self and narrows his eyes.

"What?" he asks, his hellfire lighting his eyes. "I'm not in the mood for bullshit, Raven. Your rejection is getting on my nerves."

I hurt his pride by leaving. Of course I did.

My mouth takes on a mind of its own and I smile despite my good senses. "You think I was ever in the mood for your bullshit, Satan? Stop acting like I pegged you without lube."

He growls.

I grin wider. "And I won't apologize for leaving. You need to learn that you're not entitled to me, even if you turn me on. Your asshole deals ruined your chance for me to give in...but there's time to fix this crap. Find Elias for me, and maybe I'll reward you. End my contract, and maybe I'll fuck you how you imagine. Let me control the deal for once."

"No," he snaps. "Your manipulation won't work when your soul is mine and I know you'll give in."

I narrow my eyes. "Not if I find Elias first. Which we're close. We're going to find him today, and then I'll be one step closer to getting my own power."

He remains expressionless. "Sounds like a damn plan. I have business I need to attend to and need Dante by my side, so we can make a day out of it."

My smile falters. I had intended to push his buttons and make him realize he won't ever get his way, not turn my day with Dante into a satanic errand. Shit. "Fine."

Is that a blip of surprise on his face? Fuck yeah, it is. He thought I'd deny him.

"I can't wait to see your face when we get Elias without your help," I add, forcing my face to obey my command to smirk. "And since you've been so unhelpful, I'll make sure to be loud enough for even Heaven to hear when I sit on his face. Bend over and plant my palms on the floor. Have Dante and Kase teach him how to use the swing and give everyone a show. He'd do it for me." Warmth builds between my legs at my attempt to make him jealous, because it reminds me of putting on a show for Andre.

Standing up, Lucian strides across the room, trying to intimidate me with his presence. His onyx eyes smolder like coal, and he braces his hand on the doorframe above my head.

His scent, like smoky incense, engulfs me. It might be the first time I've paid attention. Breathed a little deeper. Teasing Lucian is like playing with a grenade and if I fuck around too much, he'll go off. But I don't think any sort of explosion between Lucian and I could be more dangerous than everything I've been through. If anything, it'll prove just how tough I am. I break angels. I stand beside devils. I can handle Lucian.

"Careful, Raven. You're teasing my darkness. I'd accept another whipping to taste your lips, you know. Steal a kiss that will set your soul off. That's all it would take." Lucian bows closer, gliding his tongue over his bottom lip as he studies my mouth. "One small touch will weaken your knees."

Ah Hell. "I'm starting to think you enjoy me hurting your pride."

Lucian graces me with a wicked smile. "We both know you're lying to yourself. You won't reject me. You already shift your legs open in anticipation. You imagine what it would be like if I licked every inch of you. How you could hold onto my horns. Feel my power in every nerve ending of your clit."

Shit. Shit. Shit. He's getting to me, putting the exhilarating, filthy thoughts in my mind. It takes everything in me to shove my hand to his chest and push him back. "Not today, Satan," I say, grinning. I've always wanted to fucking say that. "Today belongs to my sexy devil of envy. If you haven't noticed his tongue...hmm, maybe I'll go sit on his face for a bit. He loves that."

Lucian releases a deep growl, practically shooting fire from his nostrils. If Dante didn't hiss from behind me and engulf me in his arms, I'm nearly certain Lucian would've done something crazy like drop to his knees and show me the truth of his words.

"Damn straight, I do." Dante sticks out his tongue slowly, moving each side in a way that sends tingles exploding through me. "You love it too. I could bury myself between your thighs and rest in peace for eternity."

Lucian growls again. "She won't want you to after she experiences me. I'll prove it." Turning to me, Lucian reaches out and touches my hand, surprising me. "Say yes. We'll have a competition."

I can't get my mouth to work, the sudden intensity of both devils staring at me setting my soul ablaze.

Dante breaks first and grins. "You heard Raven. Not today, Satan." Bellowing a laugh, Dante whacks Lucian on his back. "We have shit to do. Soulmates to find. A new manicure for my pretty soul, too. Glorious sex to have. TLC for a little something-something." He winks at me.

TLC doesn't ever mean what I think it does as Dante adds his own damn words to the acronym. Last time it was Tasty Long Cock. Before that, it was Tight Little Cunt when he mentioned needing my TLC. I figured that one out quickly. This time? Who fucking knows what he means. Hopefully Tighten Lucian's Collar or something. That devil needs a damn leash.

"The Lube Collection," he whispers in my ear. "Him and Her. For some training." And by training, I don't think he means what he usually means. We're not preparing and stretching. Shit.

"After we fucking check in at the Demon's Den to make sure your bullshit stays in line. I've had two fucking locations hit by guardians." Pushing past us, Lucian heads to the hallway and abandons us in his doorway. "I want to set a trap somewhere they haven't hit."

Dante dramatically rolls his eyes. "What a fucking waste of time. Gia keeps things tighter than an angel's asshole. The guardians won't try."

"Prove me wrong." Lucian flashes his devil façade. "If my trap proves to be unnecessary, I'll lick your damn a—"

"No deals," I snap, dangling my arms on Dante's shoulders. "Just be a good, quiet devil and I'll let you tag along as a third wheel. If you can do that, maybe you can watch me sit on Dante's face later. See what you're missing for being an outrageous dick."

"I need more than a maybe." Lucian graces me with a wicked smile.

I glare. "No. That's not how this works. I already told you what I want in exchange for a possibility of me even humoring your twisted fantasy about me."

"You say that now, but you'll see. I'll give you a few

hours. You're going to regret denying me and then you'll beg." This bastard. "I guarantee it. I know something about you that you haven't realized yet."

"What's that?" I hate my curiosity.

"You're selfish. Needy. Greedy like your soulmate. And I'll use it against you." Lucian pulls his phone from his pocket and taps the screen.

I glance from him to Dante, waiting to see what he's talking about.

"Hey, babe. Want to meet up?" he asks, smirking at me. "Cool, yeah. At the Demon's Den. Wear something hot."

I frown, wondering what the fuck is going on.

Lucian disconnects the line and grins. "You all set? Now I'm fucking ready to go."

I could kill him.

I will kill him.

The next time I find myself locked in his room with him, I'm going to get on my knees, pretend that I'm finally giving in, and then I'm going to use the force of Hell to bite his fucking cock off.

I can't believe he pulled this shit. Or that Tamia has fallen for his charm.

What's even worse is that I'm jealous. He was right about me. I'm needy and greedy, and even though Lucian pisses me the hell off, I don't want to see him with anyone else. Even if it's just to get to me. He hasn't done anything to make me think he's slept with her or anything, but if he has? He's not going to ever have a piece of my eternity. He still might not. I don't want a jerkoff who manipulates my emotions already, and this is crossing a damn line.

And I blow up.

"Lucian, I need to talk to you." I snatch him by the front of his shirt and use my Hell strength to drag him away from Tamia before he has a chance to sit in the booth beside her.

Dante slides up against my back, towering behind me, looking fully ready to restrain Lucian so that I can hurt him in a way I hadn't expected him to hurt me. Turning slightly, I press my hand to his chest, silently getting him to stay behind. I know he's worried about what happened after the last time I went off on Lucian at the bar and grill, but I need to handle this myself. He needs to be put in his place by my terms.

"I don't think so. We have nothing to talk about." Lucian tries to join Tamia again.

I slam my hands into his chest, nearly pushing him to the floor. I'll tackle him if I have to. Because I'm over this.

"Like fuck we don't," I say, herding him with my body, feeling the dozens of gazes of Hell-bound humans and demons alike bearing witness to me manhandling the one everyone is supposed to be afraid of.

Lucian snarls at me, his eyes lighting with fire. It takes everything in me to keep pushing him, but I refuse to back down. My actions strike a nerve, because he only lets me get in one more shove before lifting me off my feet and slinging me over his shoulder. I pound my fists into his back, wishing he would've just grabbed my hand, but this is typical devil behavior. Even Kase and Dante choose to carry me everywhere I let them. I don't know if it's because they feel like they're protecting me better or what, but with Lucian, it's definitely him flexing power back. He won't let me humiliate him in front of bottom feeder demons.

"Stop fighting or you're not going to like how I restrain you," Lucian says, kicking the door open to the back room and where the kitchen is. A few people scatter and duck as if they expect to receive the fury of Hell with our arrival.

"Lucian, damn it. Put me down!" I yell, yanking his shirt up. I scratch my nails along his skin until I feel the rough bumps of scars. Not just any scars. These are where his wings used to be.

He freezes at the touch of my fingers turning from all-out vicious to curious, and I can't stop myself from exploring him in a way I've never been allowed. Kase and Micah no longer show their scars, and I've never felt them with their human forms, but Lucian likes the reminder, I guess.

"Put me down," I say again, my voice softer than it was before.

Lucian finally flips me off of his shoulder and sets me on my feet. I glimpse his rock-hard abs as his shirt falls down again, and I can't stop myself from staring. Damn his sexy body. It shouldn't get to me the way it does.

Strolling closer, he pushes me, herding me this time until I hit my back on a counter. He locks his fingers to my hips and picks me up, plopping my ass down, and gets right between my legs. I peek down between us and glower at the bulge hardening in his pants. He was utterly wrong about me not liking how he planned to restrain me. Which is actually worse for me.

"Go on and speak your mind, Raven," Lucian says, the heat of his power buzzing over my skin. "Tell me how you're going to try to send me to Hell for inviting your cousin here. Or how you'll never be with me because of it. Tell me you have plenty of other devils to choose from and how you'll bend over and let them train bang you while leaving me out."

This fucker. He's not even letting me get a word out. I want so badly to tell him that he's right about all those things, but another more dominant part of me just wants him to stop. I want him to truly listen to me. Because I don't like this game of cat and mouse. He toys with me over and over again, pushing my buttons, and then he'll show me a glimpse of his softer side. I can't stand the hurricane of emotions warring between us.

"Lucian, why do you have to be a godforsaken dick all the time? Of course I didn't want you to call my cousin and to bring her here. You think I'm jealous or whatever, but I just don't want her involved. I don't want her getting hurt. What I wanted was for you to fucking be nice to me and show me that I'm not wasting my damn time with trying to figure you out. I'm pissed because you're too stubborn to realize that it's not about me or the other devils. I love them. I love being with them. And I fucking would love to have that with you but with the way you act? I can see it'll never be. You can't get off your fucking throne and pull that stick out of your ass that keeps you believing you're above everyone when you're really just stuck and miserable." I blow out a breath and hang my head, letting my hair fall into my face to veil me protectively.

"Raven, I—"

I cover his mouth with my hand. "I'm not done. You're going to let me speak. What you've done is take things too damn far. You know, trying to manipulate me and seduce me into having a physical relationship is annoying but whatever. Trying to use my cousin to do so? If I find out that you've even so much as thought of fucking her—" I point between us. "This will never, and I mean never, fucking happen. You can't prove you want me this way. You know my place and what I'm trying to accomplish. You can agree or disagree in building an eternity alongside me and the other devils. But just know that I draw a line."

He blows a hot breath against my palm and snatches my wrist. Fire burns over his face eating away his handsome features and turning him into his monstrous form. His horns jut out from his forehead and he snarls. My hair flies from my face, leaving me eye-to-eye with him.

"You hypocritical little soul," he mutters, stretching to tower over me. His dagger nails carve lines into the counter at my sides. "You want everything yet want us to share. You tell me that I have a chance, yet you put rules in place that will always leave me the bad guy in your eyes. You make assumptions about things without asking. But guess what? I'm not wasting my time on a mortal who will never benefit me or be able to handle me in all of my sexy glory. Tamia isn't here to push you closer to me. She's here because I want to make a point."

His words sink into me. With the heat in his voice, he should warm me up but fear cools me from my heart outward. "What point, Lucian? Haven't you made enough already? You're here not because you demanded to come but because I've allowed it. I'm trying to reason with you."

"You're trying to play me!" he shouts, growling in my face. "All of you are damn liars, standing against me. I know that Elias managed to escape my brother and is now in hiding. You think you're smart in that regards, but guess what? You've only pissed Heaven off. Do you have any fucking idea what your soulmate has put at risk not following through with the one damn mercy I granted him? Your soul was going to be free no matter what. Now, you face Heaven's vengeance."

"You're a fucking lying bastard. I don't believe you. There

are stipulations to Elias's deal. I know you will try to see him fail." I ram my hands into his hard chest, trying to force him back but he doesn't budge. "You're mad because he outsmarted you and your asshole brother."

"You know, I no longer care about possessing your soul. You will be mine by your own free will. When you fail, and you will fucking fail to bring the rest of Heaven to its knees, your unbound soul will be coveted and fought for. The rest of the devils and demons alike will battle for it. They will tear you apart and make you wish you'd have just given in to me." Lucian's skin ripples as he calms his devilish nature and shifts back into his normal form. "Heaven will never be able to save you. You will beg me."

Rage explodes through me and I swing my arm, slapping him across the face hard enough to startle him. "Fuck off. I'm done trying to crack through all your darkness. You've stolen enough of my light. I'll create a new contract with my devils and be theirs, even if I fail."

A smile twitches across his mouth, turning his sharp features more handsome. "Which brings us back to the reason why Tamia is here. You might change your mind about your decision when you realize what I have in store for her soul. Perhaps offer it to whoever thinks they're most powerful."

His words steal my breath. "You fucker. I'm not going to let you do that."

I manage to push past him and run through the kitchen

and back into the bar. Lucian's heat follows behind me as he stalks me like the mouse he thinks I am. But he's wrong. I'm not a mouse to his cat. I'm a fucking snake and I'll attack. I'll bite.

Tamia sits across from Dante, who watches my every movement as I storm toward him. I reach the booth and blink, trying to keep my anger from making me cry.

I suck in a few breaths and hold out my hand to Tamia. "Come on. I want to catch up. Go somewhere else."

Tamia frowns. "What, I—"

"Now. Seriously. We need to go. Trust me. You don't want to be around Lucian." I snatch her hand and try to pull her from the booth but she resists. "Tamia."

"You can't pick who I hang out with, Raven." Tamia glowers. "Sounds familiar, right? Except Lucian isn't a fucking possessive psycho. He arranged this for us. He's trying to help us mend things Joel fucked up. He's a nice guy, and I don't know why you have such a problem with him. He's probably better than your boyfriend." She motions to Dante. "Or are you with the other guy? Lucian said you didn't want to be with him because you—"

I scream in frustration, spinning on my feet only to slam against Lucian's chest.

With one look into his eyes, I know he's already brought Hell to Earth for me. He's going to force me into an impossible decision.

I jab him with my index finger. "I meant what I said. If you even so much as touch her soul, her body, or even get to her mind, any chance you think you'll have will be over."

He can't manipulate me anymore.

I'm stronger than that.

My devils taught me something I never knew before I met them—everything I'm capable of. Everything I'm willing to do.

They taught me how to fucking win.

18

MICAH

VOICE OF REASON

ELIAS PARKS THE black Maserati along the curb instead of pulling into the drive leading toward the eight car garage. His hands shake as he clutches the wheel, and I nearly didn't allow him to drive. But it was on his list of things to do before he succumbs to his cancer. Which will happen soon. I can see it in his soul. Hear it in his heart and lungs. My once-angelic companion and now mortal friend will soon join us by taking his throne in Hell.

Unfortunately, Elias can't see things the same way I can. He's fallen into a mortal cycle that has stolen the knowledge he once had, and now he carries fear in his mind. Death has been a part of living beings life cycles since creation. Yet despite knowing what happens after his final breath, he can't grasp things completely. I just hope I can help him the same as I would've as an angel. I'm not sure I'm capable of such things any longer. I can barely control the vile darkness tainting my essence with Raven.

"Are you sure we should be here?" Elias asks after a quiet moment. "Maybe we should stay away a bit longer. I'm feeling fi—" His coughing fit gives away his lie, and he rests his head on the steering wheel.

I reach over and rub my hand over his back, unsure of what to do. "Dante said it was pointless. Lucian knows we have you."

Elias groans and clutches his chest, his pain obvious on his scrunched features. "I hope the bastard stays the fuck away. I don't trust him."

"Then trust me. I made Raven a promise to protect you. I will not let either of you down. Why don't you stay in my room? I can take the floor. We can share my time with Raven." I fidget in my seat, messing with the hem of my shirt. "I don't want you two worrying about anything you don't have to."

Elias cranes his neck, meeting my gaze. "Damn. I'm dying soon, aren't I? Give it to me straight. You're acting like a damn angel because of it."

I sigh and lean back in the seat. "Not even I can tell you when for certain, but yes. I think things are wearing on your mortal body and the light that you carry wants to free itself. If you'd—"

"Raven, don't walk away from me!" Lucian's holler rumbles through the crack in the window.

Flinging my door open, I rush from the vehicle, missing whatever Raven says to Lucian. He roars and explodes into his true body, charging forward in an attempt to grab her. Raven flips him off and slams the front door in his face. He tries to chase her inside, but Kase materializes in the doorway, blocking his path. They threaten each other in silence, Kase blindly daring Lucian to do something.

Annoyance rushes through me as he stomps closer to the mansion and where Raven wants to only find reprieve from his intolerable behavior.

"Lucian! Lucian, face me! You will leave Raven alone!" I summon my hellish nature and erupt into my devil form. "Face me!"

Kase smirks and closes the door, not bothering to get involved, letting me handle it. I don't know what happened between Lucian and Raven, but she obviously doesn't want to be bothered by him.

Snarling, Lucian jerks around and swings his fire chain, trying to lash it at me to keep me back. All he does is push me to move forward. I wasn't afraid of him when I was an angel and I'm far from fearful now. He thinks he's above us but now without his tether to Hell, he's on equal ground. But I have something he doesn't. I have the need to protect Raven and her beautiful soul. I haven't gone through everything I have, risked losing her light and affection to ensure I could care for her, or make the decision to be the best devil I can for nothing.

"Stay the fuck out of it and go back to your useless, dying boyfriend, Micah. Leave Raven for those who know how to control her." Lucian whips his chain in my direction again.

I summon a sword, one glowing with my Hell power, from the depths of my kingdom and swing it. It cracks against Lucian's whip, sending his chain toward him. The second he spins to regain control of it, I catapult from the ground and slam into him with my weight. In my devil form, I'm taller and broader. He might have horns, but I have tusks, and I will gut him.

I impale the ground on each side of his head, caging him down. He roars and fights beneath me, trying to flip me off his back but it's no use. We're matched in power and he struck a nerve deep within me. Seeing him chase after Raven and then trying to tell me to stay out of their fight set me off. He doesn't have the right to tell me such things. He doesn't have a mutual claim on Raven like I do. Her fight with him is my fight, and I won't tolerate it anymore. I only complied to appease him and to keep my name on her contract. That no longer matters. Elias proved his love and loyalty not only as Raven's soulmate but also as a devil by managing to end the contract with his death. He outsmarted Lucian and Cassius—all of Heaven and Hell for that matter—and I will ensure things continue to go Raven's way and that her freewill will no longer be compromised by forces that think they're as mighty as the Higher Power or more so.

"Tell me what you've done, Lucian," I growl, pressing into him with my weight. "Raven has been trying to give you a chance, so if you have ruined it, you will face the consequences."

"It's none of your fucking business. This is your last chance to control yourself or you will regret trying to overpower me. I'm not fighting at my full power." Lucian vibrates with a deep rumble of annoyance, humming from his core. He's lying and we both know it.

"It is my business as one of Raven's kings. I will protect her and do anything on her behalf, including dragging you back to your kingdom and figuring out how to keep you there." I blow out a breath of hellfire, singeing the concrete around his head in a cloud of black residue. "I have tried my best to help you make amends and have encouraged her to give you a chance. All you've done is waste my efforts."

"I never asked for your help, you wannabe angelic bastard." Lucian breaks his arm free of my restraint and jabs a blade into my side, sending pain exploding through me.

I roar and rip my tusks free from the ground. Lucian doesn't have the chance to move, roll, or even speak a word as I stomp my hooved hand into his back. He howls in pain, his bones cracking under my force. I swing my arm and turn him over, towering over his wretched form. His black eyes smolder with lava-like light, and I punch him in the face, yearning to see the power fade from his expression completely.

"You will learn your new place!" I shout, swinging my hoof and clobbering him again. "You will accept that Hell will change and grow. You are no longer in complete control. You gave up your incomparable power the moment you handed over the tether to Andre. You will obey our agreement. I will ensure it even if it means taking control and giving up my time here."

"You wouldn't." Lucian heaves a breath, no longer fighting me. We both know that I'm right. He can act like he's the epitome of Hell power, but the Mortal Realm has in fact weakened him.

"I already plan to. Elias will need my guidance in taking his throne. His descent into power to help Raven rise to her rightful place is all that matters." I summon a sword once again. He will feel the truth of my words.

Lucian clenches his jaw, his body rippling with his fury.

In this moment, I feel his fire burning out. He's officially realized the consequences of letting his desire to join the Mortal Realm consume him. Without the tether to Hell, he will face the same punishment he dished out before weaseling his way here.

And I can't wait to hear him scream and beg for mercy.

Pushing up, I stand tall and aim my fiery sword at his chest. He won't die but he will suffer.

"Micah? Hey, man." Elias's voice cuts through the fury pounding in my skull. "Put the sword down. This isn't what Raven would want. Don't resort to his level. It's not worth it."

I whip my head in Elias's direction. "You out of everyone should want Lucian to face punishment for his actions. He stole so much time from the remainder of your mortal life."

Elias steps closer, keeping his hands up in surrender. His eyes flick from me to Lucian, and he remains expressionless under the weight of Lucian's glower. Reaching up, Elias rests his hand on my elbow, his height as a mortal short in comparison to my devil form. I close my eyes for a second under his touch, the gesture reminding me of our lives together as angels and how strong our companionship used to be.

"My mortal life isn't important. I'm breaking the cycle I've put Raven and me in, and when I do, the only thing that's going to matter is the rest of eternity. Just let the fuckhead go and be his miserable self. He creates his own torture fine on his own." Elias grins with his words. "Let us reap the benefits.

Enjoy Raven in a way he can't. She's probably waiting inside. Let's not waste another moment on this asshole."

He's right.

Releasing a breath, I move off Lucian and kick him in the side, sending him rolling a dozen times with the force of my strength. I shift back into my human form and let Elias grab my elbow and pull me toward the door, not waiting to see what Lucian does. Either he finally gets my point or decides to wait until he gets a chance to sneak-attack me—whatever it is, he doesn't retaliate.

I close the front door and stand with Elias in the foyer. Silence greets us, which means Kase didn't immediately take Raven to his room.

"Thanks, Elias," I murmur, needing for him to know that his interference didn't piss me off. "You're absolutely right about Lucian. I just—I cannot grasp why he is the way he is."

Elias presses his lips together, a frown turning him broodingly handsome—more devil than angel and far from mortal. His expression reminds me of the last moments before he vanished from my existence without a word.

"I can't remember the extent of it, but I believe he acts as he does because the fuckhead holds a massive grudge that I didn't jump from grace and instead fell. I think I might have tried to make a deal or something to protect Grace, and I failed to follow through." He shrugs. Tipping his head up, he stares at the glittering chandelier. "Or maybe it's all in my fucking head and he's a dickwad. Who knows? I hope that once I shed mortality and end the cycle, things will come back to me more clearly. I hate only getting tiny glimpses. But whatever. There's no point in regretting anything...except abandoning you the way I had. That was fucked up, and I'm sorry."

His apology touches me deeply in a way I never thought it would. I can't control the sudden blooming emotions unlike anything I've felt in a while, and I grab him and pull him to me, hugging him. He groans and laughs, patting my back as if he's unused to this sort of affection. I start to lean away, but then cool fingers clasp my biceps. Raven releases a light giggle, sandwiching Elias between us. Her eyes shine with unshed tears, but she's not sad. Her soul shines brighter than I've seen it in weeks. I want to bathe in the beauty of her light from what she finds and loves in this moment.

"You guys are so cute. I just want to cuddle the hell out of you." Raven laughs again and snuggles her face into the crook of Elias's neck. "Get used to it, Elias. These devils have a squishy side that will swallow you up and you'll suffocate happily in their affection. I know I do."

"You love this too much," Elias mumbles, trying to turn around to face her.

She doesn't allow him, tightening her embrace. "You bet I do. It makes me want to show you."

Rocking her hips, she playfully humps him, making him

bellow a laugh. If his exertion of his lungs didn't cause a coughing fit, she might never show him mercy. I loosen my hold on him, letting him bow forward. She shifts on her feet, smoothing her hand over his back. A frown flashes across her face for a moment, but she pulls herself together, hiding it from Elias as he regains control and straightens up.

"Always fucking ruining shit," he mutters under his breath.

"Never," Raven says softly. "I don't want you to blame yourself for things out of your control now."

"She's right." I smile and touch Raven's cheek. "It won't be like this forever."

I regret saying the words, because Raven's bottom lip trembles at the thought. I can't imagine what it's like being in her position. She must be the one to claim Elias's life to make him descend. It's their tether that will push him down.

"Maybe we can go upstairs and get this over with, darlin'? Make me a wicked devil now and put me out of this misery." Elias's face hardens with his words. He's steeling himself against his own fear of death. "We'll make it a party or some shit."

Raven doesn't respond to his comment, her beautiful eyes darkening with her thoughts. It would be the most practical thing to do, especially after everything, and all of us know it. If she took his mortal life this instant and sent him to Hell, we could move forward with our plan. I nearly agree with Elias about it.

But then a tear slips onto Raven's cheek and crushes all thoughts of reason. Murdering an evil bastard or killing out of self-preservation is one thing. Taking the life of her soulmate? She's not ready. The idea hurts her on a soul-deep level that burns through my middle. She's tough—Raven is stronger than she thinks—but it's the softer side of her that I want to protect. I never want her to let that side go, and not only because it's the side I've fallen madly in love with beyond comprehension. It's the part of her that will make her an excellent queen in Hell and the force of Purgatory.

She will help return balance to the world and give souls a chance to grow instead of getting lost in their personal Hell forever.

I drape my arm over Elias's shoulder. "Come on now. I think you're only saying that because you want to make love to this beautiful woman."

Elias chuckles, his painful expression smoothing out. "You're not wrong there." Shifting on his feet, Elias swings Raven's arm, smiling. "I'd love to pick up where we were interrupted and do things our way."

Raven's face heats with her blush, though she doesn't rush to give into him. "How about you let me make you something to eat first? Maybe cuddle and catch up on some TV?"

Elias nods his head. "That sounds even better. I've missed you more than you know."

"Then go meet me upstairs. I'll be up in a few minutes." She turns to me. "Mind giving me a hand?"

My heart falters at her words, the weight of her gaze digging deeply into me. I now realize why she wasn't quick to jump into anything with Elias. She wants to talk to me.

"Anything for you, heathen." I smile at her as she shoos Elias away to go upstairs.

I lick my lips and test the openness of his mind, seeing if he'll let me in. He does. "I think Raven needs a bit of a distraction. Might I suggest you undress to cuddle with her? She enjoys that."

Elias peers over his shoulder at me. "You just want to see my naked ass, don't you? It's off limits, Mic."

I try not to react with a laugh, feeling the intensity of Raven's gaze. It takes her lacing her fingers through mine and tugging my arm to get me to move from my spot to follow her into the kitchen.

It doesn't take her more than ten seconds to turn to me. Her blue-green eyes dart back and forth as she searches my expression.

I sigh and hang my head. "Raven, I'm sorry. I know things have been hectic and a bit strenuous between us after...our act of love."

Cutting me off with a kiss, Raven stops me from apologizing. She brushes her lips softly, sliding her tongue across mine to ensure I don't continue. Confusion swirls through my mind, but I don't question her intentions or need.

Raven pulls away and puffs a breath through her pouty lips. "Micah, I can't fault you for what you did and how you handled things. I know this whole life is new for you. It's new for me. I never expected to find myself in this position. I care about you. I care about Kase, Dante, Elias, and Andre too. I might even care a bit about Zade. I can feel his shift. It's like how it was with you before you abandoned grace. And it's all so fucking crazy."

I swallow and play with her hair, pushing it behind her ear. "But is it? I've known since the second you begged for help that you were extraordinary. You have so much light and love that I believe deep in my very being that it's impossible for you to only give it to one person despite my dark desire to keep you all to myself. I know it's wrong. I know it's something you don't want. I just—I can't stop questioning my worth and being enough."

Raven drinks me in, taking a moment to gather her thoughts before speaking. My heart pounds, my whole body buzzing in anticipation. Perhaps I was too honest. I know she appreciates the openness, but she's mortal. She's been trying to save her soul and I haven't been helpful for my own selfish reasons, but I'm done with that behavior. Seeing the ring I gave her still glittering on her finger gives me hope.

"I know it's wrong," I add, breaking the silence. I can't help it.

She offers me a whisper of a smile, her nose scrunching. "Oh, Micah. You are absolutely enough and everything I need you to be. And I know this is hard. It's hard on everyone, but like you told Elias, it won't be forever. We're going to learn and adapt to things, and once I can stop worrying about Elias and Heaven, I think things will get better."

"You mean even better. Because they're all I can hope for right now. I was concerned that you'd turn away from me because of my actions." Heat burns through me as I think about how selfish I was to take initiative to change Raven's contract without her permission. "But even so, I want you to know that I will stand beside you regardless. You're my purpose and always will be."

She laughs breathlessly, her surprise over my words obvious. "All right, you sweet, sometimes naïve devil. Listen up. People make mistakes. Devils too. My ability to forgive might be seen as a fault, but I don't give a fuck. I'm far from the perfect soul you all talk me up to be. If you think that I'm going to give up on you because of the bullshit with my contract, then I should bend you over and spank you with Dante's spiky paddle. This is more than about me. It's about all of you and Hell. About humanity and the souls. It's more than about just saving me."

"I love you, Raven," I say, the urge to declare my feelings in this moment all-consuming. "I love you more than anything. It's unfathomable."

"And to think I've spent who knows how long being afraid of the devil. You are all just a bunch of squishies." She steps closer and hugs me, resting her head against my chest.

I chuckle. "Don't let the others hear you. Kase would love to prove you otherwise."

"It's impossible. I figured out how to make him purr. He's lost to my light forever." She bites her lip between her teeth.

"We all are." If only she knew the extent of it. "You'll make the rest of the angels fall in no time."

She kisses me again. "After I get Lucian to drop to his damn knees."

"I'll help you with him, even if I have to break his legs to force him." I flare my nostrils, trying not to breathe out fire.

Something indecipherable crosses her beautiful features. "You might have to. I'm afraid that if he continues this bull-shit, he'll fight until my very end for control. We need him on our side. I know it's possible, but damn it. He's stubborn."

She has no idea.

I ease away from her and guide her to follow me to the fridge, hearing Elias's thoughts in my mind as he wonders what's taking so long. "It's hard to break something already broken."

She bobs her head, her eyes suddenly lighting up. "Micah, you're brilliant. I think I know how to get to Lucian. I'm not supposed to break him and force him to bow. What I need is to pick up his pieces and help him get himself back together. But how?"

I don't respond. Breaking angels is one thing, but trying to fix a devil who doesn't see his faults?

Impossible.

"I'll do what I can," I say, trying not to giveaway my true thoughts.

Standing on her tiptoes, she kisses me once more. "I'm going to need all of you to work together for me. He's broken now, but I need him shattered. It might be the only way he'll ever truly give in to my light."

19

LUCIAN

BREAKING POINT

HELL, HELP ME. I no longer know which fiery path is the right one to take. A soul should not get under my skin so deeply, twisting and twining, tying up my insides and leaving me weak. If I wanted to be weak, I'd have stayed on Heaven's Army like a good fucking little angel, helping humanity see with my light.

But the Higher Power ignored me. It left me dim and dying for an eternity where I didn't have to suffer through cycle after fucking cycle of mortal souls making the same mistakes over and over again. Before my kingdom rose, the souls rejected from Heaven would be given another chance, another life, another blasted opportunity to fuck up and ruin the beauty and the gifts we worked hard to provide them in the name of the Higher Power.

What a huge craptastic mistake. I saw the shift. I saw the power of souls spreading across their beloved yet uncared for world. How is a soul ever to learn if they have no consequences and endless opportunities to try to gain their chance to enter and steal the light that shines because of angels—because of me?

The Higher Power was far too proud to admit Its fault. It couldn't see how no matter how many souls were born, only a few would live to meet Heaven's standards. It would leave those unfit for such paradise to continue to worsen and destroy the creation of the Almighty. I couldn't stand it. My brethren couldn't stand it.

So I jumped from the high point of Heaven and from the pedestal of the godliest throne, turning my back and taking my light with me to fix what mortal souls have broken. My descent was felt across the realms. My world opened up, and I was ready to guide these souls, to teach them and stop them from making the same mistakes over and over again. With Kase and Dante by my sides on the first jump and my other brethren soon to follow, I knew I was going to change everything. I knew I'd save the world.

But then the light I had planned to use to create my own glorious kingdom vanished. Darkness stole everything. Without my light, there was no chance for souls to follow me. To follow my brethren.

And worse?

The angels I needed and relied on to help me no longer saw my light or looked at it for guidance. All they saw was a scorned angel now forced to not teach and guide souls, but a power that would devour all of those rejected by Heaven. And fuck did the souls get pissed off, losing their ability to cycle over and over.

It's what made me the devil.

I had no choice but to use fear and fire—the only light I could control in the pitch darkness of my new kingdom—to put the wayward, disgraced souls into place. They would not ruin what I gave up everything to create. Humanity blames me for their destruction and punishment, but they should fucking blame the Higher Power. They should blame themselves.

Just thinking about as much and about Raven's mission to change things brings up the animosity that burns through my veins. It was easy before, knowing that no matter how hard Dante and Kase tried and kept to their convictions, we'd never have the place we had envisioned. And I no longer wanted it. I still don't. Humanity hasn't proved anything. They deserve my Hell and my Hell alone.

"Brother, I find it curious that you've been hiding from me." Cassius expands his wings, setting the night aglow. Fucking show off. His comment yanks me from my thoughts, igniting my hatred for the angel who was supposed to stand by me.

"You think I'm fucking scared of you? Hell no. I've been busy trying to get your savages in control. They're bad for my businesses." I clench my fingers into fists and meet Cass's smug expression. His iris-jeweled eyes sparkle in the glow of his wings, turning him way too righteous for me. Jabbing my fist, I punch him in the gut, knocking him away. "Get them under control or I'll add to my collection in Hell."

Cass clenches his jaw, his anger hot enough to nearly convince me that he might have jumped from grace and taken a throne while I was busy trying to get into Raven's pants. The little tease is wearing me down with her hot and cold attitude. She'll never admit how much she wants me to bend her over and spread her open to slide my satanic cock into her wet ass pussy.

Damn body. Damn boner.

I need to get her off my mind. She makes me want to be nice, and I fucking hate it.

"Brother, what you've done...you can only blame yourself with how Heaven's army reacts. As you know, they're only after your contracted souls. Return those warriors you've imprisoned in your kingdom, and perhaps, I can settle the guardians down. After you give me Elias." Cass flares his nostrils and launches toward me.

I dodge out of the way before he can shove me into the side of my car. I should've stayed home and just pestered Raven until she gets too fed up to show me attention, but fuck that. Micah's grown some massive balls and won't let up or let go. He might even have a damn hard-on for Elias.

"Lucifer, I mean it. I've come to give you one final chance to make things right. You know you don't want Elias to take a throne nor do you want Raven to succeed in getting him there. We had a deal. I'd keep him away, and you'd get to keep Hell running as you please. I'd get the guardians to return to their posts where they belong. Humanity suffers with them having to cater to you and your selfish ways." Cassius unsheathes his flaming sword. "Don't make me fight you to make you hold up your end of the deal."

A wicked smile crosses my face at his words. "Fuck, Cass. Are you sure you're still in Its light and grace? The words you speak sound demonic. You know as well as I do that your agreement was with Elias, and I don't have control over his soul or freewill. You can thank the Higher Power for that."

"Of course I fucking am." Cassius intakes a sharp breath at his devious mouth.

I knew the bastard had it in him. He's my worse half after all. Flapping his wings, he looks like a scared little boy about to get the smiting of his life, but he won't. The Higher Power's special angel wouldn't have been given the gift of my favorite language if he wasn't allowed to use it.

I snap my head back, howling a laugh. God, you hear that? This asshole doesn't do things in your name. He's a little bitch and just scared of your punishment, but we both know I'm the only one capable. And I will make him regret ever trying to threaten me.

"Luce, I'm through with your games. Your darkness is seeping into me, stealing my light and I won't allow it. Bring Elias to me by tomorrow or you will learn the true meaning of God's almighty wrath. It is in our army's hands." Cassius bends his knees, preparing to launch into the air.

But I can't just let him go so easily.

Summoning my Hell power, I swing my fire chain and knock his feet out from under him. I propel forward, transforming into my true form midair, and smash my hooves into the concrete, cracking it under my weight. Cassius tries to impale me with his sword, his features hardening in his anger. Snatching it, I clutch it in my hand, fighting against the pain of touching something holy. I will not let him threaten me.

"Cass, you will regret ever trying to fight against me. Elias is under the protection of the very devils that left your side, and I will not fight them just to appease you. If you want Elias, go fucking get him yourself. Try and take Raven too. I'd return to Hell and let your warriors go if you can manage that." I blow a breath of fire, stinging his face. "I'd love to see you t—"

I don't get a chance to finish my threat as Kase lashes his tail at me, slicing it across my leg. I snarl and twist. Cass jabs another sword into my thigh, getting far too close to my devil cock. It's one thing to have a hot woman slap and punch it—I like that—but to have my brother try to impale my fucking nuts with his holy blade? Fuck that.

I stumble back and slam Cass's stolen sword into the concrete inches away from his wings. If Kase didn't yank me with his tail, I could've cut off my brother's precious wings. Catapulting to his feet, Cass runs like the coward he is and flies away. He shoots angelic light in my direction but misses me, dodging Dante as he tries to cut him off. I expect Dante to chase Cass, but he doesn't. He lands with a thud in front of me, hissing with his anger.

"What did I say, Kase?" Dante asks, stretching his wings out. "You owe me a blow job."

Kase growls and shoots his red Hell power at Dante's boots, sending the bastard flying a few feet into the air. The two of them square off, but Kase gives in and flips him off. "You're lucky Raven would fucking get a kick out of it."

I shift, looking for an opening to dodge past them before they fucking start kissing. I know them far too well. Being in the Mortal Realm for so long, isolated and exposed to mortal desire—I know they find pleasure in fucking around. I can appreciate getting sucked off, especially by someone far superior than a needy soul just wanting to appease their master.

But now that they mentioned Raven...I can't wait to stretch her mouth with my girth and see the outline of my dick through her neck.

Kase winds his tail around my hands, binding them together. God damn it. He shouldn't be able to fucking lift me off my feet and swing me—

I heave a breath as the air escapes my lungs. Summoning my Hell strength and power, I try to open a portal to knock us both into it. If I can manage that, I can refill my source and show him that his wrath has nothing on mine.

"Keep trying and I will lift you up by your nuts, Lucian. You're going to be my good fucking boy and let me drag your ass home. I knew you wouldn't resist trying to get Heaven involved again." Kase drops me and slides his damn tail between my legs.

I clench my ass as if the gesture could help me suck my balls into my body. "Would you like to fuck my ass with your tail while you're at it?"

It wouldn't be the first time he slid it in and rubbed me just right to make me blow a load. I can't let his ability to get me off put me on my knees and bent over asking for it. I know that's what he's attempting. That happened four fucking times and he will never let me forget it.

Laughing, Dante steps forward and gets into my face.

"You would love that, wouldn't you? Sucks for you that you're not worthy of his power tail. It's Raven's now. It only goes where she asks, and this shit you pulled tonight? You are fucking done. We have given you enough chances."

"Wai—" I open my mouth to argue and tell him I was clearing my head and giving Raven the space they demanded, not secretly meeting with my featherhead brother, but Dante surprises the fuck out of me by shoving a damn rubber gag into my mouth.

"We're not the ones you need to face. You can make this easy or hard. I have no flying fucks to give how I deliver you as long as you end up on your knees and bowing to the soul that's far more worthy of the power of Hell than you." Kase's eyes glow red with his threat.

My first instinct is to fight and show him that he's not as strong as he thinks he is, but then the glow of angelic light flashes in the sky above me. Fucking angels. Tonight reminded me exactly why I abandoned Heaven, and as much as I don't want Hell to change now, I don't want Heaven to have Raven even more. Or Elias. The guardians and the saviors think they're as mighty as the Higher Power that they worship and fight for, but all they are is a bunch of scared angels.

"Get moving, asshole. If your cock-sucking angels come swooping down, you'll be the one they fight. I'll hold you down and let them smite your dick right off of you. Then I will hand-deliver it to Raven myself, coated in the finest silicone that she can fuck herself with to experience Satan's cock without having to deal with you. That's the only reason she even gives you a second thought, you know." Dante shoves his hand into my back, pushing me forward.

I don't react.

He's jealous as fuck, which means I might be getting closer to claiming Raven as mine. He thinks it's about my body, but he has no idea. The allure of my darkness will continue to tease my light. It's that connection that draws her closer. It'll be that connection that she will fall for, even if I have to get on my knees.

But I can't make shit too easy. I want her to want it. To ask for it. I want her to see that her lovers are no different than me. We're all devils in the end.

Dragging me the few blocks back to the mansion, I remain stern and closed off. They want a reaction from me. They want to see me fight and threaten their dicks. They want to see me break like the many times I've broken them. And maybe that's what I want them to do. Break me. Force me out of my shitty head. Teach me how to get the pussy and soul I crave so that I can keep her for myself. All of this will backfire. I'm a sadist and a masochist—getting off on getting and receiving pain. It's the most addicting pleasure in the universe.

"Kase, Dante? What's going on?" Raven's soft voice echoes through the living room as she rushes down the staircase. Her wild midnight hair blows behind her, giving me a good look at her beautiful face and perky tits with her nipples so tight and cold that I'm certain they'll pierce the fabric at any second.

"We caught this bastard with Cassius. They were arranging a deal to hand Elias back to the angels." Dante sweeps one of his wings to the back of my knees, sending me dropping to the floor.

I remain stiff and quiet. If I act like a dick, Raven will never listen to me. I know her. I know what buttons to push to set her off. I also know what to do to make her pity me. She can't stand the sight of a man she knows contains a helluva lot of power suddenly helpless. It's why she tended to my wounds after the guardians attacked our place.

The memory ignites something hot in my belly, and I can't help thinking about it over and over again. How her lips tasted like Heaven though they kissed like the hot passion of Hell. I had almost given in to her then. I almost controlled my devil nature. But—I can't. I need to be all she wants and needs.

"Lucian?" Raven's bare feet step a foot away from me as she looks down at me on the floor. Glittery polish in Dante's favorite red color sparkles in the light.

Do I have a fetish? Not usually. But right now, I can imagine her feet walking all over me, kicking and stepping on my cock, and how she could pinch the skin of my balls between her toes—and now I want it. I want her to use and abuse me.

To whip me with all her fury. And then when the torture is over, I want her lips to brush against every part of me with sweet whispers that she loved it as much as I did.

"Lucian, fucker." A heavy boot kicks my side and rolls me onto my back as Dante manhandles me. "When Raven speaks to you, you fucking acknowledge her."

I tighten my jaw and tip my head back. And it's like Heaven strikes me in the balls, setting my body aglow at the sight of her smooth, perfect pussy right in my line of view. She wears only a long shirt and no panties, and I can't help marveling in the sexiness that stands above me. With her hip cocked and her hands planted on her sides, I can spot her clit peeking out and teasing me.

"Lucian, you have five minutes to explain yourself before I let the other devils do what they feel is necessary." Raven speaks, but I don't meet her gaze.

Is she wet? Does seeing me on the floor excite her? I need to find out. If Kase or Dante wouldn't sever my arm and send it into the bowels of Hell, forcing me to look high and low for it, I would risk finding out. I crave to get to the point with her that I could act first as a quiet question and see if she lets me continue.

"I'd take whatever punishment to prolong the sight of your sexy pussy forever. If you come a bit closer, I'll make you drip. You'd love it." I lick my lips and draw circles with two of my fingers.

Instead of scowling and getting pissed, she sighs. She doesn't even move or try to cover herself, and I realize her flashing me thrills her. She loves seeing me turned on for her. Loves getting caught.

"The fuck you'll get to touch her." Kase slides his tail around her waist and down her ass. Raven bites her lip, shifts her leg, and lets him slip his tail into her pussy.

My nuts throb, the fire in my being exploding. I can't take my eyes away from the slow, sensual penetration. Kase's tail slides out, glistening wet, and then he teases the seam of her body and enters her ass.

My muscles clench and I reach down and grab my aching cock, desperate to rub one out. I get within inches of taking care of the pain in my balls, but my arms snap up as Kase restrains me.

"You think we're here for your pleasure? Fuck no. You must earn it. Start with explaining to Raven what the fuck you were doing with Cassius." Dante hisses and sticks out his tongue, the barbells glittering in the light.

"No, I think you're here to fucking torture me even when I've done nothing wrong. You have been carrying a damn grudge because I see the world as it is. I've given up on our mission long ago because humanity no longer deserves an eternity outside of the torturous pits. You want me to stand by and suffer for my actions—ones that you aren't innocent of doing." I keep my eyes locked on Raven's, watching her reaction. "You think they're better than me because they give you what you want. But you know what? They can't give you everything you need. You were intended to be mine. Elias and I had an agreement that I would take you and care for you as my queen to save you from Heaven. And then the fucker never followed through. He set your souls on a cycle, ruining everything."

Raven's expression morphs from annoyance to confusion. "What?"

"Your soul was supposed to be mine. Grace was my intended. Had I known from the day I laid eyes on your soul about whose light you had stolen, I would've done things differently. I would've taken you immediately instead of letting mortality ruin you a moment longer." Anger snaps through me the more I think about it. "I was supposed to be your savior from the clutches of Heaven, and you turned to them instead." I glower at Dante and Kase.

Raven clenches her fingers into fists and jumps on top of me, straddling my waist. "I'm not a fucking possession! I'm not Grace! No one can fucking make these kinds of contracts on my behalf. No angel. No devil. No one in Heaven and Hell. I don't fucking belong to you and I never will, Lucian. The same as I don't belong to Kase and Dante. To Micah and Andre. And soon to be Elias. No one owns me! They earn the right to my body and soul, and if they do something and fuck it up, they will face the same damn consequences of losing my affection and love until they can earn it back. Eternity is a fucking long time, and I know people make mistakes, but I also know that you can fucking do better. I want you to do better!"

"Then fucking make me!" I roar, thrashing against Kase's hold.

Raven slides off of me and crosses her arms over her chest. "I shouldn't have to. You should want to do it on your own."

"I can't," I say, feeling the fires of Hell burning through me, stealing away the light Raven's presence alone pushes into me. "I don't have the same freewill as you, Raven. My sins rage too deep. Hell consumes everything inside me."

"You're lying, Lucian." She heaves a few breaths. "You're trying to manipulate me, and I won't stand for it."

"I'm not. Make me fucking do better. Show me! Come on, Raven. You give yourself the Hell of many. Do it! Force me. Beat me. Hurt me. Break me! I want it." I snarl and thrash, my skin smoldering as I lose control, freeing my beast.

Kase and Dante both hit me with power, shooting me off my feet and away from Raven. Micah materializes in the room, his heavy footsteps shaking the world. He stomps his hoof into my gut, stealing my yells of anger away. I writhe on the floor, taking their power and pain, their frustration and annoyance that I failed to keep any sense of a promise. Raven stands in shock and silence, and I refuse to shift my eyes off of her. Nothing could be worse than when the Higher Power denied me and turned me into the most hated being in the universe. Mortals perished if they were even thought to have a connection to me. The world blames every awful thing that happens on me like I could possibly summon nature to do my bidding or possess a soul and steal their freewill. That's not devils or demons. That's other mortal souls and the ones who manage to slip away from both punishment and paradise. Those who get the chance to cycle again but choose to remain lost between realms.

All my thoughts crash through me, stealing the world away and leaving me in a dark place of misery like my kingdom had been before I found the fire in Hell to light it up. Ice slithers through me, the sensation as painful as the Higher Power's rejection. It's as if I fell back into my own personal Hell again. But this time I'm without Kase and Dante. I don't have them to help me to my feet and remind me why we started this in the first place.

"Lucian?" Raven's voice cuts through the darkness, and a pinprick of light glows in the distance. "Let me in."

Her voice chases away the cold, away the loneliness, and suddenly, Raven's glowing soul stands before me in a halo of the most brilliant light. It casts away the darkness, leaving us standing in a world of white nothingness together, untouched by Hell and the Mortal Realm, leaving us exposed in body, mind, and soul.

Her naked beauty entrances me, but not in the same way

it would on a physical level. I can see behind the power of her light and the chains of darkness keeping her close to me. She's the most stunning entity I've ever laid my eyes on, and I intake a small breath. She remains expressionless and silent in front of me, not shifting under the weight of my stare. For the first time, it's me who squirms, unable to stay still as her vibrant gaze drinks me. Her whole soul calls to me, but not in the way most do. It doesn't ask for my mercy and forgiveness. It asks for attention and respect. It asks for the power it needs to be able to take a throne like my brethren. Raven's soul asks for me to finally see its light and ability to drown my darkness instead of letting it consume the both of us.

"I denied Cassius his demands," I finally say, unable to win the staring match. "He threatened war, and I still denied him."

Raven's face softens as her brows crinkle together in curiosity. "Why couldn't you just say that? I gave you a chance to explain yourself but instead you tried to unleash Hell."

I sigh a long breath. "Like the others struggle to contain their hellish nature, I too sometimes get lost in it and can't escape. Your soul does things to me that I'm not used to. You blind me and light my way, Raven."

"You're blaming me for your actions?" she asks, her voice sharpening. "You're blaming your nature and Hell. But Lucian, you need to blame yourself. I'm tired of trying to come up with excuses. This connection I feel to you—it's not enough for me. Denying Cassius one time doesn't make things better either. I spent far too much of my life getting broken by a man who would apologize and kiss me to make things better. And for too long, I allowed it. I accepted it. And then he tried to destroy me. I'm not perfect and I might never be intended for Heaven, but I will not stand for your shit anymore, hoping you come around and will be a part of the Hell you wanted."

I bow my head. "I just—"

"No. Don't speak. I can hear another excuse without you even forming the words. I'm no longer going to fight with you or let you manipulate me. You're either going to be a part of our team or you can fuck off and go back to your kingdom. This is your last chance. I'm not your possession or reward. I'm not obligated to you at all. You must earn your place and learn that we're one power under the name of Hell." She steps closer and clutches my cheeks. "I know you have it in you. I can see it and feel it now. It's the only reason why I'm here. The others might have given up, but Lucian, I don't want you as my enemy."

"You were never my enemy, Raven," I say, letting her light engulf us. "But I resist and fight because I know your power. You will be my ruin."

"If that's what you need. I heard your prayer, you know. Your desire to be broken, so you could rebuild. I'd like to help you." Raven leans closer, her lips mere inches from mine. "What do you say, Satan? Be my bitch? Succumb to my power? I'll even give in for a power switch once I know I can trust you."

I test her resolve and close the space but don't kiss her. I won't. Not until she does it first. "I'll be none of that fucking shit, but I will accept your offer for help. After the shit with my brother...it reminded me why I left Heaven."

"Then come back to us. Make amends with the others. Show them you're ready to be part of our team." Raven must sense my desire to kiss her, because she teases me with her lips, caressing her light to my darkness until we're merely shadows.

I nod, caressing my fingers to her cheek. "What have you done to me? I haven't felt like this in...I can't remember in how long."

Raven smiles. "Savor it, Satan. It's your one free pass to my soul. From now on, if you want my attention and closeness, it must be earned."

In this moment, Raven reminds me why I created Hell in the first place.

I'm ready to give in to Raven's light.

With her, we'll be Heaven's undoing.

20

ZADE

DEMONIC BONDS

LAUGHTER FILLS THE air, the glow of fire illuminating the patio of the devil's estate. It looks as if they're having some sort of gathering, but only among themselves with Raven. She claps her hands and squeals, letting Dante spin her around and into Micah's arms. I drink in the sight of her brilliant soul, the chains of Hell barely visible. Something has shifted, and I can feel it deep in my essence. I'm nearly entranced by Raven's swaying hips, how her dark hair sweeps with her sensual movements, and how everyone, including me and Cassius beside me, watches her shine like the star Lucian was intended to be.

"Is it possible for a mortal to steal angelic light even after they've abandoned it long ago?" I ask, keeping my voice low. I swing my legs, feeling anxious in my spot on the wall surrounding the property. "Doesn't Raven remind you of—"

"Blasphemy. Utter, despicable, blasphemy. I don't understand." Cassius cuts off my question with his complaint, but he's not talking to me. He closes his eyes and summons access to Heaven, lighting his palms aglow. "Why didn't it work? I gave Lucian what he wanted. He could've done as I asked and thought of the world for once."

I fold my hands in my lap and shrug without verbally responding. Cassius is far too upset to think outside of what he believes is his failure. He was so certain that Lucifer would bring Elias to us that he even managed to get the guardians to fall back already. He had used his knowledge of Lucifer to convince them that he had it under control.

Now, he's at a loss. I can feel his emotions radiating from him as if they're my own. Instead of trying to encourage him to keep pushing on, I decide to drape my arm over his shoulders. Sometimes, he just needs to feel I'm here and know I won't abandon him or grace. He's always felt responsible for Lucifer's undoing the same way I feel like there should've been more I could've done for Andre. Maybe if I hadn't let him make his own decisions and kept reminding him that there is a bigger purpose outside of one soul. Maybe I could've gotten more involved and helped him guide her away from Hell instead of letting him follow her down. I... There is no point in holding onto the negativity that burns my chest. It's too late. All I can do is continue to follow the light of the Higher Power.

Cassius groans and shoots his heavenly light away, letting it fade on the grass below. "Something must be done. Lucifer cannot lose himself in Raven's light. We're doomed otherwise."

"Cass," I say, squeezing him. "Don't think like that. Have faith. Hell cannot rise like they intend unless Seven Sinners take their thrones with Raven and Lucian. I'm not going anywhere, and neither are you."

"Hell doesn't need us to put Heaven at risk, Zade. Look at the damage it has already caused." Throwing his arms out, Cassius motions to something invisible I can't see. "The guardians have followed new paths, leaving many, many souls unprotected. The legions of Hell will start to notice. They will ruin everything."

"Give humanity credit." I frown at his words, watching him drop down to his feet. "The Higher Power does."

"And look what happened because of it. Because of Lucifer. I need to fix this. It is my purpose. Now stay here and call me if they leave." Without waiting for me to respond, Cassius launches into the air and disappears into the night like a shooting star heading toward the atmosphere.

I bow my head and clasp my hands together. Please give Cassius the strength and the hope he needs. My prayer hums through my body, igniting me aglow, and I savor the connection to home.

Another melody of laughter trickles through the air, and I watch Raven grab Kase's tail and draw him to her. He scoops her up into his arms and kisses her, blindly heading toward the back door where Elias holds it open. Dante smacks Kase's behind, getting him to move, and the other devils shove each other and play-fight, fooling around until Raven shouts that the last one to the couch has to act like a footstool for her as she catches up on her show with Elias.

The roars and growls mixed with swears and chuckles draw me from my spot on the branch. I know I shouldn't abandon my place at this safe distance, but it's like Raven's soul pulls me to her like a magnet. Seeing her interact with the devils and how they treat her like a lover and plaything, and also the most important being in the universe...I must find out why. I've kissed her lips and felt her soul. She opens something deep and new inside me, but a part of it scares me. I can't comprehend just giving up my eternity for another moment of her time.

Yet here I am, strolling across the lawn to peek through

the window of the entertainment room where Lucian rests on his hands and knees, glowering in humiliation as Raven stayed true to her word and props her bare feet on his shirtless back.

"You shouldn't be here, Zade." Andre's deep voice rumbles behind me. My heart sinks into my stomach, his familiarity cracking open my essence, spilling out the wave of hurt I've done my best to suppress.

"Neither should you," I say, keeping my back toward him. If I turn and face him, I'll have to see him for the devil Hell made him. If I keep my eyes on the window and Raven, I can pretend a moment longer that he's still my angelic companion. "I'm merely keeping an eye out and ensuring Lucifer doesn't destroy the world. Someone must do it now that you've lost sight."

Cruel? Perhaps. But I've been silent for far too long.

"Don't you ever regret it? You can't be happy with the eternity you've chosen. Look how the other devils relish in the light of Raven's soul while you remain tethered and bound like Lucifer himself." I clench my fingers into fists, the heat of Andre's fire warming up my wings. If he could stroll through the ring of hellfire caging him, he would. I imagine he'd do more than chastise me. He'd try to blaze my wings and make them look like his. Dark, evil, and as far from light as possible.

"The only thing I regret is not claiming my throne sooner." Andre's firelight sets the house aglow. It's a wonder that none of the other devils come looking. "You think I need pity, but really, I'm the one who pities you. You fight a losing battle. You choose a force that doesn't even acknowledge anything you accomplish, always silent and judging. Never showing anything other than light. We create our own light and kingdoms, Zade. Our purpose is far better than watching humanity fuck up over and over again. And with Raven? You have no idea what's to come. I won't be tethered here forever. I'll get my time on Earth."

I try so hard not to react but the darkness of his comment stabs me right in the gut. He should regret abandoning grace and leaving me. I know somewhere inside him the capability to see it is there. I just need to remind him. I need to show him that he's lost and confused. He has no idea what he's talking about and in the end, his mortal desire and lust isn't worth it.

Gathering heavenly light in my hands, I scowl and fly forward, risking the ring of hellfire to launch at Andre. He expects me and opens his arms wide. I chuck my power at him, hitting him in the chest and sending smoke wafting through the air. His back hits the barrier, not letting us slide out of the summoning circle, and I land on top of him, straddling his waist.

"How does it feel being so close to me?" Andre asks, his touch alone doing strange things to my body.

With one breath of the air in his space, my body buzzes.

With two? My pants tighten with my lust, and I jerk back

and clutch my erection through my pants, the sensation of my hand alone zinging me with pain and pleasure and an undeniable need to rub myself in prayer, hoping my body returns to normal instead of threatening to bust through my clothes.

"You love it, don't you? The pleasure? Imagine what comes with it if you just accept where your place should be." Andre pushes from the ground, his form rippling with the movements. "Imagine what it could be like with Raven. You think you know what Heaven is supposed to feel like but what we've known is truly a false deity. The divine lingers between her legs. In her mouth. Everywhere on her body. Just one taste and you'll be on your knees, Zade. You'll be begging for her affection and love more so than you ever thought possible."

I fall on my back and lie frozen with Andre towering over me. He expands his leathery black wings and smiles, his handsome face lighting up with the fire in his eyes. I suck in a few breaths, trying to push away my lust and desire. I'm so unused to these things that it makes me question whether or not Andre speaks the truth. That maybe I've been misguided all along.

I shake my head, forcing the strange thoughts from my mind. No. That's Hell talking and trying to lure me into its dark and fiery depths.

"Maybe if I showed you something Raven might be willing to share with you...if you're brave enough. I haven't forgotten our former companionship. I see things clearer. Hotter.

You would make a good pool of pleasure for Raven and I. We'd love to explore you." Andre's eyes close into half-slits, heavy with his fantasy about...

I clutch myself and squeeze my backside together, the thought both thrilling and exciting.

And completely and utterly impossible.

"Isn't that right, little hellion?" Andre asks, his voice turning from dark and dangerous to light and teasing. "Don't you think Zade would have a great time with us? Perhaps in the middle?"

Raven's soft intake of breath draws my attention to her and away from the throbbing pulse shuddering through my groin. I never even felt such desperation in the Kingdom of Lust when I traveled through Hell with Raven. But something about Andre and Raven's closeness, his words, her quick breathing and the soft moan...I nearly give in.

"I—No. I must go." I scramble to my feet and attempt to run out of the summoning circle before Andre tries to capture me and pressure me into something I still struggle to grasp.

Grabbing my leg, he yanks my feet out from under me and I stumble forward, crashing into Raven. We both fall to the ground together with me on top and her legs open and hooked around me. I drop my gaze to her naked body, exposed with her shirt rolled up.

I moan at the heat of her seeping into me and roll off her, but she doesn't let me go. She matches my movements, getting on top of me, and I gasp and squeeze my eyes shut at the sight of her beautiful body bare and open, her light dimmed by Andre so that I find myself yearning to stare at her.

Raven's gentle hands touch my chest. "Zade, open your eyes. You don't have to be ashamed of looking at me. It's just a body, remember? I find it far more intimate when you prod at my soul."

It takes everything in me to open my eyes and glance into her smiling face. She slides a bit closer until her hair veils the world around me, blocking Andre. I blow a breath at the sudden quiet of the world and how Andre doesn't try to push me into a lust-filled haze. I honestly don't think it would be a push in this moment. I'd willingly give in as long as Raven keeps smiling at me like this. As long as she tames Andre's wild side and helps remind me of him as an angel. Because I miss him as my companion. I miss talking to him and just being in his company. The devil version of him runs hot and cold and everything in between, and I just—I don't know. I can't. I won't. I don't see the worth in changing my eternity like he has.

"Zade, I just wanted to say thank you for trying your best to bring Elias back to me. I know the task was difficult." Raven touches my blond hair, twisting the strands in her fingers. Her gentle touch does nothing for the unfortunate state of my body, and I can't help imagining what it would feel like if she sits on me while I'm naked too. Is Andre right about the feeling? Could a connection with her body truly compare to Heaven?

"You should give him a little reward, little hellion," Andre murmurs, breaking the heavy silence. "Maybe a little kiss. Tease him. Show him what he's missing."

Raven glides her tongue over her bottom lip, drawing my attention to her mouth. "I do love kissing you, Zade. I think it's the perfect way to show my thanks, especially because you helped us prepare for the attack by the guardians."

"You like kissing me?" The question sounds breathy coming from my mouth. I never thought I'd want such a confirmation. She's the only one I've kissed, and it felt so sinfully intoxicating yet also heavenly. Nothing about kissing Raven could ever be bad or wrong.

Her smile widens and she hums her agreement. "I do. Can I kiss you now?"

I don't respond with my voice and instead arch up and pull her close, clutching her cheeks in my hands to guide her mouth to mine. She releases a small breath of a laugh and slides her arms around my neck, risking burning herself on my feathers but teasing me anyway as she maps out the muscles of my shoulders. Her warm lips caress mine lightly at first, testing and teasing me, sending an even greater ache to my pelvis. I drag my hand down her back and pull her into me, feeling the smooth skin of her butt cheeks.

"You taste amazing," I murmur, easing back only to have

her nip my bottom lip between her teeth and tug me close again.

Her desire ignites a passion in my soul, lighting the two of us ablaze, and I glide my tongue into her mouth and kiss her deeper, harder, and with everything incredible in my soul. The weight of her body rubs against my excitement, and she rocks her hips harder, grinding on me like she wants and needs more. I want it too. I want to give her whatever it is she needs from me. Perhaps our affection wasn't intended to be my undoing. Maybe this is how I bring her back into good grace and away from Hell. This could be why I'm drawn to her.

"You're so hard," she whispers, reaching between us.

"For you," I murmur, breaking away from her mouth and licking her throat.

Andre's wide smile smacks sense into me, his devil form peeking through as he drinks in breath after breath of our lust. His power is getting to me and twisting my desire for Raven into something dangerous. Something I worry that will leave her broken. She could like me as an angel and show me this attention because our light attracts one another's. Nothing is certain until I can unhook Andre's claws from her and have time to see her without his fire shining so brightly with ours.

"Zade? Zade, what's the matter?" Raven frowns, her breath panting. "Why have you stopped?"

I swallow the burning in my throat. "I...I can't do this to you. You're far too beautiful and pure."

Her mouth twists to the side and she continues to clutch me, hanging on for dear life. If I wasn't afraid to fly away with her, I would. But I know she hates that. She fears Heaven's warriors—her worry valid and warranted. The guardians won't stop. Cassius won't either. The thought of such a brilliant, hypnotic light getting snuffed out hurts me deeply.

"Me, pure?" Raven's face brightens with her amusement. "I've probably sullied your virgin, sweet angel baby existence by just sharing a breath."

I might not have the mortal experience of a physical relationship, but I know what one could lead to. I already find myself drawn to Raven. I don't know if it's because Andre has a claim on her or if she's just dug into my light and I can't imagine a life without her in this realm. Whatever it is, I know that I can't in good faith give in to Hell. There is no place or throne for me in Hell.

"Raven," I say softly, petting her hair away from her shoulder. "The condition of my mortal form does not contribute to what I mean. I'm—I'm worried about other things."

I can't bring myself to admit why I carry such reluctance apart from knowing that my path is intended to remain in the light of the Higher Power.

"Like what? You're a tough, buff, intimidating savior. What are you worried about?" She presses her lips together, keeping her stare locked on mine. "Maybe I can help ease your worry."

It's my turn to chuckle. "It's not your job to take on such burdens. They are for only me to bear."

Andre growls from behind Raven, stealing my attention from her. "If you dare reject my beautiful hellion because of some mundane bullshit, you better get your ass out of here. I'll not let you steal an ounce of her light with upsetting words. You were only welcome here because Raven desires you."

I huff a breath. I should go. I really should. But Raven's soft kiss to my jawline begs me to stay. So I hug her a moment longer, basking in just her presence as she gathers the thoughts on her mind to speak them aloud.

"Don't let the big dick get you down, Zade. I know you don't want to reject me," Raven murmurs, brushing her lips to my ear. "But I want to know, why? Why are you resisting something that will be so perfect and powerful between us? Your companion is here and would enjoy having you around. I don't even think he thinks you're rejecting me. I think he feels it."

I close my eyes and droop my shoulders. "I still care very much for Andre. It pains me in the depths of my being not being able to turn to him whenever I need him...but this life?"

"It's not evil like you think, Zade. It's only different. The devils want a way to help humanity as a whole. I mean, look at me. Look at how quickly the Higher Power forced you to reject me. Look how Andre had to abandon grace to save my life. How Micah only wanted to save my soul. Those aren't acts that should damn someone, but here they are. You have to see what I see, Zade. Andre wasn't a bad angel. If anything, he was better. Braver." Raven tickles my ear with her breath. "I need you to help me understand why. Why fight for something so unfair? Why not take your eternity into your own hands and do something that feels good and right, even if it's unholy?"

Her words stab into me, tightening my chest. A part of me wants to deny the truth she speaks. If I do, I'd just be lying to myself.

"I—I can't answer your questions, Raven. I'm sorry." Sliding her off me, I set her gently on the ground. "I need to leave. Please be careful. I think something dangerous is heading your way."

Raven tries to snatch my leg, but I stumble out of her reach and flap my wings, propelling myself into the air. I soar higher and higher, losing myself to the night and the beauty of the world around me until the midnight sky shifts to azure, and I land on a sparkling, rainbow prism-like pathway leading into my home away from home.

Soft murmurs sound through the tranquil air, the beautiful hum of a melody from long ago strummed on strings of the most precious lines of creativity from some of history's most talented souls. I stride into my sanctuary and slow, inwardly groaning at the intrusion when I've come here to find tranquility. My emotions run far too hot and wild, and I just wanted some peace.

"You ignored my first call, Zade," Cassius says, tightening his jaw. "Is something the matter?"

I shake my head a little too furiously and slump into a seat made of light and ethereal stone but feels like the sky engulfing me in the lightest clouds. I didn't ignore his call. I never heard it. My ears still ring with Raven's laugher. Her breathless moans. I can't get her out of my mind even with Cassius penetrating me with a nearly painful gaze.

"Nothing is the matter. I'm sorry if I wanted to make sure the devils weren't causing havoc." I cringe at the snap of my voice.

"We won't have to worry about them much longer." Mikail's voice strikes me like lightning, and I straighten my back to peer at him. I nearly tuned him out with my arrival, my disconnection to the grace of light taking a bigger toll on me than I had realized.

Cassius plops onto the seat beside me and bumps me with his shoulder. "The time has come, Zade. The devils are far beyond reason. It's time we take them down by force."

I blink a few times, the strange feeling of danger hitting me sharply in the gut. How could I have known to warn Raven? I just hope she heeds my warning and doesn't put all of her faith in the devils.

Because with Cassius's words, I hear the thundering sound of Heaven's army gathering. I sense the static of heavenly power crackling in the air.

"It's time for war, Zade. The devils must be sent to Hell. It must be done. The portals to the Mortal Realms will finally be sealed off and guarded how they always should've been. Our universe depends on it." Cassius stands and unsheathes his dagger. "I'm going to need you by my side. Can I depend on you?"

Does he know? Does he feel my hesitation?

I open my mouth to convince him that there has to be another way, but the sound of Heaven's army turns deafening. It turns all-consuming and unavoidable. This isn't just a war. It could be the end. Whether it's Heaven or Hell? I pray for neither. I pray for the Higher Power to shine a new light over us, to guide our way.

"Zade? Are you with me?" Cassius repeats. "I can't do this without you."

I clench my fingers into fists and dip my chin in agreement. "I'm always with you."

Cassius flaps his wings, launching up, breaking through the ethereal ceiling created out of pure light. Standing in my spot, I look up at his silhouette in the shining world.

Dear God, please have mercy on all of us.

Please have mercy on my fallen brethren's and Raven's soul.

21

RAVEN

ALL GOOD DEEDS

TALK ABOUT ONE helluva slumber party.

A hot, heavy arm hangs over my waist as Dante's gigantic boner rests right between my legs as if he uses it to better align my body for sleeping on my side. Kase nuzzles his nose to my neck, probably awake all night like he tends to do, silently asking me to wake up and give him some morning attention.

"If you two start fucking out here, be prepared to get shot

with my load," Lucian mutters, staring like a creepy bastard from the recliner in the corner. "I'll aim for both of your faces."

Kase ignores him, continuing to lick my throat and test my resolve with his finger, rubbing my clit despite Dante's hard-on blocking his access to enter me.

"Do it, and I'll bite you in your balls. You'll be so high you'll think that you're blowing glitter bombs from your dick hole." Dante's fangs tease my shoulder, and he nips my skin, molding his mouth over the bite mark, sucking a bit of my blood.

I can't stop the giggle from escaping my lips. "Shhh. He's going to think you're going to suck him off while you're at it."

Dante hisses. "Fuck that. Only if you asked, and even then, we'd have to trade something. Maybe a ride in that tight ass." The horny bastard eases his hips back and aligns the tip of his cock to my asshole.

I relax instead of clench and arch my back just enough to get him to stop. He damn well knows if he tries to fuck me without lube, there will be equal punishment.

"Sounds like a fair trade, Raven," Lucian calls out, getting up from his chair. The bastard adjusts his cock in his pants a little too much, snagging my attention.

It takes Kase biting my boob to snap me out of it. "You'll take a bite to the balls and a blowjob so that Dante can fuck me in the ass? What the fuck is wrong with you?"

"I have to get my rocks off somehow, and I doubt your pouty mouth will open wide for me today." Lucian tries closing the distance, but Kase silently stops him with a whip of his tail, keeping him back.

"Not only today. Maybe this fucking decade. Now go get the door. Someone triggered the barrier. Pay more attention next time. You're supposed to be on fucking guard today." Kase doesn't pull away from my boob, shifting my shirt with his chin, attempting to suck my nipple into his mouth.

"I am on fucking guard. It's Vincent, and I'm not going to act like his damn bitch by rushing. He can wait outside until I'm good and fucking ready to deal with his bullshit." Lucian's eyes light with fire, but Kase shifts onto his elbow, blocking my view.

"Just fucking answer it and send him away. I don't want him within a five mile radius of my angel-girl. He should be decapitated and strung out through Hell for what you made him do." Kase growls and sits up. "You know what? I'm going to deal with him."

Sliding off the couch, Kase embraces his devil side and morphs into his monstrous beast. Dante tries to roll me over him to sandwich me with the back of the couch, but I want nothing more than to watch Kase disembowel Vincent and throw his guts across Hell. Call me twisted. I'll accept it. He's such a disgusting piece of shit demon that he deserves far worse. Someone should rip his damn fangs out and shove a bunch of dismembered demon cocks down his throat until they come out his ass and start the process all over again.

Damn. Maybe I'm not intended for Purgatory with these thoughts.

Or maybe...I wonder if one of my devils will let me help them remodel part of their Hell kingdoms. Who knew such a thought would excite me when it came to people who hurt and tormented me. Joel can join the fuckhead and they can take turns feeding each other.

"Kase, damn it. Wait. I will handle it. His power surge is with me, and not you. If you fuck with my legion, you'll ruin bullshit I've been working on putting into place here for weeks." Lucian pushes from the recliner and tries to whip Kase's paws out from under him. "Please, fucker."

Did he just ask Kase semi-nicely?

Kase freezes and twists his torso, his eyes glowing ruby with his power. "Come again?" Yup. I thought I heard Lucian correctly. "Did you just say please?"

"I don't think we all heard him correctly," Micah says, stretching his arms over his head, woken up by Kase's quaking footsteps. "Repeat yourself, Lucian."

I cover my mouth with my hand, hiding my smile. Lucian deserves to get hassled by my devils after all of this bullshit, and I'm all here for it. Lucian knows it too, because he glowers but doesn't argue or start a fight.

"Kase, please let me handle my bitch-ass demon," Lucian

says, practically spitting fire with the words.

Dante chuckles and adjusts me in his arms. "I think our pretty soul would love to see exactly what that means. You better manhandle him like the fucker he is, Lucian. Give us a good show."

Lucian glowers even more, but once again, he keeps his internal fury to himself. And actually, I think he might like the humiliation, though he doesn't admit it. How do I know? His hand hasn't left his cock. He's not rubbing it to get my attention anymore. He's rubbing it because he's turned on.

Throwing his arms out, Lucian summons his Hell form. "Fucking fine, but you all better be quiet. If you even think of trying to fuck with me in front of Vincent, I'll—"

A pillow flies across the room, smacking Lucian in the face. Elias rubs his hands on his cheeks, pretending like he didn't just shut Lucian up.

I lose it. Laughter bubbles from my throat, and my whole body shakes with my amusement. It must be contagious, because Kase and Dante bellow laughs, and Micah holds out his hand to high-five Elias. Lucian looks on the verge of exploding, but an annoying thudding bangs on the door, sounding as if Vincent might be trying to break it down.

Grumbling, Lucian storms away, gathering power in his hands. I grin like a maniac at Dante, motioning to him to carry me and follow Lucian. Kase sticks by our side and Micah helps Elias to join our audience.

"You better live up to your satanic expectation for Raven," Kase goads, whipping Lucian's ass with his tail. "Consider this round two of your initiation."

Lucian flips us all off, adjusts his cock once more, and yanks the door open. Fear seizes through me at just the sight of Vincent, and I regret thinking I was ready to see the bastard again. Angry tears burn in my eyes, blurring the world. I hate myself for not being as tough as the devils. I hate that just the sight of Vincent drags me back to the warehouse where he tortured and killed me, sending me to Hell.

"Oh, shit!" Elias shouts, laughing. I think Lucian does something, but I still can't see.

"My liege, please! Let me speak. The guardians—" The door slams, startling me and cutting off Vincent's pleas.

"Micah, you and Elias make sure Lucian handles his bitch ass. Let us know what the bastard angels have done. I have to get Raven out of here." Dante's warm hand rubs on my back, smoothing my trembles. "She wasn't ready."

The world shifts and bumps, and I hide my embarrassment and fear the best I can by kissing Dante's throat. I can't believe I had such a strong reaction with just one look at Vincent. It was the same when I glimpsed Joel in Hell. How can these bastards still take up even an ounce of my headspace? I can't stand how vulnerable I feel.

My ass plops down on the cold marble countertop of Dante's gigantic bathroom, snapping me out of my wild, emotional haze. I hear Kase turn on the bathwater, and a fresh lavender scent wafts through the air.

"Hey, pretty soul. Look at me," Dante says, cupping my cheeks in his warm hands.

I lick my lips and stare at his diamond-shaped pupils. Rubbing his fingers under my eyes, he smears away tears I hadn't realized splashed onto my cheeks. His fangs peek out from his full top lip, drawing my attention to his kissable mouth. We breathe together in silence with only the sound of the filling tub and calming fragranced air around us until my muscles loosen and I suck in a breath.

"I'm sorry. You looked so ready to watch a beat down that I didn't think about what you'd have to face first to enjoy it." Dante hisses under his breath.

"I want him dead," I say, my voice shaking.

"He will be by tonight." Kase's deep voice rumbles through the air. "If Lucian wants even a chance to make amends, sending Vincent back to Hell will be his first requirement. The fact that he still lets him think he's in charge of this realm already has me wanting to change my mind."

I nod my head, grabbing the front of Kase's shirt, getting him to step close enough that I can cradle his head next to Dante's and share a three-way kiss with them so neither has to wait for my affection.

"Good," I murmur, tracing each of my hands down their bodies, loving the different sensations I feel on each of them until I reach their bulges, hard and throbbing just for me. I half expect either a sword fight to ensue or their swords to cross and stuff me, testing my flexibility. "Now distract me. I've missed you both."

Kase releases a deep purr, the vibration enough to zing tingles between my legs, spread wide and exposing my body the way they want. "Fucking finally, right? I've been dying to get a piece of your ass."

Dante whacks him. "Don't start. I know you two have a deal, but Raven needs her way right now. She needs to know that she is powerful."

Kase's face lights with a wicked smile, and he leans into Dante and whispers, "Maybe finally give our soul the power switch you always tease her about."

Oh, boy. I don't know exactly what that means, but my body is totally on board to skydive into the Kingdom of Kink with Dante. I have a vague idea of what Kase is suggesting, and the idea thrills me more than I realize.

Slipping a warm finger inside me, Kase hums. "Just feel how excited she got by the thought."

Dante's expression smolders me to my soul, burning me in passion as he tests my body, adding pressure by joining Kase in fingering me. And damn it, it feels amazing. I lean back and rest my head on the mirror, letting Kase adjust my legs so my heels rest on the counters by my sides. I moan at the stretch of my muscles waking up from sleeping, and Dante kisses me again and tells Kase to take care of me while he gets things ready. He crosses the bathroom and shuts off the tub, leaving it steaming-hot and waiting for when we're ready. I'm sure I'm going to need it. I can already tell the second Kase drops to his knees and buries his face into the heat of my body.

"Oh, fuck," I moan, the intensity of his mouth's desperation sending pleasure through me in one amazing wave after another.

Grabbing my hips, he curls me more, going straight for my ass. I gasp and tug his hair, dropping my hesitation after only a second. Kase always makes me feel utterly and completely comfortable doing what he wants and pushing boundaries to discover new things he thinks I'll like.

"Fuck, you're going to feel so good, angel-girl. I can't wait. You have no idea how hard it's going to be for me to not do what I fucking want." His words hum as he licks and teases me with his finger, strumming his thumb over my clit until my muscles lose control, and I bang my head on the mirror with my orgasm.

I gasp and pant, squirming with my need for more. "You know, it doesn't have to be only my way right now," I murmur, joining my hand with his, craving to see his excitement as I touch myself.

He tips his head up, his whole face brightening with his lust. His excitement battles with mine, and I laugh and shriek as he buries his face between my legs again like a wild beast. Lifting me on his shoulders, he manages to blindly make his way out of the bathroom as I clutch onto his head for dear life, the sensation of him devouring me like I'm all he's going to get for the rest of eternity making my heart race and my stomach flip, the adrenaline hitting me hard and where it counts. I screech as the world blurs and Kase drops me onto Dante's bed. I can't even breathe a moan before he flips me over and spanks my ass, dropping to his knees once more. He slides his tail into me, rubbing me just right that my body explodes with an orgasm.

"Fuck yeah!" Dante shouts, his voice echoing through the room. "I fucking love a good soaking."

"So do I." Kase rolls me to my back and grabs my ankles, yanking me to him. His roughness turns me on. His power exhilarates every nerve-ending in my body. "This is our chance to celebrate. Ride the kink train into pleasure oblivion. She said I can take her ass."

Dante's smile widens, and he flops beside me. "What? Fuck yeah. I'm ready to give our soul what she wants and needs while you give her what she has yet to realize she will desire when we're through with her."

"You ready for this, Raven?" Kase says, yanking his belt off, the act alone shooting electricity through me.

I inhale slow breaths, trying to control my body. "I'm so fucking ready. You have no idea how much I needed this right now. Needed you."

Dante follows Kase's lead and kicks out of his pants and flexes his muscles, showing off his massive boner. I can't stop myself from wanting to tease and please them, so I slide off the bed and crawl the few feet toward them on my knees. Taking each of their cocks in my hands, I suck on them, taking turns, tasting the different sweetness of their bodies. I savor the sensation of their fingers combing my hair and how Dante rolls my hard nipple between his fingers. Kase ties his tail around me and slides it between my legs fucking me in a way that leaves me trembling.

And then Kase fists my hair in his hand and yanks, slowing me down. He tips my head back, towering over me, his dominance as hot as ever. I release an uncontrollable whimper, my body begging for him to keep going. This is a moment I never expected to feel so incredible and exciting. Being with two devils is always a test of my body, and they have proven how strong I truly am.

"That's enough for us, angel-girl. It's time for Dante to give you the one thing you don't know how much you need." Kase's heavy-lidded gaze shifts from me on my knees to Dante. "I will be here for both of you as you need. You're in charge, Raven."

Dante helps me to my feet while Kase climbs onto the bed and watches, stroking himself. I know how incredibly hard it is for him to give up an ounce of control, and if Dante didn't dangle some kind of underwear—no, not underwear, a strap on—and a big ass dildo with thick veins adding texture.

I stare at the piece in surprise and excitement. I knew that Dante wanted to give me his power and to have me peg him, and damn. Who knew I'd be down and ready for this.

I can't stop the silly smile from lighting my face, and Kase cracks up from the bed, watching me stroke my fake cock the size of a devils' as Dante helps me strap in. And then the cute little bastard hits a remote and I realize that this is more than just me getting ready to embrace Dante's power. He's getting me off too. I squirm and shift, clutching his shoulders as he inserts the much smaller toy into me. I rock my hips, messing around and nearly fall over from pleasure because it penetrates me deeper.

"I don't think I've ever seen our soul so excited. You sure you can handle her having all the power, Dante?" Kase asks, grabbing a bottle of lube to slick over himself, masturbating in front of us.

I step closer to Dante and grab him by the cock, standing up on my tiptoes. "You want my big cock in your ass, don't you? You can't wait to feel what it's like to be at my mercy."

Kase's laughter fades with the look Dante gives me, all hot and bothered. "Damn."

"Damn is right. I'm ready, my soul. My queen. Show me your power. Fuck me how you want." Dante slides his fingers through mine and guides me to the bed.

Kase moves to the edge as Dante flips onto his back instead of remaining on his knees. Now that we're so close, and he exposes his body more to me, nerves bunch my stomach. Am I really doing this? Fucking a devil in his ass to experience his power? Fuck yeah, I am.

"I want to watch you fuck me for a bit," Dante says, reaching up to take the lube from Kase. "I love you, my pretty soul. I've been dreaming about you."

I bite my lip between my teeth and rest my hands on his bent knees, just drinking him in. "You're so sexy," I say, channeling words I know he would enjoy. "So hard for me. I want to make your dreams come true."

"Come here. Give me that big dick. Show me how you love power. You know our word in case. Don't be afraid to use it if it's too much or you realize it's not what you want, okay?" Dante wags the bottle of lube, waiting for me to take it. "I want you to do the honors. Learn my body. Savor my power."

I release a breath, my body, mind, and soul going out of whack. Dante turns off the vibration of the double penetrating strap-on, letting me take my time while he silently guides me. I've never thought much about fucking anything, either with my finger or a dildo, but damn. I'm ready. It's not even about power or getting to try something new. For me, in this moment, it's about solidifying the trust I have with Dante and my need to give him what he needs as much as he gives the same to me.

Kase remains silent, but he shifts closer for a better look. Dante strokes his cock, lifting it up a bit as he adjusts his hips and opens his legs wider for me. His ass is so smooth and tight. Every muscle on his body ripples. I start by squirting some lube on him and add more to my hand, slicking it over my finger. The need to explore him first consumes me. I take over stroking his cock with one hand and use my other to slip it inside him, watching his face the whole time as his eyes flash green with his desire.

"You like this, don't you?" I tease, drawing my finger slow and sensually, wanting to make sure he's absolutely ready for this beast of a cock even knowing that he's a pro at this kind of thing. This isn't his first time, and I know right now that this isn't going to be the last time. He loves a good stroke of his P-spot and he silently adjusts my hand to guide me to it.

His cock pulses in my hand, hardening even more. Kase groans with his lust, watching me pleasure Dante until I'm ready to give him more. To take more.

"Tell me you want my cock," I say, pulling my hand away to massage my slippery fingers to his thighs.

"I want that big, beautiful dick in my ass, pretty soul. Show me your power. Take mine." Dante's fangs extend with his lust, and I slowly, teasingly drip more lube on his ass and cock. I add more to the dildo, turning everything I touch slick and ready.

Kase grazes his fingers over my nipples and kisses my

neck, silently reminding me that he's here. "You two are so fucking hot. I can't wait to join."

I grin and wag my finger. "The power is mine until I'm ready to share, but enjoy this. Watch his face with me. He's going to take my cock like the beast he is."

Kase and Dante love the hell out of my words, and I find it easier and easier to play to their needs. Grabbing one of Dante's knees, Kase shifts him a bit, giving me complete easy access to fuck Dante how he craves. I lean forward, grazing my stomach along Dante's hard-on, and take a moment to kiss him, gliding my tongue into his mouth and showing him my love and appreciation teaching me things about myself I never knew existed.

"I'll start nice and slow, but get ready, Dante. Your ass is mine. Your cock is mine. I'll fuck you like the queen I am. You're mine." I align the dildo to his body and test his resistance, watching with intensity as I slide it in an inch.

Dante clutches the blankets and moans, arching his back in pleasure, and I follow his body, not pushing too fast or hard until he welcomes the dildo completely and with ease. His moans fill the air, and I rock on my knees, jerking him off at the same time, losing myself to the pressure and pleasure I get with each of my thrusts. The vibrations ignite against my clit, the strap-on buzzing to life, and holy shit. I scream out and thrust faster, deeper, feeling the pleasure coursing through me.

"You fuck me so good, Raven. I want it harder. Give me

what you got," Dante says, moaning and letting me have complete control.

I drop all my reserve and do as he says, humping the fuck out of him until he grunts and cums, blasting his load into the air to rain down. Kase ducks, rolling off the bed and sheltering himself with a pillow as if a storm is trying to take him out. I don't know if it's the power zapping through me or what, but I tip my head back and open my mouth, bouncing on my knees in celebration for getting my devil off in a way that I'm nearly certain neither of them expected.

"Unholy Hell, that was fucking outrageous," Kase says, popping up beside the bed.

"You want to go next?" I tease, slowing down and gently sliding the strap on out. "Feel the power of my big ass cock?"

Dante releases a whoosh of a breath and snatches me, pulling me on top only to roll me over. His mouth crashes against mine, our bodies slick and sticky, and porn-like messy, but I don't care. All I care about is tasting Dante's mouth and soaking up his pleasure and love.

"No fucking way, pretty soul. I want more. I want to take it again while Kase takes your sweet ass." Dante nips my throat, his hot body sizzling my skin in the best way.

I nearly forgot about what I offered Kase, and though I should be nervous, I'm totally and completely ready to dive into their darkly delicious desire. I'll let Dante be the engine and Kase be the caboose of a real fucking Kinkland Express.

"You want that, don't you, angel-girl?" Kase says, shifting the bed with his weight. He rolls Dante off me, flips me onto my stomach and uses his big hands to spread my ass cheeks wide.

I gasp at his tongue licking up my body, tasting me how he likes. "I do. More than I thought. If Dante can take my new mega dick, I know I can take yours. I want it."

He hums under his breath. "Let's feel that hot pussy first." Shifting the strap-on out of the way, he sinks into my body and thrusts a few times. "Damn. That feels good. I can't wait to fuck your tight ass."

I grin and practically coo at his anticipation. Peeking at him over my shoulder, I say, "I want you to first bow to me and thank me for spreading my cheeks for you to go on an ass-venture."

The look Kase gives me, raised brows and then a smile that warms me up even more, nearly makes me tell him I'm kidding.

But I don't have to. He spanks my ass and gets me to straighten up to make room for him to lie forward.

"I will worship your ass like the deity it is. And as an offering, I give you my cock to stuff you with the Hell you crave and my almighty tail to ensure orgasms aplenty." Kase chuckles and meets me for a kiss, squirting so much lube onto his cock it's like a slippery sleeve that makes it look even thicker.

"All aboard the Ass Express," Dante says, his humor and

passion ensuring that my nerves remain locked away. "Time to swap out for a new dick, pretty soul. Kase will take care of you completely."

"Damn straight, I will. I don't have a tail for nothing." Kase swats me again and he and Dante help me switch to a different strap-on with...shit. The Andre 3000. I laughed when he told me its name, but now he wants me to use it on him...well, okay. He is always down for a pounding, and he knows what he likes.

I let Dante lube it up for me, watching him have way too much fun playing with my big, thick, realistic dick that could really have been modeled after Andre. Kase takes care to tease me, working me up with his fingers, adding pressure to my ass while I kneel. One thing is for certain, I'm glad I'm no ass-virgin, and Kase knows exactly how to treat me while getting what he wants.

"I think it'll be best for Raven to be on her side this time so you don't accidentally get balls deep too quickly. Also, don't you fucking forget her word is Halo. If you hurt her, I'll shove something comparable up your ass. Got it? This is a privilege and an honor. I will not let you ruin my future chance at slipping into that dainty winking star."

I expect Kase to yell at him for threatening, but all he does is nod and listen, taking complete care to follow Dante's instructions. This is his room after all.

Before lying down, I clutch each of their cheeks and pull

them to me, kissing them. "I love you both. So, so, so much."

"My love for you is as strong and hot as my desire to remain in this bed, fucking each other forever," Dante says, guiding me to lie behind him. "Now have at me first. I want you in place for Kase's turn. It'd be easier for both of us."

"My two favorite beings," Kase says. "I fucking hate how grossly romantic you've made me. Stop it."

I laugh and let Dante help me guide the dildo inside him, until he moans and grabs my hand. I reach around him and play with his cock, anxious as Kase adds even more lube. He really took Dante's threat to heart and I love it. I love everything about this moment, experiencing something new and exciting and utterly and completely perfect. The trust we have is incomparable, and I hope to get to this point with all of my devils.

"Relax, angel-girl. If you clench, I can't get in." Kase aligns his boner to my ass and pushes slightly, testing my resistance.

I release a breath and kiss Dante's shoulder, clutching him as Kase slips in an inch. Sucking in a breath, I close my eyes, feeling the intense pressure of him stretching my body. It hurts for only a moment, but not in a bad way. It's just me getting used to it.

"You okay, Raven?" Kase asks quietly.

I hadn't realized how quiet the both of them became, listening and paying attention to my every noise and movement, ensuring I'm good. Their attentiveness gets to me in a good way, and I wish I had realized this was what I've always deserved in a lover and a mate. We deserve the world and each other, and everything we want.

"I'm perfect," I say, slowly rocking my hips to fuck Dante and at the same time encouraging Kase to do the same.

Kase and Dante both moan in unison, and I smile and stay in sync with Kase's movement as we nearly turn this train into a goddamned choreographed ass fucking production. Draping his tail over my hip, Kase teases me, rubbing my clit while slipping it into me, in what is reverse to his usual double penetration.

The three of us lose each other to our passion as we swap power and pleasure, love and affection. What starts as sensual turns utterly and completely passionate and I summon my bravery and roll Dante onto his stomach and allow Kase to sandwich me to him.

Dante pants and moans, clutching the blankets as I follow his pleas to fuck him with the power of Hell. We all fall into a hurricane of lust and bliss, and Kase increases the pressure of his tail until my muscles tense and I hump the Hell out of Dante until he hollers with his orgasm, the intensity of it shaking the entire bed.

"Dante, hurry and watch. I'm going to fucking blow," Kase says, surprising me.

I'm too lost to the sensations of pleasure and fiery passion to fully grasp Dante shifting out from under me to get the best view of Kase fucking both my holes until I cum again and scream into the blankets. With one more thrust, Kase releases the loudest moan I ever heard from him. My eyes roll back in my head, my body weakening. I remain panting and aching in the best way possible until Kase gently rolls me over and uses the sheet to clean me off the best he can.

"I'm going to give you a little venom bite, pretty soul, if that's okay," Dante murmurs, snuggling close to my side. "It'll help with the tenderness of your body, okay? I want you to just relax and let us take care of you. It's all we want now. A soak in the tub. A massage. Some food and a damn good cuddle."

I nod my head, my eyes heavy with lust still. "That sounds like Heaven."

Kase groans and chuckles. "Far from it. It's our paradise. Just you wait, angel-girl. You'll see. When Hell rises, we'll have everything we could hope for."

"I already do," I say. "I couldn't ask for more."

22

RAVEN

ANGELIC VENGEANCE

"TAMIA, I DON'T know what to tell you. I haven't seen Lucian in days. What's so important you need him now?" I tighten my jaw and stare out the front window, wishing I wasn't so jealous that my cousin called me to ask about Lucian. "I hope you don't think he's available."

"Fuck, Raven. It's not like that. He's...not my type. Not with how much he's asked about you. I just—can you tell him

I called? It's important. I found the name of the guy he was looking for."

"The guy? What guy?" I ask, tapping my fingers to my knees. "What did he involve you in?"

"Seriously, stop. You can't demand to know everything about my life when you shut me out of yours for years." Ouch. Her words cut me deeply, but a part of me knows it's true and it's still true. Still, it doesn't hurt any less.

"I'm sorry, Tamia," I say, lowering my voice. "I wish things could be different."

"Me too, cousin. I miss you. I miss how things were. I just—maybe we can have lunch next week. Just the two of us?" Tamia's line crackles with static, her words coming in and out with her question. Then she swears, not giving me a chance to respond before adding, "I have to call you back. Let's plan something, For real."

"I'd li—" I sigh and drop my phone on the couch as she disconnects without hearing my response.

I nearly forgot Elias was beside me until he drapes his arm over my shoulders and pulls me into his side. I rest my head against him, trying to be careful how much weight I put on him. He won't admit it to me, but he's having a bad day already. The fact that one of Dante's venom bites glows on his bicep this early proves as much.

"I think taking some time to hang out with Tamia might be exactly what you need, darlin'," he says, gliding his hand down my arm until I twine my fingers with his. "You don't have to babysit me twenty-four seven. I swear on my cock that I won't die without you, and that thing is important to me."

I giggle at his words, knowing it's what he was trying to do, but I can't feel it deep in my soul. He's right. I am babysitting him, remaining glued to his side. I will not risk everything we've worked toward, but especially Elias's chance to claim his power and throne in Hell. If I have to ignore Tamia a few weeks longer, I will.

"Tamia's fine. She only called because of something with Lucian. She wouldn't even tell me what. It's better this way, anyhow." I shift and meet his gaze, forcing my mouth to smile.

"But is it? I know the importance of a companion that doesn't want to fuck your brains out every second." He chuckles at his own words until he coughs, the wheeze and crackle noise coming from his throat sounding worse than even last night when he was coughing in his sleep.

I thump my palm against his back, hoping to break up or fix even a bit what's irritating him. "I will reconnect with her...just not until everything is in place. I won't jeopardize my cousin. I'm already pissed off that Lucian dragged her into this in the first place."

"Just remember, pretty soul. She chose to stay. And Elias is right. With everything a bit out of control, it might even be better to keep her close. Lucian and basically everyone in the damn universe is unpredictable." Dante strolls from the kitchen in only a pair of boxer-briefs just because Elias would complain otherwise if he were naked. "He was also right about giving him some space. The bastard will be fine for a few hours. Let him have his privacy to hack up his lung, fart, take a damn shit, and just groan and complain like he wants instead of acting fine for you."

I can't help pouting.

"He's wrong about all of that," Elias says, flicking Dante in his muscular thigh before accepting one of the plates of pasta he carries. "Except maybe the shitting. Hard to compete with fuckers that don't use the bathroom and can just empty their bowels in Hell or what the fuck ever."

I grimace and whack him, unable to stop myself from laughing. It's not like I haven't thought about it. I'm barely ever alone and learned really quick that I was the only one using the toilet when Dante mentioned I was lucky they were too lazy to remodel the bathroom without one. "You asked Micah about it, didn't you?"

Elias chuckles. "What else would we talk about besides you, sex, and his ideas of the meaning of mortal lives?"

"We should really create better boundaries." I flick my gaze up to Dante, who winks at me, clearly amused. He knows as well as I do that after our ass train, boundaries are nonexistent. I mean, I was too out of it to want to do anything with his venom bite. My mind has officially blocked out his helping me with what he insisted was important aftercare.

"Good luck with that one," Elias says, bumping his shoulder to mine.

Dante extends his arms out, wiggling his fingers. "No luck is needed. You'll both realize how special it is to have a boundary-less bond for eternity." I give in and let him pull me to my feet. "Now go enjoy a good shit, shower, and nap. Watch some porn and get some ideas of how you want to celebrate your descent."

I try not to react to Dante's words. Descent means death of Elias as a mortal. Planning his demise is just as morbid as it sounds, and the idea stabs me in the heart, knowing it must be by my hands.

I bend over and kiss Elias, hugging him a moment longer. "Call me for anything. I mean it. I'll make sure Dante brings me back ASAP."

"I love you, darlin'. Don't go misbehaving and being naughty. They like that too much." He grins with his words and slumps back on the couch.

I watch in silence as Dante offers another venom bite, which Elias accepts without complaint. Kase materializes in the room and holds out a jacket and pair of heels for me to wear with my short, cotton dress. By the time I'm ready, Elias already dozes off on the couch and Micah joins him, shifting him on his side.

"He's going to be fine, angel-girl. Taking you out will be

good for both of you. You're depressed as fuck just sitting around and waiting to kill him. It's fucking twisted that you have to, and I want to distract you until it's actually time, okay?" Kase links his fingers through mine and guides me to the door with Dante behind us.

I think about his comment for a moment, knowing he is right. I need to stop thinking about this as killing my soulmate and more as helping him rise in his rightful place and finally breaking our cycle.

"And what better way than to hunt Lucian's ass down to kick it? The fucker has ignored my calls all day now. He's too damn proud to admit he fucked up with Cassius and needs help cleaning up his mess." Dante spreads his wings wide in the front yard and holds his arms open. Without giving me a chance to prepare, he snatches me and Kase and launches into the air, soaring so quickly toward the sky that I can't even squeak a sound.

Like he's determined to make my soul leave my body, he dives down just as fast, twisting my insides and making it impossible to think. Kase growls and cusses him out, somehow managing to speak over the wind and his chaotic flying. Dante only laughs and throws the two of us in the air before only catching me. Kase transforms into his devil self, landing with ease outside the familiar bar they own together.

The ground quakes with Dante's landing, but it's not from our weight. Kase charges ahead of us and to the broken door, shattered and hanging by only a hinge. The tinted glass window doesn't fare any better. A human-sized hole sends cracks fissuring to the frame. And the smell. Fuck, is it bad. Something rotten permeated from inside like a portal remains open, letting the stench of Hell out. It's even stronger than when the devils open a summoning circle.

"Shit. What the fuck happened?" I ask, stretching to peer behind me as Dante picks up his pace to follow Kase inside the building.

All it takes is one look to make me wish he had left my ass outside. My stomach heaves and I bury my face into Dante's shoulder. I've seen some pretty fucked up shit involved with Hell's affairs, but whatever happened here can't even compare.

"Throw up on the floor and not me, please," Dante says, shifting me in his arms. "Unless you're trying to get me to fly us home naked."

I groan and touch my heels to the ground, thankful they're tall enough to stop any guts—both human and demon—from splashing across my open toes. I thought watching Dante slaughter the contracted souls who tried to take me was the worst I could see. But I guess when it's the aftermath of a gruesome attack and not unfolding before me while I'm high off his bite that makes a difference.

"It's about damn time you two showed up." The sharp, feminine voice cuts through the air, pulling my mind away from the pile of intestines on the floor a few feet away. "The fucking angels cut off my communications. They suggested all these bitch-asses could possibly get salvation if they stood against Hell. And then some fucking guardians kept healing the damn injured, so look at what they made me do!" Gia throws out her arms and spins around. "I had to fucking take everyone apart to stop it. These damn souls were forced to break their contracts."

I bring my jacket up to my face, securing it the best I can over my mouth and nose. "Oh, God."

"Yeah, fucking God. I liked this guy." Reaching down, Gia picks up a severed head and dangles it in front of me. "James was my fucking favorite. Do you know how hard it is to find a man who can get me off?" Spinning, she chucks poor James's head at the wall, pulverizing it with her force. "I am so not happy. I've been stuck here for what feels like years."

Kase roars and swipes his dagger claws, flinging a bunch of guts and body parts toward the wall. "I'll take care of it. Where are the souls?"

"Cooking just how you like, which is why I've been stuck waiting for you assholes. I haven't sent them to Hell yet. Maybe you can squeeze more answers out of them than I could." Gia motions toward the back of the room. No wonder the scent of Hell taints the air. Who knows how long she's been holding souls prisoner within a portal.

"You've served us well, Gia. I think an expansion in your territory is well deserved." Kase motions to Dante with his tail.

"Stay out here with Raven. Make her a drink or something. She looks like she needs it."

More like twenty shots until I turn blackout drunk and melt this image from my mind.

"I'm going to stand by the window, Dante," I say, keeping my eyes glued to his to stop from looking around. "Bring me something strong, okay?"

Ruffling his feathers, he dips his chin in agreement. "You got it, pretty soul. Just keep your eyes open for bastards. If you spot one, I'm going hunting."

Dante swats my ass, getting me to stroll the dozen feet to a bouncer podium with a stool. It's thankfully still intact and not covered in guts.

Like the fucker was waiting for me to appear, Cassius shows up across the street. He expands his brilliant wings and glares at me. The asshole. It only takes me a minute to realize that this might've been a set up. But there's nothing I can do as Dante charges through the broken window and into the street.

Dante doesn't make it far before two guardian angels, with their gold wings, jump in his way, stopping him from going after Cassius. Hissing, Dante spits venom at the two bastards. All it does is piss them off. Each of them grabs one of his arms and launches into the air with him.

I'm out of my seat and rushing outside before I realize my mistake. Cassius materializes in front of me and grabs my hand. I scream out and swing my arm, punching him in his smug face. He doesn't falter. He doesn't block my attempt to hit him again and lets me slam my fist into his jaw. I actually think he likes it. I swear to unholy Hell that he purposely turns his face in the other direction to let me smack him on his other cheek.

Fear crashes through me as his bright light engulfs the world, stealing my vision away. My stomach flips and flops, and I lose sight of the bar. I can't hear Dante fighting above me either. And now that I have a chance to look around, I notice that Cassius not only flew me away, but he also shifted me between planes. Kase and Dante might not be able to find me here. Oh fucking hell.

I shove my palms against his chest and push them away, making him stumble with my Hell strength. The cocky bastard has the nerve to smile at me like he's won. But he has no idea what he has done, taking me away from my devils. I won't stand for it. This is his fault. The massacre inside of the bar wouldn't have happened had he intervened. Many people died because of him and because of the guardian angels.

"Do you have any idea how hard I've been trying to get you within arm's reach?" Cassius flares his nostrils and expands his wings sending a gust of stinging heavenly light in my direction.

"Not as hard as it's going to be to escape me once I twist your fucking balls in my hand and drag you back to the mortal realm." I swing my fist at his groin and try to grab them through his pants.

He finally realizes the threat I really am to him and hops out of my reach blocking me from trying to grab his cock and rip it off. I'd love to give my devils an angelic dick bouquet in celebration of finally being able to see Hell rise. It'll be so sweet, and I'm sure they'll reward me for it in the way I love.

"Raven, control yourself. I will not let you seduce me." Cassius shields his body with his wings.

I halt mid-punch, throwing my weight to not burn myself on his damn wings. "I wouldn't fuck you, even if you promised to abandon Heaven for the chance."

He has a lot of damn nerve to think this is me trying to seduce him. It's nearly laughable. Does he think this is what devils like as foreplay? Taking a serious beating to attempt to be as close to humans as possible unlike the devils who do it to fit in? Maybe only Lucian likes to have his cock whacked...well, they are born from the same essence or whatever. This little bitch ass probably has the same kinks.

I store the thought in my mind to think about later. Right now, I need to figure out how to get him to merge realms so I can cross back through.

"You're lying. I know about your seductive ways." Cassius glowers at me and flaps his wings, nearly brushing them to my face in the process.

He's seriously asking to get dismembered and have a piece

of him hidden within every one of the devils' kingdoms. I can just imagine how they'd react to him branding my face with one of his feathers. Dante still gets upset about the one Micah gave me on my palm, a striking contrast to Lucian's mark on my other. I know how much he loves my hands and lusts after them. Especially now that I did something new to him with my finger...

I shake my head, snapping out of my wandering thoughts.

Cassius continues to glower at me, waiting for me to respond to his comment. Instead of doing what he expects, I spin on my feet and stride away. I might be on another plane, but there is one thing that I can access regardless of where I am—the Hell portal Gia has open inside the bar.

"Raven! Raven, stop! Accept that this is over." Cassius tries to chase after me, but the second I cross into the strange, red-lit bar, he freezes.

He can't cross the protective barrier. His ass is stuck outside.

This might be childish as fuck, but I stick out my tongue and flip him off. "You need to accept that Hell is rising no matter what you want. You've lost, Cass-hole." Elias would be so proud to hear me use the nickname he gave the dickhead angel.

"Do you really want to jeopardize all of humanity? You can't be that evil, Raven. Your soul shines too brightly. Even your mistakes and faults are hard to see beyond the pureness of your morality." Cassius toes the line of the barrier like he might risk getting the shock of an eternity to get to me. And who knows? He might.

"Me? You think I'm the one jeopardizing humanity? Are you that dense? That high and mighty with your damn halo so tight around your balls that all you can think is that you know best." I heave a breath in anger, his accusation setting me off. I know I shouldn't cross back over the line. He could do something crazy like fly me a thousand miles away and leave me in the middle of nowhere to ensure Elias dies without me, but damn it. I have faith in myself and the devils that he will not be able to overpower me.

I have hope that this is my time to fucking knock him off his heavenly cloud and bring him back to Earth.

"I do know what is best," Cassius snaps, fisting his hands.

I lose it.

Charging at him, I plow into him and knock him onto his back. I jab my fist into his perfect face with enough force to feel his nose give way under the fury of my strength. He doesn't move. He doesn't fight back. It annoys me even more that he just lies beneath me and stares at me like I'm the most pathetic thing he's ever seen.

"You're a fucking bastard! These people were slaughtered because of you and your army, Cassius! They were torn apart limb by limb. They broke their contracts because you lied to them, giving them hope that they could be redeemed. Some of them had a chance to get their souls back!" I slap and hit him over and over, my eyes burning with my tears. "None of this would've happened if you would just realize that I'm trying to save humanity! I want to give souls a chance to find their way out of the depths and torture of Hell and give them somewhere more deserved since Heaven rejected them."

"They wouldn't be in that place had they—"

"Shut up!" I screech. I gather the front of his shirt in my fingers and shake him. "You're not listening. Do you even care? You claim that you're doing all of this for humanity, but I know for goddamn certain that you're only doing this because you're too proud to admit that things could—no, they would—be better if the kingdoms could rise." I heave a few breaths, gathering my nerve to shove off of him and get to my feet. "It's no wonder your brethren left you and your own brother abandoned you. You truly are a piece of work."

Cassius catapults to his feet, growling in anger. He unsheathes his holy sword, setting it ablaze with his righteous fury. "You've been consumed by evil. You can't see what I do. I wanted to save you, Raven. But I no longer think you deserve it. You don't deserve another moment alive because everything you do will—"

Anger explodes through me, and I kick him so hard between his legs that he jumps up a foot into the air. Crashing to his knees, Cassius clutches his groin and attempts to grab me, but he's not quick enough. I scramble out of his reach and back into the bar. He's so blinded by his kill-mission that he forgets he can't cross into a Hell-protected place. I squeeze my eyes shut and brace myself. The whole world quakes and rocks as he smashes into the shield. Cassius hollers in pain, and his blinding light steals all of my senses. My skin buzzes and stings at the explosion of heavenly light, but there is nothing I can do but hope for the best.

Silence fills the world before my eyelids turn from red to all shadows, and Kase's familiar growl vibrates through me.

"Fuck, Raven. What happened? Are you okay? How did you get back to this realm?" Dante's questions fly from his mouth as his warm hands lock onto my hips and he lifts me up.

My whole body turns into mush at the comfort of his embrace. I was so angry and scared. So furious at Cassius and his righteous accusations. I nearly ruined everything...or maybe I struck a nerve sharp enough to get through to him. Why would he react so violently otherwise? I can't start questioning my instincts now. They've grown more powerful and clear with guidance and help from my devils.

"I—I—fuck that fucking fuck fuckhead fucker." I wish I could spit out something more coherent, but damn it.

"Did he hurt you?" Kase asks, coming up behind Dante. He peers at me from over his shoulder. "I'll cut his balls off with a butter knife and shove them up his ass so far that they'll eventually exit his throat with enough of my Hell power. Then I'll use his cock to shove the shitty sack back down. After that, I'll fucking stuff him with all the nut sacks in this room until—"

Gia laughs and cuts Kase's threat off. "My liege. You should let some of that be a surprise. I'm sure your queen would love to watch such a show without spoilers. She'll bask in your brilliance. Why don't I help you and start collecting them now."

This demon bitch. I want to hate her for her bullshit last time, but I enjoy her psycho attitude far more than I should.

I turn to her. "Leave them to rot in the sun a bit."

Clapping her hands, Gia grins. "Marvelous, my queen. Perhaps I might've underestimated you. Would you like to help me pluck the biggest of the bunch?"

I try not to react and open my mouth to say okay, just to play it cool, but Dante squeezes my ass cheek.

"We must find the bastard savior first, don't you think?" Dante says, his rumbly voice vibrating against my chest. "Go on and finish sorting the souls and keep a couple extra for your own personal bidding."

"Yes, my liege," Gia says, pouting but not arguing. "Call me if I can be of any service to you."

Without responding, Dante turns and strides outside with Kase close behind them. I peer up at the sky, afraid to see the silhouette of angels, but they're thankfully not there.

"Take our soul home," Kase says, straightening his back. "I'm going to hunt Lucian's bitch ass down."

"You found him?" I ask.

Kase nods. "The fucker is preparing for something downtown. One of the souls was responsible for delivering a message to us, but the guardians got to him first. Lucian's being his paranoid self, so...just try not to worry. I have it handled, okay?"

I know better than to question him and just nod my head. "If Cassius confronts you, tie him up for me, okay? I want to handle him."

Kase grins. "Better be good."

My heart clenches at the thought of everything I want to do to break that angel, and none of it will be good. "He's going to learn exactly what it's like to face my version of Hell."

23

RAVEN

KINGDOM COME

"HEY, SATAN! YOU are so unlucky that you chose now to show your damn face." I glower and point in Lucian's direction, but he ignores me to focus on the others.

Dante sets me on my feet on the back lawn. Kase, Andre, Micah, and Lucian stand huddled together in what looks like a dramatic conversation. Lucian and Kase must've taken a Hell portal from wherever Lucian has been hiding, because I don't think me and Dante have been gone that long. I mean, sure, he convinced me to join the Mile High Club with him devil style, but it was a fast and furious quickie—by his standards. It was long enough for me to get off three times.

Too bad seeing Lucian waving hands at Andre steals my good mood right out of me. "Lucian, you better give me a good reason why Tamia called me asking for you." I storm away from Dante, feeling the heat of Hell radiating from the devils.

Lucian smiles, showing off his perfectly straight teeth. "You're jealous already."

Micah punches him in the gut, wiping the grin off his face. "Fucking respect her. You know she isn't jealous. She wants to keep Tamia safe. I should gut you for continuing with whatever the fuck you think you're doing."

"Relax, both of you. I was merely sounding my appreciation over Raven's possessiveness already." Lucian breaks away from the circle and makes it all of two feet in my direction before Micah grabs him by the back of the shirt.

"You damn well know it's not the time or fucking place to bring the Hell out of her." Micah jabs his ribs. "Whatever you plan to say next better be an apology and an answer that pleases her. You know our agreement."

Lucian huffs out a breath and yanks himself free. "Like I could ever forget when you assholes will beat it into me every other second for the rest of eternity."

I slow as Lucian strides toward me and a mixture of emotions threatens to turn my mind to mush. "I don't want you near my cousin. No calling. No texting. Nothing."

He lifts an eyebrow. "Why do you think she called you? I've been an angel, Raven. It has been excruciating ignoring someone who has information I seek. Did you know she has connections to some of the wealthiest people in the area?"

I never thought about it much, but I guess she would as an event planner. It's been so long since we've really connected, so things were easy to slip my mind. "You're trying to use her to network? Are you serious? You're fucking Satan. Don't you know every bastard?"

"I do in a sense, but...it's complicated. I'm sure you have far better things to do than listen to me ramble on about devil affairs." Reaching up, Lucian risks his hand by touching my chin. My first instinct is to bat him away like always, but something about the dark depths of his eyes locks me in place. "I heard you had a confrontation with my brother."

I slump my shoulders, letting my guard down a little. "I beat the fuck out of him and then kicked his balls hard enough to send them inside of him, which by the way, I'm nearly fucking certain got his rocks off just like your masochistic ass."

Lucian releases a low growl under his breath, his eyes sparking with fire. His anger isn't directed at me though. I'd feel it deep in my soul if it were. "Did he hurt you?"

His question surprises me. I can't tell if it's because he cares about me or wants another reason to unleash Hell on Cassius.

"He tried to fucking kill me." The memory explodes through my mind as I replay the bullshit Cassius pulled. "He took me to another plane while the guardians went after Dante. He got pissed off because I called him out on his bullshit, and he can't see his wrongdoings. Kind of like you." Low blow? Maybe. Warranted? Absolutely. This little truce is in place as a test. We all need to see if Lucian is truly on board with following through with his original plan when he, Dante, and Kase first abandoned the Higher Power.

"I guess I'll have to continue making it up to you. How would you like me to catch a guardian, and I can teach you the most effective way of breaking my brother?" Lucian leans in a bit more. "Could be fun."

Whacking him on the back, Kase nearly knocks Lucian into me. "Don't let him fool you, angel-girl. The fucker already has captured a featherhead. We were discussing how to proceed. Heaven's army is up to some bullshit, so we need to get it out of him."

"The twats are circling and waiting for their chance to grab our prisoner," Andre adds. His jaw tightens with his words.

"I want to fucking break every bone and pluck every feather to get him talking." Lucian jerks his head to Andre.

"But this soft fucker still carries damn feelings toward them. He wants to take our prisoner to Hell instead and try things his way."

"I hate—and I really hate to admit it—but I think Lucian's way would be faster." Micah rubs his hand over his stubbly jaw. "We don't have much time to deal with a battle."

Something about his comment stabs me through the heart. It's now that I realize that Elias would usually be with him, especially discussing things that will affect his future. I don't get a chance to ask him though. Lucian's cocky bastard smile lights up and he holds out his hand and gets Micah to fist bump him, the gesture weird but somehow cute. Who knew I'd love the truce between everyone.

"I think it's bullshit and will only cause more fucking problems." Kase's eyes glow with his red power. "Plus, I know you, Raven. You'd have to hear every second of it. We can't do it anywhere else except here. We're the strongest force of protection."

"She shouldn't fucking care! This is what we need!" Lucian gets in Kase's face, and the two of them break into a fight.

Okay, so not so much a truce as it is a sometimes they tolerate each other type of situation.

I step forward against my good senses, planning to separate the two of them, but Dante cuts me off and Micah grabs my shoulders and pulls me back. I spin and look at him, his eyes flicking across my face with thoughts he doesn't freely let me hear. Once again, my nerves bunch, sensing something unfamiliar but a lot like dread.

"Micah? What's wrong?" I ask, my soft words sounding through the air.

"Why don't we go inside? We need to talk." Micah drapes his muscular arm over my shoulder.

I stiffen, my whole body cooling. Oh, no. Oh-fucking-no.

Pulling away from him, I prepare to bolt to the backdoor, but Kase calls my name. I heave a few breaths as tears fill my eyes. Micah hasn't even said anything, but I know something is up with Elias.

"You guys figure it out. I have to go." Panic tightens through my muscles. "And Micah, you shouldn't even be out here. You should be with Elias. What if—"

Micah cuts off my words with a kiss and pulls me into his arms, hugging me. His heat eases the ice in my veins a little, but it also sends my emotions over, and I can't control the sob that escapes my lips. Silence fills the air as the other devils stop fighting and focus their attention on me.

"Lucian, bring the angel out and give him to Andre. Now. He will handle it. When you're done, meet us at the apartment." Kase points at Dante. "You're coming with me. We're going to sweep the area and make sure no one besides Zade lurks around. He's our next target, and I don't want anyone scaring him off. He's already in tune to Raven, and now is the time he's going to try to use his angelic charm to help her. Everyone understand?"

The others all nod their agreement. Each of them take a second to hug me, including Lucian, and I finally manage to get my quivering mouth under control.

"I can't do this alone," I say, swallowing the burning in my throat. "Please hurry back."

"We wouldn't miss it." Kase plays with my hair, tucking it behind my ear. "Just let Micah take care of you two for now, okay?"

My voice stops working, so I only nod and kiss him one more time. Hugging Micah tighter, I let him carry me inside and to the elevator. I breathe in his familiar scent, summoning the comfort he brought to me when he was an angel. The same comfort I still feel with him even as a devil.

"Raven, this might be one of the hardest things for you to bear in your mortal life. It hurts me on the deepest level of Hell that you're in this position and must face such an act on our behalf," Micah says, breaking the silence yet keeping his voice at a whisper. "I'm truly sorry, but I want you to know that I'm here to guide you through everything. Elias too. We were once inseparable, and it was fate that your soul brought us back together. I don't even know where to begin thanking you."

Stopping outside his bedroom door, Micah sets me on my feet. Music hums through the air, trickling into the hallway. I grab his hand, stopping him from opening the door right away. The uncertainty scares the living shit out of me.

"Being here is enough for me." I hug him, sinking into his embrace. "I'm scared. More than scared. I'm terrified. Is he really that bad? He was still joking and laughing with me this morning."

Micah sighs. "Sometimes things happen so quickly. A disease like his is unpredictable, and no matter how much you think you're prepared, you might never be. He's conscious, but he's not speaking vocally. Just in my mind."

I steel myself, trying to keep my eyes from spilling a waterfall of tears. Micah is right. Nothing could've ever prepared me for this. No amount of reasoning with myself or assurance that things are going to work out. Even knowing that Elias suffers in this state and once his mortal life ends, he'll finally regain his health and power, does nothing for my grief. He'll be stronger than ever. A devil. But he'll never be the mortal man who kidnapped me, pissed me off, and somehow still managed to make me fall in love with him in this life. What if things change in the next?

"Oh, God. Help me," I whisper, my silent prayer humming through the hall. I slap my hand over my mouth and stare at Micah with wide eyes. "I'm sorry."

He chuckles, his voice helping to lighten the heaviness of my mood. "My beautiful heathen. I might have turned my back on the Higher Power's grace, but it wasn't because Heaven and the almighty are my enemies. I'm here because of you.

It doesn't bother me if you feel the need to find faith in the light of your soul. It was born from Heaven, after all."

"You should still punish me later for that. I don't want them to think I want help. Their kind of help is shittier than the torture Kase and Dante plan for Cassius when they find him." My voice stops shaking with my comment, and I manage to get myself completely in control. I'll just have to summon some extra strength by thinking about all of my devils. They swore I won't go through this alone, and I believe them with my entire being. They've been the ones to prove their worth and they haven't let me down yet.

"I'll think of something if that's what you truly want," Micah murmurs, his voice turning breathy and sexy as Hell. "Maybe you can help me teach Elias what it truly means being a devil."

I lick my lips and nod. "I bet he'd love that."

Sucking in a deep breath, I finally turn the doorknob and ease it open, peering into Micah's room. It's smaller than Kase and Dante's but still large enough to feel more like an apartment rather than a tiny guest room.

"Darlin'." Elias's soft whisper sounds out before he groans and wheezes. Lying on Micah's big bed, he looks so frail and weak. I hate seeing him like this. I hate that he's going through any of this, especially because of a man who never deserved such a gift he gave him.

I rush to the bed. "I'm sorry I took so long to return, but

I'm here now and I'm not going anywhere, okay?"

His chest heaves as he tries to respond, but he gives up and offers a small smile instead.

"He says don't you apologize and what he wants most is for you to cuddle with him." Micah comes up behind me and rests his hands on my shoulders. He leans forward, staring at Elias's heavy-lidded gaze for another moment. "And...I'm not saying that Elias. You'll get the end you want when the others return."

I raise my brows. "Tell me what he wants."

Elias's smile widens and he wheezes with another cough.

"He wanted to perform cunnilingus on you in hopes that you'd suffocate him and let him descend into glory." Micah's voice remains even. "He's over his mortal life and is ready."

"Fuck," I whisper, trying not to sob and laugh at the same time. "Elias. I'm...just let me cuddle you for a bit."

"That's a good idea, heathen. I wanted to talk to you both anyway." Micah remains expressionless, though it does nothing to ease my worry. No one likes hearing that phrase. It's usually followed by something negative like a breakup from someone you love or reprehension from an employer.

I climb into bed beside him and try my best to hug him without touching him too much. I know he wouldn't let me know if I was hurting him. "Micah, he's cold. Will you take his other side? You're like a giant heater."

Micah smirks and nods, easing onto Elias's other side. He

helps him readjust, positioning him on his side to keep weight off his back. I hold Elias's cool hands between mine while Micah plays the big spoon. Any other time I'd be amused as fuck, and maybe even tease him, but all I want to do is kiss Elias and fill him with my love.

Micah chuckles and nuzzles his face on Elias's shoulder. "He wants me to tell you to behave because he's afraid you're going to give me an erection—er, a boner."

My laughter fills the air, and I bow in and kiss Elias. "And to think I was going to strip naked so you could use my boobs as pillows. Sucking my nipples might distract you for a bit. But if you're that worried—"

Again, Micah chuckles. "He's changed his mind and will accept the risk as long as I promise not to rest it between his legs and tuck it up."

I smile against his lips and ease back just enough to peer into his beautiful gray eyes. He blinks them slowly, the effort to keep them open obvious. He's out of it, but manages to remain a bit alert, which helps. If he wasn't, I wouldn't be able to maintain composure. There is definitely no way I could give him the end he wants.

Reaching over Elias, Micah surprises me by running a flaming finger up my back, burning my shirt in half before doing the same to the short sleeves. I'm not sure if it was Elias's idea or not, but I can't stop grinning, seeing a new spark light in Elias's eyes.

"Your tits give me life," Elias whispers, his words coming in gasps. "You give me life."

"I told him you were worried that he wouldn't be up to having sex as he goes," Micah thinks to me, keeping it between us.

I'm still not sure about the whole thing. I realize that I'm kinkier than I thought, but to ride him until he dies...? I might need a couple shots of tequila to make his dream come true. Maybe a venom bite from Dante. Possibly some edibles on top of it all.

I don't get much of a chance to think about it, because Micah tugs me a bit higher onto the pillow and jiggles my boobs, caressing them to Elias's face. The two of them have way too much fun with this, and I squirm and laugh until Elias gets a burst of energy and sucks my nipple into his mouth at the same time he reaches between my legs and strokes my clit, my panties long gone, ripped off by Dante on our flight home. Luckily, the horny bastard pulled out to make sure I didn't drip.

"You're right, Elias. She's so beautiful and sexy. We're lucky to have her." Micah murmurs, keeping my eye contact as I fall into the sensations Elias creates on my body. "I'm incredibly thankful to you, my friend. Your leap of faith in this irresistible soul brought her to me. To us. Which is why I'm going to accept the tether to Hell as a thank you. I want to be here for both of you through this the best I can. I will ensure your kingdom rises."

I gasp at both the pressure of Elias's fingers rubbing my clit and Micah's words. "What? I thought you all made an agreement to swap places yearly?"

"Things changed. I believe that you're in need of Andre on this plane. I'd like to personally see to Elias as well. It's time for me. Being here...it's hard, heathen. I struggle with many things, and you don't need the stress." Micah leans over and touches his fingers to my chin, guiding my chin upward. "You will never miss me. I will be here upon your request. Always."

"But Micah—" A sharp zing of pleasure steals the words from my mouth as Elias slides his fingers into me.

Micah groans. "No buts and no more discussion. Let Elias take care of you, okay? It's what he wants today and until his descent is about him."

They're lucky that my body trembles and my mind numbs, stopping me from arguing.

"I love you," I murmur, taking turns kissing each of them. "If this is what you want..."

"It's what we need. What you need." Micah cuddles close to Elias's back, smiling at me from over his shoulder. "We're going to be amazing, you know. You'll see. Maybe by tonight, Elias's kingdom will finally come."

I can't stop thinking of the familiar prayer my parents would say at bedtime when I was a kid.

Elias's kingdom...Zade's. Cassius's. Once their kingdom's come, I will be done. With Earth. With Heaven.

Purgatory will win.

The angels will see.

24

ANDRE

ADVERSARIES

"PLEASE, I—I can't. Just untie my hands. I won't fight. I just need to touch myself. The ache—you're a monster." Christian rolls his hips as he tugs against the restraints locking him to the stone wall of my kingdom.

"A monster? You're mistaken. Lucian had far worse plans than restraining you in his kingdom." I step closer and get into his face, seeing the familiarity of desire lighting his eyes.

Things could be easy for him if he would just tell me what I want. "All you need to do is give me the Mortal Realm location of your superiors. If you do that, I will release you. It'll be up to you whether or not you leave my kingdom."

"I—they've acquired the Sycamore Apartments on Playa Heights and Celeste Drive in Cloud Canyon. That's all I know." Christian grimaces with his words, his revelation hurting him on a level he probably never imagined. He just betrayed Heaven, and without realizing it, it will now be his downfall.

I grin and grab his wrists. "Was that so difficult?"

The bastard thrusts his hips toward me in an attempt to rub his uncontrollable hard-on against me. No one is immune to my kingdom. My approach is far different than that of the others. While Lucian thinks torture and pain work faster, desire not only affects someone in the moment. It will linger with them, teasing and taunting, begging them to give in. How could something that feels so good be bad? For Christian, it'll be that he'll want more and more until it turns all consuming. He will never be able to leave my kingdom once I release him.

"Please, just release me. You promised." Christian's heavy-lidded gaze searches my face and he bites his lip. "Please."

"Just remember, do not even consider trying to touch me. If you do, I will resort to Lucian's form of punishment...but if you'd like to touch my souls, they'd be happy to find some reprieve with you." I tighten my jaw, stopping myself from smiling. His mind is gone already as the thoughts flicker across his eyes. "Do you understand?"

"Yes," Christian whispers.

Using my Hell power, I break the restraints on Christian. He dashes past me and launches into the air, taking flight for only a few seconds. The lust-filled air captures him immediately. Diving down, he skids his boots across the soft ground where my souls wriggle and connect, humping and sucking, penetrating anything and everything in their paths, lost on their eternal desire in a world that they'll never find relief.

A shock of energy zaps me right in the balls, tightening my body as I watch Christian trying to control himself. The second a man breaks from his place amid the masses, sensing the fresh lust of the angel, Christian loses it. I lick my lips and grip the railing of my balcony, inhaling a deep breath.

I watch in satisfaction as Christian strips out of his pants and rubs his hard-on only a few feet from the soul. He's going in without a care, without a second thought, ready and willing to experience pleasure unlike anything Heaven could ever give. The soul smiles and turns around, dropping to all fours. Christian's light dims with each of his steps toward the man, slowly at first, curious yet anxious. Bowing forward, the soul rests his forehead on the ground and grabs his ass, spreading his cheeks wide. All it takes is his puckering asshole to get

Christian to rush the rest of the way, thrusting right into the man's invite, the lack of lube not fazing the soul.

Christian moans at the act of falling to his desires, not realizing that he's set off every soul around him. My skin prickles and the deep hunger inside me roars. I wave my hand, sending a gust of wind through the air, ripping the souls apart. Christian hollers in annoyance, only to be shut up by another soul crashing into his back and locking his arms around his hips before he buries his face and licks the angel's ass.

The glorious sight before me leaves my whole being burning.

I can't watch another minute as Christian falls completely into the lust and power of Hell. The tornado ends, sending the souls back to the ground, and the angel enters a woman next while another man mounts him from behind, the sounds of their moans and aches getting to me more deeply than they should.

Closing my eyes, I push away the image of the train of bodies humping and licking and kissing and stuffing every hole possible as they remain trapped in their aching desire. I break through the haze and open up a portal, tapping into the summoning circle that allows me to access what will soon be my home away from home.

I shudder and discard my hunger, hoping that Raven might sense me and peek out the window of Micah's room. All I need is one glimpse of the most enchanting woman and soul in existence. One glimpse of the desire she carries for me is enough to satiate me for days at a time. I can't wait until Micah takes the tether and frees me. Raven and I can finally get everything we desire together and more. I'll never be hungry with access to her all the time.

"Andre, you have an angel in your kingdom. Please let him go." Zade's voice drags my attention away from Micah's window and the faint scent of desire steaming across the glass. "You're only fueling the smite of Heaven."

Rage rushes through me, and I glower and press my palms to the summoning circle, feeling the barrier caging me inside. "The angel is no longer a prisoner. Be my guest to enter my kingdom and bring him out yourself."

Zade shifts on his feet, his face sharpening as he considers my words. "I cannot risk it. I just—I..."

"What?" I snap. "You show up and demand things but you never follow through. All you do is watch in silence. Why are you even here? Why bother?"

Sadness crosses his face, and for the first time in a long time, I get hit with a strangely familiar emotion. I've spent eternity protecting humanity by Zade's side. I'd recognize his grief and longing anywhere.

"You know why I abandoned Heaven. What I can't grasp is why you don't join me." I cross my arms, trapping him in my gaze. "Why do you hate the idea of redemption so much so that you're willing to just stand by and—"

"I don't hate redemption, Andre!" Zade gathers heavenly light in his palms, his rush of anger nearly intoxicating. "I hate that humanity faces devastation because of you. Don't you get it? Heaven's army isn't backing down. There will be a war. They won't stop. I—I don't want to see you or anyone else get hurt."

"Which you can only blame them for. Join us and help us. Make the right decision." I press harder against the barrier.

"Andre, please." Zade slumps his shoulders. "Think about what will happen. I didn't come here to start anything. I only wanted to warn you. Heaven will sacrifice humanity in the name of the Higher Power to stop you. The consequences will be apocalyptic. Devastating. Is that what you want? To destroy the world?"

I bang the barrier, sending flames dancing toward the sky. "You're a lying coward. The guardians would never. I believe you came here because you—"

Tensing with anger, Zade rushes toward me and breaks through the barrier, unsheathing his flaming sword. He tackles me and aims his sword at my neck. "I came here because I care about you and humanity! I care about Heaven and the warriors. I don't want things to be this way, Andre. You would have agreed with me before Hell consumed you."

"I would've only done so because I was lost in my light. With Raven and Hell's rulers, I can see better. You now cast light over the truth." I heave a few deep breaths and grab his flaming sword, pulling it closer. "If you can't accept the truth, then do what you need. Cast me back to Hell. But remember, it's not changing anything. There is nothing you can—no—nothing you will do about it. I know you, Zade. I know exactly what will be your downfall."

Zade scowls and rips his sword from my fingers only to aim it at my chest. "I don't want to fight you, Andre. I want everyone to back down."

"Never. Humanity needs someone who fights for them and not the Higher Power. They need Raven. After being in Hell even this short time, I know that these souls deserve to grow and change and learn. Lucian, Kase, and Dante were right. They don't deserve Heaven but they also don't deserve to be trapped in a cycle that allows them to just keep doing wrong. They need the chance to work through things and make it to Purgatory. Why Heaven is so against this is beyond me." I arch my body, purposefully forcing the tip of his sword to Hell's tether, glowing in my chest.

"You know why. The balance needs to be in Heaven's favor." Zade bares his teeth at me. "It can't fall in Lucian's hands. He'll destroy it."

"You're wrong," I snap. "You have no idea of what the Mortal Realm needs. It is time for Hell to rise. Show humanity mercy, you righteous asshole."

Heaven is afraid of losing any of its power and strength. Though I get my power from Lust and souls, it will never be as strong as the brightness of pure, light energy that comes with Heaven. The worse the soul, the weaker it is, which is why those who lived moral lives but end up in Hell can be reborn as our army. If we can complete all nine kingdoms, we can grow and thrive. That's what Heaven's afraid of. Of letting us be equal.

"That's what I'm trying to do!" Zade growls, igniting his heavenly glow. Closing his eyes, he prepares to stab me with his anger and annoyance, triggered by my hellish presence. "Why must I remind you who you truly are?"

"This is who I am." I smile with my words, feeling the agony of his blade sink deeper into my chest. "It's time for you to realize it. Send me to fucking Hell and accept it. Stop coming back. I will drag you here myself if you do."

"Damn it!" His swear rings through the air, and he sends his light radiating over me at the same time he jabs his sword deeper as if he wants to punish me.

"Zade! Zade, you fucker! Stop!" Raven's high-pitched voice echoes through the air, freezing him in place.

I stare in amusement, unfazed by Zade, as Raven crashes into him, knocking him out of the summoning circle. He spins her midair, landing on his back only to use his wings to push up. She looks sexy as Hell, wearing only one of Micah's shirts, flashing her body at me. I groan and prop up on my elbow, hoping they land close enough to drive her a bit wild. I'd love to see her wrestle him until he can't resist her. I can already taste the memory of her excitement, even as she slaps him in the face.

"Get out of here! I don't have time for this bullshit. My soulmate is dying, and I want fucking peace with him." Raven shoves him away, getting him to release her. "You shouldn't be here, baiting Andre either. What did you expect to accomplish? He's been forsaken. He can't even get his white wings back, and I wouldn't want him to. So go!" Again, she rams her palms to his chest. "Leave us alone."

Zade ruffles his feathers, tightening his jaw. "Raven..."

"I said go!" she screams.

Engulfing her in a hug, Zade surprises her by lifting her off her feet and whispering something into her ear. I half expect her to give in to his affection, losing herself to the aphrodisiacs permeating the air around me, but she remains strong-willed and determined.

"Zade, I mean it. I know you're trying. I know you want to be here for me and Andre, but I can't take it another minute. All you're doing is instigating. Just let us be for a while. I mean it. I can't have you around, knowing you're never going to even try to understand. All you do is nothing." Raven wiggles in his arms and puts space between them, backing up until she enters the safety of my Hell circle.

"You know why I can't," Zade says softly. "You both know. I just—like I said to Andre. I'm only here to warn you. Heaven's army is coming and they're not going to let anything stop them."

Raven fists her fingers. "Then you try. Give me my day with Elias. Show me you can be an angel of action."

"I can't," Zade repeats.

"Then go. We're done here." Raven heaves a breath and turns toward me. "Call the others, will you? Let them know about the bastard guardians. Micah is going to help me prepare a circle inside. You can use that one instead. And then you can give Micah the tether before Elias goes."

I touch her cheek, brushing my fingers on her jaw. "This is a good thing," I remind her. I tilt my head and catch sight of Zade still lingering but near the wall and out of hearing range.

Raven shifts and follows my gaze, and we watch as Cassius lands beside Zade. I grab onto Raven, preparing to take her to my kingdom, but Cassius grabs Zade's hand and forces him away. It's the only thing that makes Zade go.

"Do you think he was exaggerating?" Raven asks, pressing her lips together.

I shake my head. "No, there is a war coming, little hellion."

"Shit," she mutters.

Pulling her into my arms, I hug her and kiss her on the lips, savoring the taste of her mouth for a moment longer. "Don't stress about it. We're strong enough to handle it, and once Elias descends, it won't be long. We will get Zade to his knees."

She blows out a breath. "That'll be so satisfying."

I grin. "For both of us. Just wait. Now go enjoy your soulmate. He needs you. I will handle everything else and be inside shortly."

"I love you, Andre. I hope you know that." Pressing her hand to the power in my chest, she feels my heartbeat. "Once you're free of this tether, I'm going to make some time for us."

I kiss her once more. "I can't wait. An eternity with you is all I'll ever want and need. We'll have each other for the rest of time."

25

KASE

WAR

CHRISTIAN HOWLS AS Lucian uses Hell power to sear the long cut shut across his torso. The angel isn't in pain, doped up by Dante's venom bite, but he's frustrated as shit because Andre dragged him from the eternal orgy after informing us of Zade's warning. I can't exactly blame the fucker. Christian was having the time of his eternity fucking and getting fucked, able to navigate the Winds of Incompletion that Andre set up to stop any soul from reaching their peaks.

"Hey, horny bastard. It's okay. I get it. You weren't done." Dante pets the angel's hair and grins in amusement. "But don't worry. You'll get to go back soon enough. Andre's going to need you to babysit his kingdom. You'll get to do whatever you want. Maybe even get a brand new cock that'll attach you to a nice pussy or ass so you don't have to constantly chase the souls through the wind. How would you like that? Once you complete your mission, you can have access to Hell's power."

I nearly lose my shit, my laughter silently shaking my shoulder as he talks to the angel like a fucking teacher or some shit. Dom Daddy Dante to the rescue, though I know he prefers to be a master.

Christian heaves a breath and nods his head, finally relaxing. "I won't let you down."

The second Christian's hand is free, he touches his cock, jerking off so fast and furiously that he could damn well rip it off. At least it distracts him from the unholy bomb of Hell power that will detonate the second he returns to Heaven's army. They'll take him in without question and try to push the darkness of Hell out of him with their light. That's all it'll take.

"Easy, friend. Let me give you something a bit more hands off. You have to go." Dante summons a vibrating butt plug from his stash on a plane Raven would cream over if she could see. "Remember what we told you."

Christian moans, not even waiting for lube to shove the fucking plug in his ass and turning it on at high power. It's right now that I realize how fucked he is after being in Andre's Hell. Who knew the level of Lust could be torturous, even to me.

"You can count on me, your majesties. I understand the importance of your cause, and am happy to finally see things as they are." Christian stretches his frazzled wings and manages to launch out of the Hell circle and into the air.

It's so fucking satisfying hearing an angel bow.

"Think it's going to give us enough time?" I ask, watching the damn naked angel disappear into the sky.

"Plenty. I'll check on a few others from my collection and set them right as a backup plan. It's what we need. Put a rift in the army and make it so they won't know who they can trust." Lucian rubs his hands together and grins. "Elias better fucking appreciate this."

Dante growls and swings. "It's not about him. It's about Hell. Now go. We'll call you when it's time. Be thankful Micah is handling the new tether, because if he hadn't agreed, it would've been back to you."

Lucian mutters under his breath. "I'll be thankful when this is over."

"Then get to it," I say, whacking him on the back. "Break those motherfucking angels and be ready."

"Don't fuck up, either," Dante adds. "This is your chance to prove your worth, Lucian, understand? You won't get another."

"Damn straight. Fuck up, and you'll be with your little angelic pets imprisoned back in Hell."

"She doesn't need this bullshit," Dante mutters, twisting the head of a dead man until it finally snaps from its body. He hisses and chucks it at the wall of Hell's Ink, one of our shared tattoo parlors. "We don't deserve this bullshit."

My mind barely processes anything. Andre's presence is the only reason I remain calm, which is weird as fuck. Lust works two ways with me. It either drives me crazy or chills me out, and now, it distracts me from what I really want to do—catch every angel I can and turn them into bombs against Heaven.

"Heaven will get the threat. I'll feel Christian re-enter Hell." Andre stands in front of the body of my favorite piercer, who was on call for me the second Raven agreed to wear the pussy ring I created and infused with an exquisite soul just for her. Not that her pussy needs more power, but damn it. I want my jewelry on her body.

I can't even suggest she get a couple's tattoo instead, because my favorite artist is in two pieces, slaughtered by the overzealous followers of the guardians who sent their fresh mortal warriors here to ruin us.

These fucking bastard angels are making a damn mess with our businesses, and I won't stand for it. If they want a war, they're getting a war. I don't think the angelic army grasps what we are capable of. We've kept the darkness at bay for a reason. We can and will let Hell loose on their asses as revenge.

I'm not some heartless fucker like them. Everyone in this damn shop was under contract and satisfactory enough that they'd have all been great bottom feeders. But fucking Heaven stole that too, granting unwanted miracles. I know damn well that Malory would've never agreed to let some angel sweep her off her feet. She understood things beyond cultivated religions of the Mortal Realm. Our contracts were forced into begging the angels for mercy because of their followers' brutality. This is low, even by Hell's standards, and we don't have many.

"I want to know the second he does. Raven needs to know that we've handled things accordingly. This stress is going to ruin her fantastic sendoff bang with Elias." Dante throws an arm at the wall next. "I want—"

"Goddamn it. Keep it together, Dante. Raven's going to be fine. But our business? Fuck. Anyone call out today?" I ask, trying to suppress my anger over Dante's pity party. Raven doesn't need pity. She needs me to fucking gut every shitty angel I come across and collect their damn feathers to stuff in our duvet cover or some shit. Fry up some wings to feed to the masses. Creating an angelic delicacy that mankind will add to their menus when I'm through will be the only perfect recourse for this bullshit.

Dante rubs his bloody hand across the back of his neck and leans over the counter, looking at the glowing computer screen. "Looks like we got lucky. Lazy Lou and Tish canceled their appointments."

"That's the married couple?" I ask, verifying. I only know the names of the ones I let put their hands on my body. Everyone else is just a contracted soul to me.

"No, the twins." Dante motions to the collage of photos on the wall, pointing out a man and woman who completely contrast each other as the guy wears bold colors and the chick wears all black with hair as dark as Raven's. "Beau and Barbie were fucking in the backroom and were definitely not allowed their damn happy ending. The disgusting angelic dick suckers have a place in Hell because of it. What they did to Beau...they're going to have a real fucking shocker when they die and realize that Heaven tricked them into sacrificing their souls to us."

If Dante mentions what happened to Beau, then it must be worse than I thought. "And Beau will never get his personal revenge. The poor bastard. We'll have to ensure we handle it appropriately." I throw an energy ball at the wall, shattering the glass of one of the framed posters. If I didn't want my shop up and running again, I'd burn the place down. "We need to call upon our legions. If Heaven's army is getting this bold, we need to act fast. Next it'll be the church we acquired, and those souls are damn important to our business model."

Andre clears his throat, quietly listening to my conversation with Dante without butting in. He's a clueless fuck when it comes to devil affairs on this plane. Luckily for him, it won't be for long. When Micah informed us that he wanted to take Hell's tether, I almost cheered. I know angel-girl has a bond with him, but he's still on my shit list. I tolerate him for her sake, but I'm way fucking more excited that the Ruler of Lust is about to turn our estate into an endless orgy of stuffing Raven. His presence alone soaks her panties, and I can't wait for that celebration.

"What would you like me to do?" Andre asks, shifting under the intensity of my stare.

I shake my wandering thoughts away, trying not to think about what watching him with Raven would be like if she let him stretch her ass a bit. Watching the slight resistance before easing in was the fucking hottest thing I've seen between me and her, and I can already imagine watching it with her and him. I'll have to make sure to film it, because I know it might only ever be once. She'll need a damn icepack after he's through.

Dante whacks me on the arm. "What the fuck? Get it together. We have shit to do that isn't fantasizing." Reaching down, he flicks me right in the cock.

I growl and punch him in his side. The fucking bastard

knows me too damn well. "Fucker, I'm thinking," I lie, snaking my tail around his waist, preparing to whip him in the balls. "I don't know whether to have him wait for Christian or return to Raven."

Locking his fingers around my tail, Dante strokes hard and fast, shooting pain and pleasure right to my dick. I recoil and tuck my tail away, forcing myself to suppress my need to retaliate. Andre groans in annoyance, and I realize the bastard might be a bit jealous. As much as he denies his feelings, he misses his bond with Zade. But right now, it's not my damn problem that he bonded with a wishy-washy savior a millennia ago. He should've found someone who was a ride or die, fuck and get high, love but not in love, down for anything companion like Dante. Down to fuck. Down to fight. Down to share. Down for eternity.

Ugh. Now I'm getting distracted and mushy in my balls. Time to suck it up, tighten up, and fuck it up.

"Go wait for the angelic bastard and catch him before he enters the orgy pit so we have some good news to take back to Raven. We'll meet you at the house with Lucian." Dante tightens his jaw, glancing at me in his peripheral vision, taking charge.

Without waiting for me to confirm, Andre returns to Hell through his portal. The flames dissipate, and I link my fingers to the back of my head and holler, letting my voice ring through the air.

Dante surprises the fuck out of me by hugging me from behind. He tightens his arms, restraining me in place, not letting me go until I stop struggling against him. Thank fucking fuck he doesn't have a boner for once threatening the resistance of my pants. I hate that shit and don't understand how he or Raven love a big cock pressed to their ass cracks.

"You need to swallow that fucking wrath and put it toward something useful before you accidentally destroy our shop. We're already going to be down a few weeks because of the massacre." Dante digs his chin into my neck. "Channel that rage into planning another counterattack. The angel bomb won't work a second time."

I groan and scrub my hands over my cheeks. "You're a bastard."

"You love me," he teases, finally releasing me.

"I wouldn't go that far." I grin with my words and take a deep breath, appreciating that Dante got my dumbass to focus before my wrath consumed me completely. "Why don't you call Gia to come clean up this disaster while I summon Lucian? Gia can put out an alert to all our Mortal Realm bottom feeders to prepare. If Heaven wants a war, they'll get a damn war. Demand our legions attack first. No mercy. No avoidance. Have them trap and drag every damn angel they can to Hell."

Dante's face lights up with the flash of his devil façade sparking with green light in his gaze. "Fuck, Raven should hear you now. She'd be on her knees."

I flick my tongue between my index and middle finger. "And you'll be on yours for her."

I motion for him to hurry the fuck up and handle our devil affairs as I stroll toward the center of the shop, kicking body parts out of my way. Using the ash Andre left behind, I ignite a new summoning circle and focus on the deepest of Hell's levels, knowing that Lucian has other guardians there that he's been collecting for weeks. They're not useful for what currently happens, but Lucian needed something to focus on after following the lead Christian gave Andre and ended up empty handed due to his lack of a tether. That's why the bomb.

Serves the bastard right to get a reality check, though. He's not the almighty Satan he thinks he is.

"Elias better be fucking dying for interrupting my fun." Lucian materializes in front of me, dangling his fire whip from his clawed fingers as he remains in his devil form. "These featherheads are weaker than I thought. We'll have them ready to fight against Heaven by the week's end."

"Cass is going to shit his pants," I say, rubbing my hands together. "What did you do to break them?"

Lucian chuckles. "They went for a swim in the pits. Got greased up by all those fucking souls."

This smart bastard. And here I expected him to sever some wings to give to the hounds as chew toys. "I'm not admitting your brilliance, but damn."

"I knew that if they saw what we did without the damn light blinding them, they'd get it...at least some of them. There are a couple hanging with the hounds until they're ready for another dip." Lucian cracks his neck and contains his devil form, turning into the handsome bastard he is.

"Gia's on her way." Dante expands his wings at the same time he flexes his muscles, dragging my attention to him. "Let's fly. Be a little bait. I'm in a mood to fuck something up."

Lucian lifts an eyebrow. "So this is it, yeah? We're getting Greed's Kingdom?"

I forgot I didn't respond to his threat. "Close. We just have one thing to take care of first. We need to create his Hell circle."

It's time for Elias to take his throne.

It's time Heaven gets the message loud and clear.

Hell is coming, and they're about to feel the power of my wrath.

26

ELIAS

DESCEND

FUCKING BODY. I'VE never wanted to hurry and die more than I have in this moment. Everything hurts. It feels as if I'm suffocating and drowning at the same time yet my lungs still try to work.

Raven's warm palm rubs fervent circles around my back, trying her best to do something to bring me comfort. All I do is try to think about the taste of her lips, the sensation of her wet pussy craving to have me inside her—something, anything, to stop thinking about wanting to die.

She splashes in the tub, shifting to move from behind me and back in front between my legs. Micah left us a couple of minutes ago, and I wish I had his ability to communicate with her telepathically. I want to tease her and make her smile. I know she chose to move behind me so I couldn't see the sorrow in her blue-green eyes.

"I want you to know how much I love you, Elias," Raven says, nestling between my legs and sliding close enough to feel the softness of her pussy brushing my cock. "I can't even imagine the pain you're in. Is there anything I can do while we wait?"

I slowly nod my head and reach for her hand, guiding it underwater to my cock. Only she can bring me back to life. I know it's twisted and probably hard for her to think about this or want to even do this—I'm sure my coughing and wheezing will cause her a dry spell—but I fucking need something.

She giggles and laces her fingers around my cock, stroking it until I feel my body harden and pleasure finally reaches my brain to get me to shut the fuck up with my complaining. I rest my head on her shoulder and concentrate on licking her throat and caressing her hard nipples as her tits bounce from her movements.

"How's this? I can do more if you need. We can drain the tub." She tilts her head and kisses me softly, trying to give me the affection she craves without stealing my breath away.

I nod my head, willing to do anything she wants. Agreeing to her suggestions means that she's willing to do them compared to me asking.

She reaches behind her with her free hand and pops the stopper from the drain. The water hums as it swirls away, and Raven continues to work her hand up and down my shaft, the sensation of going from hot to cold as well as the slippery bubbles zings a wave of ecstasy right to my balls. Fuck, she knows how to give me just what I need.

I moan softly, clutching the side of the tub with one hand and use my other to comb her wet hair out of the way. She rinses the both of us off with hot water, sending even more goosebumps over my skin.

Sliding to her stomach, Raven gives me a killer view of her ass, keeping it in the air and just in my reach as she sucks my cock between her pouty lips and deep throats me all the way down. And fuck, she truly knows how to blow more life into a guy. The aches in my body ease and she manages to turn my pain into pleasure in a way I had no idea was possible. Every place she touches comes to life, and even the sensation of her fingers digging into the sides of my hips as she bobs up and down sends bliss zapping my balls. I groan and grab her ass cheek, wanting so desperately to give her any pleasure I can.

A knock sounds on the door, but Raven doesn't stop

sucking me in and out even as the door cracks open. I feel too good to care that it's Dante coming in and not Micah. His diamond-pupils expand and retract, and he flashes his fangs. I scrunch my face, triggered by the mere thought of his bite, and I can't stop or warn Raven about my balls about to explode.

Grunting, I cum in her mouth and tangle my fingers through her hair, hanging on to her as she slows and swallows, unfazed by my lack of warning. It's like my lungs decide this was what I needed to breathe easily again, and I manage to take my first breath without wanting to die.

"Quick, let me bite you and keep those endorphins pumping." Dante crosses the spacious bathroom and kneels beside the tub, admiring as Raven flips her hair from her face.

She smiles up at me first before flicking her attention to Dante. "Do it on his neck. Maybe it'll kick in faster."

"I think you just want to watch me suck his throat," Dante teases, touching her under the chin to get her to sit up.

I bend my head lazily to the side and flick Dante, bringing his attention to me. "Hurry, fucker," I manage to whisper.

Dante lifts his eyebrows and grins, chuckling as he extends his fangs a bit more. Raven leans in closer like she needs the best view she can possibly get, and I reach out and slide my hand between her legs at the same time Dante sinks his fangs into my neck. Raven and I moan at the same time, and Dante hums under his breath. He eases away only to watch my fingers slide in and out of Raven. He joins me for a second, spreading her open with his fingers to strum his thumb over her clit. And damn. The sound she makes sends lightning straight to my balls, making me want to push her back and fuck her with my new wave of energy coursing through me.

"Shit, you fuckheads. Wait for the circle." Kase's deep voice bellows through the bathroom and the once grand bathroom gets a bit crowded as he and Micah stroll in.

Micah blocks the door, keeping Lucian in the hallway despite his complaint. "What do you say, Elias? Are you ready or do you need some more time with Raven."

"Let's get this shit over with. We don't have fucking time to wait." Lucian smacks his palms to the doorframe, making me jump.

It sets off all the devils at once, and a collection of deep growls vibrate through the room. Raven sighs and glowers, stretching to grab a towel off the rack. If I thought I could survive yelling at Lucian for being a douche, I would. But instead, I watch Raven's hot ass wrap herself in the towel and use Dante's big shoulders to help her climb out of the tub.

"You impatient little dickhole." Raven strides toward Lucian, but Kase blocks her way. "Do you need me to remind you that this is my day with Elias and we'll do everything at the pace he wants?"

Damn it, do I love her and her protectiveness.

I don't get to hear Lucian's response to her because two

hot hands grab under my pits and haul my naked ass from the tub. This truly has become a bonding moment for me and these fuckers, because Dante doesn't even react that I still have a fucking hard-on, induced by his venom and my lust for Raven as he cradles me like a big-ass naked baby in his arms. This gives me a thought that makes me nearly choke, thinking about how I came into this life through a pussy and will leave this life trying to get in one.

"What's so funny, Elias?" Micah asks in my mind, helping Dante dry me off and slide a pair of boxers onto me like Raven isn't going to just take them off downstairs.

"I was just thinking about death," I think back to him, still grinning like a fuckhead, flying high on devil venom. "Raven's pussy is going to welcome me back home."

Micah chortles and shakes his head. "Elias is ready and content with his decision," he says, glancing to everyone else. He extends his arms and takes me from Dante, turning me slightly, so I can see Raven slipping into a sheer, lace nighty that accentuates her sweet-ass cleavage.

Strolling up to us, Raven strokes her finger along my jaw and kisses me. "I'm okay now too. I was scared, but I want nothing more than to see you take your throne. I can't wait to see the kingdom you build."

All I do is smile and nod.

Kase shoves Lucian down the hall, getting him to lead the way, and Dante stops in the doorway and faces us. The fucking devil summons a butt plug into the palm of his hand and shows it to us.

"Before you two get started, I wanted to suggest you let me put this in you, Elias." Dante remains straight faced. "Give your P-spot some action while also...stopping certain aspects that could come with death."

Shit. I pucker at just the thought. Why did the bastard have to bring that up? I know he's thinking about Raven, but I'm nearly sure Raven isn't going to fuck me once I die. She's going to smother me with her damn tits or something. Her pussy.

"Could be fun," Micah says, inspecting the piece.

Raven tips her head back and laughs. "You guys, stop. If he doesn't want his ass to vibrate, then don't try to convince him. This is a celebration, and I'm not going to worry about any of this shit."

Dante closes his hand, hiding the plug. "Fine, pretty soul. Whatever you two want. We're just here for the show."

"He means support," Micah corrects, whacking him.

I wave my hand at Raven, getting her attention. Summoning my strength, I whisper, "Kill me fucking now."

"Fuck yeah, let's do this." Dante spanks her ass and lifts her up, rushing ahead of us and out of the bathroom.

Micah doesn't even make it to the staircase before we watch Dante jump over the banister with Raven screeching in his arms. The second they're out of sight, I close my eyes and concentrate on the sound of Micah's beating heart. It's a strange thing to think about. My heart will stop beating and my essence will leave this body and get taken to Hell. What happens after that? I have no idea. I was scared to find out, but now I'm just anxious.

"I'll be with you every second of the way. Raven will carry your soul down and put it to rest. How you choose to be reborn as a devil is up to you. How you create your kingdom and throne will come naturally. Do not worry. I want you to focus on just being with Raven and freeing your soul, okay?" Micah's soft voice helps relieve my nerves. "Just remember, you're powerful. This is how it should've always been for you."

The scent of Hell permeates through the air as Micah takes two steps at a time downstairs. I struggle to focus on the hazy room. All of the lights are off apart from the ring of hellfire, which Andre stands within. He towers in his devil form, freaky as fuck, and I can't stop from glancing at his giant cock still hanging in his Hell form.

"I'm going to be taking the tether to Hell first," Micah says, remaining expressionless as the others watch Micah stroll me on a damn death march toward the place I will get to fuck Raven one more time as a mortal. It's really all I want to think about—or maybe all I can think about—with the sudden desire triggered by Andre getting to my cock.

"I don't know how long I can wait," I think to him, training my gaze on Raven. Dante must've brushed her hair in the short time they were waiting, because the silky tresses cascade down her back.

Micah chuckles at my comment, understanding that I'm not talking about clinging on to my life. "Just a minute. You won't see it as it happens in Hell."

Raven closes the space to us first, and she stretches up and kisses Micah. "Thank you for doing this for us. You have no idea what it means to me."

"I'm sure you can thank him later, angel-girl," Kase says, winding his tail around her waist. He extends his arms to Micah. "Now let me take your soulmate and get him settled. You two don't have to wait for the switch to get started. I don't mind lifting your humping asses into the circle."

Raven's face flushes, warming at his words. "This should be way more awkward, you know."

"Nah, pretty soul. We're all down and comfortable for any and all things. Maybe the Jizz Master will get a new nickname while he's at it." Dante stands outside the circle and lays down a pile of blankets.

The sight of him setting a few toys around and within reach breathes new life into me. Because unholy Hell. I should really learn to accept that this is my eternity. Standing up for my asshole while also trying not to question myself whether or not my resistance might be a waste. What if I do like what's being offered? Fuck. I'd say that I only live once, but that's a damn lie.

"Shit, you really are kinky," I say to Dante, my heart picking up speed and thrashing out of control. I try not to react, though my hand flying to my chest gives me away.

"Haven't you been paying attention? Our soul loves pushing the boundaries and trying new things. These are just a couple of her favorites. You don't look like you might be up to the challenge of reciprocating with what you have, so I've decided to make things easier." Dante grabs some weird-ass toy that looks nothing like a dick and more like something women use on their faces. Clearly it's not, because Dante turns it on and holds it up to Raven's tit first. "Nipple, nipple, clit." He holds it to each part of her, making her shiver. Bringing it down to his groin, he adds, "Balls."

Damn it. Raven's reaction alone has me extending my hand out.

"Let this be fun. Adventurous. Not like you have anything left to lose except your ass virginity. And you know, Raven and a strap-on—"

Raven's face reddens more and she whacks Dante in the shoulder, making him laugh. "Thanks for your help, but I think we got this."

Kase helps me the rest of the way to the blankets as Raven remains by our side. She was right about thinking that this situation should be more awkward than it is, but it's not the first time we gave one of the devils a show. And now? I just want Raven to love and fuck and enjoy our last mortal bang with the time we have.

Dante grabs Raven's hand, pulling her to him. "We're all right here. Our focus will be on the tether swap. Just say my name if you need me. If you don't, we won't interrupt, okay?"

Raven smirks and kisses him. "We'll be fine...for now."

I sit propped up on my elbows and offer her what I think is an easy smile, but part of my face remains numb from Dante's venom bite and I could possibly look awkward as Hell. Raven joins me on the blankets and surprises me by pulling one over the both of us, blocking out the world around us. Even with the crackle of Hell popping through the air, and the sound of the devils murmuring close by, with the blanket around us and Raven filling up my line of sight, I can pretend it's only the two of us in this moment.

She smiles and caresses her fingers to my cheek. "Can I be honest?"

"Always," I mumble, keeping my voice low, afraid if I talk too loudly, I'll start coughing.

She smiles, her beautiful eyes watering. "I don't know if I should cry or laugh in this moment. I—I feel like my emotions are out of control. I know what we need to do, but it's so damn hard to even think about it. I just—I love you."

I pull her to me, getting her to sit between my legs and face me so that I can hug her. "I don't want you to laugh or cry, darlin'. The only thing I want to hear come from that pouty mouth of yours is moans of pleasure. I love you more than I ever knew possible. From the glimpses of our past lives, the one thing that sticks with me is how truly, madly, and deeply I'm in love with you. You're my Raven, but you're also my Grace. I'm just relieved that we found each other when we did. I can't imagine another life without you in it."

She blinks her glassy eyes, and I swipe a stray tear from her cheek. Leaning in, I kiss her with everything in me, guiding her to sit on my lap without worrying about hurting me. She hangs her arms over my shoulders and plays with my hair, following my lead and giving me whatever she thinks I can take.

Like a switch flips on inside me, I deepen our kiss, sliding my tongue into her mouth at the same time I reach for the hem of her lacy black nightie and tug it over her head, letting in a stream of cooler air. She reaches between us, her hands desperate to wrap around my cock, and I groan into her mouth at the pleasure rolling through me. She adjusts herself, lifting her hips and giving me room to raise up to pull my underwear down. And damn it, do I want her more than I ever have in my life.

Feeling around the blankets, I find the toy Dante had showed me and blindly get the thing to turn on. Raven gasps and clutches onto me, trembling the second I feel my way to her clit. The quiet vibrations buzz over my hand, and I swear I've never seen Raven react as she does now, panting and squirming as I adjust the toy until she grabs my wrist and stops me where she likes it.

"Oh, fuck. Fuck," she whispers, slightly bouncing on her knees. Her mouth goes to war with mine as she kisses me again, sucking my lip and kissing me with the intensity of her pleasure.

With my free hand, I grab her ass and lift her a bit, aligning our bodies until she sinks onto my cock, releasing a loud moan of pleasure. The vibration from the toy zings through my body, setting off an indescribable pleasure that turns my brain numb. The last time I fucked Raven was incredible and this is goddamned mind-blowing. Her pussy drips over my balls, her excitement turning her into a slippery pool of fucking amazingness, and I grin as she screams out, her orgasm intense enough that her pussy tightens like it's not going to release me.

She starts up again, moaning and panting, bouncing harder and faster, and I fall back to the blankets and hold her hips, watching as the light of the room around us engulfs us in Hell's firelight.

Neither of us pays attention to the devils, though the ground shakes harder and harder. Raven's eyes widen for a split second, but I grunt and cum, flinging myself forward with the intensity of my body reacting. The edges of my vision shadow. My heart pounds out of whack, furiously and irregularly. Raven mouths something I can't hear.

Roaring, Kase pounces beside us and bites down on the

blanket, dragging the two of us toward the summoning circle.

Raven slides off me and kneels beside me, trying to pull me into her arms. Her brows pucker together and she whips her attention somewhere else, but my body remains frozen.

I can't move.

I think this is it.

Hell, accept me as your newest ruler. I'm ready to descend.

27

DANTE

FIRST BATTLE

"KASE! SHIT! IS he breathing?" Raven's voice screams through the air. "Oh, fucking God. Elias! Wake up!"

"Watch out, angel-girl. He still has a pulse. His heartbeat is fucking nuts." Gathering flickering red light between his palms, Kase shocks Elias in his chest.

Raven cradles Elias's head on her lap, her beautiful face stained with hot tears. "He groaned. Fuck, Elias. Open your eyes."

The room shakes, dragging my attention away from Kase and Raven and back to my phone as Gia yammers on with a warning that comes a little too late. An angel managed to get past the Hell barrier we put in place around the whole neighborhood and blew out a window.

I hate that I knew this shit was coming.

I knew that the angelic army would still somehow manage to get through all of the defenses we've put up, but I thought we'd have more time. I've underestimated my legion and their ability to fight Heaven off, and it makes me question everything I've worked for.

"I don't know how they're doing it. They're possessing pure souls, Dante. Did you know they could do that? We can't tell who to fight." Gia's voice rings over the line as I stand protectively in front of Raven and Elias as Kase helps them dress. Lucian remains with Andre and Micah, finalizing the power shift.

These fuckers better hurry, because if what Gia says is true, then we're about to go to battle. "Of course I knew it was possible but it's unheard of. A mortal has to be willing and there has never been a reason for it." I hiss and clench my fist, trying not to shatter the phone with my strength.

"What should I do? We have boundaries. Expectations," Gia says, groaning.

"Show no mercy. If they stand in your way, take them

down." I disconnect the line, trusting my first in command with handling the attacks as we finish this shit.

Bright light glows from the window as the angel tries to attack again. Glass sprays over the floor, causing Raven to screech and swear. If she could spit fire, she would burn the fucking guardian to a crisp.

"Hurry the fuck up with the switch!" I yell, extending my fangs and striding toward the window. My skin stings at the heavenly glow radiating in but I push through and spit venom into an unfamiliar bastard's face.

The mortal man, glowing with angelic light, doesn't even scream. He has no control of his body as one of the bastard guardians uses him as a vessel in an attempt to crack our shields. With enough force, it's possible, and the angel pushes the man to keep trying even as his body smolders under the heat.

"Fuck, I need some help here," I call, spotting another possessed mortal striding to the broken window.

Another angel stands behind the woman, using her as a shield. Gathering holy power, the angel blasts it at the barrier at the same time the possessed woman slams her palms against it. The room quakes, humming against the power.

"Just keep them back another minute," Kase calls, growling in his devil form.

"I'm going outside," I snap, stretching my wings.

"Don't." Launching a ball of red energy, he blasts the

woman and angel back a couple feet, but it only slows them down. "There are too many for you alone."

I can handle my damn self and he knows it. If Raven didn't say my name, I'd ignore Kase and lunge, taking out as many angels as I can while dragging them to Hell with me. It would be their mistake. I can return from Hell after a recharge in power. But them? They'd suffer under my punishment.

A low rumble quivers under my feet, and I peek over my shoulder and watch the summoning circle shoot up toward the ceiling. Fucking finally. My whole body tingles with the exchange of the tether. Even feeling it uncaged for a second rattles me to my core, the wild, immense power that runs Hell so palpable that I get a fucking boner from it. I've never taken the tether before, but I can imagine how good it feels getting filled up with it. If only it didn't trap you. I'm not exactly looking forward to my time. Because fuck. I've never been away from my angry half and I never want to be away from my pretty soul.

"Dante, the shield. The shift cracked it," Kase says, sending another burst of power toward the window.

"Shit." I expand my wings, using my body to create a wall between the angels attacking the shield and the Hell portal. Heavenly light burns my skin, smoldering away my human façade until I stand in my devil form.

What the fuck are the angels doing?

Light seeps in through every crack, turning night into day

outside. Hellfire explodes behind me, the force knocking me forward. I slam my hands to the wall. My palms sear against the now blessed wall. They're not trying to get in. They're trying to banish us from the Mortal Realm.

A furious roar echoes through the room, and Andre bursts from the summoning circle in his devil form. His scorpion-like form fills the room, his sharp appendages cracking the wood with his heavy footsteps. Swinging his tail over his head and at the window, he impales one of the possessed mortals and drags them through, sending guts spraying everywhere. The remnants of being tethered to Hell make him stronger, faster, and nearly unstoppable.

Screams ring through the air as the light that explodes from the mortal gathers to form an angelic silhouette on the floor. Lucian climbs from Hell and whips his fire chain at the angel, dragging it closer to him. Raven gasps and spins away, covering her eyes. Lifting his hoof, he smashes it into the angelic light, breaking the floor open. The angel tries latching onto the edge only to have Lucian blast him right into a legion of demons waiting.

I spit venom at the gathering forms, threatening the entire mansion. I can't see them, but there must be at least a hundred guardians. I can sense them. Hear them. They're surrounding the estate. "Raven, we're out of time. You have to hurry—"

An earthquake rocks everything, knocking furniture over

and sending the pictures and vases Raven picked off the tables and from the walls. The ceiling cracks above us, and Lucian and Andre fight with their power, pushing back hard.

"Dante," Raven calls, shouting over the noise. "Please, I need you."

I spin and rush to her side, entering the summoning circle. Kase stands on one side of her while Micah holds his arms out, waiting to grab Elias. I join the four of them, using my wings to create a barrier.

"Everyone touch her. Connect to her soul." Kase rests his hand on Raven's shoulder. "Raven, I need you to follow my instructions exactly. We don't have time to smother him with your pussy like he wants."

She frowns and shakes her head. "I don't know if I can do this."

"He's strong. Take my blade. Pain is fleeting," Micah says, keeping his voice low. "Elias agrees."

Kase grabs Micah's wrist, stopping his attempt to give Raven the Hell blade. "You're going to break his neck. Now listen. It'll be fast."

I reach down and carefully adjust Raven's hands on Elias's head. Tears spill from her eyes, splashing his face. "You can do this, Raven. We're here. Use our strength to help you."

Andre's hollers boom through the air, the intensity of his pain slapping against Raven, making her hesitate. I jerk my attention toward his yells and watch the protective barrier shatter with Heaven's light and strike Andre, blasting him from the room and out of this plane. And fuck. It could take him minutes to recoup from that.

"Now, Raven—" Kase's voice fades with the boom of the plane shifting.

Shit. Fuck. Cunt. Cocksucker. I extend my fangs and launch forward, crashing into the next angel to make it inside. A gust of holy wind whips around, extinguishing the flaming circle around Raven and Elias, cutting Micah off.

Without it, Elias can't descend. Micah can't guide him.

"Raven, this is your last chance to do the right thing." Cassius holds a flaming sword and pushes past two guardians, gathering enough power to keep us back. "Give us Elias and let us save your soul or burn for eternity. Those are your only options."

Fury bursts through me, and I glower, clenching my fingers into fists.

Lucian snarls, reacting before I do, and he charges toward his brother and tackles him, shoving him hard into the wall. The world trembles, Lucian's fire against Cassius's holy light bending the foundation of the plane.

That's it.

"We need to attack at once. It'll break the holy shield they're trying to trap us in," I tell Kase, watching as Lucian and Cassius throw punches, trying to get an opening for their weapons.

"Angel-girl, hold onto Elias. Use your whole body to protect him the best you can. This is going to hurt." Kase throws a blanket onto Raven, getting her to shield the two of them even though it won't protect him. He does it to help lessen her fear. He doesn't want her to see what's about to happen.

"Lucian, the veil!" I yell, standing beside Kase and spitting my venom, watching it eat away at the world in front of us.

Kase throws orb after orb of red power, sending crackling electricity through the room, turning it from shadows and the light of Heaven to a ruby color the shade of blood. The light shimmers and twists, the whole world shaking. Punching Cassius one more time, Lucian knocks him back through the window. Gathering fire from the depths of Hell, Lucian shoots it at the veil, the force of our power battling against Heaven enough to crack this plane open, letting it merge into the Mortal Realm.

Light and fire explode through the room, knocking all of us off our feet. I crash into the wall behind Raven and use my wings to push up. Kase whips his tail, keeping an angel back, and Lucian blasts more power at the burning wall, using it to keep Cassius away.

"Raven, we have to move," I say, pushing to my feet. "We need a summoning circle."

She rips the blanket from her and Elias and bobs her head. "I'm going to fucking destroy them! You hear me, Cassius!" Her voice rings through the air. "You're fucking going to know what it's like to experience Hell on a level you never imagined."

Lucian strides forward, heaving a deep breath. Uncoiling his chain, he hands it to Raven. "This will protect you and keep the fuckers back."

"Lucian, I want you to lead." Kase nudges me with his hand. "Dante, help Raven get out. Elias was knocked unconscious. She needs you to carry him. Go straight to the summoning circle. Watch your back and let Raven handle anyone she has to. Elias's life is the most important right now."

It's like a kick in a dick to have to agree to that, but he's right. Elias can't die without Raven taking him out. If he does—fuck. It's not happening. My pretty soul is determined and strong. We can manage to get a couple dozen feet. She made it through fucking years with a serial killing psycho and abusive douche. She survived being on Lucian's bad side. She's handled Heaven's attempts to destroy her. Fuck, she's even walked through fucking Hell and made it back to us. She is far more powerful than she might even be aware. The angels wouldn't fight so hard otherwise.

"Stay close and alert," I tell Raven, adjusting Elias onto my shoulder and covering him with my wing protectively. "Treat these fuckers how they deserve. The second we get into the summoning circle, put your hands on Elias's head where I showed you. We must be fucking fast. Once he dies, then we'll have the strength of another devil to empower us."

Raven licks her lips and nods, covering her mouth and nose with the blanket Kase hands her. "I'm ready to fuck some assholes up."

I smile. I can't help it. "Good."

Lucian growls, leading the way toward the back of the house. There is no way we will be able to easily exit through the back door, so Lucian stomps his way toward an empty wing of the house near the back corner. It was supposed to be another living quarters for either Zade or Cassius, but this place is now trash. We're going to have to relocate and hide for a bit while we get shit together.

"Be fucking ready. I'm going to get fucking blasted. I'll run as far as I can to give you clearance." Lucian rams his horns into the doorframe, breaking through part of the wall without bending down. "Someone is going to fucking owe me for this."

"Fuck right we will. This is your fault." Kase whips him on the back with his tail. "If anything, you're going to fucking owe us."

"Blowjobs!" Raven says, her word coming out far sexier and breathy than she realizes. "You're blowing every single devil and swallowing their damn loads."

Lucian growls and flares his nostrils. "You'd love that."

"I'd love getting the fuck out of here alive even more." Raven swings the fire chain, smacking it across the floor. "So prove your damn power already."

Backing up, Lucian gives himself space and flexes his muscles. He extends his hands and blasts fire at the wall, choosing to break it open instead of using the window. The angelic army would expect us to use the easier approach, so this should give us the chance we need.

Kase runs behind him, preparing to attack the second he has an opening, and I nudge Raven to get ready, acting as a shield to her back.

The wall explodes, sending smoke, fire, and debris raining through the air around us. Raven sucks in a deep breath and jets forward, staying just a few feet behind Kase. I expect to see a thousand warriors lined up and ready to blast us all to Hell. I expect the world to break open and for guardians and saviors to push us into the pits.

Unnerving silence greets us.

Lucian spins, blasting power toward the sky anyway.

"What the fuck," Raven says, her voice a whisper.

I push her between the shoulder blades. "Keep moving."

Bright light flashes through the sky above us, and Lucian and Kase both blast power at an angel that crosses in between planes, trying to fuck with us. They're here, but we can't see them unless they want to reveal themselves. To hurt us, they'd have to do the same.

Something's up, and I fucking brace for the worst.

Another angel breaks between planes, and once again, Lucian and Kase attack.

"Raven, you have ten seconds." Cassius thumps down in front of us, wielding his flaming sword. His amethyst eyes sparkle with his heavenly light. "I can't let you do this."

Peeking at me over her shoulder, Raven crinkles her nose in a frown. "Get him to the circle," she mouths, sending a burst of pain right to my middle with her words. I don't like the look in her eyes, but I can't stop her. She's going to do what she thinks is best, and I trust her.

I nod without a word.

Raising her hands, Raven says, "I surrender. Please, just let me say goodbye to my devils. Please."

Cassius's hard features soften. "To Dante only."

Raven fakes a cry and swivels toward me. "I love you. You need to trust me, okay?"

My mouth dries at her words. "Always, pretty soul."

"Then run!" Jerking back around, Raven swings the fire whip, slashing it across Cassius's chest. His eyes widen and he automatically raises his hands protectively. Raven launches at him, jabbing the chain into his neck, pinning him down.

I don't wait to see what happens. I use the chance to do what she asks. Flapping my wings, I race forward and toward the summoning circle. Micah growls and shouts, waving his hands, pointing behind me.

Tossing Elias to him, I spin and spit venom, getting an angel right in the face. But two more materialize and blast me with power. Then another and another. I can't do anything as heavenly light engulfs me, burning my skin and eating away at my being. The ground shakes beneath my feet, and I holler, unable to control my voice as I sink down.

Raven screams out, punching Cassius and then scrambling away.

But the angelic power is too much for me.

The world shifts and Hell opens up.

I fall into my kingdom.

28

RAVEN

DARKNESS

MY HEART SMASHES into pieces as fire consumes Dante and he vanishes right before my eyes. I scream and run forward, stepping over the ash left in his wake. I can't believe these angels. I can't believe Heaven. They're monsters and far worse than anything I could've imaged. These blessed beings are vicious. They're ruthless. They're going to ruin everything.

"He's fine. Go!" Kase hollers, shooting an angel with

power from the sky.

Lucian jumps on top of the angel and slices his claws across his wing, severing it. "Go!" he shouts, repeating Kase.

I summon my speed and strength and race toward Micah and Elias. Micah blasts his orange power, fighting the angels from the ground as they try to swoop toward me. A short, buff angel drops in front of me, and I whip the fire chain, lashing him from his shoulder to his leg, searing his clothing.

Micah roars and flings a dagger, piercing it into the angel's golden wing. I swing the fire chain again, aiming for his other wing, stopping the angel from trying to tackle and fly away with me. Channeling my devil strength, I bow down and ram into his stomach, knocking him onto his back. I punch and slap, slamming my palms to him so quickly that he doesn't get a good hold on me.

"Run!" Micah yells, roaring with his words. "Five feet!"

I shove my hands to the angel and stumble away, catching my balance enough to run the rest of the way to Micah. Heat engulfs me for a split second, and the world around me blazes with the fires of Hell.

Like all of Heaven is seeking vengeance, a flock of angels flies toward him. Lucian spins and blasts fire, catapulting into the air. He rams his horns into one of the angel's stomach and flings her over his head. The female angel hits the ground and rolls. She unsheathes a short dagger and sets it aglow with holy fire. I scream out in warning, but it's too late. The flaming dagger sinks into Lucian's ass cheek.

He snarls and rips it free, throwing it back to the angel, hitting her in the chest. His moment of distraction leaves his back open, and four angels dive toward him and each one of them stabs him—his shoulder, torso, leg, and neck.

Summoning a huge orb of red Hell power, Kase thrusts it at the group of angels, but it only stops them for a second. More fly down, lighting up the night like falling stars shooting toward Earth.

"Kase, leave him!" Micah shouts, releasing a loud whistle.

Kase roars and bounds away, using his tail and horns to clear a path. "I'll hold them off. Raven, take his life. Now!"

Don't fuck up. Don't fuck up. Don't you dare fucking fuck up. I chant the words to myself over and over, dropping to the ground at the same time bright light blinds me as the fires of Hell swallow Lucian, sending him back to his kingdom.

Kase circles our summoning circle, blasting angels away, but they don't stop. They keep trying over and over.

"Raven," Elias says, his soft voice sounding through the air. "Hurry."

I swallow my nerves and take deep breaths, cupping his head in my hands. Leaning in, I kiss him, using his love to push me forward. The world crashes and booms around us, light and fire shaking the foundation of the summoning circle.

"Raven, shit. Shit!" Kase tumbles across the ground and

lands on his back a few feet away.

A loud gunshot rings through the air, hitting Kase in the chest. He roars and tries to get up, but a couple more bullets spray across his body.

Angelic light streams above, turning the yard as bright as day. I shield my eyes, my mind whirling. Everything happens so fast that I can barely think. Micah roars and shoots his power toward the sky. Kase thrashes, getting hit with orbs of heavenly light. The ground opens up, and the fires of Hell drag him into a portal but not without him lassoing an angel and dragging him down too.

"I can't focus to guide you. Protect him. Stay low! I'm going to channel all the devils," Micah shouts, blasting his power at the shield. The fiery barrier grows higher and higher, finally cutting the angels off.

"Raven," Elias says again, shifting his body as he tries to sit up. "Raven, watch—"

Fire and agony swallows my leg, the pop of a gunshot echoing in my ears. I screech and clutch the back of my leg, feeling the warmth of blood. What the actual fuck?

"Mi-Micah," I gasp, heaving through the pain in my leg.

Micah doesn't get a chance to respond because the angels hit the barrier full force. Their power can't get to us, the protection of Hell too strong, but damn it. It didn't stop the damn bullet. Where did it come from? I...

A rumble quakes the ground and dirt explodes toward the

sky, raining down on us. Andre's beautiful leathery wings expand out, and he launches from his Hell portal, flying toward the sky. His monstrous form fills the world above, and he impales angel after angel with his huge stinger, dropping them to the ground.

Micah growls and cuts off his wave of power, not wasting even a second to drop to his knees beside us. Helping me lift Elias upright, he holds him against his chest, propping him up. Elias's head lolls as his eyes struggle to focus.

"I know you're in pain, but you'll heal. We have to finish this now." Micah reminds me where to place my hands on Elias. "One quick motion. Use all your strength."

I nod, tears pooling in my eyes, a mixture between heartache and agony from the bullet lodged in my leg. With a soft whisper of love, I summon the strength of all my devils. A soft smile crosses Elias's lips, and I squeeze my eyes shut. I can't watch. I can't think about it. All I can do is pray to Hell that I don't fuck this up.

"Raven, stop! Stop! Don't do this!" Tamia's voice rings through the air.

I snap my eyes open and watch as an angel drops her from above. She lands in the grass and scrambles to her feet.

"Raven, please," she calls, waving a hand.

I can't believe this shit.

"Micah, behind you!" Andre swings his tail, trying to knock Cassius out of the way, but another angel crashes into him.

Wielding his flaming sword, Cassius enters the circle, his whole body set aglow. Micah punches his heavy hoof-like hand, trying to knock him away. Another angel joins him, and the two attack Micah as Andre tries to get them away from the barrier.

Elias squeezes my arm. "Raven, she's possessed."

His words jerk my attention away from the battle between my devils and the fucking angelic army to where Tamia strides closer and raises a gun. It was her. She was the one shooting at us. She was the one who shot me.

I throw myself in front of Elias protectively. "Tamia, stop. I don't want to hurt you."

Tears shine in her glassy eyes, the same shape but bluer than my teal irises. "I can't. I can't stop. Please, you have to move. The angel is giving me only twenty seconds to convince you to move. She will make me shoot you otherwise."

"Fuck," I breathe, stealing myself. "Fight her. Kick her fucking ass out of you. It's your body."

Tamia clenches her jaw, her whole body shaking. "Please, Raven. I have to kill him. If you don't let me, she will make me kill you too."

Well this isn't going to fucking work for me. Elias must die by my hands. It's the only way. Right now, he must descend for Hell to rise. If the angels take his life...it's over. Everything is over.

I gather my courage and raise my hands. "Then fucking do it. Shoot me."

"Raven," Tamia begs. "Ten seconds."

"Shoot me!" I scream, stumbling to stand upright, the agony in my leg nearly sending me back down. "You can't fucking kill him! He's mine! He will descend!"

Tamia's whole body trembles as her eyes flash and light up with Heaven's glow. Anger and rage course through me, and I flip the angel possessing my cousin off. Aiming the gun, the angel forces my cousin to pull the trigger. I screech and clutch my stomach as she shoots me in the abdomen. Shadows edge my vision, and I fall backward and onto Elias. I do the only thing I can think of and twist around, lacing my fingers to his throat. This is it. I have to do this. It has to be now.

"Micah! Get ready!" I scream, begging for him to risk losing the circle to help carry Elias to Hell.

I squeeze harder, feeling Elias's muscles tighten and spasm. His body fights against my strength, but I don't let go. I can't. The ground rumbles and splits open just outside the circle, and Dante catapults from his kingdom in all his hellish glory. He spits venom, sending a cluster of angels scattering, giving Micah the chance to turn to me.

Something firm taps the back of my head.

"Please, Raven. This is your last chance." Tamia's voice cracks.

I don't stop. Micah roars, gathering his power.

Heat courses through my veins, the power of Hell snaking around me. The world slows and I look down at Elias, his eyes wide, his head shaking. Like he summons strength from the kingdom his death will build, he jerks his hands up and rips my fingers from his throat. He hollers and shoves his hands to my chest, knocking me onto my back.

I can't even process what's going on. Elias climbs on top of me and shields me with his body. Angelic light illuminates the world around us, cutting us off from Hell.

"I can't let you die first. I'm sorry, darlin'. I'm so sorry." Elias pushes on his hands, his neck struggling to keep his head up.

My ears ring, deafening me, and I stare in horror as Tamia shoots Elias in the chest, sending him sprawling forward and onto me. I scream, my vision turning red. My whole world collapses and burns around me. Fury snares my thoughts, refusing to let me go. Yells cut through the air as the angels retreat, shouting their joy.

Happiness.

They stole humanity's chance at changing.

They stole Hell's ability to rise.

They stole my throne in Purgatory.

"Raven," Tamia whispers, shaking and crying, standing a foot away. Suddenly, her face hardens and a smile crosses her face. I spot the glow of the angel shining in her eyes, stealing control from my cousin. "Your sacrifice will not be forgotten.

You've done a great thing for Heaven."

Something dark and dangerous stabs me in the soul, and I reach out and grab Tamia by her ankle, yanking her over the barrier completely. She lights up in flames as the holy power of the angel explodes, dragging the fucking bitch from my cousin's body. A gust of wind puts out the flames of Hell from Tamia's clothing, but she stumbles, trying to escape.

Except the ground crumbles beneath her feet, and there is nothing I can do as Hell swallows the essence of the angel and drags my cousin with her into its fiery depths.

I stare in shock and horror, my whole body roiling with a thousand emotions as I try to process what happened.

"Angel-girl. Take a breath, okay. We're going to figure this out." Kase materializes beside me, slinking his way closer to where I stare at Elias's bare leg, praying with everything in me for his toes to curl or something, anything, to show me that Heaven failed.

But I know in the depths of my being that they didn't. They forced my cousin to kill my soulmate. They forced her to sacrifice herself. And for what? What did they truly accomplish? Hell isn't going anywhere.

"Raven, please. Will you look at me?" Micah drops to his knees beside me, taking my hand. "I'm so sorry I've failed you. I tried to grab his soul and guide him, hoping that he was strong enough."

My mouth quivers with his words. "I just don't understand. Why did he do that? Where is he?"

Micah doesn't respond right away, and the other devils close the space, circling me. I raise my gaze to meet his, but he looks at the other devils instead. Reaching out, I grab him by the chin, forcing him to look at me.

"Micah, tell me. Where is he?" I heave a few breaths, my nerves getting the best of me.

"He died unbound," Dante says, speaking up. He scoots close to my other side and drapes an arm over me. "But don't worry. We'll find him."

I blink a few times and release a breath. "Fuck. Go now. He can't be there by himself!" Fear flutters through me. "Get him!"

Kase's tail wraps around me and drags me from my spot on the ground and into his arms. I slap my hands against his shoulders, my mind swirling with the memory of me walking through Hell. If he's unbound, then any demon can get to him. He is at the mercy of those who torment Hell.

"Let me go! I need you to find him!" I screech, thrashing. Kase only holds me tighter. "They're going to torture him. Your fucking legions are going to steal everything good he carries."

Another hot body presses against my back. "Raven, Elias is strong. He's not an ordinary soul," Dante says, sandwiching me to Kase. "He will be okay until we can get a good sense of him. Right now, his soul is finding its place. Even if we scoured all of Hell this second, he could still be between planes. He might not even realize what's happening or what he needs to do yet."

I breakdown, a sob stealing my breath and sending unbearable anguish crashing through me. "Why?" I ask, my words stuttering with my sobs. "Why did you do this, Elias? How could you just leave me?"

I push away from Kase and Dante until they finally let me go. My eyes burn with my hot tears, and I crawl across the charred grass to where Elias's body lies, his chest ravaged with bullet holes and blood. I bow beside him and rest my head on his cool shoulder, hiccupping and bawling more tears than I knew were possible.

"Why did you protect me? You were more important," I say, feeling the heat of the devils surrounding me. "I'm so fucking pissed. I would've been okay. I could've survived."

Micah clears his throat and rests his big hand on my back. "You might not have, Raven. If you had died before him, you'd have failed to uphold your contract. Elias protected you because with his end, your soul would be free from Hell. He was saving you."

His words zap me right in the heart, and I whip my head up and glower at Lucian. My body reacts before my mind has a chance to comprehend what I'm doing, and I throw myself at him. I scream in his face and whack him, hitting him as hard as I can over and over again.

"This is your fault!" I screech, punching him in the nose.

I expect him to shove me off. To react. To do something. It pisses me off that Lucian lies placidly beneath me, just accepting my wrath.

"You should've just ended my contract! You should've just accepted your damn place. Now Elias is lost in Hell! Heaven has won. This is what you wanted, wasn't it? I was so stupid!" I swing and hit him one more time before two hands hook around my waist and pull me off.

Lucian scrubs his hands over his beard and gets to his feet, striding to stand in front of me while Andre tries to settle me down with his presence alone. Fire flashes in his eyes, and he flicks his gaze toward the stars once and back to me.

"You can blame me all you want, but it doesn't change things. You damn fucking know that I was on board." Flaring his nostrils he leans even closer. "There was a fucking reason I never ended your contract. You had to be bound to Hell for Elias to descend. Not to mention, if I had freed your soul, Heaven would've taken it immediately. You're already fucking close to Zade. You probably wouldn't have realized it until it was too late. I re-negotiated the contract with Elias so that upon his unbound death, you'd be free. It was the only way to give you time to negotiate something with someone you prefer. So like I said, hate me. Blame me. I don't give a flying fuck if it makes you feel better, but don't accuse me of trying to sabotage Hell."

We remain in a staring match until I break first, hanging my head and letting the silent tears leak from my eyes. I thought I survived the worst day of my life, but it could never compare to this moment. My eternity is ruined. Purgatory can't exist without the power of all eight of Hell's kingdoms.

"Okay," I manage to squeak out.

"And I hope you know I am sorry. Not for everything, but for some things. I will fucking find the bitch who possessed your cousin. She will pay." Lucian tightens his jaw and reaches up, caressing my cheek. "That, I promise you."

I only nod and push thoughts of Tamia away. What the fuck convinced her to allow an angel to possess her? Was she tricked? Manipulated? Does it even matter?

"And we will fucking ensure Lucian stays good on his word," Dante says, staring around. "Heaven thinks they fucking won, but we're the damn rulers of Hell. This isn't over."

"Damn straight." Kase takes me from Andre, gathering me in his arms. "You can still be the queen of our kingdoms. Heaven will regret their decision to put a stop to our plan."

"They assuredly will, especially when they realize we're strong, and will only continue to grow in power. Just because we don't have Greed's level doesn't mean we still can't take Sloth and Pride's." Andre motions with his finger, pointing toward the trees at the back of the property. I spot Zade's familiar glow as he watches us from a distance. "He can't keep away."

I tighten my mouth. "I want to take the guardians down. I want the saviors to pay."

"I'll help you get my brother to his knees," Lucian says, gathering hellfire in his hand.

"I don't want just him to fucking bow." I clench my fingers into fists. "I want every last angel."

As I stare at Zade's glowing light disappear, I realize there is only one thing certain in my life now. The angelic army will pay.

I'm no longer going to rule Purgatory.

I'm taking Hell as my devils' queen.

Hell, the world, and Heaven will be ours.

EPILOGUE

GONE

WARM LIPS CARESS my bare shoulder as I stare at the blank wall of our temporary home. I haven't left my room, remaining wrapped in Elias's blankets I demanded someone retrieve since he died and his soul went to Hell. It's the last thing I have of him from his mortal life and I just wanted something that smells like him—like comfort and familiarity. Like love.

I thought his death would be the worst of things. But it was supposed to be as fleeting as the pain of taking his life. Not this. Not the uncertainty of what to expect. He was to rise and claim Hell and be my new king. Now? I still don't know.

He made a deal with Lucian to serve him on his army. Lucian damn well knows that I'm not letting that happen. As soon as Micah finds him, he'll be in his kingdom. Then Kase's. Dante's. The one thing I know is that he will never be alone. The thought helps ease my fears, but it doesn't do anything for the ache in my very soul. Who knew I'd be able to tell that a part of me was missing from the Mortal Realm? Even though we haven't known each other long in this life, our bond was always there. But now?

Fuck. I need a distraction.

Turning over, I meet Andre's beautiful velvety dark gaze as his eyes search mine. His brows pucker together, and he reminds me of himself as the angel he was before he jumped from grace. He strokes his warm fingers over my cheek, his desire and hunger prevalent with the enormous amount of unwanted space between us. But he hasn't pushed me. He hasn't offered to fuck my brains out to forget.

And now, I want him to know that he can. He doesn't have to be careful with me or sensitive to what he thinks I need. All I need is his cock inside me. I don't care if he gets stuck. That will help me think about something else.

Rolling on top of him, I surprise him by crashing my mouth to his, giving in to our rampant desire sending tingles exploding between my legs. Andre releases the sexiest groan in existence, the deepness of it vibrating across my lips. His hands glide down my back and to the hem of my nightie, not wasting even a second to allow its flimsy fabric to create a barrier between us.

"Fuck me like you need me," I murmur, shimmying down until I feel the thickness of his girth against the apex of my legs. "Fuck me until I can't think."

"I always need you, little hellion. I crave you every second of every day." Andre locks his fingers to my hips and moves me back and forth getting me to grind against him. "You're so intoxicating. Almost infuriating how naïve you are about teasing me. Tempting me. I've never understood true torture until watching you just exist and manage to go even an hour without letting me pleasure you."

I smirk and slide down farther, hooking my fingers to his cotton briefs to pull them down. I watch in my lusty haze as his enormous cock bounces free. I scoot back up until I feel the softness of his balls touch the heat between my legs and use both my hands to stroke him. Fire lights his eyes, and he sits up and tests my flexibility by shifting my leg to rest on his elbow to give his other hand better access to my body. Sucking his fingers into his mouth, he wets them, adding more slickness to sink into me. I moan at the sensation of him fingering me in both holes while managing to strum his thumb to my clit.

I follow his initiative and spit on his tip, using it to slide both my hands up and down his shaft. He moans and shifts like he can barely handle me giving him pleasure, and I love the hell out of his intense desperation as he kisses me while he fucks me with his hand until my body tenses and explodes with an orgasm that makes him cum at the same time as if our bodies are connected.

But it's not enough for either of us.

Andre pushes me back between his legs and rips my sticky panties off with the hellfire that dances across his finger. His eyes rove over me inch by inch, his whole body ripping and flickering between his human and devil state.

"I want to fuck you with my tail," Andre says, his words breathy.

I intake a small breath as his long, ribbed tail curves over his back. The stinger he uses in fighting remains hidden within the smooth bulbous end, and I automatically wrap my fingers about it and memorize the bumpy texture, imagining what it would be like inside me.

I lick my lips and slowly nod, clutching the blankets in my hands. Andre's eyes close with his desire and we both watch as he spreads my knees wider and slowly glides his tail into me. I don't know how or why or what the fuck it is about the sensation, but I scream with a wave of a sudden all-consuming orgasm that makes me squirt all over him unlike anything I've even done before. Andre grunts, once again cumming, triggered by me, and I watch as he uses the mess to slicken his tail and glide it into my ass next. The sensation makes me moan and arch, unleashing the darkest, dirtiest part of me that just wants to be used and fucked and appreciated for bringing my devil the lust he needs.

Slowly pulling his tail out, he smiles and grabs me by my hips, flipping me over onto my stomach. I catch sight of the two of us in the wall mirror, and I moan in anticipation, feeling Andre's big hands massage my ass cheeks and spread my body open.

"Fuck me with both," I say, pushing onto my knees and wiggling my ass. "Fuck me hard like I want. I want to feel it for days. Show me what it's like to give the king of Lust his way."

Andre flares his nostrils and meets my gaze in the mirror. His lips puff with his panting desire, and he aligns his cock to my body, teasing me with the crazy pressure of his thickness. His slow push inside me makes me gasp as my body gets used to the stretch, and I moan and savor every inch of him that nearly feels like he's rearranged my insides to fit in as deeply as he likes. I knew he had power and control with his lust, and the buzzing power stealing my breath confirms it.

"Tell me how it feels," Andre says, his voice rasping with his desire.

"Huge," I say, gasping. "Teasing. Fuck me, Andre. I can take it. I need it."

Like my words set him off, Andre grabs my hair and twists it with one hand while using his other to brace on my shoulder. The power of his thrust sends an intense zing right to my clit and my eyes roll back for a second as the pressure intensifies like his cock swells even bigger.

And then I swear I feel him orgasm. Like a shock of power, I moan and feel every muscle on my body tighten with my release. Andre thrusts hard and fast, never feeling as if he's even close to sliding out of me. I lose myself to the haze of his desire, enjoying every sensation and every sexy word that escapes his mouth. He adds even more pressure to my body with his tail again, fucking me in the ass like he wants to stuff me with all of the pleasure he needs for his power.

A bright light flashes on the balcony, turning my eyelids red, and I open my eyes and see Zade's figure creeping outside the window. Andre notices it too, because his fingers dig more into me and he bows and licks my earlobe.

"I can't stop yet," Andre says softly, though annoyance lines his words. "I've been starved."

I nod my head, letting him know I don't give a fuck if the bastard angel wants to enjoy the show. But I'm going to let him know it doesn't come without a price.

"If you plan on just standing out there like a perv, then leave. If you want to come in and help Andre release me, then you're welcome to have a couple minutes of our time. Andre will break the ward on this room for you." I clutch the blankets, my voice high and drawn out with my moans. I wait in anticipation to see what Zade chooses to do.

Zade's light dims but he doesn't move from the window.

Surprising the fuck out of me, Andre lifts me up and carries me, still humping me like it's in his nature to fuck me regardless of interruption. Flinging open the curtain, I tip my head up and laugh, catching Zade's shocked expression as I hang like a damn sex doll attached to Andre.

"Get undressed to enter our room." Andre sears the marking on the wall by the window, breaking the barrier.

Grabbing the front of his shirt, Zade strips it off and climbs through the window as if he's caught by his dick on a line that Andre reels to us. Plopping down, Andre sits with me on his lap, purposefully grabbing my knees and giving Zade one helluva show. Dante and Kase are going to beg for a replay later once they hear about this. I can't even speak as he bounces my body onto his, now sitting on his tail so it can still reach my ass.

"Show her your cock. She needs to cum at least once more. My body won't release her otherwise." Damn it, does Andre's command drive me wild.

I bite my lip and watch as Zade remains silent but does what he asks and finishes undressing. My hands stretch out without my consent, and I wiggle my fingers, trying to bait the blushing angel to come closer. His abs ripple, his eyes wandering from my body taking a devil's pounding to my face where he might mistake my look of pleasure for pain until he truly understands me.

"Do not deny her after everything Heaven put her

through. You know that we've lost and if this makes her forget that you belong to a legion of righteous bastards, then you'll do whatever it is she wants...or leave." Once again, Andre growls the words and sends tingles bursting through me.

Zade steps closer, his chest heaving. Licking his lips, he stands beside us and brings his hand up like it's now him who has lost the ability to control his need to touch me. "Tell me what to do to help her. I'm unsure of how to proceed."

"She likes it rough. A bit more pressure on the side of her clit. Back and forth in a fast, consistent motion. It makes her cum the quickest. If you prefer to draw it out, use three fingers and rub her up and down and softer." Andre drags his hand across my hip and between my legs, my body stretched and giving a clear view without even having to spread my lips. "Like this."

Oh, fuck.

I jerk back in his arms and nearly knock him onto his back, the sensation zapping me with immense pleasure and on the verge of exploding. It's intense enough to knock my questions from my mind, because I really want to fucking know how he is already familiar enough with what I enjoy. Maybe Kase or Dante told him.

The second Zade summons his bravery, he does what Andre instructs, and I scream and arch again, scaring the fuck out of Zade. Andre roars a laugh and snatches his arm, tugging him back to us.

"You don't fucking stop when that's her reaction. We don't deny orgasms in this room." Andre bounces me harder and faster, his cock pulsing and stretching me, still unable to pull out more than an inch or two.

Zade takes a breath, closes his eyes, and rubs my clit again, nearly lighting up the room with his glow. I reach out for him and stroke my wet hand across his cock, setting him off. He gasps and grunts in surprise, shocked by the pleasure I arouse in him that he doesn't even know what to do as he explodes with an orgasm right onto my clit.

The shock of his heavenly load burst bliss through me as if he went and sent my damn vagina to Heaven for a second, and once again, I squirt. And not just a little bit. I soak Zade right back, the clear liquid glistening off his sexy body.

Both our orgasms ignite the power Andre needs, and my whole body quakes with his cumming. The pressure eases between my legs, and he manages to slide out, his massive cock, dripping as bad as I am.

"Whoa," Zade whispers under his breath, still clutching his cock. He unveils his white wings and ruffles his feathers like he needs to assure himself his wings are still there.

"Ready to join us?" Andre asks, scooping me up and taking me to the small bathroom.

I can't think or speak or do anything in the moment except replay the pleasure he gave me over and over again. Zade stands in the doorway, watching in silence as Andre takes his time wiping me off and cleaning me off. He must've had some lessons in how to handle me after such a pounding from Dante, because I love how attentive he is.

He even stops to hug and kiss me and whisper his love and appreciation in my ear as Zade tries to pull himself from the lust still hanging in the air. Starting the tub, Andre throws some scented powder in, ignoring Zade as he finishes up.

Should I be embarrassed that I'm sitting on the damn toilet in front of a devil and angel after getting my thoughts fucked out of me? Maybe. But I'm beyond caring. They're beyond the scope of humanity and they know my body has different needs.

I quickly finish cleaning myself up and stand, wobbling on my feet. Andre comes to my side and lifts me back into his arms. Zade finally clears his throat, realizing that the only way any of us will say anything is if he speaks first. He was the one to creep around outside after all.

"Raven," he finally says, whispering for my attention.

I force my gaze away from Andre and give Zade a long look as he stands all sticky and glistening completely naked, not bothering to hide himself.

"I just want to say that—"

Andre growls and lunges at him, grabbing him by the throat. My side hits Zade's stomach as Andre doesn't let me go "Your next words better not be an apology about Elias. That would be a slap in the face because you did nothing to stop it.

You stood by and did nothing."

"I had no choice. I couldn't stand against Heaven, nor could I help you. I had to stand by and do nothing or risk my wings." Zade tightens his jaw. "Please, I just wanted to come here and let you know that I had nothing to do with the attack. I did not agree with what Cassius allowed to happen."

Anger hits me hard and fast, and it's me who grabs him next, yanking his hair with my fingers. "You didn't agree! You fucking didn't agree! Yet you are still on Heaven's side? Why? Tell me fucking why?"

His eyes glass over. "I—"

The room rumbles and quakes, cutting off his words. I whip my head toward the bedroom and listen as the familiar sound of the Hell portal opening up crackles through the air. I shove against Zade and wiggle, finding my strength to ignore the good ache in my body and hop from Andre's arms. It's Micah. He's back. He swore to me he wouldn't return until he found Elias's soul, and it's been the longest week of my existence.

"Raven," Zade says, trying to grab me. "Wait, please."

Andre growls and shoves him against the wall. "She has been fucking waiting."

I yank away and switch between jogging and hobbling like I still have a damn tail up my ass, rushing as fast as I can to the hallway of our new townhouse. Zade is the only angel we allow within miles, and all demons are instructed to attack on sight. Before, I'd feel bad. But now? I plan to see them all crying and begging for mercy in Hell. I look forward to the day I can stand in front of them and deny them like they had me.

"Micah!" I call, heaving a breath.

I don't make it all the way into the living room as Kase steps in my way, a frown knitting his brows together. A few feet behind him, Dante tightens his jaw. He tries to remain expressionless, but the green flash in his eyes screams at me that something is incredibly wrong.

I whip my attention toward the glowing fire and catch sight of Micah and Lucian quietly arguing with each other.

My heart freefalls into my stomach as their gazes jerk to mine.

Lucian scowls and disappears, abandoning us and jumping back through the portal into Hell.

"Spit it out right now. Where the fuck is Elias?" I ask, my voice quaking. "If I find out that one of Lucian's bitch-ass minions has him, I'm going to destroy his kingdom."

Micah opens and closes his mouth and shakes his head.

I flick my gaze to Kase and Dante and back again. Andre comes up behind me without Zade, probably scared off. "Okay, he's not a demon's bitch. That's good." It takes everything in me to keep prying. "So where is he?"

Again, Micah doesn't respond.

Dante steps closer, taking charge of the situation. "Raven,

I don't want you to freak out, because this is a good thing in the long run."

I blink my eyes, trying to control my emotions. "Just fucking tell me."

Dante opens his arms, quietly asking me to step into them. "When a mortal's life is brutally taken before its time the way Tamia took his, a soul gets reborn and the cycle continues. The same happens for those who take their own lives. It takes someone of either terrible darkness or pure light to end a cycle when they die outside of their time. Elias was unbound and teetering between Heaven and Hell. His decision to protect you is most likely why it happened. Like I said, this is a good thing."

My mind whirls with a thousand thoughts, and I clutch his shirt between my fingers. "How? How is this good? Elias is gone! He's gone and could end up anywhere in the fucking Mortal Realm. Even if we find his soul...I'm fucking thirty-four! It'll be like nineteen years before he's an adult. He could be anyone."

"He can also still take a throne," Micah says, getting the nerve to speak.

My heart aches, and the edges of my vision shadow.

I want to scream and tell them that I don't care about that. I care about my soulmate and the life that we had together now. The one that will stay with me for eternity. Who knows what will happen in twenty or thirty years. I could die before then.

There is no point in arguing or telling them how I feel.

There is nothing I can do.

Bowing my head, I let my burning tears sprinkle over the floor.

"We will find him. We'll do whatever it takes," Kase says, hugging his arms around me and Dante.

If only they could rewind time.

Because in this moment, even knowing we have another chance to help humanity and Elias isn't trapped as a soul in Hell, I can't help feeling selfish. I can't help wanting Elias as he was. As we were together. And I damn well can't stand the thought of being without him for what could be the rest of my life.

"Raven?" Andre whispers from behind me. "Say something."

I suppress my anger the best I can, trying not to scream my anger. "I—I have nothing to say. It is what it is."

My chest tightens and something dark rises in my soul.

It steals my light.

It devours me whole.

To be continued…

Other Reverse Harem Novels by Ginna Moran

THE VAMPIRE HEIRS WORLD

La Vega Vampire Showstoppers

Vampire Nights

The Divine Vampire Heirs

Blood Match

Blood Rebel

Blood Debt

Blood Feud

Blood Loss

Blood Vows

The Royale Vampire Heirs Series:

Rebel Vampires

Rebel Dhampir

Rebel Match

Rebel Heir

Rebel Fight

Academy of Vampire Heirs Series:

Dhampirs 101

Blood Sources 102

Coven Bonds 103

Personal Donors 104

Blood Wars 105

SERIES IN THE MATES OF MAGAELORUM WORLD

The Pack Mates of Lunar Crest:

The She-Wolf Games

The Wolf-Mate Trials

The Omega Hunt

The Witch Chase

Winter Wolf Games

The Inmate of the Dreki Dragons:

Maximum Magical Penitentiary: Falsely Accused

Maximum Magical Penitentiary: Deadly Fugitive

Maximum Magical Penitentiary: Death Row

THE SEVEN SINNERS OF HELL'S KINGDOM

Her Personal Demons

Her Deadly Angels

Her Darkest Devils

Her Sinful Saints

A Date With Her Devils

ABOUT GINNA MORAN

GINNA MORAN IS the author of over seventy novels, including the popular The Pack Mates of Lunar Crest, The Divine Vampire Heirs, and The Royale Vampire Heirs Why Choose novels.

She always carried a fascination for all things paranormal and wrote her first unpublished manuscript at age eighteen. Her love of the supernatural grew stronger through her adult life, and she now spends her days with different creatures of the night. Whether it's vampires, werewolves, dragons, fae, angels, demons, or mermaids, Ginna loves creating and living in worlds from her dreams.

Aside from Ginna's professional life, she enjoys binge watching TV, crafting and design, playing pretend with her daughter, and cuddling with her dogs. Some of her favorite things include chocolate, mermaids, anything that glitters, learning new things, cheesy jokes, and organizing her bookshelf.

Ginna is currently hard at work on her next novel and the one after, and the one after that.

www.ingramcontent.com/pod-product-compliance
Lightning Source LLC
Chambersburg PA
CBHW030524310726
48979CB00010B/1788/J
9781951314514